P9-EDM-428

THE RESORT

SOL STEIN

THE RESORT

WILLIAM MORROW AND COMPANY, INC.
NEW YORK 1980

Library of Congress Cataloging in Publication Data

Stein, Sol.
  The resort.

  I. Title.
PZ4.S8195Re   [PS3569.T375]   813'.5'4   79-21781
ISBN 0-688-03541-8

Printed in the United States of America.

First Edition

1 2 3 4 5 6 7 8 9 10

for
Elizabeth and David
every other cell

ACKNOWLEDGMENTS

I owe a debt of gratitude to Ernest van den Haag for permission to use one of his theories in a context he would abhor if it happened in life.

Hillel Black, my editor in America, and Claire Carleton, my editor in Britain, both gave me valuable advice. Patricia Day was, as always, helpful through every draft.

Marilee Talman had a profound influence on the texture of this story and on the development of several of the characters. Judge Charles L. Brieant, Jr., helped me, as many times before, to understand the sometimes strange workings of the law.

Michael Burke, who has fought fires in California professionally, was good enough to let me interview him. Benton Arnovitz's expertise in Judaica was useful to me.

My work also benefited from the advice of Renni Browne, Wallace Exman, George Greenfield, Ernest Hecht, Henry Schwarzschild, Claire Smith, and Jeff Stein, to all of whom I am grateful, as I also am to Joan Searle, living litmus for a work of fiction.

"There is no real proof that the Holocaust actually did happen."

> —George Pape, President, German-American Committee of Greater New York, a cultural organization with fifty chapters in the metropolitan area, as quoted in *The New York Times*, October 8, 1977

"Do you want us to put you in the ovens? We will. . . . We say one more time, all you Jews are going to get it."

> —Michael Allen, St. Louis, Missouri, Nazi leader, July 9, 1978, at rally in Chicago, Illinois, quoted in *The New York Times*, July 10, 1978

"The 'deep irrationality' of the Jewish people and the Jewish religion were apt to 'trigger confusions, fear and eventually bloody aggressions in almost all host nations.'"

> —Dr. Otto Scrinzi, neurologist and member of the Austrian Parliament, as reported in *The New York Times*, March 29, 1979

"Hadn't he said he wanted only justice?"

> —of Kurtz, in *Heart of Darkness* by Joseph Conrad

PART 1

1

Dr. Margaret Brown, a wise woman, was in as much a minority among physicians as in the rest of the world. To become a doctor twenty-five years ago meant much memorizing, which she considered a low order of accomplishment, and a willingness to work long hours at low pay as an intern in preparation for a life's work observing not the beauty of the human race or its accomplishments, but blotchy skin, swollen joints, and much worse. When asked why she had chosen medicine, she said she was curious about people. Why then did she not become a teacher? Because, she said, she was interested in formed people rather than masses of children conceived by others. Once her fellow students had learned the exact location of the pancreas and spleen, they were content. Margaret was not until she could confidently determine the precise cause of a patient's discomfort or pain. Her curiosity made her an excellent diagnostician and constantly got her into trouble. At a lecture covering conception and prenatal care, the instructor, possibly a thwarted preacher, talked of the first human miracle, gestation. Margaret raised her hand and, when recognized, said, "Wouldn't the miracle of tumescence come first and couldn't we discuss that?" In a class that was predominantly male, Margaret was a frequent cause of nervous laughter.

She was thought to be attractive, which was an asset, and very smart, which was a liability. In those days few males enjoyed the idea of dating a woman who, whatever the splendor of her physical virtues, seemed to be intellectually superior. Especially cautious in this respect were young physicians-to-be, whose idea of accomplishment was playing not Hippocrates but Houdini.

Margaret realized much too soon that the ultimate organ, the brain that harbored the mind, was *terra incognita* for most of her fellow students. Her wisest instructor, Dr. Teal, once asked her if brain surgery attracted her as a specialty.

"No," she said much too quickly.

"May I ask why?"

"I find surgeons boring."

Dr. Teal, a surgeon, blushed. Margaret quickly apologized, explaining she meant those of her fellow students who, bereft of leeches, had already opted for the surgical response.

Soon afterward Margaret decided that there was really no medical specialty for her to pursue. Her field, clearly, was wherever her curiosity might lead her. Some avenue of research perhaps. Psychiatry was not the answer; she was a talker, not a listener. Even internal medicine seemed restrictive, and so, *faute de mieux*, she became a general practitioner, with the whole human being her field of play. Dr. Teal thought, somewhat sadly, that the brightest medical student he ever had might as well have majored in philosophy.

One of the things that attracted Margaret to Henry Brown was that when he learned she was a physician, he said, "That's convenient for emergencies." Otherwise, it seemed, he was not impressed. "Doctors," he said, "are like politicians. Status before content. Physicians, like teenage magicians, know a few tricks and expect minor deification. Politicians are assholes attended by proctologists."

Margaret thought this young fellow pompous, bright, and

intriguing, impertinent, and wholly unsuccessful in putting her off. Or did he think he was being attractive? She led him on.

After two hours, Henry had decided that Margaret was smart. When he stopped goading her unsuccessfully, he was doomed. She turned on him. She, at least, had a vocation in which if one failed totally, and was drunk all day long, one could still practice as a ship's doctor. But he was a what? A businessman? What did that mean? An inventor? No. A creator of new markets? No. From what he reported, he was not even a successful exploiter of labor.

Their skill at brickbats cemented their friendship. They found themselves teaming up against others who were less skillful in verbal offense. Given the customs of the day, marriage began to seem inevitable.

Margaret got him interested in medicine as she saw it, a potpourri of neglected nutrition, wonder drugs, and common sense. Henry got her interested in his eccentric business, mailing things that other people made, that went by the charming name of order fulfillment. For their off-hours they collected a group of friends who joined them on Friday evenings for drinks and talk. No bridge, no chatter about hearth or progeny was ever ventured. The sports events of the upcoming weekend were never alluded to by the men. The women never discussed meals they had prepared or were thinking of preparing. One heard few references even to medicine or business, unless the point was of general consequence and of interest to the group. An evening's conversation might range from the sixth to the fourteenth century, with no mention of the twentieth, or might be spent in debate about the one subject that was of more interest than physics or history or *a capella* music. Human nature, though it varied not from century to century, was a subject worth infinite dissection, and Friday evenings at the Browns' frequently turned to that topic. It was not for the ears of children, of which the Browns eventually had two. Ruth and Stanley, when young, accused their parents of always *talking*.

One spring morning Margaret awoke before Henry and pulled the drapes of their bedroom windows apart to find a sky that was overcast for the third day. She had hoped for sun, and failing that, a rainstorm that would relieve the sky of its lowering burden.

"God isn't listening," Margaret said.

Henry, stirring from sleep, said, "What's that?"

"If the weather's not going to change, I am," she said. "Let's go to California."

"Where?" Henry said, sitting up.

"Let's visit Stanley."

Their son was finishing his freshman year at the University of California at Santa Cruz.

"He was here for Christmas."

"That was months ago," Margaret said, coming to sit beside Henry on the bed.

"He'll be back here in a few weeks," Henry said.

"We could rent a car in San Francisco, see Stanley, then drive down the coast on Highway 1. We could stop at Carmel, Big Sur, Santa Barbara, and fly home from Los Angeles. Everybody who's ever done that trip says it's marvelous."

"I can't take a week away on such short notice," Henry said.

"Neither can I. Let's do it anyway."

"Insane," Henry said. He had to admire her talent for electives. "California is like another country."

"What's wrong with that? Look at the weather here."

"What makes you think the weather in California is going to be any better?" California, Henry told himself, is movieland and Disneyland, with pockets of elderly Neanderthals and drug-culture communes, surfboarding and tripping, lush groves and vineyards, the best and the worst of climates, the magnificent sierras and the valley of death. He'd been to a convention in Los Angeles. He'd visited San Francisco with Margaret long ago. Between them, he felt, would be like going up the river looking for Kurtz.

"Please?" Margaret said.

"It's not to visit Stanley," Henry said. "It's for us."

"What's wrong with that?" Much later she was to think *I wished it on ourselves.*

Their five-hour flight from Kennedy was uneventful. As

they emerged into the San Francisco terminal, they were both startled to see Stanley behind the roped-off egressway. Quickly they came around to where Henry could pump his son's hand, releasing its enthusiasm so that Stanley could put his arms gently around the woman who had been his first love. God, how much taller than Margaret he was! In fact, Henry noticed, Stanley was now a smidge taller than himself. If each generation was a mite taller, where would it all end? The field of genetics escaped him. He felt the wonder of a father at the miracle of a son who had so recently been a child leaning down to embrace his mother.

"Did Mom worry all the way?" Stanley asked.

"I'll tell you about Mom," Margaret said. "Mom is a completely rational human being except on Ferris wheels and airplanes, and I haven't accepted an offer for a Ferris wheel ride since I was sixteen. I trust airplanes even less than most people trust doctors. I know what doctors don't know. How do I know what airplane pilots don't know?"

Stanley and Henry laughed, as they all headed for the baggage area.

"How did you know where to meet us?" Henry asked.

"You told me the flight number."

"But how'd you get here from Santa Cruz?"

"The way I always do," Stanley said. "I took a thumb."

Margaret was thirteen, walking home from school when, in a sudden rain, she saw the pickup truck and the driver stopped for her. Her wet middy blouse made her feel almost naked. She apologized for getting the cab seat wet. He said *never mind* and patted her knee, leaving his hand there, a signal for terror. At the light she got out against his protests, running all the way home in the rain. She scrubbed her knee and thigh with soap and water over and over again to remove the memory, determined never ever never to hitch a ride again.

"It's easy out here," Stanley said, "and you get to meet people. You know, not everyone who drives a car is a child molester." He laughed, hoping she wouldn't deliver the lecture again. "Of course, if Dad would spring for a car . . ."

"You'd only drive around a lot and get yourself into an accident," Margaret said. "They say half the drivers in California are crazy."

At the Hertz counter an ambitious clerk saw the coded rating on Henry's credit card and said, "We've got the Granada you reserved, Mr. Brown, but I thought you might be interested in the special we have on Mercedes right now. They're very popular in California."

"Thanks for the suggestion," said Henry. "We'll stick to the Ford."

As they left for the parking lot, the men each carrying a bag, Stanley put his free arm through his father's and said, "I reserved a tennis court for eleven A.M. Tuesday. Think you can drive down in time so we can play before I show you around?"

"Terrific," said Henry, who always played tennis twice a week at home. From his friends Henry heard horror stories about their adolescent sons; Stanley seemed to have bypassed all the conspicuous pitfalls. So far.

When they checked in at the Highgate, the clerk behind the desk, a sixtyish stout man with a slight accent, asked, "You'll be staying just the one night, Dr. Brown?"

"I'm Mr. Brown. My wife is Dr. Brown. It doesn't matter. Yes, just the one night." The clerk reminded him of someone.

"Will the young man be staying with you? We can provide a folding bed or . . ."

"No, no. He's going back to Santa Cruz." A Lillian Hellman play? Or was it the film? Maybe he used to be an actor.

"Will you need a reservation at your next destination?" the man asked politely. The Highgate really deserved its reputation for considerate service.

"We'll be driving south along the ocean. First stop is Carmel."

"As your second, may I recommend Cliffhaven in Big Sur? It's a new place, excellent view, three-star restaurant."

"Yes, yes," Margaret said, overhearing.

"Good," the stout man said. "I'll leave the confirmation in your box."

As they followed the bellhop to the elevator, Henry looked

over his shoulder once at the desk clerk. He wasn't paying attention to the next person in line. He was staring straight at them. Embarrassed, Henry proceeded to the elevator without looking back again.

"Anything the matter?" Margaret asked in the elevator.

"No, no," Henry said.

Margaret, out of long experience, knew Henry was lying to spare her something.

If you asked any of Margaret's patients about why they went to her, they'd say her self-confidence was catching, you felt better after visiting her, even if the news was bad. You felt whatever was bothering you was under control, hers and yours. As for Margaret, she took pride in being a perceptive diagnostician of emotional as well as physical needs, needing only the tiniest clues to give her insight that helped. And so when Stanley took them via cable car to Ghirardelli Square, she sensed her son wanted a private talk with his father. Ghirardelli's wonders offered a perfect excuse; for Margaret, useless shopping was a perfect recreation, and here there were dozens of attractive shops beckoning.

"I'll have a look around if you sports don't mind."

"Great, Mom," Stanley said. "Dad and I can have a beer."

So Margaret went off, while father and son settled themselves at a sun-shaded table in an outdoor café.

"I'll be back in twenty minutes," Margaret cried from a distance. People turned to look at her.

"Take your time," Henry said, but she was now too far to hear. Henry, for it was his nature to do so, wondered for a moment what their lives would be like if Margaret did not return. There would be a search, an investigation, nothing. Hundreds of people disappeared that way each year.

"Your mother," he said to Stanley, "enjoys shopping more than anyone I know."

"You might as well enjoy what you have to do."

"No, no," Henry said, "I'm not talking about necessities. It's her way of making up for the past."

"Because Grandpa was so poor."

"You got it. She even enjoys window shopping, she says,

because she *knows* she can buy what she's looking at."

"I'm glad you two like each other," Stanley said.

"What makes you think that?"

"It shows. Dad, it's real neat having you both visit." He nodded his head several times the way young people sometimes did.

His son, Henry thought, had evolved into an interesting looking young man, with Margaret's best facial features. And yet one could easily see Henry in his son. Wonder where the reddish glint in the hair came from? Margaret's mother? Wonder if it's the sun out here?

"It's good to be here," Henry said. "I'm really pleased about the courtesy."

"I wanted to meet you."

"I mean the tennis."

"*De nada,*" Stanley said.

"You pick up a bit of Spanish out here?"

"Picked that up from Hemingway. Didn't you ever read Hemingway, Dad?"

Henry was tempted to say *before you were born.*

Henry let some silence settle between them so that Stanley could organize whatever it was that he had in mind.

"Pop," he said finally in a form of address he always reserved for moments of feeling, "I've been hit."

"What does that mean?"

"A girl."

"A friend? How nice."

"I've got lots of friends, you know, fellows I hang around with, and girls I see. This is different."

"Not like Marjorie what's-her-name?"

"No," said Stanley. "Not like any of the others."

"Tell me about her."

"Actually, I met her when I was on line for registration. She was in front of me and I asked her a dumb question."

"What kind of dumb question?"

"I don't recall, but I remember she turned around—she is just sensational-looking—and said, 'That's a dumb question.'"

Henry had to laugh.

"Pop, I have been seeing her every day."

"I hope it's not interfering with your studies too much."

"Yes and no. I think about her when she's not there, you know what I mean?"

"Has she got a name?"

"Yeah, sure, I'm sorry. Her name's Kathy. They call her Kathy Brown."

"That's a coincidence!"

"No, no, that's not her name, just what they call her. The guys here have a thing—if a girl's going sort of steady with a fellow they call her by his last name. It usually makes the girls mad."

"I can imagine."

"That's why they do it. Kathy doesn't mind too much."

"You haven't done anything hasty, I hope."

"What do you mean?"

"Look, Stanley, you haven't secretly gotten married or something. Mother would . . ."

"No, no, Pop, it's just a thing with the name. Wait'll you meet her. She's into ballet, and she likes the same music I do, and we like being together. Pop, I'm in trouble."

Henry thought *abortion.*

"You need money?"

Stanley nodded uncomfortably. "Sort of."

"How much is sort of?"

"Sixty bucks. Please?"

"That's outrageous."

"I don't want you to get angry."

"I'm not angry. What kind of medical attention do you think she'll get for sixty dollars? It's got to be a first-rate hospital and a first-rate doctor. You have . . ."

He stopped because Stanley was laughing.

"Oh Pop, not that. It's just, well, I buy her presents, little things. She used to refuse them, but I have to buy them even if I can't squeeze it out of my allowance. I take her to different restaurants. It's like an insane thing, a compulsion."

First love, thought Henry, remembering.

"I borrowed sixty from two guys to cover myself and I've got to return it. I'd rather owe the money to you. I promise to pay it back out of summer work."

"What are you doing?"

"I'm writing an I.O.U. on the napkin."

"You don't need to do that."

"It's in case I forget."

"I'd rather you remembered."

Henry took three twenties from his wallet, folded them twice, and handed them to his son.

"Thanks, Dad."

"I know how irrational love can be. And how expensive. Just don't do anything rash like getting married without at least talking about it first."

"Not too many people get married just like that, Dad." He put the still-folded bills into his wallet stuffed with papers and crammed the billfold into his jeans.

"Will we meet Kathy?"

"She's got classes Tuesday morning, but I had an idea. You in a good mood?"

"Good mood," Henry said. It was a ritual with them.

"We're always talking about going down to Los Angeles. Kathy comes from there. We could fly down Friday after her class—PCA is real cheap—and we could all go out someplace together, she knows the spots, and then I could meet her family, that sort of thing. All I'd need is like . . ."

"The air fare," Henry volunteered.

"Just for me. Kathy pays her own way."

"And some spending money?"

"A little," Stanley said. "I'll repay all of it out of my summer job."

"Can you cash a traveler's check at school?"

Stanley nodded, trying to contain his joy.

"This is a hundred. I'll endorse it to you."

"It's too much," Stanley said.

"I don't have smaller ones," Henry lied. "We'll settle up in the summer, okay?"

"Dad, you are something. Thanks." Just then Margaret came into view out of the ambling crowd, a bit breathless, her face touched with a blush of excitement.

Seeing her, Henry and Stanley both laughed. "What have you bought, Mom?"

"This place is fabulous," Margaret said. "Not buying in a place like this is sinful."

"You mean virtuous, Mom."

"I know sin when I feel it," Margaret said. "Take it from me, extreme virtue is a great sin."

"I expected to see you carrying a lot of packages," Henry said.

"Just looking," Margaret replied as Henry paid the check, "except one little thing I bought for you. You know how you struggle over a dry cork when it breaks in the wine bottle. Well, they have this European shop—I guess it's an American shop full of European gadgets—and they have a Swiss or a German twin corkscrew. It's this tiny little thing"—she took it out of her purse—"and the way it works, it's guaranteed to get a broken cork out. Aren't you glad I looked around?"

Henry had once had a dream he was in a desert, dehydrated, parched, desperate for water, and had come across a bottle of wine, or water—he didn't know which—lying at the foot of a large cactus. He remembered trying to get the cork out of the bottle with his bare hands, which was impossible. He was going to die for want of a corkscrew. Had he told Margaret about that dream? He was certain he had not.

"Thank you," he said to her. "It's a marvelous present."

"A little nothing," Margaret said, and extended an elbow in the direction of each of her men. They went off arm in arm to inspect the temptations of Ghirardelli Square.

Later Henry seized an opportune moment to say, "Margaret, I've got a surprise. Stanley's flying down to L.A. Friday. He's got a friend who comes from there and they want to show us around a bit, isn't that nice?"

"Your roommate?" Margaret asked.

"I wish she were," Stanley said.

"I guess I automatically assumed a male friend," Margaret said.

"I'm into girls, Mom," Stanley said, and then laughed at the implication in his language. Stanley was glad his father and mother laughed, too. Some parents were impossible about things like that.

"Where are you staying in L.A.?" Stanley asked.

"Glad you reminded me," Henry said. "The Beverly Hills was full when my travel agent checked from New York, but they advised me to call to see if there were any cancellations. Now we need, what, three rooms?"

"No, no thanks. Kathy's parents, we'll stay there."

"While I'm thinking of it," Henry said, "will you excuse me a minute?"

He made a credit card call. The man at the desk of the Beverly Hills was very polite, but said he wouldn't know about cancellations till Thursday.

"What are the chances?" Henry asked.

"Oh very good, Mr. Brown. There're almost always some cancellations and you're first in line."

Henry reported on his conversation to Stanley and added, "I'll call them from the Beachcomber in Santa Barbara Thursday, then I'll phone you. If they have a cancellation, you and your friend get a drink at the Polo Lounge. If not, I'll let you know where we're registered."

"You won't forget to call?" Stanley asked.

"I always keep my promises," Henry said, glancing at Margaret. "Especially if Mom reminds me."

Stanley scribbled down a phone number. "You don't have to get me on the hall phone anymore," he said. "This is a private phone I share with my roommate."

When darkness had descended on San Francisco, Stanley said, "Tomorrow's my hectic day at school, but on Tuesday morning, when you come down, I'm okay."

"Can we walk you to the bus station?" Henry asked.

"Afraid I'm going to hitch a ride?" Stanley said, glancing at his mother. "Honest, I was taking the bus back."

They accompanied him to the bus station anyway.

The next day the Browns took in the waterfront, ate lunch in Di Maggio's, rode a cable car, crammed in as much as they could.

Tuesday morning they got up early, packed, checked out. Henry looked for the clerk who had checked them in. He was nowhere in sight.

They breakfasted on the road, arrived in Santa Cruz in time for father and son to play an hour's tennis before the three of them went sightseeing on the spectacular Santa Cruz campus.

"You like California?" Henry asked his son.

"Are you kidding? This place is so beautiful I feel guilty."

"Guilty about what?"

"It's like a resort, not a school."

"It's simple," Margaret said. "Paradise is a gestalt. It's hard to concentrate on mundane particulars."

"Like homework," Stanley said.

I don't belong in California, Henry thought. Young people in their twenties here acted as if they were still teenagers. So many of the young women one saw in the street looked like cocktail waitresses, the young men like beach attendants with dyed blond hair. Older men looked not mature but merely wrinkled, wizened by the sun, in need of prunes for regularity. Older women in California suffered from obtrusive cosmetics and arteriosclerotic opinions. What am I doing here, Henry thought. It was the natives who drove Kurtz insane.

Margaret gently put her thumbs on Henry's eyelids. "Incipient melancholia," she diagnosed. "Snap out of it. *We* don't have any homework to do. We're on vacation in Paradise."

Henry put his hands on Stanley's shoulders and said, "Take care of yourself. And kiss your mother. She doesn't get kissed enough these days."

Henry and Margaret stopped only briefly to inspect the waterfront in Monterey, then drove on to Carmel. There they checked into an idyllic motel that had groups of rooms at different levels, tiered to conform to the sloping ground. For an extra five dollars, Henry got a room on the topmost level with a splendid view of the Pacific. Margaret wouldn't take time to unpack, and they were off exploring.

For dinner they searched out a small Italian restaurant a friend had told them about. They had *spinace en brodo, fettucine verde*, a bottle of Barolo, and shared a single *zabaglione* afterward.

"Spirits better?" Margaret asked, as they walked up the steeply inclined street, a bit light-headed from the Barolo.

He nodded. When Margaret had gotten ready for bed, she found him on one side, his hands under his cheek, fast asleep.

* * *

In the middle of the night Henry woke to the sound of angry thunder. He pulled the curtain to see lightning striking at the ocean. Would the squalls reach the land, which was dry as tinder?

He turned toward the bed to see if the noise had awakened Margaret, too, and discovered her writhing. Quickly, he woke her up. She sat up, hugging him.

He knew it had been her medical school dream. Dr. Tate giving her Charley, her own cadaver to work on. In the dream Charley screamed that he was alive, pleaded with her to restore his body to its original condition. The first time she had told Dr. Tate about her dream. He admonished her. "Doctors are scientists," he had said, "they are not supposed to dream."

"Tate was an idiot," Henry said. "The best doctors are dreamers."

"A lot you know," she said, still clasping him.

"Why now?" asked Henry.

"Probably the storm," she said, though she wondered if that was really the reason.

They woke later than they'd planned, dressed more casually than they had for San Francisco, breakfasted in the coffee shop, sauntered around town, and took in the shop windows. Margaret was attracted by a scarf in a window, went in, looked at two or three dozen different ones, suddenly realized that Henry was not with her, and felt the familiar, momentary alarm. It wasn't a phobia, she told herself. If she were ever to be separated from Henry, the worst would really happen. Their lives were too intertwined. She rejected the idea of widowhood as intolerable. Her private deal with her Maker was either she went first, or they had to go together. Margaret excused herself to the clerk, went quickly out, and immediately, with a wave of relief and a reprimand for her anxiety, saw Henry coming up the inclined sidewalk holding a single flower wrapped in green tissue.

It was midafternoon before they drove out of town to find Highway 1. They stopped at a lookout on the edge of the craggy cliffs that plummeted to the white-flecked breakers below.

"The weather around here is supposed to be the most perfect in the world," Margaret said.

"If you don't like to see the leaves turn."

"Oh Henry, you're a spoilsport."

"Just kidding. The views are fantastic," he admitted.

"I have a feeling California will be good for us," she said.

I have a feeling California will be bad for us, Henry thought. What he said was, "I'm not sure."

"Think of it," Margaret said, "the Pacific, the palisades, the redwoods, and views like this, all in one state."

"Including the desert."

"Henry, you're talking yourself into a depression. This is a vacation. We're supposed to be having fun."

He strolled back to the car alone. Margaret was right. He turned to look at her, standing at the cliff's edge, her back to him, looking out over the most magnificent ocean in the world. *You fool,* he thought, *it is she and not the view that is your aphrodisiac.*

As they went around a curve on the winding road, Henry spotted the green camper up ahead followed closely by a yellow highway patrol car, its roof lights flashing.

"The next lookout should be very soon," Margaret said, looking up from the map to see the vehicles ahead. "What are they doing?"

"I think he wants the camper to stop," Henry said, tapping the brakes as he closed in on the slowing vehicles. The camper pulled into the lookout area. The police car followed. Henry stopped fifty feet behind the police car. He saw the trooper emerge, take his gun out of his holster, and approach the driver's window of the camper.

Henry got out of the car.

"Stay here, Henry," Margaret said.

"Maybe I can help."

He stopped when he saw the trooper point the gun directly at the driver's face as he lowered the window. The driver, a young man with longish hair, handed something out to the policeman. The policeman glanced at the card, keeping the gun inches from the driver's face. Henry couldn't hear what the driver said.

With the gun the trooper motioned the driver out of the car. Henry could see that it was a boy of about Stanley's age. He turned toward the camper, put his hands on the roof, as the trooper felt the sides of his pants and along the inseams. Then, motioning with the gun, he had the young man open the rear of the camper. He peered in, lifted something, dropped it back. The trooper glanced back at Henry, just for a second, as Henry instinctively stepped closer.

The trooper had the young man open the driver's door wide. Still pointing the gun at the kid, the trooper peered inside. Then he gave the license back to the young man, holstered his gun, and drove off, tires screaming.

Henry went over to the young man.

"Anything wrong?" Henry asked.

The driver shook his head. "The usual. If I cut my hair, they wouldn't stop me. They stop Chicanos, Blacks, longhairs, and—for different reasons—cute blondes."

"Why the gun?"

"They always do that. At least he didn't put the cuffs on me while he looked in the van."

"What was he looking for?"

"Grass. Anything. Trouble."

"Were you speeding?"

"Nah." The young man looked at Henry. "Where you from?" he asked. "East?"

"New York," Henry said.

"Well," the driver said, getting back into his camper, "this is California, mister."

"You should have stayed in the car," Margaret said. "It could have been dangerous."

"I thought I might help."

"Who? The police or the driver?"

They arrived in the Big Sur area, content but tired, glad they had reserved a room. Within minutes they spotted the huge orange-and-blue sign off the road on the left: CLIFF-HAVEN, RESERVATIONS ONLY. A double chain hung from posts blocked the dirt road leading upward. What Henry thought of as a sentry box, also in orange and blue, opened the moment they drove up, and a fair-haired young man of twenty-six or -seven with a clipboard under his arm bounded out, his hand reaching for Henry's as he opened the door. "Welcome to Cliffhaven," he said. "You're Mr. and Mrs. . . . ?"

"Brown," Henry said. "Mr. and Dr. Brown. We reserved from San Francisco."

"Yes, indeed," said the young man, checking his clipboard. "The Dr. threw me. I guess I assumed you were two men. My name is Steve Clete, and I'm your guide. How do you do, Dr. Brown," he said, coming around to Margaret's side of the car and shaking her hand through the open window.

Well, they're friendly here, aren't they? thought Henry. Out loud he said, "I guess it's a good thing we reserved. You don't take people who just wander by, like a motel?"

"Well, we'd like to, of course," said Steve, "but we really can't, sir. We're pretty full up with reservations since we opened six months ago—word gets around, you know—and if we didn't have the sign and the chain, people would drive in. It's a good fifteen minutes getting up to the place, three S-curves on the way, and it's pretty much one way except in a few spots. They'd get angry being turned away after the drive up, and we wouldn't know they were coming so we'd have cars going up against cars coming down, awful. Let me buzz them that we're on the way."

The young man went back inside the sentry box and into the wall phone said, "On the way." Henry saw the books on the rocker inside the sentry box.

"I see you have something to read while you wait," he said.

"Oh yeah," the young man said, "it's great. Gives me a chance to catch up on all those books I was supposed to have read in college, you know, Spengler, Joyce."

"What school'd you go to, Steve?" Henry asked, feeling the necessity of reciprocating the effusion of hospitality.

"Call me Clete," the young man said. "Everyone does."

Clete latched and locked the sentry-box door.

"Mind if I ride in the back with you?"

Henry thought Clete was a very nice, California-looking young man, down to the blue jeans and orange T-shirt saying "Cliffhaven."

Clete unhooked the chain, waited for the car to pass, and put the chain back up, then clambered into the back seat of the Ford.

"Nice car," he said.

"Rented," Henry said.

"That's good," Clete said.

Why good?

Henry drove up the dirt road slowly in order not to stir up too much dust.

"You'll probably find it easier in low gear," Clete said. "Don't worry about the blind curves. They'll hold any car coming down until we get there. Who recommended Cliffhaven to you, Mr. Brown?"

Henry told him.

"That's good," Clete said.

Henry kept his eyes on the rock-strewn, curving road.

"Oh look," Margaret said, "there's a baby redwood."

"Right you are, Dr. Brown. Actually, if you want to stop a minute here, it's worth looking. The redwoods go down almost as far as they go up."

They got out of the car, and, true enough, the redwoods at the side of the road went all the way down into a ravine for fifty or sixty feet. It was an odd sensation looking down and then up to get the full length of the trees.

"The lay of the land gives us plenty of privacy up there," Clete said.

"Yes," Henry replied.

"Off we go," Clete said, clapping his hands.

Henry wondered whether Stanley would be like that when he was twenty-six or -seven. Well, he wouldn't be that blond or that California-looking. Stanley was not likely to be working at an inn. At least he hoped he wouldn't.

"Be a bit careful on this next turn," Clete said. "You've got a boulder on each side, but you can squeeze by. We get small trucks by them."

"It's a long way," Margaret said. "Does anyone walk it?"

"Not usually," Clete said, a sober tone in his voice. "Especially after dusk. We get some mountain lions in these parts."

"You do?" Margaret said.

"They never attack a car," Clete said.

When they finally reached the top of the road and passed another sentry box, Henry was able to pull over and the three of them got out of the car. Cliffhaven was miraculously beautiful.

The four largest buildings seemed to Henry triangles greatly extended vertically, one side thrusting straight at the sky, and at the apex sloping at a sharp angle almost to the ground. Though the design was stark and modern, the graying redwood used in the construction seemed natural atop the hills overlooking the surf far below. An artist-architect with a nature-defying boldness had implanted new houses atop hills accustomed only to wilderness.

Henry turned to Margaret. Her eyes were registering astonishment and praise.

"You folks dig Cliffhaven?" Clete asked.

"Yes," Henry said.

"It's like I imagined Norway would look like on a sunny day without the snow and ice," Margaret said. "Or Switzerland."

"Terrific, isn't it?" Clete said.

Margaret looked at Henry. "How much is this a night?"

"I think it's around eighty," Henry said.

"It won't seem high," Clete said, "when you see your room. It's not like a motel or a city hotel."

They got back in the car, and Henry followed Clete's instructions, pulling up and around the second triangular edifice to its rear, where a graceful wooden staircase went up to a landing divided into small patios overlooking the redwood forest and, far below, the breakers of the Pacific.

"If you'll give me your keys," Clete said, "I'll get your bags out of the trunk."

"I'll help," Henry said.

"No need." Clete opened the car trunk. "You've only got two small ones. Traveling light?"

When they reached the landing, Margaret, taking in the

view, said, "I wish we were going to be here more than a night."
She looked at Clete, who set down the bags, hoping he would
say that they might extend their stay. He looked straight at
her but said nothing. *Strange young man,* she thought. But
so many of the young men she'd seen in California looked like
that, lean and muscular, bronzed from the sun, walking on
sneakers as if they were balancing on a surfboard.

Clete opened the door of their room with a key. He let
them go in first. The wall opposite the entrance was a con-
tinuation of the ceiling, an angled line of solid, sloping glass
through which they could see the cloudpuffs drifting in the
blue sky.

Clete entered behind them, carrying the bags.

"Everybody says it's fantastic. Here. If you'll just sign your
name on this card and put your home address in, I'll register
you downstairs."

"That's very considerate," Henry said.

"One moment," Margaret said to Clete. "How do you open
this huge window?"

"The room's air-conditioned, Dr. Brown, and it works perfectly."

"I prefer fresh air unless it's very humid," Margaret said.

"I'm afraid it's part of the architecture," Clete said.

"Too bad," Margaret said. "Well, we'll live with it, I suppose."

Only then did Henry sign the registration card. He handed
it to Clete.

"Will you be paying by cash or credit card?" Clete asked.

"American Express okay?"

"Sure thing," Clete said. "If you'll let me have your card,
the girl at the desk will get you squared away."

Henry rummaged in his left pocket where he kept his singles
folded, peeled off three, and gave them to Clete with his
Amex card.

"Oh thank you, sir," Clete said, as if he hadn't expected to
be tipped. "You'll find towels in the bathroom. The phone's by
the bed. It rings in reception when you pick up. The beds are
firm. I hope you like firm beds. Breakfast is included in the
charge. It's served from seven A.M. in the main building—that's

the flatter one over there. If you need anything, just ask reception for me. I'm your man," he said. "Take care now."

The moment Clete had closed the door behind him, Henry put his arms around Margaret, happy they had discovered a place like this.

He kicked off his shoes and took in the king-size bed with its inlaid headboard. It looked, like the outside, very Scandinavian modern, but the wood was Californian, like everything else. He stretched out on the bed, clasping his hands behind his head.

Margaret, her head supported on an elbow, was on the bed beside him, looking at her contented husband. "I wish we weren't staying just the one night," she said, "despite the window."

"Yes," Henry said. "Yes, yes, yes."

When Henry woke, Margaret's face was so close to his it blurred in his vision. They must have fallen asleep in each other's arms. His stirring stirred her. He took her chin in his hand and kissed her gently just to the side of her mouth because Margaret, as a courtesy, always wanted to brush her teeth before being kissed, even if she was waking from a brief nap.

"Oh Henry," she said.

"Oh Henry what?"

"I love you, and I'm hungry. It must be dinnertime."

Henry glanced at his watch. It was still on his wrist. It must have been the drive. He always took it off when sleeping. It was almost seven.

"Let's change," Margaret said, swinging her legs off the bed. "Put your elegant blazer on. We'll have a drink at the bar—I assume they have something that does for a cocktail lounge."

"In this healthy atmosphere, they probably serve only orange juice," Henry said, checking to see that he had his wallet, his comb, his—then remembered Clete had not returned his car keys.

"I guess he moved the car to the parking lot. I'll pick up the car keys at the reception desk. I'll bet that's where he left them."

He looked on the dresser for the room key.

"Margaret, did you see the room key?"

"Hmmmm," she said. "It had a triangular orange-and-blue plastic tag on it. I saw it in his hand when he opened the door."

"Could he have forgotten to leave it? Check the bathroom, will you?"

Margaret said, "I didn't see him go into the bathroom."

"Don't be difficult. Just look."

"I'm not being difficult." From the bathroom Margaret called out, "Come look."

She was pointing to a typed index card taped to the bottom of the mirror over the basin.

California is experiencing a water shortage. Please make sure the tap is turned off tight.

"As long as there isn't a wine shortage in the dining room," Henry said cheerfully. "I'll check at the desk about the room key, too."

At the door he said, "Come on now."

"Coming."

The knob turned, but the door did not open. He tugged at it.

"That's odd," he said.

"Is it stuck?" Margaret asked.

Henry tried again, then went to the room phone.

Within a second of his picking it up, a woman's voice with a marked California accent said, "I'll connect you with Clete."

Henry heard a buzz like an intercom, and then Clete's voice. "Yes, sir."

"This is Mr. Brown in room twenty."

"Yes, sir."

"I'm sorry, this is silly, but I can't seem to get the door open."

"I know, sir."

"I don't understand," said Henry, who believed in patience.

Clete's voice changed just the slightest when he said, "You're Jewish, aren't you?"

2

Once when Henry had been asked if he were a practicing Jew he had answered, "Practicing for what?"

When asked if he were religious, he'd say, "I have the same beliefs as God." Pressed, he would amplify. "The notion that God is everywhere in nature is bullshit. That's an idea that confuses the Creator with the creation. Nor is God a plant superintendent, overseeing us all. If you believe that God had a hand in making all this"—Henry's gesture would encompass the world—"He had to be the most energetic Force around. Please understand, God is not a democrat. In the animal world He distributed his energy unequally, a modicum to the sloth, a lot to frisky puppies. Now, if you look at people you can see how undemocratic He is. The superenergetic who have been great leaders have seemed to others godlike. If you want something done, the saw says, give it to a busy man. If you want to understand God, you have to know the Devil, who keeps road gangs standing around as each man takes turns working a bit, like government workers everywhere. Firemen and policemen start out as energetic types, and the Devil grants them twenty-year retirement. All over the world the Devil is winning out. That doesn't make me a Republican, it makes me a believer in the source of energy. Call it God, it's okay with me. If you realize there's been a battle out there between God and the Devil since the beginning of time, you don't get so uptight about human nature, you don't become a zany perfectionist, you take life and other people as you find them."

It was Henry's gentle father who had taught him to respect competence rather than authority. In his business, for instance, Henry made a special point of being able to do almost anything any of his employees could do except reprogram the computer. When they saw him roll up his sleeves to help the foreman get a stuck conveyor belt moving again, his employees fortified their belief that in this company at least authority derived from ability not rank.

Henry saw to it that his family had enough of the necessities, including love. Other men demanded from their business life always *more*. Henry did not want to expand, acquire, or make more money. "Unlimited ambition," he told Margaret, "is for artists or athletes who compete mainly against themselves. In business and in politics, unlimited ambition is dangerous."

If, now that Henry had reached fifty, people felt relaxed in his presence, it was because he had learned to relax himself. He was not an optimist or a pessimist, he thought, but a realist poised to consider whatever life would offer.

Now, whenever a moment of panic presented itself, Henry would think *There has to be a net.*

It came from passing a crowd in New York City some years ago, everyone staring upward to the lip of the roof of a six-story tenement, where a stout lady was hanging on perilously. A policeman on the roof was trying to talk her into giving him her hand. Faced with the decision to accept or reject the helping hand, the woman suddenly let her grip go and started to tumble through the air. Henry didn't want to believe what he was so clearly seeing, a fat lady on her way to momentary death.

But the firemen were below with their safety net. The six men holding it braced themselves for the impact. The fat lady bounced high, then bounced less, then stayed, safe from the concrete and herself.

"Let me try that," Margaret said, turning the doorknob. She pulled on it. Nothing happened. "Some people," she said, "would get angry about a practical joke like this."

There has to be a net. "Give me a moment," Henry said, as Margaret stepped aside. He bent his knees to peer between the door and the jamb, separated only by a vertical hairline of light. He could see two locks.

I wish that were true, Henry thought. On his knees in front of the door, he seemed fascinated by the hardware. "The top lock is a deadbolt," he said, "but Clete locked only the bottom. The bottom's a spring latch. Watch me," he said, turning to look up at her.

Of course, there was anxiety in Margaret's face. She was unprepared by history. "Don't be nervous," he said. "It'll be all right."

Henry was good at fixing things around the house. She thought *This isn't our house.*

"Thank heaven for credit cards," Henry said. He still had his from the Diners Club. It just fit between the door and the jamb. He moved it carefully until it was under the spring latch, then gently pushed upward, moving the latch back into the door. "That's why deadbolt locks are safer," he said over his shoulder to Margaret. "These can be opened by an amateur."

As soon as the plastic card was up an inch, he said, "There," and with his right hand turned the knob and opened the door.

Clete was standing three feet from the door, his arms folded. Henry felt the blood rise to his face.

"You've passed the first test," Clete said gaily. "I'll have to use the deadbolt also from now on, Mr. Brown."

"What the hell kind of nonsense is this?" Margaret asked.

Clete ignored her question. "Dr. Brown," he said, "you're not Jewish, are you?"

Henry remembered when on his second date with Margaret

the subject they had avoided on their first date came up.

"I have an impertinent question," Margaret had said.

"Go ahead."

"You're not Jewish, are you?"

"Would it make a difference?" Henry asked.

"Not to me," she said. "To others."

"I'm Jewish."

"You don't look Jewish," Margaret said.

"That's okay," Henry said. "You don't look Methodist."

"How'd you know I was a Methodist?"

"All Methodists have a certain look."

It was then she realized he was kidding, and they both laughed.

"I looked you up," Henry said. "Your father's a minister. Is he the one it would make a difference to?"

"Yes, but he'd like the idea. Reverend Kittredge's Sunday sermons are about his private conversations with God. They got him transferred to the poorest church in Omaha, which had no choice but to take us. He'd say things like, *I'm going to open a clothing store. Why should the Jews make all the money?* He hated our poverty and couldn't do anything about it. He'd be pleased we're going together. He'd say, *Latch on to a Jew, they always know where the money is.*"

When she saw Henry's face, Margaret added, "You have to think of it as half a joke. He'd never lift a hand against another human being."

"It's a joke that is not a joke," Henry said. "The essence of Jewish humor."

"My mother was the big proponent of brains in my family. She would adore you."

By the time they made that first trip to Omaha, Henry remembered, her mother was dead.

"I'm not Jewish," Margaret was saying to Clete. "What's that got to do with anything?"

"But you married a Jew, right?" Clete asked.

"Listen, young man," Henry said. "You were polite when we arrived and now you're being discourteous."

"I'm sorry," Clete said. "I was just getting some facts straight. We don't like making mistakes."

Damn thought Henry, as he went back into the room to pick up the phone. He was prepared for everything but this.

The girl at the other end sounded alarmed. "Isn't Clete with you?"

"I want to talk to the manager," Henry said, trying to calm his voice.

"Mr. Whittaker doesn't talk to guests," the girl said. "Isn't Clete there?"

"We were locked in our room."

"You'll have to talk to Clete about that."

"I'm afraid he's been rude to my wife and to me."

"Oh, sir, Clete's very polite. I'm sure you must be mistaken."

Henry put the phone back on the cradle. What kind of a place was this? He turned to see Clete standing in the doorway. And he remembered the room clerk at the Highgate. *Will you need a reservation at your next destination? May I recommend Cliffhaven in Big Sur?* And the way he watched him all the way to the elevator?

"Coming, Mr. Brown?"

Henry could see Margaret's anxious face behind Clete.

"I'd like to go down to the reception desk," Henry said.

"Sure," Clete said. "Just follow me."

Outside, Henry took Margaret by the arm. "I think we'd better get out of here," he whispered.

"What about our bags, our clothes?" Margaret asked, starting ·back into the room.

Henry tightened his grip on her arm. "Don't go in there." Then, loud enough for Clete to hear, he said, "We'll come back to get our things, with the police, if necessary."

Clete stopped. Slowly, he turned to face them. "Oh Mr. Brown, you seemed so calm before. I wish you wouldn't get yourself all worked up. It's so un-California, if you know what I mean." His face was expressionless. "Please cool it."

"I don't like jokes like this."

"Mr. Brown, this isn't a joke."

"Do you have my car keys?"

"I told you they'd be at the reception desk," Clete said. "I wouldn't lie to you."

"Well, I'm going straight to the reception desk." Henry took Margaret by the hand and went down the stairs, Clete right behind them.

"Don't try to stop me, young man," Henry said.

"I wouldn't do that, Mr. Brown. And I wish you'd call me Clete, not young man."

Henry turned to look at him. Clete was serious. The name meant something to him.

"You wouldn't want me to call you old man, would you?" Clete asked.

He led Henry and Margaret around to the front of the building. Three other blue-and-orange T-shirted young men, blond like Clete, were lolling in front of another building.

Where were the other guests?

Henry started walking at a fast pace toward the nearest of the staff members. They wouldn't all be crazy. But the young man, seeing him coming, glanced over at Clete, then went into the building behind him. As if on signal, the other two did the same thing.

There wasn't another human being in sight. Behind the building, encircling the distant perimeter of the built-up area, was redwood forest, the trees like stiff sentinels almost all the way up the mountains behind Cliffhaven. Turning toward the Pacific, Henry saw seemingly impenetrable foliage that went all the way down to the whitecapped surf sounding against the rocks. Between the brush and the roiling water there had to be the curving highway they had come on. They had to get back down there.

"I'll be happy to show you where reception is," Clete said.

Henry looked over at Margaret. "There are times," she said, "when a good mind is of absolutely no use."

"Nonsense," Henry had replied, though Margaret, who on occasion had to release a patient to death, was demonstrably right.

"Take your time," Clete said. "I've got all the time in the world."

"Well, I haven't," Henry said, motioning Clete on. He

waited for Margaret, then followed Clete to the side of the next building. The young man leaped up the three steps onto the porch and held the glass door open for them, waiting.

The reception room was plain, just two couches at one end, with a coffee table in front of each, and some extra chairs. At the left as they entered was a large desk with a young lady seated behind it. She, too, was wearing one of the orange T-shirts with "Cliffhaven" stenciled on its front.

"Good evening," she said cheerfully.

"I'm Henry Brown."

"Yes, I know," she said.

"I'd like my car keys, please."

"Oh they're locked up, Mr. Brown. I'm afraid I can't give them to you without Clete's permission."

It is useless to lose one's temper.

"Miss," Henry said, "that Ford belongs to the Hertz people."

The girl looked over at Clete. "Haven't you briefed them?"

"I told him no keys. He's just being stubborn the way some of them are."

Henry turned. "Some of who?"

"Mr. Brown, don't act naïve. You're a very intelligent man. Come now, I'm going to take you and your wife for a real treat. The restaurant is three stars, you know."

"Is that supposed to be the chief attraction of this place?" Henry asked, a touch of sarcasm in his voice.

"It wasn't at first," Clete said. "We got lucky. One of our first guests was a restauranteur—did I get that word right?— you know what I mean, who used to be a gourmet chef, and Mr. Clifford, he's the most intelligent man I ever met, he immediately saw the potential."

"You mean he hired the guest as cook? Why would the man be willing to work here?"

Clete smiled. "Willing is irrelevant, Mr. Brown. Our guests never leave us."

3

An hour earlier, while Henry and Margaret were taking a nap, Clete had decided on a siesta, too. Siesta meant one thing to him. He went to his room and buzzed Charlotte's.

"Come on over," he said.

"I thought you weren't calling today."

"Don't get sore," Clete said. "I got held up with some incomers. You coming?"

Charlotte let his phrase hang in the air a second. Then she said, "Not yet," and they both laughed.

Clete was lying on his bed when Charlotte knocked. She came in without waiting for his response, and locked the door behind her.

"Suppose I had someone in here?" Clete said.

"I'd kill her," Charlotte said.

Charlotte was blonde, young, and extraordinarily tall. Clete, who believed himself to be a connoisseur of female bodies, admired Charlotte's proportions. Even her height pleased him, he just didn't like *standing* next to her.

"There's room," he said, beckoning to the place beside him on the bed. "I like you better horizontal."

"No finesse." She lay down next to him as she had done so many afternoons before.

"No finesse, eh?" Clete said, touching the tip of her left breast through the orange T-shirt. He moved his finger in a small circle around the perimeter of the nipple, barely in contact with the nipple itself. As always, it aroused her, and when he saw that it had, he withdrew his finger. A little at a time, was his motto with women. Make them want it.

"Got myself some beauts," he said. "Henry Brown. Wife's a doctor."

"Is she cute?" Charlotte asked.

"She's old enough to be my mother, for Christ's sake!" Clete said.

"So's Mrs. Clifford."

"You watch yourself." He returned his finger to its circling motion, this time on Charlotte's right nipple.

"You can't always tell when people are Jewish," Clete said. "They ought to wear signs."

Charlotte pointed to her nose.

"Oh, some of them have nose jobs," Clete said. "But some just in their natural looks, you can't tell. This guy Brown doesn't look it. If anything, his wife—that's the doctor—she might look a little, but I'll bet she's not."

Clete had moved his hand to Charlotte's belly, expanding the circular motion.

"I'm glad you find me attractive," Charlotte said.

"How do you know I find you attractive?" Clete said.

Charlotte quickly flicked her fingers at his hardened crotch.

"Hey, don't do that."

She moved her hand gently across his jeans.

"Better?"

"A lot better."

"You ever fuck a Jewish girl?" Charlotte asked.

"Not that I know of," Clete said quickly, thinking of the Minter woman.

"You don't sound sure," Charlotte said, removing her hand from his jeans.

"I'm sure, I'm sure."

Clete had eyeballed Phyllis Minter on her first day in the dining room. He'd have guessed her to be thirty-five max, though her eyes and carriage conveyed the self-confidence Clete associated with older women. It wasn't just her tits, ass, and legs, it was how it all came together, even the way she held her fucking head high. If he was ever going to sample Jewish pussy, it ought to be hers. He'd bring her head down to where she could see what he had for her.

It was a simple matter for him to find out her room number. A small favor got him the key from someone who would never tell Charlotte.

Phyllis Minter was born two years before World War II ended in a part of Brooklyn then inhabited almost entirely by Jews. Her father, a good-looking man as proved by a World War II photograph, returned from the army safe, got a job driving a cab in Manhattan on the swing shift. As an ex-serviceman, when he cruised for customers, Morton Minter naturally gave preference to men in uniform. During his second week, his cab was hailed by a man in soldier's uniform, who had him drive to somewhere under the El-tracks and there pointed a pistol at Morton's head and said, "Let's have your dough." Morton turned to tell the man he was an ex-G.I. trying to make an honest living, but as he turned around to do so, the man fired. It was the last sound ever heard by Morton Minter, who became the first cab driver casualty that February in New York City. The thief got less than six dollars.

Phyllis was told that her father had gone back into the army. Though only four, she refused to believe it. He hadn't said good-bye, and his uniforms were still hanging in the closet. Phyllis's mother, a fragile woman, let her sanity be shrouded in grief. Unable to cope, she let relatives place Phyllis, kicking and screaming, into a Hebrew orphanage run by an Orthodox sadist, who had an excessive interest in barely pubescent children. He kept his eye on Phyllis. When she was almost twelve, the director called her to his office and offered her twenty-five cents to do something Phyllis had only read about in a book that circulated clandestinely among the girls for under-the-cover reading late at night. Phyllis, a cynic at twelve, was quite prepared to sell the only thing she possessed that was of interest, but not for twenty-five cents. Though the director preached socialism—which he called "sharing"—Phyllis was the possessor of a remarkable intelligence and had read the counter-vailing literature. This was a society in which one sold for the highest possible price, which wasn't a quarter. She ran away to try her luck.

By the time Phyllis was seventeen, she was well-to-do, though she had slept with only four men in all that time, and with each of them a few times at most. The first two were easy—older men, married, with a penchant for youngsters—who learned to their dismay that Phyllis understood not only what jailbait meant but was quite prepared to trade their freedom from prosecution for a fair sum. The sum, which seemed unfair to them, was designated as fair by Phyllis, who pegged the amount to the largest sum she thought she could get away with. She was not a pirate, but a canny businesswoman who never overreached herself.

Her third mark was a popular crooner, who enjoyed the groupies clustering around him in his dressing room at the Paramount. Through a friend of a friend, Phyllis infiltrated this group, attracted the crooner's attention, whose mistake was to assume this very bright and pretty young girl was one of his worshipers. He allowed himself to be seduced. When the time came—which Phyllis put off as long as possible in order to raise the price—she surprised him by confessing that she was not interested in his passing affection but in endowment. He told her to git, whereupon he was visited a day later by a policeman in uniform, who didn't threaten arrest or anything unpleasant, provided the crooner paid Phyllis Minter her due. "You her pimp?" screamed the crooner. "Get the fuck out of here!"

The police officer, a man thoroughly at home in the ways of the world, patiently explained that his role was not unlike that of the theatrical agents the crooner was used to. There was a certain amount of money to pay each month—it wouldn't make a serious dent in his income—and the policeman, who would see to it that it was paid, took, with permission, ten percent before turning the balance over to Phyllis, who was now sixteen and looked several years older. It was the stink bombs—rolls of camera film wrapped tightly in cardboard—that caused the management of the Paramount to urge the crooner to settle with the aggrieved.

When the policeman next showed, the crooner offered a deal. Instead of monthly payments, five thousand dollars cash, a bounty at the time. After the transfer of the money, they shook hands, as businessmen will.

The policeman, prepared to turn over Phyllis's share to her, thought of negotiating his fee upward to twenty percent. The expression in Phyllis's face in response to his proposal was fearsome. He'd seen men—but never a woman—look like that.

"What's the matter?" he said.

With a minimal movement of her lips, which she'd seen women of menace do in movies, Phyllis reminded the policeman of his wife. She said, "I'll visit the police commissioner first, then her."

That was all it took. The policeman, having worked with Phyllis, believed her. He not only turned over her ninety percent, but to show his continued good will introduced her to a man he had only told her about, a stockbroker who was having a particular run of postwar luck with laundered dollars.

They were still in bed when Phyllis suggested that the stockbroker invest her forty-five hundred dollars cash in whatever was his best going deal.

"You can't always guess perfectly in this business," the broker said, not wanting to put her off entirely because he wanted a repetition of the pleasure he had just experienced.

"Oh that's easy," Phyllis said. "Whatever turned out best for the year, you'll consider the first forty-five hundred mine and the rest whoever else's."

It took a little persuasion, but Phyllis became the most fortunate investor on the street. Whatever was the most productive deal of the year, turned out to be what she had "invested" in, even if her friend had to make up the difference out of his own pocket.

Her eventual affluence decided her. There was no point to getting married; she already had what she considered her "alimony" from several men. She moved, at twenty-three, to Los Angeles, where an acquaintance introduced her to the prospects of real estate. As one might expect, she turned into a terrific saleswoman because she never seemed to need to make the sale. Phyllis Minter was thirty-five when she went to that new resort she had heard about—Cliffhaven—to rest and reflect in an environment she suspected would suit her: she was told everybody went there in couples. She, as usual, would go alone, and by that very fact be both exceptional and, just in case, desirable.

When Clete inveigled a key to Phyllis's room, she thought she'd found her exit visa from crazy Cliffhaven.

"You're a terrific looker," Clete told her.

These California beachboy types, thought Phyllis, had the style of a preformed hamburger. He was examining her with his eyes. That part was free.

Clete had come in with the express desire of having what he thought of as his first Jewish pussy, but when he saw the way Phyllis moved her mouth, he thought he'd try another avenue first.

"I've got something for you," he said. "You hungry?"

"What's in it for me?" Phyllis said, biding her time.

Clete decided to show her. He let his jeans and shorts drop.

"Don't you think you ought to take your sneakers off?" asked Phyllis.

Clete looked down. It was kind of ridiculous-looking. He had to sit down on the edge of the bed to untie his Keds. When he got them off and pulled his pants and undershorts off, he stood up. But the process of undressing on order had minimized his tumescence, and she was staring at it, which didn't help.

"Okay," he said, figuring thirty seconds of that chick and he'd be back in form.

"What's the quid?" Phyllis asked.

"Quid?"

"Quid pro quo. You give, you get."

He wasn't about to get involved in affectionate foreplay with a Jewess. He made that clear.

She laughed, which didn't help his rigidity any.

"What the hell do you want?" Clete said angrily.

"Out of this place," she said.

"Nobody gets out of here."

Phyllis went into the john and started washing her face, ignoring him.

Clete tapped her on the shoulder.

"Okay."

"Okay what?"

"You do what I say and I'll get you out afterward."

"You take me out and we'll do it on the outside. That's my condition."

"You've got to be kidding. I'd lose my job."

"You've lost more than your job," she said pointing.

Clete wanted to shove a crowbar up her ass, the fucking Hebe!

"Why don't you put your pants back on," she said, "so neither of us has to look at it."

"You bitch!" he said. If he struck her now the marks would show. There'd be an investigation. That stupid broad would tell them everything.

"There must be somebody on the premises who'll put up with your droopy miniature," Phyllis said. "Vamoose."

He got his shorts and pants on, tied his sneakers. He would have slammed the door, but he didn't want to attract attention.

When he left, Phyllis Minter lay on her bed, thinking. She'd encountered men who asked her if Minter was a Jewish name, adding that she really didn't look Jewish. Was that anti-Semitism, curiosity, or just a compliment? She'd never taken the subject seriously till her door was bolted shut in Cliffhaven. Maybe whatever her father had run into in Europe had affected him the same way.

As for this place, Phyllis thought, she didn't doubt for a minute that she'd get out, maybe using the orange-and-blue uniformed *putz* she'd just humiliated. He'd be back. She wasn't afraid of any man whose baton she could lower. Other women she'd met sometimes boasted of their ability to give a man a hard-on real quick. To Phyllis that was child's play. Making a man lose his by talking him down, that was a skill she was proud of. What she found strange, as she lay with her hands clasped behind her head thinking, was that in all of the previous ruminations of her life, she'd centered her ambitions on succeeding financially, showing the orphanage and her crazed mother and dead father that despite their abandonment, she could make out. All that seemed behind her now. She wasn't the once-poor kid, or the mark for lechers who'd turn the tables on them. She was, by the definition of others, a Jew. Okay, she'd show them. She'd not only get out of this place, she'd kill at least one of the bastards on the way.

Clete wished Charlotte hadn't asked him about whether he'd ever fucked a Jewish girl. All it did was bring that brass-balled Minter woman into his mind. He was glad Charlotte wasn't like that. He was on track with her, a really good two-way street. Maybe she'd asked the question because . . .

Clete looked at Charlotte. "You ever fuck a Jewish guy?"

Charlotte didn't answer immediately. That was a mistake.

Clete sat up straight. "Didn't you hear me?"

"I heard you. Take it easy." Charlotte patted Clete's crotch, not sensually as earlier.

"Yes or no?" He was standing.

"Come back down here."

"Answer my question."

"Come back down here and I'll answer." Clete sat down on the bed.

Charlotte pulled him down to her. With her face close to his, she said, "The only Jewish so-called person I ever got close to before Cliffhaven was a girl in my dorm. Arlene. Forget her last name. Itsky something, I think. She used to go around without a top a lot of the time. I don't blame her. Fantastic tits. She once came to my room to ask me something about some course, I forgot what, and when she sat down on the edge of my bed, I couldn't help myself, I reached down and touched her breasts."

"You what?" Clete said.

"You would have, too," Charlotte said, laughing. "It was

nice. Don't worry, I'm straight, it was just a thing of the moment."

"Sometimes I don't understand you."

"Ditto. Like now. You going to get out of that uniform?"

Clete loved it when Charlotte sort of ordered him to undress in front of her. It reminded him of shows he had seen in Vegas, only he was on stage.

"Come *on*," she said. "You're keeping me waiting."

He didn't know what it was, but just her words, maybe the way she said the words, got him going. He could feel the tightening.

He got off the bed in a rolling motion. Then, standing close to her head, he lifted his T-shirt slowly past his face. He unbuckled his belt, first the flap, pulling it hard, then let the stem ease out of the hole. He unsnapped the top button of his jeans. He took the tab of the zipper and slowly pulled his fly down, watching her watching him. Next, the moccasins, kicking each off in turn. Letting his jeans fall, he stepped out of them, standing in his nylon brief that showed his now-hard equipment off to advantage. He took off one sock, then the other, then expanded the elastic waist of his brief so that when he quickly lowered them, his member would twang upward, something Charlotte always appreciated in a way he especially liked —getting on her knees and opening her mouth, never letting her eyes stray from his eyes as she licked, then sucked, feeling she had him in her power more in these moments than at any other time.

"Hey," he said, meaning he didn't want to come just yet, and he pulled her up and helped her take her clothes off. Her own nylon bikini panties matched his, one of their first conspiracies, since they were never allowed leave from Cliffhaven together.

Afterward, once Clete was sure Charlotte had also had hers, he almost always drifted off for a few minutes. When his eyes opened, she was on her elbow staring at him as if she owned him. He liked the feeling.

"Question. You ever ball Mrs. Clifford?"

Clete wondered what Charlotte was getting at.

"You go to their place," she said, "when Mr. Clifford's not there."

Some things Clete did not trust Charlotte with, much as he liked her. His relationship with the Clifford woman was *his* relationship.

"You taking the Fifth Amendment?" Charlotte asked. She had never met Mrs. Clifford.

"She's a terrific lady," Clete said. "Real smart. Real class."

"I don't understand," Charlotte said, stretching, letting her hand touch his shrunken member on its descent.

"Understand what?"

"Why you want to be Mr. Clifford's gofer?"

"Who says that?"

"George Whittaker says that."

Clete slapped Charlotte's face hard. "Why'd you say that for?"

"George Whittaker said it!"

"Don't you repeat any of his shit to me."

Charlotte remembered the rabbit. Once, behind the pot farm, they'd seen a rabbit up close. Clete boasted he could run as fast as any rabbit. Charlotte dared Clete to catch the rabbit, which was parked, ears up, no more than thirty feet away. Clete gave her an angry glance, then bolted toward the rabbit, which took a second too long to figure out where to run, and Clete scooped it up in one hand, then twisted its neck around. He waltzed over to Charlotte, light on his feet, a mocking expression on his face, and dropped the corpse at her feet. "Satisfied?" he'd said.

Clete had the same crazy expression now, so Charlotte, frightened, said, "I'm sorry, I didn't mean anything by it." She put her hand up to her red cheek.

"Well, okay," Clete said, panting. "Whittaker's just jealous. Clifford said I was his fair-haired boy right in front of George once. He said he could always count on me. What's wrong with that?"

"Nothing."

"Jesus." Clete glanced at his watch, which was the only thing he had on. "My new ones have probably found they're locked in by now. I'd better git."

"Kiss me first," Charlotte said.

For a moment, Clete stood his ground.

"Kiss me," Charlotte said.

Obediently, Clete slid down lower on the bed and with parted lips kissed Charlotte where her legs met, but when she started moving her pelvis up and down in rhythm, he stopped. It would do her good to leave her hanging for once, he thought, as he hopped off the bed. She'd had one, that's enough. He pulled his shorts and jeans and socks on, put on his shirt, slipped his feet into his moccasins, and, brushing his hands through his hair, checked himself for a second in front of the mirror and was out the door. Women were just like Jews, he thought. You had to keep them under control or they'd give you trouble.

4

"Excuse me," Clete said, stifling a yawn with his fist, "I meant to get a nap while you were resting."

"Don't you have other guests to look after?" Margaret asked, suddenly curious to know everything possible about this place before they were out and gone.

"Not till you're fully briefed," Clete replied. "This place," he said, spreading his arms wide, "is one of the newest deluxe resorts in the United States. You have to admit the geographic location is exceptional. Now, is everyone ready for dinner, or would you care for a drink in the lounge first?"

"Why did you lock us in our room?" Margaret asked.

"A signal. Let's call it a tip, from me to you. You gave me a tip. I gave you a tip." Clete smiled. "Let's discuss it over dinner, like civilized folks. Shall we have a drink first?"

"Are you suggesting," Henry said, "that Dr. Brown and I have a drink before dinner?"

"I was thinking of all of us."

"Oh. You're allowed to socialize with the guests?"

"Please don't be sarcastic, Mr. Brown. It's part of my job."

"I'll forego a drink tonight," Henry said.

"I agree," Margaret said, who liked a predinner drink even more than Henry did.

"I see," Clete said.

He seems hurt, thought Henry, as if *we* were being rude to *him*. He felt suddenly as if he were in a foreign country, trying to pick up the customs.

"Look," Clete said affably. "Let's be realistic. You have to eat, right?"

Henry's gaze wandered. There was no fence that he could see. No guards, guns, nothing of that sort. Everything looked so normal.

"If you're thinking of running away," Clete said, "that's perfectly okay with me, as long as it's just thinking. You need energy to run away. You need energy to live. There's no place else to get food than the dining room."

One eyelid lowered, Clete looked at Margaret. "You are thinking you might rather skip the meal and go hungry."

"Exactly," Margaret said.

"Three squares a day, Doctor."

"No harm in skipping a meal once in a while," Margaret said.

"Ah, but if you thought that tomorrow you might not get any food at all . . ." Clete stopped to observe their reaction, then continued, "No breakfast, no dinner, no anything, you might not want to skip your meal tonight. It's just logical."

"Is that a threat?" Henry asked.

"Oh Mr. Brown, we don't make threats around this place. Please be reasonable and come to dinner before the kitchen closes down. I intend to eat. If you don't want to eat, you can just sit there and watch me."

He went on ahead.

Why is he so cocksure that we won't just walk out of here? Henry thought. He noticed Margaret's shoes. If only she hadn't changed from her walking shoes.

"What do you say, Margaret?"

Clete was now well ahead of them.

"He's certainly got self-confidence," Margaret said.

"He knows a lot that we don't yet know," Henry said, remembering, as he did in times of stress, the words of his father, telling him that the role of a man was to keep his senses and intelligence tuned to the nuances of events so that in the event of danger he could walk faster, turn a corner, look up in time, do something that would by his conscious act avert catastrophe. *Look both ways before crossing the street. Watch out for incompetent drivers, drive defensively.*

"Coming?" Clete called.

Henry made up his mind. "We might as well eat."

"If you say so," Margaret said.

"You don't sound as if you agree we should. We'll be out of this place in no time."

"I'm sure of that," Margaret said, her voice less certain than her words. "It's just that I can't believe we are voluntarily following him."

The path to the restaurant crossed the road they had come up on. Henry glanced to his right. He could see no one in the sentry box. Were they expecting no more guests this evening? Did they need no traffic control for the one-way road? When they had a new order-processing problem at the plant, a product that wouldn't fit one of the standard shipping cartons, he'd pull together the available facts, consider the alternatives.

Clete had stopped. When they caught up to him, he pointed. "Over there's the Olympic-size swimming pool. If you don't give us any trouble, you can use it once a day."

"Why, thank you."

"Dr. Brown," Clete said. "I think you'll find sarcasm counterproductive around here." He turned and walked ahead of them again.

They were a hundred yards from the entrance to the low, flat building that housed the restaurant. Henry noticed that the path leading to it was made up of small white stones that crunched under their feet. Was it that way on purpose, noisy, to betray the sound of running? Mustn't get paranoid. When he'd seen hostages on a train on TV, he'd thought, what would he do if Margaret were held captive? He hadn't thought of them both being trapped.

At the entrance to the restaurant, Clete waited for them to catch up, then beckoned for them to precede him.

Inside, they were immediately greeted by a maître d' in a tuxedo—a tall man, handsome, with a trace of accent. "Ah, you must be Mr. and Mrs. Brown of New York," said the maître d', extending his hand. Why did Henry shake it? *You didn't get rid of civilities in an hour.* "Welcome," the maître d' said, but Henry's gaze was beyond him, taking in the splendor of the dining room with its many levels, each a few steps up or down from the next, aesthetically pleasing geometry. On all sides there were green-tinted picture windows looking out on the natural magnificence that surrounded Cliffhaven. But Henry's attention was riveted on the other people.

There must have been more than a hundred guests seated at the tables, and every one of them had turned to stare at them. It wouldn't have happened in a restaurant unless they were movie stars. Why were they looking? Because we are the newcomers.

The maître d' led the way, Clete bringing up the rear. Very few of the tables had someone like Clete in attendance. The orange blouses of the waitresses fluttered through the dining room.

Henry stopped at a table where an older couple, in their sixties, were looking at them with sad eyes.

Henry bent to the man and, in a half-whisper, asked, "What is this place?"

Clete immediately stepped forward, touched Henry on the arm, and said, "I'm sorry, Mr. Brown, but conversation with the other guests is not permitted for the first three months."

The old couple looked away, their faces reddening, as if the reproof had been for them. Gradually the other heads in the dining room turned back to their meals, and resumed their broken conversations.

"This way, please," the maître d' said, showing them to a table for four on one of the higher platforms. "You'll have a good view of the mountainside from here," he said, "even at dusk. This will be your regular table from now on." He gestured for one of the busboys to remove the fourth chair.

Margaret sat on Henry's side of the table, Clete opposite Henry. He moved his chair toward the middle so that he might be opposite both of them.

Clete said, "I'll join you for meals during the break-in period, perhaps a week."

"We're only staying overnight," said Margaret, her voice sliding out of her usual pitch.

Clete smiled. "Provided your conduct is exemplary. After three months another couple might be allowed to join you for the evening meal. Breakfast and lunch is served cafeteria style."

This is insane, Margaret thought. She was moving to get up when she felt Henry's constraining hand. Damned if she'd be quiet. "What the hell do you people think you're doing here?" she said.

"I'll be happy to answer that question," Clete said.

"We're on vacation," Henry said. "We'd prefer to eat by ourselves."

"I understand," Clete said. "But that isn't possible right now."

"We can just leave."

"I don't recommend it. Why don't we order?"

"I won't pay," Henry said.

"Oh, you don't pay for my dinner, Mr. Brown. Just for the two of you, as you normally would. We'll put it on your American Express card. Please let's order. Very few guests really give us any trouble."

"You locked the door of our room," Margaret said.

"It's a security measure."

"You locked us in," she said.

"I told you it's a way of apprising you of your status."

"What the hell do you mean?"

Henry interrupted her with his hand on her arm. *Cool it,* it always meant. *You accomplish more if you're cool.*

"Henry, these people are committing a crime."

"I beg your pardon," Clete said.

"This is kidnapping."

"Oh Dr. Brown, we haven't taken you anywhere. I'm disappointed in you."

"It's a federal offense."

"Dr. Brown, we want you to think of this place as hospitable."

"We are not going to stay here."

"Yes, I know." Clete glanced at the diners in the room. "They all said that at the beginning. Why don't we order now?" He handed two menus across. Margaret refused hers.

"You have to eat," Clete said. "You might as well take advantage of the circumstances. You'll see how quickly time will pass."

Henry now found Margaret's hand under the table, patted it with a minimum of movement. They'd have to play out the string.

A trace of amusement wrinkled the corner of Clete's mouth. There would come a time when they'd do without touching. "What would you like to start with?" he asked.

I have to think. I'm reacting emotionally. Margaret and I will have to use our heads to get us out of here.

"I can recommend the California avocados," Clete said. "You can have them with shrimp filling, or neat with lemon. Why don't I order them with the shrimp for all of us? That'll set us up for the chef's special. It's a fish mousse, it comes with buttered asparagus."

Clete motioned to the waitress and ordered for them.

"While we're waiting," Clete said, "let me tell you about some of the other guests. That man you stopped to talk to? Which, by the way, you shouldn't have done, right? He used to be a prize-winning composer, poor as a churchmouse, then went to Hollywood to do movie scores. We're all corruptible, right?"

Henry didn't answer.

"Dr. Brown," Clete said, "we have four or five other doctors here. We've also got some actors. Way over in that corner, see, that's—he played the lead in—"

"I recognize him," Margaret said.

That's right, Henry thought. *Play along so he'll let down his guard.*

"Just in front of him," Clete said, "that man with the prominent nose," he tittered, "I guess there're quite a few like that here, he's from your part of the country—Pelham, I think. He owns a chain of groceries, small chain but lucrative."

"How long has he been here?" Henry asked.

"I'm not allowed to answer questions like that. Sorry."

"Hasn't anyone come looking for him?" Margaret asked.

"We're very selective in the people we invite here. None of your taxi drivers, you may have noticed, or mom-and-pop candy-store types. No Las Vegas types either. Middle class and up, people who will appreciate the environment."

"I think you get people who can afford to stay in a place like this," Henry said.

"And their kids who come looking for them," Clete added as the appetizers arrived. "Teenagers, young twenties. Sometimes a brother or sister, but mostly younger people."

Margaret tried to keep her hand from trembling as she squeezed lemon on the avocado. She glanced around.

"I know what you're thinking, Dr. Brown," Clete said.

Margaret tried to look at his eyes.

Clete avoided her gaze. To Henry he said, "Not many young people to be seen. They're kept in a special building near the farm."

"What farm?" Henry asked.

"You'll know soon enough." Clete put his fork down. "We're not stupid here, Mr. Brown. You Jews sometimes think everybody else is stupid. Everything here is very carefully planned. Mr. Clifford is a genius. Just wait till someone comes looking for you."

"He will!" Margaret said.

"You mean your son Stanley at Santa Cruz? Sure. You'll be sorry if he comes looking. You'll wish you'd had a kid who didn't give a damn."

"I don't know what you do here," Margaret said, "but whatever it is is inhuman."

"You'll have an opportunity to critique the program some weeks from now," Clete said. "In the meantime, I suggest you eat. You'll need the nourishment. Your second week is a dry week."

"What the hell does that mean?"

"Easy, easy. No water. No liquids. Except for whatever moisture is naturally present in food. The third week, no food, but you're back on water. It's an interesting procedure devised by Dr. Goodson."

Henry waited for the explanation.

"Please eat. I'm giving you good advice," Clete said. "Dr. Goodson came here as a guest and has stayed on to conduct some experiments. We know people just don't appreciate the things they've got, you know, the most fundamental things like food and water. Dr. Goodson's findings show that after one week of liquid deprivation and one week of food deprivation, people appreciate both for the first time in their lives, isn't that wonderful!"

"You need experiments to demonstrate something that obvious?" Margaret asked.

"To prove his thesis," Clete said. "He's a brilliant man. That's him over there."

Dr. Goodson, a gray-haired, small man was eating at a long table that accommodated more than a dozen people, all wearing orange armbands.

"Those are all trusties with him," Clete said. "They have privileges denied to other guests."

"Like what?"

"They're allowed to work without supervision. They can wander around the grounds during daylight hours. We've got a terrific work project going right now down the southern end."

"What kind of work?" Henry asked.

"Oh you'll see, just as soon as your indoctrination period's over. Your wife will probably work with Dr. Goodson."

"I will not," Margaret said.

Clete smiled. "Relax. The important thing is to accept. You'll be happier here. Ah, there we are."

The waitress arrived with the fish mousse.

"I really don't think I can eat any more," Henry said.

"Oh, it's delicious," Clete said, reaching his fork over to Margaret's plate and taking a small amount. "You see," he said, flourishing his fork, "it's not poisoned."

Clete, he noticed, was not served the mousse, but two hamburgers and a side of french fries.

"I'm not much on European-type food," Clete said.

"Perhaps you'd better try eating something," Margaret said to Henry.

The doctor is being sensible, Henry thought. Nourishment

was necessary. *Eat, eat* was the refrain that sang in his head. Were Jewish mothers who pressed food on their children the harbingers of catastrophe? Did they think man was made like a camel so that he could store food for the uncertain future? Margaret wasn't like that. She was practical. He had to be practical, too. Get the facts. Know your opponent.

"Tell me about yourself," Henry said to Clete.

Clete looked up with the expression of a child just handed a present. "I'd love to."

"If it's not against the rules," Henry said carefully.

"Oh no," Clete said. "We've really got to get to know each other, don't we? To start with—go on, you finish that marvelous fish mousse and I'll talk. My father drove one of those sixteen-wheel interstate rigs, and he used to come home maybe once a week and say how awful Texas was or Illinois or someplace like that. My mother always told me he was lying, that he had a woman in most of those places and talked them down just so she'd think all he did on the road was drive the rig, eat, sleep, and think of her. My own opinion was that he didn't think of her even when he was home. Sure, he'd shave, eat a tremendous meal, then take her into the bedroom, but if she was anyone else female and handy, he'd have taken anyone else into the bedroom. He got laid the way most people—gosh, Dr. Brown, I'm sorry, I forgot myself."

"That's all right," Margaret said. "Go on."

"He offered to take me on one of those trips when I was thirteen or so, but Mom said I couldn't miss school for a week. I think she was worried about what I might see on the road. It's a terrible place, when you think of it. I mean bus stops and diners and other truckers for company, and nothing to do all day but stare through the windshield. I couldn't do it. I wanted to enjoy life. I used to go out to the beach with a group of boys —we started out doing this on weekends and ended up playing hooky sometimes so we wouldn't have to wait for the weekend. People would park at the lot near the beach, and we'd offer to watch their cars for them for, you know, a quarter or a half-dollar, depending on what kind of car it was. I guess they figured it was worth it to have air in their tires when they finished at the beach. Well, as soon as we had, say, five dollars each, we'd forget our car-watching and go to some other part of the beach ourselves, sun a while on borrowed towels—we borrowed more towels!—and have chili or tacos for lunch, and then go hunting for snatch."

Clete looked at Margaret to see how she would react.

She maintained her neutral expression, interest without commitment; Henry seemed to want to hear this story for some reason she didn't yet understand.

"Our big thing was older women."

"How old were you at the time?" Henry asked.

"Oh thirteen, maybe fourteen later on," Clete said.

"How old were the older women?" Henry asked.

"Oh," Clete said, laughing. "Everything. Seventeen or forty, it didn't matter. You know those planes would come over the beach hauling some ad? Well, we had our own way of advertising. There'd be four or five of us, and we'd walk down the beach just where the sand meets the water so we'd attract the most attention, and, well, it's hard to put this, we were all at attention in our bathing suits, and believe me people would notice. And you didn't have to walk too long or too far before some chick would say something and you'd be going somewhere, sometimes one for each of us and sometimes we'd share. We learned something, which is there are a lot of women in California, some of them real good looking, who want something different than a vibrator once in a while. Sometimes we'd get money, too, but that wasn't it. We could make all we needed off of the car-watching."

Clete took time out for a bite of hamburger.

"I thought surfboarding was the big thing in California."

"Oh, yeah, sure," Clete said, munching. "Excuse me," he said, holding his napkin up to his mouth. "Shouldn't talk while eating."

When he finished he said, "Down around where I lived, south of L.A., you just didn't let good waves go by as virgins. We had to chip in for a surfboard at first, but after a time, we each had one, and one of the guys was sixteen and got himself a heap, and we strapped our surfboards to the roof—you should have seen us in a wind—and we went out to the beach to collect the dough, and the chicks, and the waves. We had some bad times with a truant officer, though, a real snitch. He told my mother a whole bunch of lies, like he gave her more dates that I was supposed to have missed school than I really did—I kept track, you know—and he said we were into dope, which we weren't, not then anyway. Next time my father came home, my mother laid it on him how I was into a bad bunch, et cetera, et cetera, and he took off his two-inch belt. His pants were too wide for him, and he tried to strop me with one hand while holding up his pants with the other. Well, I just grabbed the belt and yanked it out of his hands and stropped him. You should have seen my mother yell."

Clete looked to see how his story was going down.

"Had to leave home after that," Clete said. "No two ways about it. I came back later when my mother was out, shoved the stuff I wanted into a suitcase. I wasn't going to be on my own bareass, excuse me."

"I would estimate that to have been about eight years ago," Henry said. "Am I right?"

"Close."

"What have you been doing since?"

"I got chased a lot—cops, storekeepers who saw me lift something, you know. Worst was the creeps. Can I be frank?"

The waitress brought coffee and a moment's surcease.

Clete watched the waitress leave. "They've got some mighty fine young women working here, I can tell you that. Oh yes, creeps. Well, you know there are types, men I mean, who cruise looking for boys on the loose. It's not just California, I'm sure you've got people like that back home. Well, if you're hung up for bread, you can close your eyes I suppose. Hell, if you close your eyes, how can you tell whoever's down there is a man or a woman?"

"I think we ought to go to our room now, Clete," Margaret said.

"You don't like what I told you?"

"It's a pathetic story, Clete. I'm sorry you had to live such a life."

The truth was she felt light-headed, relaxed, compared to the way she had felt at the beginning of the meal.

It hadn't been Clete's story.

Could it have been something in the food? She glanced over at Henry. His eyes looked the way he always looked after he'd had two or three drinks quickly at a boring cocktail party. But they'd had nothing to drink.

"I need to use the washroom," she said to Clete.

"It's over there," Clete said. He didn't like Margaret. She looked down on him, just the way Jews did. She had no right.

There were two women in the ladies' room, a dark-haired pretty woman in her thirties, and a graying woman of Margaret's age.

"I'm Dr. Brown," she said to both of them. "We just arrived."

The older woman walked right past Margaret and left the bathroom.

"She's afraid," the younger woman said.

"I hadn't said anything."

"Newcomers always try to ask questions."

"Is there anything they put in the food?"

There was suddenly a splash of fear in the young woman's eyes. She nodded her head quickly, as if not speaking words might keep her safe.

"It was in the fish mousse, wasn't it?" Clete had taken one small bite. But he'd eaten hamburgers. "What is it?"

The young woman bit her lip and started for the door. Margaret put her hand on the woman's arm. "What is it?"

"From the farm," the woman said, a catch in her throat. "Please let me go."

The young woman's eyes, a beautiful dark brown, had deep circles under them.

"How long have you been here?"

She said, "More than four months. Please don't ask me any more."

"Four months! Was anyone with you?"

The young woman was silent.

Margaret took the young woman's hands. "Please tell me."

"My husband."

"Yes."

"And my child. A boy."

It seemed to Margaret that the young woman was on the verge of tears.

"I haven't seen children here," Margaret said.

"They remove them to the nursery," the young woman said.

"During the day?" Margaret asked.

The young woman looked frightened. "I must go."

"When did you last see your child?"

"When we arrived. Four months ago."

Margaret put her arms around the woman. "Oh my dear. I'm sorry."

The door to the ladies' room opened. An orange-and-blue uniformed young woman came in. "Lesbian conduct is not permitted here," she said.

Margaret dropped her arms from around the young woman and approached the staff member. "Where is this woman's child?" asked Margaret.

The staff member glared at the young woman. "You've been talking. Out."

The young woman seemed terribly frightened. She glanced at Margaret, then swiftly left.

"You, too," the staff member said.

"Just hold your horses," Margaret said and went into a booth. She could see the staff member's feet just outside the booth, waiting.

When Margaret was finished, she came out of the booth, washed, and left the room. The staff member was following her.

When Margaret resumed her place beside Henry, the staff member said to Clete, "You'd better keep an eye on her, Clete. She's trouble."

"I'm sorry to hear that," Clete said to Margaret as the staff member left. Margaret looked around the dining room, trying to spot the dark-haired woman, whose name she did not know. There she was, eating at a small table all by herself. Where was her husband?

To Clete, Margaret said, "Where are the young children?"

"There are no children, Dr. Brown."

"What about the nursery?"

"There is no nursery," Clete said. "Oh, by the way, your

husband and I were just exchanging notes about New York and California."

"Clete's never been out of California," Henry said.

"Don't feel sorry for me," Clete said. "California's a big and varied place. I like it here. And the people. I don't mean movie Jews or students, people with real values about the world. There was this one couple who were like a mother and father to me, not just talkers and doers, people with ideas to put into practice, and they taught me a lot more about life than I ever learned in high school."

"Who were those people?" Henry asked. He thought it a good idea to keep Clete talking, but wondered why Margaret was sitting as if carved out of stone.

Clete's eyes glistened. "Mr. and Mrs. Clifford. They had more than a dozen of us on their ranch, fed us, gave us horses to ride, taught us what we had to know. Mr. Clifford it was who had the connections and the money to get things started. That's why this place is named after him. Cliffhaven. Now, Mr. Brown, while we're having our coffee, tell me about you."

This is insane, thought Henry. This is the United States. We don't have things like this here. But at the same time he felt no anger, as if the problem was an abstract one or concerned other people.

He doesn't realize about the food, thought Margaret.

For a long time Henry had put out of his mind what had happened to him at Fort Benning, Georgia, toward the very end of the war. They were housed in two barracks, the officer candidates in his company. On the bottom floor of the first barrack were the trainees whose last names started with Acker and ended with Fielding. Opposite his bunk, across the aisle, lived a tall, slightly pockmarked boy from southern Illinois named Cooper who, one night, brought a clip of live M-1 ammo into the barracks and, without the stimulus of alcohol, stood up on his bunk while everybody was cleaning their weapons, shoved the live clip into his rifle, and, looking straight at Henry, announced at the top of his voice, "The only mistake Hitler made was he didn't kill all the fucking Jews."

They were bedded in alphabetical order. The bunk to

Henry's right was the province of a young man named Brownell, who had admitted to Henry during one of their late-night chats that, before the army, he'd never met a Jew. It was Brownell who slowly got off his bunk and strode across the aisle. Suddenly he grabbed Cooper's rifle away from him, pulled the bolt back, unloaded the M-1, threw the empty weapon on Cooper's bunk, and said so he could be heard by everyone who was staring, "That's not a toy," and that was that.

Except the next day Henry had, with some trepidation, sought out his platoon leader, a certain lieutenant from Virginia, and told the officer about what had happened the night before.

"Why are you telling me this?" the officer had said.

"Cooper just could have shot somebody."

"He broke the rules, bringing live ammo into quarters," the officer said. "If you and he and Brownell want to make an issue of it, I can tell you none of you is going to get your bars two weeks from now. If I were you, soldier, I'd just forget you came to see me."

Two weeks later to the day, Cooper and Brownell and Henry Brown were all made officers and gentlemen by act of Congress, second lieutenants of infantry in the Army of the United States.

"Hey there," Clete said, "you're daydreaming. I asked you to tell me about yourself."

Henry stood up, got behind Margaret's chair so she could rise easily, then walked with her through the dining room toward the door. Some of the guests pretended not to watch. Others couldn't keep their gaze from the familiar spectacle of a first-nighter's behavior.

Clete followed along, ten or fifteen feet behind them, not hurrying.

Out-of-doors, Henry trod on the crunching white gravel as if he were wearing sneakers with very soft soles. He knew what he was doing. He was leaving.

Margaret had to walk quickly to catch up to him. "It's something in the food," she whispered, but Henry wasn't really paying attention.

"It's their method of control," she said.

When they came to the road going down, Henry turned left, walking a bit faster. "Come on," he said to Margaret, who was having trouble with those shoes that weren't meant for fast walking.

Behind them Clete picked up his pace, but only enough to stay the same distance behind the couple.

It was very dark on that road.

"I can't walk this fast downhill," she said to Henry.

Henry slowed a bit, glancing behind him to see if Clete was closing the space between them. Clete seemed in no hurry, as if Henry were doing nothing unexpected.

Around the first bend Henry saw the object across the road, then, squinting, made out a camper parked sideways on the road. On its roof sat four orange T-shirted young men, all Clete's age more or less, their legs dangling. Only one of them wore a holster. It was that one who said, "Mr. Brown, would you and your wife please return to your room. Clete will show you the way."

Henry looked up at their faces. You really couldn't tell the difference between them and any other American kids their age.

"I know the way," Henry said. He took Margaret by the arm and started back uphill, passing Clete.

Clete waved a casual greeting to the four atop the camper, then turned to follow the Browns to the door of their room.

Inside, their sudden privacy seemed a godsend. Then they heard Clete lock the deadbolt from outside.

5

"I shouldn't have gone walking off down the road like that," Henry said. His head felt a bit strange.

"If I hadn't had these absurd shoes on," Margaret said, "we could have gone through the brush."

"There are steep drops in places, didn't you see? At night it would be hazardous unless we had a light. And if we carried a light, they'd find us."

"What about the mountain lions?"

"I'm sure Clete just dropped that one to scare us."

"We must get out of here, Henry."

He didn't answer.

"You heard me," she said softly. It wasn't a question.

"Yes," he said.

It was then she told him about the dark-haired young woman in the bathroom.

"Clete said there wasn't any nursery."

"Maybe there is," Margaret said. "Maybe he was just saying that to put off further questions."

"Don't be naïve," Henry said.

Had she been?

They were both startled by a sharp rap on the door. An unfamiliar male voice said, "Lights out in twenty minutes."

"Like summer camp," Margaret said.

"Like jail," Henry said.

"I thought," Margaret said, "they kept the light *on* all night in jails."

"Maybe you're right. Let's get our stuff sorted away before we're in the dark."

"We don't have to obey," Margaret said. "We can keep the light on as long as we feel like it."

It's not that she's an optimist, Henry thought, she has just never been a Jew. "They may turn the electricity off from some central place," he said.

"How long is it since we were eating?" she asked. "An hour?"

"About that."

"Don't you feel odd in any way?"

"I don't feel sick."

"I didn't mean that."

"Well," Henry said, sitting down on the edge of the bed, "I was thinking that I hadn't had a drink before dinner and . . ."

"And?" She sat down in the one armchair, facing the bed.

"Well," he said with a half-laugh, "I guess I feel as if I'd had more than one drink before dinner and wine during."

"It was the fish mousse," Margaret said. "I'm almost certain."

"What was wrong with it?"

"It had a stronger flavor than it should have. And it was a tiny bit grittier."

"Maybe it's the way they prepare it," Henry said.

"It's what they put in it."

"What do you mean?"

"If it were a chemical—there are dozens of things they could use—it wouldn't change the texture. It's probably THC."

Henry looked blank.

70

"The upper leaves and flowers of marijuana, where the resin is."

"You mean we've been eating marijuana?" Henry laughed. "I don't believe it."

"Just a touch in the food will do it," said Margaret.

"Do what?"

"It takes longer than smoking to have an effect. An hour is just about right for the high to start. And it lasts a lot longer when eaten. Four, five, six; sometimes ten hours."

Henry, who now with certainty was feeling something he had always related to alcohol, couldn't keep from laughing. "You mean after an adult lifetime of abstaining from the pleasure of the young, I've now had it in a three-star restaurant? Terrific. What would they do that for? Make you think the meal was great?"

"I doubt it," Margaret said. "If everyone feels euphoric most of the time, I suspect it's easier to keep them in line."

Henry let his right eyelid droop, in an attempt to lend a stern expression to his face. "How do you know so much about it?"

"I run into it all the time in my practice," Margaret said.

"Ever tried it?"

She remembered him saying that even alcohol was not usual for Jews in the generation that had preceded his. Perhaps a shot of whisky neat at bar mitzvahs and weddings, but as a predinner habit, never. It was contact with the Gentile world that had corrupted the original puritans.

"Once," she said. "An eighteen-year-old, daughter of someone who's been my patient forever, came to see me, nervous as hell, thinking she was pregnant. I told her she wasn't. I said I'd send her urine out for a test, just to be sure. She was so relieved, she took a handmade cigarette—at least that's what I thought it was for a moment—out of her bag and lit it. It was only when the twisted paper at the end burned off and I could smell the smoke that I knew it wasn't tobacco. She thanked me effusively, as if she had been pregnant and I, by merely talking, had undone the harm. She offered me the thing, called it a joint. How could I refuse? I took a puff and coughed. When she realized I had never smoked, she showed me how, letting the smoke sort of roll down your esophagus, then breathing in deeply, and holding the smoke way down as long as you can."

Henry reached out to take Margaret's hands.

"You are a wicked lady."

"You, my dear, are the naïve one, just an old-fashioned prude."

Perhaps it was whatever they had ingested in the dining room, a middle-aged couple bound by half a lifetime shared, experiencing something new. As they stood, Henry put his arms around her, and suddenly the familiarity was an asset, and feeling ran high. Just then the lights went out, leaving them in the dark for a split second, then came back on.

"It must be a warning," Henry said, not wanting reality to intrude on his euphoric state.

He started undressing.

"When we were coming back from our little stroll," Margaret said, "I was thinking that it must be difficult to keep a place like this secret in the middle of things. But the cults and sects do. Remember when we met the mother of a Moonie—Rose something—and we didn't believe her when she said her son was being held captive? We thought she was exaggerating."

"Some of the kids seem to enjoy their captivity," Henry said. "Did you think we're in the hands of one of those sects this part of the country seems full of?"

"Something like that," Margaret said.

"Remember the Joads?" Henry said.

"*The Grapes of Wrath.*"

"That's it. Remember that camp they came to, it was like a prison. It had gates and barbed wire and guards, and the only way they could get out was to escape. Do you remember where that was?"

"Yes," Margaret said. "California."

Henry took Margaret's face in his hands. There was no need to add anything. They were both of one mind. At the first opportunity, escape.

As he waited for Margaret, who was in the bathroom preparing herself for sleep, Henry lay stretched out on the king-size bed in his pajama bottoms, his hands clasped behind his head, trying to put the pieces together. Were all of those guests in the dining room unwillingly detained? Surely he couldn't be the first to have thought of escape. That stuff in the food, even if one couldn't avoid it, was that enough to keep everyone passive? Impossible.

He tried to let all thought drain from his head.

This place is a business, isn't it? How do they keep it economically viable? They can charge what they like to my credit cards, it won't last if there's no one at the other end paying for it. Who supports this crazy place, not the guests? Where does it come from? This wasn't a puzzle to be solved, but a place to escape from.

He let the muscles in his arms go limp, his body from the top down unwinding, then his legs. They needed rest if they were to make a break for it. They had to conserve energy, restore what had been lost during the long drive to the Big Sur area, and then in the tension of this evening. And from whatever it was in the fish mousse. Had they only been at Cliffhaven a few hours?

"What are you scheming?" Margaret asked, standing in her lavender Halston nightgown, her long hair brushed into loveliness.

He held his arms out to her. She sat on the edge of the bed.

His hands motioned her closer. She lay down at his side, and he put his arms around her, smelling the soap with which she had washed her face as he kissed her cheek, and then the side of her mouth, and then her lips gently as a lover would.

Margaret put her hands on his hair. She returned his kiss, gently.

Henry slipped his pajama bottoms off. Then she felt his hand, the familiar sensation, the excitement of his excitement.

Henry, who always wanted to look at Margaret's face when entering, suddenly saw her blanch. Had he hurt her?

Her eyes were staring past him.

He turned, the mood breaking, to follow her gaze to the place where the far wall met the high ceiling. He had to turn completely about to see what she was staring at.

It was a camera like the ones they had in banks to photograph

73

thieves at the tellers' cages at the moment of a holdup. The camera was aimed directly at them.

The sound that came from Margaret was despair.

Henry, who had rolled away from her, got off the bed, grabbed the chair at the desk and put it underneath the camera, stood on it, but could not reach it. The ceiling was too high!

Livid, he got off the chair and went to the phone. When the girl answered, he said, "Get me Clete!"

"It's quite late," the girl said. "We usually don't—"

"Get me Clete!" Henry demanded.

He was left holding the phone for what seemed the longest time. Margaret had slipped the lavender Halston back into place. Finally Clete got on the line.

"Hi, Mr. Brown," he said. "What can I do for you?"

His voice sounded as if he'd been drinking. Is that what he did late in the evenings, or was it more of that dope?

"What's that son-of-a-bitch camera doing in our room?!"

"So that's all," Clete said, woozily. "You didn't have to haul my ass over to the phone for that tonight, did you?"

"I want that camera out of the room!" Henry said.

"Listen, old man, what did you expect, a Judas hole in the door? This isn't an old-fashioned place, we're up to date as hell. If you have to fuck your old lady in private, why don't you just throw a towel over the camera?" Clete laughed.

Henry looked at the camera, eleven or twelve feet up the wall. How would he ever get a towel up there?

"Listen," said Clete. "Get used to it. Very few of the guests around here have sex anymore. After a while you won't even be in a mood for it. Anyway, the lights are going out in a minute. Now go to bed like a good fellow," said Clete, "and I'll see you in the morning."

Henry put the telephone on the cradle. He motioned Margaret to follow him into the bathroom. There he turned on both taps full blast and said into her ear, "They might have a bug in the room, too. We'd better be careful what we say."

The lights in the bedroom went out, but stayed on in the bathroom.

"How considerate," said Margaret.

The mood had gone.

Henry fished around in the dark for his pajamas, found them at last, and slipped them on, thinking how inappropriate the dacron and cotton fabric felt. What did prisoners wear?

As he slid into bed, he thought for a moment that Margaret had already fallen asleep, but she stirred and turned to put her arms around him.

"I love you," she whispered.

"I love you," he returned even more quietly.

The only sound he could hear was the tick of his watch on the night table. Sleep was a necessity.

It was Margaret who broke the silence again.

"How can they run a place like this without the world knowing about it?" she asked in a whisper.

And in a moment she answered her own question. "No one outside," she said, "knew about Los Alamos, did they?"

6

The sixty-year-old founder of Cliffhaven, Mr. Merlin Clifford, was a rotund man with pronounced ideas about genetics, which he spent much of his time and some of his considerable income developing. His wife Abigail, who not only was much younger than her husband but seemed even younger because she percolated with vitality, considered herself, with justice, the authority on the subject of Mr. Clifford's own genes.

At the age of eighteen, Abigail had come to the Southwest from somewhere in Alabama where an individual's family background was of greater consequence than his or her ability to charm adjacent humanity. When she met Merle Clifford, he was already in his late twenties and was running much of his father's oil business. As a full partner, his income was stupendous for a young man, satisfying Abigail's requirement that if a woman supported a man well in bed from time to time, it was only fitting that he support her in great style at other times.

Content that her new acquaintance Merle Clifford had enough money for her future needs, Abigail did not immediately rush him. Any man who had gotten to twenty-nine unmarried wasn't going to be rushed, she figured.

Abigail observed how her new companion effused civility in his conversations with her. Merle said *please* and *thank you* and *you're welcome* more often than any of the younger men she had now stopped dating. Though Merle didn't smoke, he carried an elegant Ronson and was quick to light her cigarettes. He would rush around to open a door before she could touch it. He always got up when she entered the room and remained standing until she herself sat. His tone of voice with doormen and taxi drivers was suitably commanding, and when he instructed a dining room captain in their wishes for their evening meal, he sounded not twenty-nine, a bleak age for most men, but every bit an authority on food, wine, and the world.

In private Merle was different, a bit shy when he kissed her cheek the first time, hesitant when he reached to secure the button of her blouse just above her breasts.

He talked to her about his desire to travel to the far reaches of the world—Bali, Surinam, Japan—and shyly expressed his hope that she might travel with him.

"Didn't you see some of those places during the war?" Abigail asked.

"I had a slight heart murmur," Merle said. "They wouldn't take me."

Abigail patted his cheek. "Don't look that way. I don't mind if you were 4-F."

It was clear that Merle minded even the designation. He led her away from the topic to his profound interest in genetics. He tried not to show his disappointment that she knew so little about the subject of his one intellectual passion. He recommended several elementary books, lending them to her as if they were volumes of poetry.

Abigail had noticed that Merle washed his hands not just before meals but at every opportunity. Thoughtlessly, she remarked on it, only to see a glower settle on his face. She had stepped over some line that protected his vulnerability. Abigail knew enough about the world to realize that whatever it was that made him vulnerable could also give her strength.

Abigail, at eighteen, had learned some things from books and much more from experience. In fact, she'd actually run into one previous handwasher in Alabama. That one had killed small animals as a boy.

One day, as Abigail and Merle set out riding over his estate on two of the thoroughbred mares Merle was proud of, she shouted across the space between them, "You ever run down an animal on purpose?"

As he turned toward her, for a second his face seemed as if she'd shot him between the eyes.

"Never!" he shouted back.

"Don't tell me you never even killed a cat?" she insisted, laughing.

"Abigail," he said, reining in his horse so that she had to stop alongside him and measure the seriousness of his words, "I have never harmed any of God's animals, so help me."

"I believe you," Abigail said, standing in her stirrups, thinking that if this twenty-nine-year-old millionaire was telling the truth, which was doubtful considering his reaction, what would account for his handwashing? She'd read in some women's magazines that mothers should watch out for children with the too-much-handwashing habit. Had Merle been one of those fanatical masturbators? Or was he still?

Abigail smiled at him. "I believe you," she repeated, and galloped off, Merle in happy pursuit, not a clue in his head that she was determined to discover all of his predilections in pursuit of her own clear goals.

The opportunity she sought presented itself when he invited her one Saturday evening to have dinner at his home instead of taking in a restaurant meal and a first-run movie downtown. The Spanish couple who kept house for him provided a candle-lit meal so rich in pepper and spices she felt the same almost painful excitement in her bladder that had been brought on once when a boy introduced her to Spanish fly. She'd washed it all down with more red wine than she'd ever had at a meal before, and Merle drank right along with her, though he'd had two bourbons before dinner and she none. As soon as the Spanish couple had cleared the dishes and retired to their own cottage on the grounds, Abigail and Merle were on the bear rug in front of the roaring fireplace, their arms around each other, alone in the vastness of the house.

The inevitable happened, of course. After the first ardent kisses, Abigail excused herself long enough to insert the diaphragm she had brought in her purse just in case. As it turned out, she hadn't needed to, for what she discovered that evening was that Merle had special preferences. While the young men Abigail had known liked to be stroked gently as part of the preliminaries, Merle wanted to have her do that for the main course. That evening, Abigail also learned that if while she was handling his needs, she permitted him to look at her virtues the way most men looked at pictures in Danish magazines, his ardor would burst like it was the Fourth of July. He was ecstatic at her favorable reaction and, courteous man that he was, soon thereafter attended to Abigail's needs with skilled and purposeful hands.

Over the next few weeks, Merle sought and obtained several opportunities to entertain Abigail at home, testing to see if she would be repulsed by the kind of things he liked best to do. Abigail used these opportunities to refine her knowledge of his wants, a few of which proved to be truly extraordinary.

For Merle had discovered, in his first decade after puberty, that some of the attractive young ladies he dated from good families were adamant not only about their virginity, but about what they referred to as heavy petting. How could he possibly go to the altar with one of them, only to have them view his special preferences with shock and possible disdain afterward? He found that one of the elegant prostitutes frequented by some of his friends accepted his needs as if he were ordering a meal in a restaurant with a menu that could suit any taste in Christendom. He didn't mind the thought of paying for his indulgences, but he wouldn't find a lifelong companion among professional purveyors. And so when he found Abigail responding to his needs with alacrity rather than disdain, he was so smitten by her sexual understanding, he declared himself in love.

Abigail wasn't sure that was the case. To her it was like a man saying he was in love because he liked her cooking. She also didn't know if she really wanted to settle down with a man who honored her with penetration only on special request and treated normal copulation as perfunctory.

In a month's time Abigail had resolved her quandary. She had decided that after sampling just a few of the benefits of Merle's fortunate economic state, if she were to marry a man less rich than Merle she'd never forgive herself. Access to luxury was to her a nonreversible addiction. And, after all, Merle did extend his courtesies to her bodily wants if she requested them. If their actual coupling was more rare than she would have preferred, she knew that if she ever felt the need urgently to be embraced with fervor in her fashion, her attractiveness insured supplements from others. Abigail therefore decided it was time to meet Merle's family. She was sure they were fine people from the way Merle described them, but her folks back in Alabama would want some personal assurances from her that she wasn't seriously contemplating a permanent relationship with just anybody who was rich. She needed details to fill them in.

And so arrangements were made for Abigail to meet Merle's father, Sam Clifford, who turned out to be as different from his son as a man could be. His physical presence was astonishing. His experience of life filled his conversation with continuous interest. Though he was a quarter of a century older than his son, it didn't take Abigail much time to decide that she'd prefer Sam Clifford to his son Merle, and not because he was richer than his son. She played at seducing him in a preliminary way; all she got for her pains was some wry amusement from the man, who finally decided that this young girl Merle was in love with needed some lecturing.

"Abigail," he said to her in private, "you are a good-looking filly. You're smart as hell for an eighteen-year-old, and you've got the figure of a racehorse. But you don't have much experience with people who are as smart as you are. I wouldn't give you a tumble, if that's what you're inviting, even if you were the Queen of Sheba because Merle brought you under this roof as a prospective bride and I have the obligations of a host, which are stronger than the obligations of a father. Besides, it would please me if Merle ended up with a wife as interesting as you because if he married a bore I'd never look forward to family visits."

Abigail was chastened, but not enough. If her curiosity about how the old stallion behaved in bed wouldn't be assuaged just yet (never count out the future, she would tell herself, the future is full of pleasant surprises), at least she could find out how he got so damn rich. She was sure that getting rich was a broth of secret formulas that the rich shared with each other in order to keep the doors closed to outsiders, but one could always take advantage of having a body like a racehorse to at least try. Trying with Merle wouldn't do much good since he was born rich and might not know.

When she asked Sam the question, he first went through the ritual of lighting his pipe, tamping the smoldering tobacco down, then puffing till he got the right draw and saw that his audience was in a suitable state of suspense. Then he said, "Abigail, child, I made my money in oil by means it would no way enlighten you to know because you couldn't use that information to your advantage. I made it before there were income taxes, so I kept what I made and made it grow. When the loonies in Washington put taxes in, I had to be in two businesses at the same time—oil and avoiding taxes. Oil is oil. But avoiding taxes is a sport, and I relish not only the game but getting back at all those people lazy enough to want to work for the government."

Abigail knew he hadn't given any secrets away and it just increased her admiration for him. She thanked him with a hug that brought her racehorse form in close contact with his body from about where his string tie was in a bow to just above his knees.

"Hey there," he exclaimed. "If Merle sees, he'll be jealous."

The truth was that Sam felt just the least prickle in his loins from the moment of contact, and he decided to hold the lady's attention by satisfying her curiosity a bit more and giving himself a chance to think a few harmless lewd thoughts while gazing keenly at her.

"I will tell you something about the oil business that might be useful to you, child, 'cause it speaks to the fundamentals of business life. There's more money to be made in having the oil than in doing anything with it. Now, we know oil is in the ground under someone's feet, but the only time it does an outsider any good is when the fellow whose feet it's under doesn't know it. Lesson one. Lesson two is to find out who that fellow is and make a friend of him. Tell him he may think he's standing on a piece of fertile farmland, which is true, but that someone with geological know-how like yourself might be able to find a crop underground on little patches of his land that won't disturb his farming the rest of it. You tell him you'll spend the money to find out if you're right and if you're wrong, you'll take the loss of it, and if you're right you'll share with him, and if he's a fellow like most he'll say yes, what's he got to lose? Lesson three is that a fellow like that has got one piece of land, but your geological know-how can be applied to the land of two fellows or three fellows or ten fellows, and if you're sharing with all of them, you're collecting on ten shares while each of them is collecting only from one. I see you smiling, so I guess you get the point."

Actually Abigail was smiling because she was thinking of Sam stark naked in the shower, and wondered if he exuded as much authority under a spray of water as he did standing there in his string tie looking like he owned half the world.

"Lesson four," Sam said, "is when you've got something to sell. In my case it was oil. You got to find at least two customers. That's called creating competition. And then you don't go calling on them like you was a peddler or something. You see to it that they find out what you've got from some third party. That's called public relations. It makes them come to you. Lesson five is that when they come to you, no matter what they offer, you say no. Then you wait for the other fellow, the competition, to come to you, and you tell him about that crazy fellow you just saw who offered you X. X is just plain silly. So the new fellow offers you Y, which is more than X. So you thank him for his offer and say you got to think it over. What you do is go back to the first fellow and say guess what, I got offered Y for my oil, and he's bound to say he'll offer you Y plus something since he was first and he'd like to make the deal. Lesson six is to know when it's time to stop. Make your deal. Then the next time you've got something to sell, you go to the other fellow and say listen here, I owe you something because you didn't get the deal the last time. You make me an offer and no matter what anyone else offers me, I'll come back to you so you can make the last offer and get the oil at whatever the market really is. You get the point, child?"

Abigail rewarded him for his lesson with a further hug, and told Sam enough was enough about business, she wanted to get acquainted with Merle's family background, could Sam tell her how he came to marry Lucinda. She knew that the best way to get a fellow thinking about you is to ask him about his wife.

"You're not going to like this story," he told her.

"Tell it anyway," Abigail coaxed.

"Well now," Sam said, "when I was a young buck of nineteen, I was beginning to do real well in the oil business, and other young fellows kind of clustered around, friends, cronies, hoping some of it would rub off on them. I ended up hiring most of them sooner or later because what rubbed off was that I had the gift of talking to people. Well, in a year or two I had me the feeling that all my friends were marrying the same girl, by which I mean each one of them zeroed in on a girl who didn't fool around with other fellows, a girl who looked pretty, talked pretty, knew how to keep a house and act respectable in public. Sometimes it was hard to tell their girls apart. When I met Lucinda, I told her I didn't care if she could cook or keep house because I was going to hire help to do all that. Mind, she did know those things, but I wanted my emphasis to be elsewhere. I told Lucinda that I would never buy a car without driving it around the block. She got my meaning real quick, and so we spent some private time together, and I'll tell you something. Merle's mother was a mighty skilled woman. She could make love like a professional, and my belief was—this is lesson number seven—that if you're going to spend the rest of your life owning one car, you better make sure it's good at doing what it's supposed to do."

Abigail said, "I wish I had known you then."

"Well," Sam said, figuring he'd best skip that thought, "we got hitched in time to have a few months between then and when she delivered the first colt. That wasn't Merle, it was

Lucy. God damn it, I wanted a son to help me in the oil business, and sure enough, just as the 1918 war was drawing to a close, Lucinda give me a present named Merle. I spoiled him silly I did, bought him clothes he was much too small to wear, I got him a pony long before he could get on its back and ride. I'll tell you something."

Abigail had a feeling that Sam was about to tell her something she shouldn't know, so she said, "Why don't we go inside now and we can talk some more later?"

"No," Sam said, in a voice that brooked no opposition. "If you and Merle are going to come together, I want you to hear this. He was a small child. That was a minus point in Texas and in my life. And he always had a tendency to fat. I thought it was baby fat, but it stuck with him, that shape. I urged him to get more involved in sports. I bought him barbells, the works, and he tried all right, but Merle's real interest was in exercising his head. That kid had a real curiosity. He used to take clocks apart and put them together again so they worked. He read books like there was no tomorrow. Mind you, he was no goody-good. I caught him dissecting the family cat out of curiosity, and when I made to whup him, he said he was interested in biology. Lucinda thought he was a pervert for killing the cat. She never understood that boy. Lucinda's never been much in the brain department, and she didn't understand that people with as much curiosity as that boy had always get into some trouble now and again."

Abigail was ecstatic. Merle, the handwasher, was a cat-cutter as well as a masturbator! She swelled with the power this knowledge gave her, and Abigail never looked so beautiful as when she felt powerful.

And so Abigail and Merle were married in Dallas at a ceremony attended by four hundred people. Within weeks of their honeymoon, Abigail observed that Merle's needs for sexual recreation tapered off to once a week and then once in two weeks. She twitted him about it only once; his face red with anger, he said sex was all right in its place, but it interfered with the supply of energy he wanted to devote to his genetic studies. It was thus inevitable that Abigail would arrange her life so that she might take her pleasure from time to time with, at first, older men who entered into their business life.

Merle was not a typically jealous man, he was so preoccupied with other things, but Abigail, being prudent as well as wise, had a private meeting with a lawyer who was second only to Percy Foreman in the area and who advised her that in the event Merle Clifford ever asked for a divorce, this lawyer could make it cost him something like seven million dollars. Rage at someone's infidelity, he counseled Abigail, is one thing, seven million dollars is quite another, and a man like Merle would never knowingly choose rage. However, the lawyer was wise in the ways of the world and cautioned her to keep her adventures private, which she did with one exception. And when Merle raised his suspicions with her, she managed to deny that anything had happened and at the same time allude to the seven-million-dollar advice she had received and from whom. Merle never raised the subject again.

Merle's preoccupation, other than the oil business, derived from his feeling that he was a mixture of his father's superior and his mother's inferior genes, and the one thing he blamed his father for was the use of his mother to reproduce him. He thought that a fundamental, irreversible mistake that would handicap him for the rest of his life unless he learned to use every ounce of brains that he had. Merle continued in his father's oil business, but his off-duty hours were devoted to cramming his head full of all the learning he didn't get at Harvard Business School. His intellectual pursuits included hobnobbing with some of the more sensible faculty at the university, who were always glad to get a splendid free meal at the Cliffords, and one or two found a way to thank their hostess privately in a way that pleased them both. Merle Clifford ventured to New York, where he occasionally attended a salon conducted by a French lady that was frequented by conservative intellectuals and by more than one senator. He took Abigail with him on these excursions because her mind was good, she kept up with him as best she could, and wasn't an embarrassment in that kind of company the way so many Texas wives were.

Merle's special interest in genetics also took him to Cambridge, Massachusetts, to attend conferences, where he was always welcome as a donor and eventually as a participant. His only problem with his eastern ventures was that he suspected that a good many of the people he met in Cambridge and New York were Jews, and that bothered him somewhat more each year.

Merle was torn between his sometime need for intellectual companionship and his horror at how many faculty members and graduate students in genetics had Jewish names. Worse still, he wondered how many of the others with ordinary-sounding names might be concealed Jews. Over the years he developed a series of discreet questions that enabled him, in the guise of a discussion of genetics, to probe the true ancestry of one suspect or another.

He settled on the fact that New York was a dangerous trap, but in his travels over the next two decades, he came to the conclusion that San Francisco, Denver, Chicago, Detroit, Cleveland, Philadelphia, Baltimore were rife with scholars and wits of Semitic origin. The statistics about Jewish Nobel prize-winners was appalling! Couldn't something be done about these people?

As the years went by, Merle traveled less to Cambridge and not at all to New York. For him, in his middle age, it had become a foreign capital, fraught with hazardous encounters. By the time he was in his late forties, Merle's home-rootedness became an inconvenience to Abigail. However, he was prevailed upon to attend a not terribly important seminar in genetics at the University of Texas because of its geographic convenience. It was at that lackluster meeting, however, that he met the single most brilliant individual in his field he had ever encountered, a younger man by the name of Tarkington. Merle flowered, listening to Tarkington's incisive brilliance. He invited Tarkington to his home for a weekend of good conversation. It was only at the end of it that Merle learned, quite accidentally, that Tarkington was a changed name and that while Tarkington was not a religious man, there was no blinking the fact that he was a Jew.

Merle felt betrayed. Had he known about Tarkington's background, he might have still engaged him in conversation, but not as a friend, not in his home.

Merle thought quite a bit about Tarkington's physiognomy and build. There was absolutely nothing to give you a clue to his origins. In fact, he was quite a good-looking man, even handsome, and he stood straight, effusing strength in a way that reminded Merle of his father. The only odd thing about Tarkington was that he smoked cigarettes in an amber holder, which Merle considered foppish.

When Tarkington phoned to invite the Cliffords to dinner at the Tarkington home, Merle pleaded a prior engagement, but wished he had come right out with a definitive *never.* Three weeks later, looking for a certain letter that had been addressed to Mr. & Mrs. Merle Clifford, he thought Abigail might have taken it into her bedroom. Merle was looking for it in the drawer of her night table, when he came across an amber cigarette holder that still had a half inch of snuffed-out cigarette in it. What was it doing here? He dreaded fire, and absolutely forbade Abigail to smoke in her bedroom. Why was that cigarette holder being kept? When Abigail had not accompanied him to Cambridge the preceding week, he had thought nothing of it.

The thought that Abigail might have fornicated with a Jew —even if she didn't know he was a Jew—obsessed Merle's mind. He could ask her outright. She might lie. The whole thing might only be a further embarrassment between them. He waited another week and then asked Abigail, as casually as he could, whether there was the slightest possibility that she might be pregnant.

He saw the alarm in Abigail's face. There had only been contact between them once in recent weeks, just before the trip to Cambridge, and Merle's seed had been spent outside her body as was now their custom. Was he accusing her of infidelity openly? Did she need to consult the lawyer before they talked further?

"I have my period, if that's what you mean," Abigail said, astonished to see instant relief on Merle's face. When he kissed her on both cheeks, she could feel the heat of his face, and both his hands that held her were trembling. However astute Abigail was, she could not guess that Merle had been near an intolerable internal panic over the possibility that his wife might bear Tarkington's half-Jewish child. He felt as if he had escaped a terrible danger, a humiliation worse than death.

Even Texas was no longer safe. Within a month three significant things happened. Sam Clifford died. With his father dead, Merle relocated himself and Abigail to Orange County in southern California, where he would find the comfort of more like-minded people. And soon thereafter Merle Clifford started assembling the parcels of redwood forest that would eventually become Cliffhaven.

Something needs to be said about the death of Sam Clifford. One would never have suspected he was past eighty. Up until the month before his death, he exercised vigorously, swimming at the country club two or three times a week, playing golf without a cart, and doing twenty sit-ups before showering each morning, as he had done all of his adult life. Then one day he had what he thought of as a stitch in his side that wouldn't go away with bourbon, aspirin, or trying to walk it off. He went to see his doctor, whom he called a funeral director to his face, and the doctor sent him to a specialist who told him, after various diagnostic procedures the old man hated, that he had the disease that comes to most people if they live long enough, and it seemed inoperable.

"It'll go fast now," the specialist had said.

"How fast?" Sam asked.

"Month or two. Anybody's guess."

At first Sam intended to keep the news a secret. Then he thought it would be great fun to watch the different reactions of people in his life to the announcement of his forthcoming passage. If anybody behaved greedily or insincerely, he thought, hell, there's still time to change the will and twist a few tails. The problem was, however, that Sam looked so well nobody believed him except Abigail. And the reason she knew was that she called the doctor on her own from Los Angeles, and he referred her to the specialist, who told her that the diagnosis was locked up in the confidentiality of the relationship between patient and doctor. Abigail figured that if the news was good, it wouldn't be confidential.

Early the next morning, she phoned Lucinda to tell Sam she was coming. She caught an early plane from Los Angeles to Dallas, and a feeder from there, so it was afternoon by the time she arrived. Lucinda said that Sam was lazying.

"You mean he's still in bed this time of day?" Abigail asked. To her it was the worst news she had heard.

She went up to Sam's bedroom, knocked, heard his feeble "Come in," and entered quietly.

Sam's smile told her she was welcome, but the rest of his face looked like it had aged in Tibet since she'd seen him last.

"Close the door, girl," he said.

She obeyed.

"Turn the lock," he said.

She did as she was instructed.

"I knew you'd come without asking," Sam said. "You know, you get a vibration about something and I think it goes through your head just as it does mine."

"Telepathy," Abigail said.

"Something like that. I got something to ask you."

She came close to the bed, bent down, and kissed his forehead.

"You and me," Sam said, "woulda made a great couple. Much bettern me and Lucinda or you and Merle."

Abigail smiled. "Yes," she said.

"And we been on absolutely good behavior all along."

"Yes," she said.

"Well, can you tell what's on my mind?"

She thought about money, oil, wills, but said none of that.

"You see," he said, "sometimes it doesn't work. Telepathy. I guess I'll just have to tell you straight-out."

She sat down on the edge of the bed.

"I think it's over," he said.

"What's over?"

"Life. Mine. Couldn't get out of bed this morning without feeling I'd fall on my face. I don't want to finish off with a pratfall and have Lucinda scraping me off the floor. There's something else I want."

She looked closely at his face and thought he was in pain.

"You taking your pain-killers like the doctor said?" she asked.

"Not today when I heard you were coming."

"Why not?"

"Don't want it to interfere."

"With what?"

"With what I'm going to ask."

She began to realize what his request might be.

"I know you're my daughter-in-law, and I know it's wrong in some people's eyes, but not in mine. I want you to touch it."

When she rolled down the coverlet, Abigail felt as if she was about to perform a religious ritual. Even in those flannel pajamas he looked like a skeleton. She could see the outline of it between his legs.

"Go ahead," Sam Clifford said, his voice stronger than it had been.

And so she put her hand, the palm and all five fingers on it. She moved her fingers just a bit, then felt it stir. She looked at Sam's eyes and they were wet and bright. She opened his pajama bottoms just enough to get her hand in, and then gently stroking it on its underside and just below the corona, she felt it begin to stiffen. This man was indeed an eighty-year-old death's-door miracle.

"I always knew you'd be terrifically knowledgeable about something like this," he said.

She accepted the compliment with a nod of her head, not breaking the rhythm of her stroke. When it was firm and upright, she looked at him as if to ask what's next. She would do anything for that old man.

"That's it," he said happily. "Just wanted to see if I could get it up one more time."

"You want me to . . ." She indicated the possibility with a gesture.

"Oh no," Sam said. "It'd take too damn long and just be a frustration. This is fine."

She stroked it once more, then neatened his pajama bottoms, and pulled the coverlet up.

"Lucinda would have laughed at me if I had asked her," Sam said. "You're a lady, Abigail. I thank you."

Abigail kissed his forehead.

"Ready to take your pill now?"

"Guess so," he said. "Nothing it can interfere with now."

Carefully, she shook one of the white pills out of the plastic bottle on his night table, and let him take it from the palm of her hand. She poured some water from the carafe, and he took just the barest sip to swallow the pill and fell back on his pillow, exhausted.

"I'll go chat with Lucinda a bit," Abigail said. "She'll be wondering what we're up to here."

The old man let a hoarse laugh drift through his lips.

"Be back before I go," she said. "You rest."

Abigail and Lucinda exchanged the kind of gossip two women with nothing in common learn to manage, and after an hour or two of pretending to be civil to each other, it was getting time to catch the feeder flight back to Dallas.

"I'll go up and say good-bye," Abigail said.

"He's probably asleep," Lucinda said, "but go up if you want to."

There was no response to her light knock. Perhaps he was indeed asleep. Abigail went in quietly. When she saw the position of his head on the pillow, it reminded her of a pigeon she once saw whose neck was broken. As she moved closer, she noticed that the plastic pill container was lying on its side, empty. The old son of a bitch wasn't going to let God or anyone else have the last word. He'd got what he wanted, she thought, and now he's gone. She pocketed the empty container and went to tell Lucinda that Sam had died in his sleep. That part was easy.

The hard part was telephoning Merle in California.

"Abigail," he said. "I'm glad you called. How is the old man? Are you flying home this evening? Shall I meet you?"

"I am not coming home. Your papa—"

"What do you mean you're not coming home!" Merle's voice was indignant.

"Not tonight. You have to come on out here. The funeral's day after tomorrow," Abigail said.

"What are you talking about?"

"I was trying to tell you. Your papa's dead."

She listened to his breathing.

His voice a whisper, Merle said, "Suddenly?"

"He killed himself," Abigail said. "Your mother doesn't know. I took the empty pill bottle away. It's better this way. Say something."

Of course he couldn't speak because he was sobbing. *Like a woman*, she thought, *not like Sam*. She wanted to say *Get ahold of yourself, Merle, you're a big boy. Pretty soon you'll be old enough to die yourself.*

At long last, Merle was able to speak. "Was he depressed?"

"Hell, no, he was fine-spirited."

"You saw him, then, before—"

"Of course I did."

"Did he say anything?" Merle asked. "I mean any clue he'd—"

"No."

"What was the last thing he did?" Merle asked.

She'd have liked to tell him. Maybe one day she would. What she said was, "I heard him laugh. A good laugh. When I came back up to say good-bye, he was gone. What flight will you be taking?"

Merle knew the schedules from Los Angeles to Dallas by heart. "I'll try to get on the 7:05 TWA that connects with the feeder. Meet me."

It was an order. "Sure," Abigail said.

Merle and Lucinda went in together to view the body one last time. Abigail hung back at the door. She wanted to remember Sam when he was admirably alive.

Abigail watched Merle's expression as he bent down over the casket. That wasn't love on his face, it was pure, steaming hatred for a man who'd had no foresight, who'd been thoughtless about his genes, who'd mixed his with dumb Lucinda's, not giving Merle the heredity he still longed for. Quickly, Abigail went over and took Lucinda by the arm and led her out of the room so that she would not see her offspring's face.

Afterward the three of them sat together in the private mourner's room, next to the room where the casket had just been closed. Merle indicated to Abigail that he wanted to talk to her privately, and led her back into the heavily carpeted room, where the aluminum and brass casket gleamed as if it were made of gold and silver.

"I have to know something," Merle said. He jabbed a thumb in the direction of the casket. "Have you ever—I mean ever—done anything bad with him?"

"Bad? What are you talking about?"

"You know what I mean," Merle said.

"I have done nothing but good with your father," she said, determined to tell only the truth on this solemn occasion.

"That isn't what I mean!" Merle said, his voice rising so that his mother came to the door and said, "Anything wrong?"

Abigail took her away and returned to Merle. "Now say what you mean."

"I have to know. Did you ever with him?"

"Ever what?"

"Sexual relations."

"You mean did I fuck him? The answer is no. Never."

"I'm sorry," Merle said. "I'm sorry for suspecting you. But you didn't have to be so vulgar about it. You ought to be ashamed."

Abigail looked at Merle, who knew he wasn't half the man Sam had been. The only thing she was ashamed of was that she had never been able to seduce old Sam. All the others since, gratifying as some of the experiences had been, were substitutes for the man lying in the coffin. She was prouder of what she had done yesterday than anything else in her life she could remember.

7

"That's quite a place you got yourself up there in Big Sur, Merle," Jordan Everett said, letting his lanky frame down into an armchair.

"Why thank you," Merle Clifford responded, genuinely pleased. Though he and Jordan didn't see each other often, what with Jordan in Texas and the Cliffords now permanently in California, they'd been friends since they met over an oil deal nearly thirty years earlier. Nevertheless, Merle had taken a bit of a chance letting Jordan visit Cliffhaven. If the Cliffhaven idea was to spread, it wouldn't be like fast-food franchises. You'd have to start with trusted friends.

Jordan looked around the cavernous and expensively furnished living room of the Cliffords' Orange County mansion. "Quite a place here, too," he said. "Merle, I got to give you credit. You do things. A lot of other like-minded people I know would contribute dough to somebody else's scheme, but you did it on your own."

"Well, I have some really good staff up there," Merle said.

Jordan let a laugh be his comment, then he said, "You and I know what staff is, Merle. People you hire."

"It's a bit different in Cliffhaven, Jordan," Merle hesitated just a second. "Once in, they can't quit, you understand."

"I guess it's not that far different from sharecropping. I never knew one to pay off the company store. I'll bet you lend some of them serious money time to time."

Merle smiled. In fact, he had lent money only to Clete. He didn't want to get into the subject any further until he knew how committed Jordan would be.

Jordan liked Merle because he had no time for people who weren't successful early in life. He had some reservations about what he thought of as Merle's "polish," meaning the neutralizing of his Texas accent and the cultivation of a polysyllabic vocabulary, posh manners, and so-called intellectual interests. Jordan was satisfied to talk the way he'd been brought up to talk, to read the local papers, and to eat steak and fries as often as he liked. His quick tour of Cliffhaven had convinced him that his old friend Merle had more going on behind his eyes than Jordan'd ever given him credit for.

Abigail Clifford, wearing a floor-length gown of a sheer and luminous material, paused at the doorway of the living room until Jordan saw her.

"Why Abby," Jordan said, elevating himself to a standing position and then walking to her as she came toward him. He reached out to hold her arms, then leaned close to buss her cheek. "You get purtier all the time. I don't know how Merle lets you out in the street with all them sex maniacs you got in Los Angeles."

They'd been lovers only once, a long time ago when Merle had been briefly hospitalized with pneumonia. Jordan had gone to the hospital, but the nurse made him wave to the wheezing Merle from afar. He'd then stopped by the house to see if he could be of any help, or so he said to Abigail, with whom he had never been alone for ten seconds. He stayed two days. Abigail and Jordan had gotten out of bed only to go to the john and sneak some food from the ice box, which they ate in bed, and for Abigail to slip a cotton dress over her naked body in order to make one quick trip to the hospital to assure Merle that he'd be better real soon, and, more importantly, to make sure he hadn't recovered unexpectedly and was getting ready to come home.

Jordan remembered those two days with Abigail as one of the highlights of his life, a roller coaster of exhilaration, exhaustion, sleep, and exhilaration all over again. Some weeks later he'd phoned during the business day, hinting to Abigail could she provide another opportunity, even a short one. Abigail chose to ignore the hint. She was interested in men in general and not in acquiring a particular lover on a regular basis.

After Abigail had seated herself near her husband, Jordan said, "I was telling Merle that Cliffhaven place of his is something else."

"Did you try the restaurant?" Abigail asked.

"Wouldn't miss it after what Merle said. It's the honey in the trap, isn't it? Got a question. How do you make a profit feeding those jewbirds so good and keeping them in fancy buildings?"

"I don't know that we're showing a profit yet," Merle Clifford said, "but we're getting there."

"I'd a thought a place like that with a hundred to two hundred people at a time would cost you two and a half, maybe three million a year to run."

"That's a very good cost analysis off the top of your skull, Jordan. I figure it's been running at a rate that'll work out to two million seven, and the credit card charges and deposits cover less than twenty percent of that."

Jordan whistled. "Don't tell me even a Croesus like you is going to fork out over two million a year for his pet project. Come on, Merle, tell old Jordan what you're up to. Got a silver mine out back?"

Abigail smiled. Jordan was a clever man. Wrong, but on the right track.

"Where do you advertise?" Jordan asked.

"We don't," Merle said.

"You could advertise in Jewish publications, couldn't you?" Jordan said.

"Not a bad idea," Abigail commented.

"With all due respect, Jordan," Merle said, "advertising is a bad idea. It'd be seen by too many people. My system of steerers means that most of the people who hear about Cliffhaven actually get there."

"Steerers?"

"I've got more than a dozen now in key cities—room clerks, waiters in good restaurants, people like that."

"They know what Cliffhaven's all about?" Jordan asked.

"I doubt it. We just let them know it's a place Jews'll feel comfortable in. They get the point. They also get a small stipend per month and a bonus for every person that actually checks in as a result of their steering, when we know it. They call collect and tell us the names. Easy for room clerks. Easy for waiters, too, once they see the credit card."

Jordan slapped his knee. "Merle, you are ingenious."

"Why thank you," Merle said.

"Don't you ever get a Gentile by mistake?" Jordan asked.

"Rarely. The manager sends them on their way with apologies for being full up."

"Don't they get mad?"

"Sure. They swear never to reserve at Cliffhaven again," Merle said, laughing.

"Don't any of the guests tell others where they're going, relatives, friends?"

"Certainly," Merle said. "We get to keep the relatives who come searching. And the friends if . . ."

"If they're Jewish," Jordan said. "I'll be damned. You've got it all figured out." He stood up. "Mind if I call Mary? Didn't tell her I was going to Big Sur or seeing you, 'cause you said it was confidential. For all she knows I'm in Denver or San Francisco."

"Phone's right there," Merle said, pointing. "Behind the screen."

When Jordan returned, he said, "Damn, nobody home but the servants. No point leaving a message with them, it just comes out in Spanish with the facts all wrong."

"Why don't you try again later?" Merle said.

"Thanks. I will."

As the Japanese manservant appeared, Merle asked, "What are you drinking these days, Jordan?"

"The usual."

"Sour mash on the rocks for our guest, and martinis for Mrs. Clifford and myself, thank you."

The Japanese disappeared without a word.

"Could he have overheard what we were talking about?" Jordan asked.

"I wouldn't worry," Merle said. "He's in the United States illegally and has been with me for years. He's more loyal than a child of mine would be."

"You're lucky to have help like that," Jordan said. "Back home all we get is Mexicans, who sometimes quit by vanishing without notice."

"Yes," Merle said, "the Japanese are fortunately not like that at all. A remarkable people. A number of my geneticist colleagues have commented on their high level of intelligence and diligence. They are workers of the first order, and the smart ones are extraordinary. It's a pity we haven't devised a way of breeding out their epicanthic eyelids and the slight pigmentation. They'd make perfect Caucasians."

"And not a Jew among them," Jordan added, laughing.

Abigail said, "I'll bet Jordan's not as forgiving a man as you are, Merle. He probably still holds Pearl Harbor against them."

"Bet I do," Jordan said.

"You shouldn't really," Merle said, "once you've observed their industry after the war and their willingness to ally themselves with us."

"Hypocrisy," Jordan said. "Masters of it. The only side the Japanese are on is theirs. Now come on, Merle, out with it. You're holding back. How do you make that place of yours pay off?"

Merle smiled. Jordan had not guessed after all. "Well," Merle said, "half a mile behind the compound there are three quite separate small fields under cultivation, worked by perhaps half of the guests in rotation."

"I knew it," Jordan said. "Hash."

Abigail smiled. Jordan *was* smart.

"Actually, it's not hash. Do you know what two tons of marijuana is worth in southern California?"

"I'll be damned," Jordan said. "You always was the smartest of the bunch. If someone put Jews to good use, it'd have to be you. The staff seemed like nice people. Young. How do you keep the Hebrews from running off?"

A lacquer tray in both hands, the Japanese man appeared, offering Abigail her drink first, then Jordan, and finally Merle. Three thank-yous were the only sounds heard other than the clink of ice until they were alone again.

"It's all right to talk in front of him," Abigail said. "He's completely reliable."

Jordan wondered whether Abigail had sampled the Japanese man's favors. He had himself found Mexican women useful from time to time. Hell, she's probably as nutty on races as Merle is.

"Control is maintained in three ways," Merle said. "First, the environment itself provides a very nearly impenetrable barrier except for the one road, which is quite carefully, though discreetly, guarded. Nevertheless, we do find that we have a surprising number of troublemakers among the Jews, and not just the young ones. We've developed several stages of remedial treatment. Did George show you the lockers?"

"What lockers?"

"You'd remember if you saw them. Next time. Very proud I am of that—inexpensive and most effective. Even our ultimate punishment for the recalcitrants costs next to nothing. Was George Whittaker polite to you?"

"The manager? Very."

"Did you meet a young staff member by the name of Clete?"

"I don't rightly recall."

"Well, both Whittaker and Clete have been trained in a method of permanent disposal that is very American and very secure. However, for the majority the third method of control works best. It was Abigail's idea really."

Jordan turned to the woman.

"Whittaker doesn't sell off the entire crop," Abigail said. "About six percent is used in the food that the guests eat. They know they're being heavily tranquilized after a while, but there's really nothing they can do about it. And the high isn't bad. It makes up a little for not being able to leave, I should think."

"Very clever," Jordan said. "But what about air traffic?"

"Don't get very much that can see anything," said Merle. "The PSA commuter run from L.A. to San Francisco flies east of Cliffhaven. Most of the other planes are too high or over the ocean. Helicopters could be bothersome, but we farm under camouflage nets. I've been up in a helicopter several times. I know where the fields are, and I can't see them from four hundred feet, what with irregular edges and all that surrounding brush."

Jordan scratched his right cheek with his left hand, a reflex elicited by skepticism. "Suppose you get caught?" he asked. "You can't afford that."

"Nonsense," Merle asserted. "I've set aside a contingency fund of a quarter of a million cash for payoffs if need be. What I'm really concerned about is legalization. It'll drive the price clear down to tobacco, and I'll have to switch to something still prohibited."

"You better make sure it'll grow in California," Jordan said.

"Not necessarily. I've devised a means of transporting the labor force elsewhere if it becomes necessary."

"You sure have thought of everything."

"Not true," Merle said. "That leads straight to complacency. I test the program severely all the time. Does the name van den Haag mean anything to you?"

"Say that again," Jordan said.

"That's where the idea grew from. Van den Haag. Dutch. He's a professor somewhere east. It's his theory."

"That fancy resorts ought to be put to better use?"

Merle studied his glass for a moment. Jordan was fundamentally a lightweight. Perhaps he wasn't up to this. There was only one way to find out.

"Jordan, on the average, do you find Jews smarter than other people?"

"Clever. Shrewd."

"It's not just cleverness. Did you know that Jews are proportionately overrepresented in the best colleges?"

"Sure seems that way."

"But did you know that it's by three hundred and sixty-five percent?"

"Look here, Merle," Jordan said, "we all know they push."

"Surely it can't be pushiness alone. Jews are only three percent of the population, yet twenty-seven percent of American Nobel prizewinners are Jews. That's not just drive."

"Maybe it's the food they eat," Jordan said, laughing.

He saw it was a mistake to laugh.

"All right," said Merle. "It's about time you gave some thought to this. For over a millennium the only way a Christian with brains and drive could get ahead was to go into the Church. It was the only place that intellectual ability was rewarded in Europe, and if you were smart and not a nobleman, what the hell else could you do? But there was a price to pay." He studied Jordan's face to see if he was following.

"This is that Dutch fellow's idea?" Jordan asked.

"I fully accept his theories. Listen. The most gifted and intelligent members of the Christian population were forbidden to have offspring. Their genes, the best genes, were siphoned off from the genetic supply for over a thousand years, and while all this was going on, the Jews in Europe lived in small settlements where exactly the opposite was taking place. The most intelligent were encouraged to become rabbis. The rabbis were also the political leaders. And their daughters were the prizes for the smart young men. The whole process was directed at getting the best genes together, while their Christian counterparts were leading a monastic life. Just think, if two cars going forty hit head on, that's an eighty-mile-per-hour impact. And if the same two cars going forty are heading in opposite directions, their speed of separation is eighty miles an hour. When that happens with genes for a thousand years, it's bound to have had a tremendous impact on relative intelligence."

"Makes sense," Jordan said. He wasn't sure it made sense, but judging by Merle's high color, it was prudent to agree.

"And what we're doing at Cliffhaven, Abigail and I, is reversing the process. We're taking Jewish genes out of circulation!"

"Why don't we have dinner?" Abigail said. She knew how important it was to Merle to enlist Jordan in his plan to set up a series of cross-country links to Cliffhaven. Jordan was being polite, but he wasn't enthusiastic. Maybe the dinner she had had prepared, laced with an almost undetectable amount of marijuana, would in combination with the bourbon, relax Jordan and make him more receptive.

When coffee was being served, Jordan accepted a cigar out of the box of Havanas proferred by Merle, but turned away the cigar cutter, which he considered one of Merle's pretensions. You could bite the end off with friends, and in uncertain company you could always pinch the end off with thumb and forefinger.

"Merle," he said, "back in Pinckton 'fore I met you, we had two Jews in that town that I knew of, the fellow that run the jewelry store and the one that owned the clothing store. The clothing fellow made a fair piece of change—maybe he'd make in a year what we'd make in the oil business in a day or two— but that jewelry store sold imitation everything and not much of that. Those two, they were no Nobel prizewinners. I knew them both to talk to now and again, and they were ordinary dumb."

Abigail thought that if she had both of them in a bed at the same time, Jordan would clearly have her prime attention. But when it came to brains he was no match for Merle, who now sighed, hoping to explain.

"Jordan," Merle said, "in dealing with population groupings, one has to go by averages, trends, observable differences. Of course, there are dumb Jews like there are dumb everyone elses. What van den Haag makes clear is why Jews taken as a whole tend to be smarter than Gentiles taken as a whole. What I'm about"—he leaned forward on his elbows, bringing his face closer to Jordan's—"is reversing what happened in those thousand years."

Jordan burst out laughing. "You and Abigail are starting late if you're set on having a million smart Gentile kids before you die."

Abigail hoped Merle would be patient with Jordan.

"It's a pity we didn't have any children," Merle said.

It's not a pity, thought Abigail, it's what I wanted.

"My plan," Merle said, "is to reverse the process that handicapped Gentile genes during all the years the Church was dominant in Europe. It's not in my power to make Gentiles smarter. But there is one thing I can do."

Abigail stood. "Why don't we move back into the living room?"

"Please sit down," Merle said. He didn't want to lose Jordan's attention.

"I am going to deplete the reservoir of Jewish genes."

Well, Jordan thought, maybe he's becoming a lunatic, and maybe he's onto something real smart. Certainly that place he's got in Big Sur is working out okay.

"You probably think that my accomplishment at Cliffhaven is keeping up to two hundred persons at a time involuntarily out of circulation. Let me tell you the real significance of what we're doing there. I suppose you noticed that there weren't any children."

"Didn't see any," Jordan said.

"They are removed at once. They are useless as labor, and just make the parents sentimental and harder to control."

"Removed?" Jordan asked, letting a questioning stream of smoke escape his lips.

"Disposed of. As are the recalcitrants and the troublemakers. Or those who prove useless in the fields. But the important part —mark this—is that because of the reputation our cuisine has earned—we're very careful when food editors visit, only the best-behaved residents are allowed in the dining room—and the character as well as the price of the accommodations, we attract, naturally, mainly successful Jews who can afford a place like Cliffhaven. Many of them are past the active childbearing age, but then the interesting thing happens. Their teenage and older children come looking for them. By disposing of *them* we are gradually eroding the Jewish gene bank, do you see?"

Jordan'd seen fanaticism in religious cult leaders in Texas who'd come to him for money. Merle didn't want money.

"Look," Jordan said, "I don't like Jews any more'n the next fellow, but I really don't see devoting all that time and energy to knocking off a fraction of one percent of them. It's like the Klan stringing up niggers long ago. I said that doesn't deal with the nigger problem. You either ship them all back to Africa or leave them alone."

"You're only seeing the tip of the iceberg," Merle said. "I see Cliffhavens near Dallas and Houston, Philadelphia, Atlanta, Detroit, up past Racine for Chicago people, maybe twenty or thirty of them eventually."

"You going to run all this, Merle?"

"I envision it more as a series of moral franchises. I demonstrate how it can be done. Others learn what they can from my early experiment, and carry on in their part of the country. In a decade we could have a significant effect on the genetic capability of Jews in this country."

Jordan glanced over at Abigail. Where did she stand in all this?

"Perhaps you need some more time at Cliffhaven to study what we're doing," Merle said. "For instance, did you by any chance notice that there were no pregnant women?"

"I guess I didn't see any."

"There aren't any, at least any that are noticeably pregnant, because the second they are noticeable that's their last day. Actually, the Jews are smart, as I said, they get the point. Once they're familiar with the rules, spoken and unspoken, they don't get pregnant at Cliffhaven. It's amazing how the human race adjusts to circumstances."

"May we move to the living room now?" Abigail said.

And so they did, Jordan puffing on his cigar, wondering how much cash this was going to cost him as a donation to get out of any more involvement in this harebrained scheme.

Jordan waited till the Japanese manservant brought the brandy for them and Merle had poured.

"What's next?" he said.

"I'm ready to go national. One step at a time, of course."

"Jesus," Jordan said. "You're really serious."

Abigail, seeing Merle's color rise, interjected, "You've been there, Jordan. That wasn't an architect's plan you saw, it's a going institution."

"Jordan," Merle said, "I've taken you into the deepest confidence one man can take another man."

Well, thought Jordan, I can't reciprocate by telling you about what Abigail and I did to while away the time while you were in the hospital. You'd have a fit.

"I appreciate that," Jordan said.

"Moreover," Merle continued, "I haven't sworn you to secrecy the way some organizations would. I have relied on our friendship and your trustworthiness."

"That you have," Jordan said.

"I will work with you for the first few months. Closely."

"Merle," Jordan said, "before you give me any details, I've got my business to run."

"I didn't drop a stitch in my regular affairs during the time I organized Cliffhaven. You're a smart executive, Jordan. You know how to drop unessentials to pick up the creative parts of organization that need doing. I want you to find a suitable location within a few hours' driving time of Dallas and Houston. First priority should be given to difficulty of access, a piece of land that's hard to get in or out of except by one controlled egress."

"I know a lot of places in New Mexico and Arizona that lend themselves to that, but in my part of the country . . ."

"I don't mean a place where there's an existing resort. We'll build that, recruit a staff. It'll be easy. I know how to find like-minded individuals and test their sincerity, and I've had all the experience of Cliffhaven that should make any new location much easier to accomplish. In fact, I'd lend you some of the Cliffhaven staff to train your people."

"Merle," Jordan said, "we're good friends."

"Shall I leave the room?" Abigail asked. "Whenever I hear men start off that way, I think I may be a supernumerary."

"Please stay," Jordan said. With a possible disagreement brewing, he had long ago learned that a woman's presence was a moderating factor. Turning to Merle, he continued, "I hope we stay friends. But your thing, Merle, is your thing and not my thing."

"You don't agree with the necessity of reversing a historical travesty that gave the Jews an edge they have no right to?"

Merle Clifford hoped his friend was swinging toward affirmation. "I'm waiting to hear what you have to say, Jordan."

"If I wanted to help reverse any genetic imbalance, if I believed it was important to do something of that sort, I'd find me two or three really bright, good-looking, A-1 Christian gentlemen—any age will do—and set up a sperm bank for Christian ladies who wanted intelligent, good-looking children because they couldn't get them from their husbands, or didn't have husbands, or whatever. That could be done with a lot less expense, certainly less danger, and it could influence a lot more genes in a shorter period of time. You could go national with a scheme like that in no time."

Jordan waited for Merle's reaction. He figured he had the son of a bitch in a corner. While you're thinking about how simple my idea is compared to yours, Jordan thought, maybe Abigail and I could wander upstairs and find ourselves a firm mattress.

"Jordan," Merle said, "your idea is not bad at all. It would be an excellent supplement to a series of Cliffhavens, and would probably speed up the achievement of my genetic goals."

"I was thinking of sperm banks *instead* of compounds."

"Never," Merle said.

He should have realized Merle was too far gone. You couldn't shut down a place like Cliffhaven or turn it into a summer resort and expect nothing to happen.

"I had counted on you, Jordan."

"Old friend," Jordan said, "first rule of business, friendship, and everything else—you can't count on anything in this life till you check it out."

"I had not expected you to welsh, Jordan. I was counting on our friendship."

Jordan had spent an adult lifetime finding ways to control his anger because he believed it never helped accomplish one's objectives.

"You calling a marker on our friendship, Merle?"

"In a way I did that by showing you Cliffhaven."

"Maybe we should have talked first."

"You wouldn't have believed I could do it without actually seeing it."

"True," Jordan said.

"Would you believe then that this plan means so much to me that I would be willing to sacrifice a friendship to see it succeed? Please reconsider. We could be partners all the way. We did it in oil, we can do it again."

"Now look here, Merle, I don't like Jews any more than you do probably. I don't spend much time looking for them or avoiding them, and I don't see much of any of them, and that's that. Life is too goddam short to go chasing after crazy ideas that don't make sense. Please don't get me wrong. If you thought you had a strike halfway between here and Hawaii and wanted a partner to help build a contraption that could raise oil from the middle of the ocean, I'd take a good hard look at it and probably come aboard. If it didn't work, all that'd be lost is time and money. But you're asking me to invest a helluva lot more in something that gives you kicks."

"Kicks?" Merle felt as if he'd been slapped in the face. "I'm a scientist. I'm not just dealing in ideology, but in hard facts of genetic history."

"Well now, Merle, a sperm bank, as I said, is one thing. But I think you enjoy keeping Jews captive. Wouldn't you say he does, Abigail?"

Abigail looked at the two of them. Merle was smarter by far, and she prized intelligence not in general but in her man. California was a particularly dangerous climate for beliefs that turn into vehicles for death. Merle had kept Cliffhaven's real purpose from her until it was operational. What could a wife do, go to the police? Particularly a wife who'd kept her own secrets for so long? Besides, she thought, Merle was on the right track.

"I know Merle has enjoyed the success of Cliffhaven," she said.

"Bullshit," Jordan said. "He likes caging them, and he probably gets a kick out of killing off some of them. I know that look. We have people like that in Texas. Merle likes being visiting king of that little world up there, with the power of death."

"You are distorting everything," Merle said.

"I hope to Jesus Christ I am," Jordan said. He turned to

Abigail. "I appreciated seeing both of you again. Dinner was excellent." Turning to Merle, he said, "I won't say a word about what I saw to anyone. Now I'll take my leave. I assume your man can drive me to the airport."

"I thought you were staying the night," Abigail said.

"Under the circumstances, I think I'd best shove off."

Merle rang for the Japanese manservant. When he appeared Merle said, "Mr. Everett has decided he must get back to Texas."

The Japanese nodded his head in Jordan's direction as if to say he was sorry to hear the news.

"Would you be good enough," Merle continued, "to see that Mr. Everett and his suitcase get to Los Angeles International?"

The Japanese nodded.

"You are making a mistake," Merle said, extending his hand.

"I don't think so," Jordan said, shaking it.

As Merle went into the front hall, the Japanese following, Abigail and Jordan were alone for a moment.

"I got good memories of this house," he said. "Don't you worry."

"Be careful."

"I fly so often I don't think about it any more."

That wasn't what she meant, but now the Japanese had stepped back into the room as a signal for Jordan to follow him, and she could say no more.

When Merle returned from the door, she sat in front of the unlit fireplace, turning the brandy snifter in her hand.

"Another, dear?" Merle asked.

She nodded.

He poured just a touch more than he would have ordinarily.

"Aren't you having any?" Abigail asked.

"I'll join you in a few minutes, love. I have an important transaction to complete on the phone."

She thought he hadn't called her love for years. It felt ominous rather than comforting.

Seated in the comfort of the limousine, Jordan thought about Merle, a sound man, a hard-working, intelligent man, just a wee bit over the line and he's in deeper than hell. He'd read about others, but this was the first time he'd seen someone he knew who had crossed the line.

Jordan was glad he knew the way to the airport. He didn't want to be driven anywhere else. He felt a bit like a gunfighter who likes to sit with his back against the wall, facing the door of the tavern. But the Japanese man drove straight to LAX, and Jordan was mighty glad to see the airport lights. He closed his eyes. If there'd been another twenty minutes, he'd treat himself to a catnap. He wasn't worried about catching the next plane to Dallas. There was always room in first class. He'd better try phoning Mary again before getting aboard.

It was the slightly abrupt swing of the car that caused him to open his eyes. They were inside the airport, but instead of keeping on the main road to the departure gates, they'd swung off toward one of the hangars. Jordan tapped on the glass partition. The driver glanced around for a split second, nodded, and continued toward the hangar. Straight ahead a door large enough for a small plane was being swung open.

The limousine came to a stop inside. The door behind was being closed by a man in an airline mechanic's uniform. The Japanese driver got out of the car in a hurry, pointing to the back seat. Nodding, the mechanic reached into his tunic, took out a European-made gun with a silencer, opened the rear door. Jordan heard the trunk being opened. Was his suitcase being removed by these jamockos? What the hell was going on here? Jordan moved toward the other door, managed to pull the lock up, and was just pulling back on the handle that opened the door when he felt the mechanic put something against his head, and then there was an overwhelming explosion and nothing else.

8

There is between sleep and wakefulness a moment when the regeneration of consciousness causes the awakened sleeper to note his location, almost always his own bed. If it is not, locating oneself in wakefulness takes a split-second longer. If one sees, as Henry now saw, a familiar person in the same bed, there is comforting reassurance that one's own is in the bed even if the bed is not one's own. Margaret's face, whose life he usually credited to the animation with which she spoke, in repose seemed graced by the peace of heaven. If he had an artist's skill, he would paint *Sleeping Woman*.

Men who are attracted to women's bodies first, Henry thought, were shoppers, not lovers. His great initial surge of overwhelming affection for Margaret had been for her idiosyncratic mind, for whatever it was inside her head that enabled her to think and say the things that made him *know* that this woman would never be ordinary, would never, even after long acquaintance, bore him. Yes, her face was distinctive in a way that he found immediately attractive. Her shape, then, was a young woman's, remarkably unremarkable to him. It was only in time that her body, because it was hers, became a sculpture by which he would judge perfect form. Rubens had his plumpnesses, Rodin his Amazons. He had Margaret for perfect form, knowing that it was a private perfection he could not with the greatest skill share with anyone else. She was to him in his one lifetime what woman was, and looking at her, still asleep, he was yet again in love.

As he turned toward the window, the bright California light streaming through the filigree curtains struck Henry's eyes, and the reflex of closing them put him for a second in darkness. He sat upright instantly, his eyes wide open, suddenly, brutally awake, staring at the door of the room, remembering that it was locked from the outside.

Out of bed he pulled the thin curtains back. It couldn't have been long after sunrise. The cloudpuffs floating just over the hills behind Cliffhaven created the illusion of a landscape emitting wisps of steam. Would it be a hot day?

He looked down. Guests were drifting toward the dining room in one and twos, unhurried. Or were they played out, exhausted from attempting what he had yet to really try— escape? Most people accepted life as it came to them; they would adjust to Cliffhaven as to any circumstance, good or bad, into which they wandered. Henry had never respected the drones of the world. As a young man his high energy drove him to perfect his skills, to mold his growing business to design. Planning his months and years, he assumed that everyone else must feel as he did: life was there to take. Only with maturity did he accept what his senses had told him earlier, there were differences in metabolism among people, there were differences in horsepower and will.

He remembered what Margaret had said about his college friend William Perlmutter; the man was totally without ambition, a survivor scuttling along the ocean floor. As a young man just out of college, William seemed to look around and decide to let his engine idle for the balance of his life. They stayed friends, two men from different planets who looked at everything from opposite ends of a telescope. When Margaret's group of sharp wits gathered for an evening's discussion, William was always invited, and always came, as a listener. On rare occasions when he had had a bit more to drink than was his custom, William might suddenly interject a question—never an opinion —though it was clear to those who knew him that his question was an expression of opposition couched in the politest form. Whether or not his question was answered to his satisfaction, the energy consumed in getting himself to ask it so alarmed his placid core that he would sit back afterward as if exhausted, sliding back into his role in life, observing other people live. Henry sighed for his friend, a nice man everyone agreed, a thoroughly agreeable nonparticipant. How many of those people he was now watching through the window, trudging to the dining hall, were Williams, accepting their imprisonment the way they would an unjust traffic ticket—pay and forget it— the way William would?

It made him think of the time when he and Margaret had gone into the city to celebrate their anniversary and, after a posttheater dinner, had stayed the night at a hotel. On their way back the following morning, they found a ticket for illegal parking on their car at the station. He phoned the police and learned that long ago an ordinance had been passed forbidding overnight parking at the station between October 30th and April 30th to facilitate snow removal. No warnings were posted anywhere, Henry complained. Ah, the police told him, the ordinance was published in the local paper. When? They couldn't tell him, so he took the trouble to find out. The Saturday morning he spent in the library was worth it. He allowed himself to be distracted by news, as he went back year by year, and not just by the local ordinances. How marvelous to learn what had been going on in that town before he arrived, the political strivings, the fires that commanded attention, car crashes, emotional editorials about issues long dead. And then he found the ordinance prohibiting overnight parking at the railroad station—passed in 1927, the year of Henry's birth.

Though the ticket was only two dollars, while still sitting in the library Henry decided to appear in court and plead not guilty.

The judge told him that ignorance of the law was no excuse. Yes, Henry had agreed, but it was unreasonable to expect knowledge of this particular law. Did his Honor assume citizens moving into the community would read all the back issues of the newspapers? If so, how far back—1927, 1917, 1902?

The judge ordered the town to put up notice boards in three locations in the station parking lot. Henry did not pay the two dollars. The town's cost for the notice boards was one hundred and seventy-five dollars, and every time Henry passed them thereafter, he took pride in having caused government to be reasonable. When he told the story to William, William had said Henry was an innocent fool, wasting precious hours of life over two dollars. And Henry had said to William that William's attitude—don't do anything about city hall, pay and forget—led, perhaps one small step at a time, to the gas chambers.

He woke Margaret by gently kissing her cheek. As she stirred and started to speak, Henry, leaning over her, held a finger to his lips, then pointed over his shoulder. For a moment Margaret didn't remember, then realized that he was pointing at the camera up on the far wall. Henry saw dismay flicker like a delta of crow's feet from the corners of Margaret's eyes. He gestured toward the bathroom.

After they'd had a chance to use it privately, he turned the shower on so they could talk and not be overheard from the bug he had not yet detected but was sure was in place.

"Wear walking shoes and slacks to dinner," he whispered. "And something over your top that can take the underbrush. As soon as it's dark tonight, we go."

"What about Clete?"

"I'll figure out a way to duck him."

She was the diagnostician, he was the fixer. She trusted him to find a solution.

The moment they were both dressed and ready, the phone rang. It was a new voice, not the young woman he had spoken to yesterday.

"Clete will be around in a minute," she said.

Henry looked up. They were being watched on closed-circuit television, of course. Right up against the wall underneath the

camera would surely be out of its range. He motioned Margaret over to him. "Courage," he said, giving it the French pronunciation.

In a moment, as promised, they could hear the locks being opened. The door swung ajar, but Clete did not step across the threshold.

"Good morning," he said.

"Good morning," Margaret replied, a reflex she immediately regretted.

Henry'd be damned if he'd say good morning to the man.

"Sleep well?" Clete asked.

This time neither replied.

"No rule around here that you've got to talk," Clete said. "I'm heading for breakfast. You can follow me if you want to."

And off he went, nonchalantly, leaving them staring through the open doorway.

"Of course, we'll eat. We're not out to punish ourselves," Henry said lightly.

They followed Clete by perhaps twenty feet, enjoying the illusion of freedom.

Henry decided that he would look more closely at the faces of the other guests, peer for some clue of strength, determination, willingness to communicate with the newcomers. A thought occurred to him. Had the strong ones escaped already? If so, why hadn't the outside world been alerted to the goings-on in Cliffhaven? Or had something else happened to those who resisted or tried to escape and only the passive ones were left?

When the orange juice was served, Henry thought it was pointless to continue the silence game.

"Clete, how about taking us for a drive around the countryside this morning?"

"Very funny," Clete said.

"Shouldn't somebody notify Hertz? We were supposed to return the car in Los Angeles tomorrow."

"Look, Mr. Brown," Clete said, "you don't need to worry about Hertz."

"Don't they come looking?"

"Sometimes you're too much, Mr. Brown. Try the French

toast, it's really good. You, too, Dr. Brown, I recommend it. Hertz," he said, continuing through half a mouthful of French toast, "just collects the insurance. You don't think they care, do you? It's a cost of doing business in California."

As Henry slowly cut the French toast on his plate into bite-size pieces, the first shimmering nuance of an idea lured him into thought.

"You're not eating," Clete said. "Anything wrong?"

Henry looked up. "Nothing's wrong," he said, his voice trailing off.

"I meant with the food," Clete said.

"I'm afraid my stomach's a bit upset," Henry said, rising.

Margaret was puzzled. Henry always announced every complaint to her.

"Am I allowed?" Henry asked.

Clete pointed, nodding. "It's just this side of the ladies'."

"I think I know the way," Henry said.

The first door, in the modern style, showed a male figure. There was a second door less than ten feet down the hall.

The door felt as if it were controlled by a heavy spring. Inside the men's room he looked up. The door closer was vacuum-operated. Maybe. The urinals were on the right, the cubicles with their swinging half-doors on the left. So far, so good.

He went over to the double-hung window at the rear. To the right front he could see the white-stoned walkway to the dining room. His view to the left was obstructed by large bushes leading off to the woods. From outside, as they had come toward the dining room, he had noticed the window, and having noticed the approximate location of the bathrooms the night before, he assumed the window to be one of the bathrooms. The window of the second bathroom next to it was invisible from the walkway.

Henry went into one of the cubicles and listened against the wall.

Just then he heard the door open. Someone coming into the men's room. Clete? Quickly, he flushed the toilet to announce his location. He dropped his pants and sat down.

Whoever it was entered the next cubicle. It was soon ap-

115

parent that the occupant of the next booth had a purpose more ordinary than Henry's.

Henry leaned his head back against the cold tile wall, listening. Nothing.

The man in the next booth eventually left. He couldn't stay here much longer. Suddenly, through the wall he heard the sound he was waiting for, a toilet flushing just on the other side of the wall. Of course, that was the way twin bathrooms were usually arranged, the main facilities back to back, emptying into a single soil pipe between them. Okay.

He checked his appearance in front of the mirror, then went out, his eyes glancing over at the door to the other bathroom. It might work. Anything was worth trying.

He rejoined Clete and Margaret with apologies.

"Feeling all right?" Clete asked.

Henry nodded. They finished the meal in silence.

As they were wending their way out of the dining room, Henry saw a new couple being led in by one of the orange-and-blue uniformed young men with a sardonic expression just like Clete's. They were young, the woman no more than twenty-six or -seven, the man under thirty. He had red hair. Neither of them looked a bit Jewish, Henry thought. Their eyes looked like those of trapped animals.

As soon as Clete led Henry and Margaret out of the dining room, he said, "Those are the Krinskys. Nice couple. They've been here before."

No wonder the look in their eyes, thought Henry.

"And they came back?" Margaret asked.

Clete chuckled. "Not exactly. Krinsky figured his way out of here. We didn't catch up with them till near Santa Barbara."

Maybe, thought Henry. And maybe the Krinskys were a setup for them, to prove the uselessness of escape attempts.

Clete led them in a direction they hadn't been before, an area north of the dining room, on a dirt path leading away from the built-up area.

"Mind a walk?" he asked.

Ten minutes later, circling east, they came to an outcrop of rock. Clete motioned them to come look.

Perhaps thirty feet below them and stretching into the distance, Henry and Margaret could see land under cultivation. Several dozen people were working, stopping, nipping off the tops of the weedy-looking plants, inching forward, repeating the process, watched by orange-and-blue uniformed staff members.

"See how well behaved they are," Clete said. "You'd never know none of them've been farmers before."

"Who are they?" Margaret asked, suspecting she knew.

"Guests."

I've got to control my reactions, Henry thought. I don't want anything to spoil our chances for tonight.

"You'll learn more about our economy here in due course," Clete said, glancing at his watch. "In the meantime, I've got to get you back for indoctrination. I hope you don't mind walking a bit faster."

Halfway back Clete took a side road toward an area north of the dining room where twenty or so redwood lounge chairs were arrayed in two rows facing the sun as on a cruise ship. All but two of the chairs were already occupied, and Clete gestured at the two empty ones.

"Ladies and gentlemen," said the young man who stood in front of them, his legs apart like a gym instructor, "Mr. Clifford has been kind enough to donate these pamphlets, which we will all now read. Please don't speak among yourselves. Address any questions to me."

Henry glanced down at the pamphlet. *The Protocols of the Elders of Zion.* They had to be kidding.

"What is this?" Margaret said.

Henry remembered seeing a copy when he'd been seventeen or eighteen. He'd dipped into it, couldn't see how anyone could believe such garbage.

Margaret asked again, "What is this?"

A man in front of her, reddish-haired and freckle-faced, turned to Margaret and said, "It's the menu for the Holocaust."

Instantly, Clete was headed toward them.

117

"You were warned not to speak," Clete said to the red-haired man, who Henry could now see was only a few years older than Clete. "And you, too, Dr. Brown," Clete said.

The young man stood now, taller than Clete. The woman next to him tugged at his sleeve, trying to get him to sit down. He wrenched his arm away.

"You've been here nearly a week," Clete said to the young man. "You ought to know better."

"Oh fuck you," the man said, turning away, just as Clete, with the full force of his arm, slapped the man across the face with the back of his hand.

Henry found himself standing. "Now cut that out!"

Clete turned to Henry. "Mr. Brown, you're too new to get involved. This man's been trouble all week."

"My wife asked a civil question, and he answered."

The eyes of the other guests darted from their pamphlets to see what was happening. Clete waved a hand, and two of the other staff members came trotting over.

"Okay," Clete said. "Freckles goes, and Brown goes."

Henry felt the strong arms grab him from behind. "Take your hands off me," he said, watching the other staff member Clete had called snapping something on the freckled man's hands.

Handcuffs?

Henry felt the metal being snapped around his own wrists. "Cut that out!"

He tried to pull his hands apart. This was ridiculous!

"I told you good behavior was rewarded, Mr. Brown, not insolence," Clete said. "Okay," he said to the others. "The lockers for both of them."

"It was I who spoke," Margaret said, suddenly realizing that she and Henry might be separated.

"You sit down," Clete said. She wasn't a Jew. He'd need special instructions.

"Move," Clete said, and on cue the two staff members shoved their charges forward.

The freckle-faced man was trying to look back at his wife, who had tried to keep him seated.

Suddenly, the staff member behind Henry shoved him hard.

He stumbled forward. His hands, his balancing agents, were not available to him. He nearly fell. He glanced just once at Margaret's eyes, a rabbit in a field surrounded by hunters.

Then Henry and the freckle-faced man were led away around the back of the main buildings of Cliffhaven, Clete behind the group, until they came to a gray building in the rear. It looked like the kind of thing that houses electrical equipment. Clete used a key to unlock the door, then motioned Henry and the freckle-faced man in. The staff members behind them shoved them forward into the doorway.

I have to keep my head, Henry thought. The objective is to get away. Useless resistance might kill the prospect of escape. He walked into the building.

Inside it was like a long locker room, with full-length lockers along both walls. Henry could hear sounds of breathing from some of the lockers, and from one he could hear the sound of a woman whimpering. The smell was like the worst kind of public urinal.

"What the hell is this?" Henry asked.

"You'll see."

"There're people in those lockers."

"You bet."

At the other end of the room, the freckle-faced man was resisting being shoved into one of the lockers by the two staff members.

Clete swung open the door of an empty locker. There was not quite room for a man of Henry's height to stand upright.

"I'm going to be nice to you," Clete said, "since this is your first infraction. Turn around."

He unlocked Henry's handcuffs. "That's so you can scratch yourself," Clete said. He motioned Henry into the locker with his thumb.

The freckle-faced man was shouting to have his handcuffs removed. The staff members handling him turned to Clete.

"No way," Clete said. "You heard him say fuck you, didn't you?"

Henry saw the two staff members shove the man into a locker, then slam the door shut. God, it would be awful with one's hands cuffed.

"You people are crazy," Henry said.

"If every Jew in America had a taste of these lockers, we'd have a lot less trouble from you people."

"What trouble?"

"Get in there."

"How long have some of these people been in here?"

"The longest anybody's lasted is a few days. Since yours is a first infraction, I'm giving you exactly four hours. That other fellow's getting eight."

Henry wondered whether standing in that confined space would be as bad as whatever Margaret would experience in her head during the four hours of waiting.

I'm not going to do this, he thought.

He looked at Clete.

If I resist, Henry thought, he'll do something that might kill our chances to escape tonight.

"Come on," Clete said. "I haven't got all day."

He is making me my own jailer, Henry thought, as he stepped in backward so that he would face forward toward the air holes. He wasn't sure he could really turn around inside.

"Very smart," Clete said, slamming the metal door.

It was dark inside. Henry felt the metal of the door in front of him. There was no handle, no way of opening it from the inside. If only one person got out, he could open all the other lockers!

He listened to the departing footsteps, Clete's and those of the two others, then the outer door slamming.

He heard a terrible scream from one of the other lockers.

There was no one to hear except the other prisoners.

In a loud voice he said, "Can you hear me? Is there anyone in the next locker?"

No response, but Henry thought he heard the sound of movement from the locker on his right.

"Can you hear me?" he repeated.

In a whisper he could hear, a man's voice said, "Shut up or they'll double your time in here."

"Is it true you don't get liquid the second week?"

Silence.

"Is it true you get no food the third week?"

120

"Shut up!" came the voice.

"Not until you tell me."

After a moment Henry heard a barely audible rasp. "It's all true. Please don't talk."

Henry didn't want to get his anonymous neighbor in trouble, so he kept quiet, thinking for the first time that the task before him was not only to get himself and Margaret out, but to close this place down by making sure the world knew what was going on in here.

In the meantime, he thought, how long would four hours seem?

9

Phyllis Minter had long ago learned that in this world if you wanted an edge on the next fellow you had to use your eyes, not just to see but to notice. And in her first two days at Cliffhaven, she observed that between the hours of two and five in the afternoon, when the dining room was clear of guests, the outside trucks would come up the road and park near the back of the dining hall. One that she saw from her window was clearly a produce van. Another might have been delivering bottled gas, she wasn't sure. That driver was a tall fellow, wearing boots that looked like twins of hers. Could he be talked into giving an attractive girl a ride back down with him? To the drivers this place must seem perfectly normal, a fancy resort with a terrific restaurant. Wait'll she blew the whistle on it! That chief of detectives in Pasadena, he'd believe her. But first she had to get her ass out of here while it was still in one piece.

The staff member who sat with Phyllis Minter at meals was

Carol, who didn't talk much. All Phyllis had been able to pump out of her was that Carol had been an airline stewardess briefly, her plane had skidded on landing, the passengers had all got out the emergency exits okay, but Carol had panicked —something stews weren't supposed to do—and she ended up at Cliffhaven, grateful for the job. Phyllis took as much time over lunch as she could, to get as close as possible to truck-arrival time, and then, when Carol was about to lock her in her room for the afternoon, said she'd left something in the dining room and could she go get it real quick. Carol said okay, and Phyllis went strolling down to the restaurant on the deserted grounds.

The dining room was empty, except for someone with a trusty armband who was sweeping up way in the back. Everything was laid out for the evening meal. She went to her designated table and pretended to be looking for something she had left, just in case anyone was watching. She then looked under and around the next table, and, at a propitious moment, took a dinner knife from one of the place settings, holding it against her forearm and then bending, as if still looking, slipped the knife into her right boot. One of the men she knew before she moved to California, a macho type who talked army a lot of the time, told her, among other things, that bayonets were not really sharp; they did their damage by puncturing, not cutting. If that was the case, a dinner knife, even if it wasn't as sharp as a steak knife, might help persuade someone of something.

As Phyllis went around to the back of the restaurant on the outside, she gave herself a point for taking the knife from someone else's table.

There was only one truck at the dock, painted the same blue-and-orange as the Cliffhaven uniforms. It must be one of their own, she thought. Shit! She'd have to have another go at it tomorrow and dream up some other excuse for Carol.

Just then she heard the blessed noise of a large engine, and up the road labored a refrigerator truck. As the driver swung around to back up to the dock, she noticed that he was a stoutish Chicano. Too bad it wasn't the lanky one with the boots, but beggars couldn't be choosers.

* * *

She stepped as close to the cab as possible so she wouldn't have to shout. When he shut the engine down, Phyllis asked him how long he'd be.

The Chicano shook his head. "Not allowed talk to guests. Only staff."

"Oh come on, a handsome fellow like you can talk to anybody he wants to."

He seemed scared that they would be overheard.

"Can you give me a ride back down?" she said, hoping her voice was promising to make it interesting for him if he complied.

The Chicano stared dead ahead.

Phyllis turned and saw Carol, watching them from twenty feet away.

"Oh hi," she said to Carol.

"Find what you were looking for?" Carol asked.

Phyllis decided that getting out of Cliffhaven wasn't going to be as easy as she thought.

In the locker Henry Brown's worst problem was the severe muscular pain, the deep acid ache in his lower back and between his shoulders. He had tried squatting. You just couldn't get down far enough before your knees had no room to go forward. An itching sensation just below the pain between his shoulders cried out for scratching. His bladder, full from his early morning juice and water and coffee, pressed for a choice. He could urinate right where he stood, wetting his undershorts, letting it run down his trouser leg—that was probably what they wanted him to do. Or he could be a stoic; the pain was no worse than the muscular aches. It must be much longer than four hours now, he thought. What do the people do who are in here for a day or two? They foul themselves.

How long had he been in here? Time crawled. If every adult on earth spent this amount of time standing up in a cramped steel locker, would it accomplish anything? Nothing. Brothers in pain? Shared pleasure is memorable. Shared pain is forgotten. Henry thought he'd try counting again—101, 102,

103—to take the measure of actual time instead of the incredibly slow moments he felt now.

Suddenly he again heard a scream from one of the other lockers. It was a word. What was the man yelling? *Mercy*, was it? What if he started to yell *Let me out*, and urged everyone else to do the same? A thought occurred to him. *Maybe there's no one else in this place. Maybe all I'm hearing is a recording.* It can't be. There's at least the freckle-faced man. And the man in the next locker who'd told him to shut up. If I knew the freckle-faced man's name, thought Henry, I'd call it out. To keep contact. He's got guts.

It was no use. The counting, the thoughts, the plans were all diversions from the physical need, the demand of his bladder. He was about to give in when he heard clear steps, then the rattling of his door, and it was swung open.

"Hi," Clete said.

Henry looked at the face of the young man, the boy, whatever he was. *Hi*, as if nothing had transpired!

"Exactly four hours," said Clete, glancing at his watch. "Seemed longer, didn't it?"

Henry stepped down carefully from the locker, afraid that stretching the extra inch or two he needed to stand upright would cause him to collapse suddenly. He straightened out. The pain between his shoulders and in his lower back seemed worse. Margaret would rub his shoulders.

"Where's my wife?"

"At lunch."

Clete led the way out of the building.

"Who's watching her if you're here?"

"Don't be silly, Mr. Brown. Think she'd run away with her ducky still here? Besides she likes her food, I've noticed."

"Those sounds in there," Henry said. "Is that a tape?"

Clete burst out laughing. "You've got some imagination! A tape? Terrific. How the hell do you think we tape the stink in there?"

"I've got to pee."

"We're going back to your room. If you can't hold out, do it here." He gestured at the side of the building.

Henry looked bewildered.

"Nobody's looking," Clete said jovially. "Except me."

Henry opened his pants, turned a bit away from Clete, and took his penis out. Immediate, incredible relief. It seemed to take forever to finish.

"Hey," Clete said. "Want to see something?" He took out his penis. "See," he said, "you Yids didn't get everyone in this country to go in for circumcision. My father wasn't and I'm not."

Henry didn't want to get into a discussion with Clete about circumcision.

"Can I go see my wife?"

"After your bath. I've got a surprise for you."

In his room Clete showed Henry the portable whirlpool device on the side of the bathtub. "Run the hot water," he said, "and you'll see."

When the tub was three-quarters full, Henry slipped out of his clothes. Clete watched him carefully as he got into the tub, afraid of slipping. In four hours he had gotten discouraged about his body. He had trained it for sports, for standing up to emergencies. In four hours it had been made to feel helpless.

As Clete was about to plug in the device in the socket just under the mirror, Henry yelled, "Wait a minute!"

"What's the matter, love?"

"You'll electrocute me."

"You are silly," Clete said, plugging the cord in. "Why would I do that?"

The device created a gentle whirl of water. Henry let himself slip farther into the tub until only his head was above the waterline. He could feel the heat in the muscles in his back, way up near the neck where it hurt the most.

"A few minutes in this and you'll be a new man," Clete said. "It really works except for the old-timers who're just too decrepit for the locker gig. Practically everyone you see in the dining room's been there for an hour or more at one time or other, and they're not moaning about muscle pain. All they do is behave and they don't have to worry about going back. Catch?"

126

* * *

Henry put on fresh underwear and a clean shirt, for the sake of feeling clean. Why was Clete watching him so carefully when he dressed? Was Clete gay? He didn't seem to be. Was it just a way of making me feel like a thing?

"Can I rejoin my wife now?"

"On one condition."

"Yes?"

"Well, don't sound so sorrowful. It's not a dreadful thing. I just don't want you telling your wife about the lockers. If she misbehaves, I want it to come as a surprise to her."

I must warn her, Henry thought. No, Clete wants me to warn her. It'd be another infraction. She'd be able to stand up straighter, but not turn around, not be able to stretch. She wasn't in the kind of physical condition he was in.

"Agreed?" Clete asked.

Henry nodded. Tonight. They'd have to make a break for it tonight.

When Margaret, sitting alone at the table, saw him coming into the dining room, she rose to go to him, but the waitress quickly whispered something to her and Margaret sat down until Henry could join her at the table.

"How are you?" she said. Her eyes said more: *What did they do to you?*

Henry glanced at Clete, who sat down on Margaret's side of the table.

"Okay," Henry said. He hoped his tone of voice would discourage Margaret from further questioning until they were alone.

Margaret, it turned out, had already eaten. Henry was served a bowl of chowder. He poked around in it, ate some. "I'm not very hungry," he said.

"Well, stick around till I finish, okay?" Clete said.

After a while, Henry said, "Do you think I could take a nap after lunch?"

"Oh sure," Clete said. "No problem. Why don't the two of you take a nap together?"

Was he implying that Henry, after his ordeal, would not want

127

to make love to his wife? Or was he hoping they would and watch them on the closed circuit?

Clete finished using a toothpick on his front teeth, then said, "Just to keep things straight. We have no objections to any of the Jewish couples here doing anything to each other they want to in the privacy of their room, such as it is—I mean the privacy—but you two really shouldn't. You understand, right?"

"No," Margaret said.

"You're a Gentile, aren't you?" Clete said.

Margaret's expression froze.

"Nothing personal," Clete continued. "It's just Mr. Clifford, he's got very strong feelings about mismating. It's a genetic theory of his."

"We are not," Margaret said, "any longer of childbearing age."

"Yeah," Clete said. "Your kids are what, half-Jewish?"

Margaret did not reply.

"Which half?" Clete said, smiling. They weren't paying attention to him. He didn't like that.

Margaret saw the strange expression in Henry's eyes. What had they done to him? She reached across the table, taking his hand.

"Isn't that touching?" Clete said. "Get the pun?" He shook his head up and down.

Idiot, Margaret thought.

As soon as Clete locked them in, Henry took Margaret into the bathroom. The whirlpool machine was gone.

"Where'd they take you?" she asked.

Quickly, Henry turned on the cold tap full force.

"I'm not allowed to tell you."

"What do you mean not allowed?"

"It was awful."

"Do you hurt?" she asked.

Henry nodded.

"Where?"

He had to laugh. "Everywhere."

"Want me to massage you?"

Margaret's hands were expert at massage. He shook his head. *Not in front of that camera.*

"I don't know how much time we'll have. We've got to find a way to shake off Clete for a few minutes while we're in the dining room. We have both got to head for the rest rooms."

Margaret nodded.

"Once we're out of sight of the main dining room, we'll both go into the ladies' room. The window there is concealed by shrubs. I've checked it out. The shrubs go all the way to the edge of the woods. It's on the wrong side for the highway, but we can circle around as we descend. Forget everything except getting ourselves out. I've got a way, I think, of making it impossible for anyone to open the door of the bathroom from the outside once we're in. It'll take them time to figure that out, and time is what we need."

"Suppose there's another woman in there?"

"Let's worry about that when we come to it."

"I thought you always say to plan ahead."

"You're right, but listen, Margaret. There are two important things to remember right now. We don't want Clete's suspicions roused. We need to make it seem as if we're adjusting to being here."

"I will try to be a good actress."

"And second, Margaret, we both need to get as much rest as possible. Let's try to sleep. We'll need every ounce of energy tomorrow."

When Clete came to get them for dinner, Margaret told him she'd caught a bit of a chill so that he wouldn't wonder about her heavy slacks and sweater. He acted as if he hadn't heard her.

As they followed along behind Clete on the way to the dining room, Margaret whispered to Henry, "Clete seems upset about something."

After they were seated, Henry said, "Clete, is something wrong?"

Clete shrugged his shoulders.

Henry, who could have an avuncular way with younger people, wondered if he could draw him out. The more Clete talked, the better Henry's chances of finding the opening he was looking for.

"Girl problem?"

Clete looked at Henry suspiciously.

"How'd you know?"

"Oh I didn't," Henry said. "Just guessed something very commonplace."

"Well, this isn't commonplace. My girl . . ."

He stopped. Nothing wrong with telling them.

"While you two were resting," Clete said, "I thought I'd check in with Charlotte. She's my girl. Terrific girl. I couldn't get her on the phone, so I went to her room and found a note that she's taken off for San Diego. In my car."

"Anything the matter?" Henry asked, leading him on.

"You kidding? They'll never let her get down there. She's not due for leave till April. We aren't allowed to take vacations together. Mr. Clifford thinks it encourages loyalties that supersede Cliffhaven if employees are away from Cliffhaven together, and . . ."

He seemed reluctant to say more.

"Yes?" Henry asked.

"Well, Jesus, she left a note for Mr. Whittaker, he's the manager, saying she got a call her father died. What shit! Her father's been dead for years. She used to have a boy friend in San Diego. I'll bet he got through to her."

"Why don't you go after her?" Henry asked.

"I'm supposed to be watching you, right? Oh they'll bring her back, she didn't have much of a head start, but if they put her in detention, that won't do me much good, will it? They'll have to have their asshole investigation. They're always afraid some employee will get bribed by some bigass Jew to rat on Cliffhaven, something like that."

"Do you think Charlotte would do that?"

"No way." Clete glanced about the dining room. "They investigate you pretty thoroughly before you get a job at Cliffhaven. Besides, once you're in, you're in, know what I mean?"

"No, I don't," Henry said.

"This isn't like any other job. You can't just take off."

"You mean the people who work here are prisoners, too?"

"Now don't get me sore."

"I didn't mean to, Clete."

"Guests don't get to get away the way Charlotte did. Hey!"

Clete was standing. Henry and Margaret turned to see what had caught his eye.

She was a striking-looking young woman, nearly six feet tall, with shoulder-length blond hair, and very tan. She was not in uniform.

"Charlotte?" Henry asked, but Clete was already off in her direction.

Henry could see them talking animatedly. It was then Henry saw that she was in the company of two older men he hadn't seen before. Had she been apprehended? Clete seemed to be arguing with the men. Then each of them took the tall blonde by an arm and escorted her out of the building, Clete following them.

"What was that all about?" Margaret asked.

"Never mind," Henry said. "It's our chance. Let's go."

He got up.

"You go first," he said to her. "The ladies' room."

Margaret seemed nervous. He watched her leave, then slipped a fork off the table into his pocket.

The maître d' looked his way as he turned the corner toward the washrooms. Margaret had just gone into the ladies' room. Henry followed.

The minute he was inside, he saw Margaret trying to calm an older woman who'd just come out of one of the cubicles.

"I'll need your help," he said to Margaret and showed her how to twine her fingers to make a step.

"I'm going to step up on your hands," he said. "Try to hold me up there if you can."

"I'll try," she said.

Henry heaved himself up.

"I can't hold you long like that," Margaret said.

"Try!" Henry pleaded, jamming the fork into the space behind the pneumatic mechanism that closed the door. He shoved it hard, hoping it would work.

He jumped down.

131

"They won't be able to open the door," he said.

"I want to get out of here," the older woman said.

"Please just wait a minute," Henry said. "Please." He unlatched the bathroom window and opened it from the bottom. The bushes outside provided perfect concealment.

"What are you doing?" the woman said. "You can't escape."

"Please give us a chance," Henry said. "Or do you want to come with us?"

"You're newcomers. You don't know."

He could hear someone trying the door.

"Now," he said to Margaret and held twined hands for her just as she had for him. She got out of the window. He marveled at her agility.

Henry hoped his forearms were still strong enough. He hoisted himself up on the sill and flopped forward, pulling his body along, then dropped over the other side.

"This way," he said to Margaret.

In two minutes they were in the woods, which dropped down at a marked angle. The redwoods provided no grip for hands, but the small seedlings everywhere enabled them to hold on as they stumbled forward.

Henry looked up at the moonlit sky to check his direction. The thick stands of tall trees let very little light onto the forest floor, covered with many years' accumulation of slippery leaves.

"We've got to wend our way there," Henry said, pointing. "Toward the highway and the ocean." He was grateful for the distant boom of the ocean pounding the rocks.

After a while Margaret gasped, "How far have we come?"

"Not far enough. Are you okay?"

She nodded, and they were off again.

"My hands are all scratched," she said.

"Mine, too. Sorry."

He didn't hear sounds of pursuit. If they couldn't get the bathroom door open because of the fork he'd jammed into the mechanism, they'd have gone around the window side of the building by now.

"I think we'd better move faster," Henry said.

"I'm going as fast as I can."

It was like running in a nightmare, you couldn't go fast

enough. At times it seemed as if the floor of the forest descended at an acute angle to the sea, as much in a hurry to get there as they were. Henry tried to find the gentler slopes, wondering if any human beings had ever come this way before. If one was escaping alone and tripped, perhaps broke a leg, could one drag oneself out? Not likely, not through this underbrush. One would have to cry for help. Would anyone hear? What if they had stopped looking?

"Be careful," he said to Margaret.

Henry heard the sounds of himself plunging through the brush and behind him the reassuring sound that Margaret was behind him. It was like a marathon, you had to keep going, keep going. How much longer would it take?

Out of breath, he stopped a moment. Margaret caught up. When she stopped, he listened. They could actually hear the sounds of the highway now. It couldn't be far. His heart rose high with hope.

"Just a few minutes more," he said.

"I can't," Margaret said. "I'm exhausted. Go on ahead."

"No." It was absolute. He took her hand and they were off again.

"Don't try to hold on to me. I'm coming," Margaret said. "I'll be all right."

Henry guessed they were now within a hundred yards of the road. The forest was thinning. He wanted to run, but the thought of losing Margaret kept him in check. Suddenly, he could see a slope bathed in moonlight. They were nearly out of the woods.

They stopped, their chests heaving. Henry was listening for the yapping of dogs. "Let's run across the clearing," he said. "Now."

The grass was knee high. He had to lift his legs running. He could hear Margaret stumbling along behind him. Suddenly, they were out on the unpaved road. He could see the sentry box and beyond it, the highway. He hoped nobody was in the sentry box this time of night. Running on the road was easier. He waved at Margaret to hurry.

He made out the chain across the road at the entranceway. On the other side of the chain stood six of the guests of Cliffhaven, each with a club in his hand. Had they made a break for it at the same time he had? Why were they just standing there? He stopped ten feet away from them, as Margaret caught up. Their faces, some of them, were familiar.

They were people from the trusty table in the dining room, wearing their armbands. One man stepped forward to the chain. He was about Henry's age. "You'll have to go back," he said.

"Never," Henry said.

All six of them were now holding their sticks in readiness.

"Please," Henry said.

"They will take revenge on others if we let you go," the leader said. "You must return."

"No," Henry said.

"Go back peacefully," the leader insisted. "It is better for all of us."

Just then Henry heard the car swing off the highway. It spun around toward where they were all standing and came to a noisy stop on the gravel. Henry couldn't believe his luck. It was a California State Highway Patrol car.

The trooper got out of the car.

"Thank heaven," Margaret said.

The trooper looked at the trusties and then at them. The trusties all nodded at the trooper, as if in recognition. Their leader said, "This is Mr. and Mrs. Brown. They were trying to leave Cliffhaven."

Henry stretched his arms out to the trooper. "They're keeping more than a hundred people prisoner up there! Please radio for help."

The trooper strode over to Henry.

Henry dropped his arms to his sides.

"All right," the leader of the trusties said to Henry and Margaret, "come along."

"What do you mean?" Henry said. "This policeman can help us all get away."

"You," the trooper said to Henry. "You do what they say, kike."

PART 2

10

Rupert Fowler was born on his family farm in Oklahoma in time to be twenty-four in 1931. He was a broad-shouldered, restless loner of a youth who knew more about cars than country doctors did about the human body. The farming folk thought him ingenious, called on him rather than the service station in town to patch up their ailing vehicles, paid him in a lot of compliments and some cash, which he turned over to his father after deducting a tithe for himself. His father, an embittered man, told Rupert they were a farm family not a car-fixing family, and Rupert should stop wasting time on contraptions that got you from home to another place it probably wasn't worth going to.

When cantankerous Mr. Morton refused to pay Rupert promptly for a tune-up on a Model T that Rupert had nursed through every sickness an old car is prone to, Rupert decided that the car was more his than Mr. Morton's. In it he fled the family farm with one bundle of clothes and enough scrimped cash to keep him in vittles and gasoline until he reached the Los Angeles area.

He found the city bewildering—too many streets to get lost on, and if you were friendly to people you approached, they'd walk away fast as if you were crazy. The second day there a policeman looked at his license plate when he parked and asked him where he was from. Rupert said, "I'm from Oklahoma, sir, ain't that what the plate says?" The policeman said, "You a wise guy?" Rupert said he hadn't intended any impoliteness, but decided that he'd better head out of the city before he landed in the hoosegow with a lot of spicks. He was short of gas and eating money by this time, so he tried something he had imagined a time or two. He drove along late in the evening till he saw a fairly well-dressed short man walking by himself. Rupert pulled up to the curb, got out, and walking around the car to the now frightened pedestrian, asked the stranger if he could borrow five dollars.

In those days five dollars was a fortune, but when the stranger looked up at Rupert's formidable bulk, which exuded a sense of physical power, he decided not to refuse but to bargain. Rupert, who didn't want to land in the hoosegow for beating someone up any more than he wanted to be locked up for possession of a stolen car, settled for three dollars and headed north on Highway 1. The three dollars was down to a few nickels and dimes before he found himself driving up to the gas station in the Big Sur area, contemplating what would be his first holdup. The trouble was he didn't have a gun or even a knife, but he had the good sense to find a stick alongside the road that in his hands would have impressed just about anyone.

The gas-station lights were still on, but when he pulled up at the pump, no one came. He honked just as though he was a customer. Nothing. He didn't have a clue as to the distance to the next gas station. With a near-empty tank he didn't want to get stuck on the mountain road at night. Someone might decide to hold him up and, in anger at his not having any money, beat the living shit out of him.

And so Rupert decided to venture into the ramshackle building thirty feet in back of the pumps. The front room, a kind of office for the gas station, had a road-map rack and three pyramided stacks, each with a different grade of oil, a desk, a chair, and some ancient posters. Cautiously, he decided to explore the rest of the house, saying "hellooo" as he entered each room. He didn't want anyone letting a shotgun blast go at him before asking questions.

He found the man in the back bedroom, a fat fellow in his sixties, wearing coveralls and slumped not on the bed but against it. The man's face was red, covered in perspiration, and his breaths were coming real hard. Rupert thought the man looked afraid, so he put his stick down. It turned out the man wasn't afraid of Rupert but of dying. As Rupert leaned close to him, the man whispered "heart trouble" and "get the doctor." After a bit Rupert figured out that what the man was now telling him was that on the wall near the pay phone there was a card with emergency numbers, and one of them was Dr. Brooks'.

Rupert explained he didn't have a nickel for the phone. Actually, though he still had nickels and dimes in his pocket, he'd be damned if he'd use one of his and chance not getting paid back. The old man, sick as he was, looked incredulous that someone would be out on the highway with no money, but he had to take the risk and told Rupert where the cash box was. When Rupert found it, he observed that it contained more money than he had ever seen in one place in his life, maybe seventy or eighty dollars in bills, and lots of quarters, nickels, and dimes. He took one nickel and called the doctor.

The doctor wanted to know who was calling, and Rupert said, "Name's Fowler. Just came by and saw the station deserted. This fellow's real sick with heart trouble."

The doctor must have known about previous episodes of illness because he said, "Mr. Fowler, you stay right there, I'll be down quick as I can. It's seventeen miles."

Rupert was real sorry he'd given the doctor his name. That was just dumb, 'cause he could have filled his car with gas, taken the money in the cash box, and gone off into the night. Just then he heard a cry from the bedroom, more like an animal's than a man's, and when he ran back to the bedroom, he saw that the old man was clutching his chest as if someone was beating on it with a jackhammer. Instinct told Rupert to lower the man to the floor from his propped-up position. He took the pillow off the bed and put it under the man's head. In the bathroom he found a grease-marked towel and used a clean corner of it to mop the man's face. In a little, the pain seemed to ease, and Rupert went off to effect the compromise he had made with his conscience, which was to fill his car's gas tank from the pump and to take ten dollars from the cash box, figuring by the time anybody got around to counting it he'd be long gone.

When he checked the man after a while, he seemed resting comfortably, sound asleep, with the barest wheeze in his breathing. Rupert wished the doctor would get there so he could leave. While he waited, he adjusted his previous compromise and took another ten dollars from the cash box as well as a handful of change. It wouldn't be missed any more than the first ten he had taken. He stashed the box away just in time as a car in not much better shape than his own pulled up outside.

Dr. Brooks shook Rupert's hand, thanked him for the neighborly call real quick, and hurried back to his patient. Rupert wondered whether he should stay out of the bedroom or go in, finally decided to go in and when he did, the doctor, who was bent over the man on the floor, lifted his head, slipped his stethoscope out of his ears and around his neck, and said, " 'Fraid he's dead."

"What was his name?" Rupert asked.

"McDonald," the doctor said.

The doctor and Rupert sat in the living room for a while to tie things up. The doctor said he'd have the body removed by the undertaker the next day. He made out a death certificate and gave it to Rupert. "Can you stay?"

Since Rupert had nowhere pressing to go despite his new wealth, he decided to spend the night in the living room, though he told the doctor he sure didn't relish the idea of the body in the next room. "What about kin?" he asked the doctor.

The doctor looked at Rupert for quite a bit before he said, "I guess there's no harm in you knowing. McDonald was . . ." He hesitated, wondering whether the twenty-four-year-old hayseed would get his meaning. "McDonald was queer. His friend who lived here died more'n ten years back. Occasionally he'd get some man to stay here for a day or two since, but not since his first attack two years ago. He's got no kin."

For the first time Rupert began to feel that the Lord might be telling him something—like that the rest of the cash box might be his one way or t'other.

As it turned out, when cars pulled up the next morning, they weren't the undertaker's but people asking for service, and Rupert thought he might as well pump the gas and take the money. He'd taken in fourteen dollars and change by the time the undertaker showed. He wouldn't remove the body until Rupert had agreed to sign a piece of paper showing that the cost of burial would come to one hundred and ten dollars total, and that he would pay ten dollars now and ten dollars a week until it was paid off. Rupert took the ten from his pocket because he didn't want the undertaker to see where the stash was. He signed because he figured he'd be miles and miles away when the next payment was due.

In the meantime, he pumped gas, took in cash, listened to the sympathy of locals when they learned old McDonald had died. They assumed he was a relative. Rupert decided he would depart as soon as the gas ran out. But before that happened, one morning the oil company truck pulled up and started making its delivery before he came out of the john.

"Where's McDonald?" the oil company man asked.

"Dead," Rupert said.

"You one of his, er, friends?"

If Rupert had had his stick handy, he might have clubbed the man first and thought second. The man saw his anger and was quick to retract when Rupert told him what had happened. The driver knew that whenever a privately owned station changed hands, the vultures from the other oil companies would descend and he'd be in danger of losing the account, so he suggested he and Rupert have a talk, which they did, the outcome of which was that Rupert stayed on as if he owned the place. The contents of the cash box was his. But so was whatever the difference between taxes and the cost of the gas and what he took in. And with no gas station within five miles, there was no worry about customers. In fact, he'd had a chance to see the daily activity and figured he might net himself, now that he knew the costs, more than fifty dollars a week, which is a lot more than anybody paid for the labor of an ex-farmer in 1931.

Not long afterward Rupert Fowler was visited one evening by a sixteen-year-old girl with black hair and beautiful eyes, who had walked barefoot to the station from wherever she lived up in the hills and offered to fuck or suck him for two dollars cash. Rupert, whose sexual companionship since leaving Oklahoma had consisted of his right hand, hung the "Closed" sign around the pump and took her into the back room, where afterward the girl, Cindy by name, demanded four dollars on the grounds that he had availed himself of both of her offered services. He didn't quarrel too hard because he was already anticipating the next time, and, thinking of himself as a businessman now, negotiated a settlement for three dollars even. The following month Rupert, tired of the few dishes he knew how to cook, bored evenings and especially Saturday nights, figured it would be cheaper than paying Cindy three or four times a week to marry her legal so she could cook and clean and keep him company as well as satisfy his sexual requirements.

Two years later, little Joe Fowler was born, and by the time Joe Fowler took a bride, the two men had built several additions onto the original house and opened a general store to sell groceries along with gas. Moreover, Joe was as mechanically inclined as his father, and they were now fixing cars as well as pumping gas. Between them they had figured out six good ways of disabling a car while the owner was in the men's room so that a repair became a necessity.

Frank Fowler was born in 1960, nearly thirty years after his grandfather had taken possession of the McDonald place; they were now considered an old family in the sparsely populated Big Sur area. It was said that old Rupert Fowler, now in his seventies, treasured two things most: His original cash box and being a grandfather to Frank.

They were a strange sight around the dinner table, that

Fowler family, the men on one side, the women on the other, and the youngest, Frank, at the head of the table. Grandfather Rupert would have preferred to sit at the head as he had when his family was young. But the leadership of the clan had clearly devolved upon Father Joe, and to avoid a crisis that might have sent Joe with his quick temper looking for another roof, not sharing expenses anymore, Grandfather Rupert some years ago had decided that he and Joe should sit "on the men's side" of the table, and the women sit facing them, each in front of her man.

And so it was that Cindy of the three-dollar compromise, now in her mid-sixties, sat opposite Rupert, urging him to eat the Spanish rice at least if gnawing at the chicken leg hurt because of his new dentures. Opposite Father Joe sat Matilda, her auburn hair pulled back in a tight bun, not loose and long and flowing as it had been when she had claimed a pregnancy to seal their relationship, although young Frank was not born until five years after they were married. In the hospital, Joe, who used to like a joke in those days, stroked Matilda's hair and said that baby Frank's was the longest pregnancy in the history of California. Matilda, who quickly became the smartest in the Fowler clan, gave Joe a look that Joe took to mean she would deny her body to him even after the doctor said it was okay if he didn't stop wisecracking.

Young Frank was spoiled by his grandfather and encouraged by his mother. Now that he was in his last year of high school, Matilda wanted him to do what she wished she had done—learn something at a state college that would take him away from the gas pumps. Frank worked at the station after school to earn pocket money for dates and to buy spare parts for the Chevy. The car was nearly as old as he was, kept up with wax and buffing and fixing so that it looked showroom-new. Matilda didn't want him to get used to fixing cars and pumping gas into a third generation.

Matilda asked Frank why he'd come to the dinner table with a long face.

"I called Clete," he said, "I invited him to have dinner with us."

"You shoulda asked first."

"I did ask," Frank said.

"That was a month ago," his mother said.

"I been asking him ever since," Frank said.

"You should make friends with people your own age. Clete's too much older than you," his mother said.

Father Joe said, "Your mother's right." He brushed the paper napkin across his mouth. "Clete knows you're just sucking up to him to get a job up there. He ain't no fool."

"He said they hired new people from time to time," Frank protested.

Grandmother Cindy chimed in, "What you want to work in that Jew resort for anyhow?"

"It ain't just a resort," Frank said, watching their expression to see if they knew what he knew.

"You just mind your business, son," Joe said.

Just then there was the unmistakable honking of a horn from outside—first once, then three times in a row, insistent.

Rupert said to Frank, "You forgit to put the closed sign up?"

"I put both of 'em up," Frank said. "I never forget."

Outside Frank saw the young man, dressed up Los Angeles style, standing beside his Mercedes. How did a young punk like that get to earn a car only rich people could afford?

"We're closed," Frank said.

"I saw the lights inside," the young man said. "I figured someone was around."

"We're eatin' dinner," Frank said and turned to go in.

The young man followed Frank. "I'm sorry. I've been on the road from L.A. all day and didn't check the gas gauge. I'm near empty. This is a helluva road to get stuck on."

"You can't follow me into the house," Frank said.

"I'll give you five bucks over what the pump says if you'll fill it."

Frank turned to look at the young man's desperate face. He liked to see people scared like that. Owning a Mercedes was no protection against running out of gas if you're an idiot. The guy was actually peeling off a five-dollar bill and holding it out to Frank. The hand holding the five-dollar bill looked like it was manicured. Jesus, these Los Angeles people were something.

Frank took the bill. "You fill it," he said to the young man, pointing at the gas pump.

"I don't know how."

He seemed embarrassed.

The Mercedes took nearly twenty gallons.

When Frank looked up, his father was standing at the door. "Everything okay?"

"Okay, Dad. Be back in a minute."

The young man handed Frank an American Express card. "I hope that's okay. Any motels coming up on this road?"

"Where you headed for?"

"Carmel."

Frank looked at the name on the charge card: Jacob Fetterman. He shoulda guessed.

"Gotta check your name in the credit book," Frank said. "Be a minute."

Inside everyone looked up from the table. "He gave me five bucks extra to pump him some gas."

They watched Frank head for the phone. He dialed a number he knew from memory. "Can I speak to Clete?"

After a moment, Frank said, "I'm sure he'll talk to me even if he's very busy. Tell him it's Frank down at the gas station."

It seemed to take forever. Finally the woman who'd answered the phone said, "Just a minute."

"Please, hurry," Frank said.

Then he heard Clete, breathless, saying, "What's up, kid?"

"Oh hi, Clete," Frank said. "I've got another one for you down at the gas station. Jacob Fetterman. Want me to send him up or can you come down for him?"

11

Clete knew George Whittaker had it in for him ever since
Clete had knocked on the door of George's room and opened
it too soon to find George furtively stashing something away
in his desk. He's getting at me, thought Clete, by giving
Charlotte a hard time about her little bit of AWOL. He's
locked her up, *which is like punishing me.*

This time he waited till George said, "Come in."

"Hi, boss," Clete said. "Guess what? That kid at the gas
station has got another one. I told you it paid to pay attention
to the kid. Will you give him an interview?"

"Mr. Clifford says they have to be twenty-one."

"There's one favor you could do for me," Clete said.

"Like?"

"How about letting Charlotte go? She won't do it again."

Whittaker glared scornfully at Clete. "You've got nerve asking favors with Henry Brown on the loose."

"What about Charlotte? You can't leave her locked in her room like she was one of them."

"I can do anything I please in Cliffhaven," Whittaker said.

Clete stared straight at the lower right drawer of Whittaker's desk. He knew Whittaker was smart enough to get the message.

"Well," Clete said after a moment, "if you can do anything, I'd just as soon you let her out because you're punishing me, too, and I haven't done a thing. Mr. Clifford likes me real special, you know that. He wouldn't want me being punished for some little thing she did." What he wanted to do was get Charlotte into the privacy of his room, beat her for trying to get to that San Diego dude, then fuck her, then beat her, then fuck her again, that's what.

"You let your new couple get away," Whittaker said.

"I was distracted by those goons hanging onto Charlotte. You'd have been upset, boss, if it was your girl they were manhandling."

George Whittaker felt the sting. Nobody before Clete had ever dared refer to the fact that he didn't have a girl at Cliffhaven or anywhere else. He'd just have to have Clete killed accidentally. That was it.

"Okay, Clete," he said. "I'll let her out. But you talk to her the way I know you can so she won't ever try that again, right?"

"I sure will, boss," Clete said.

"Now get your ass down to the gas station. And don't lose this one, you hear?"

Getting onto his scooter, Clete was very pleased with himself for having sneaked into Whittaker's room to see what he was embarrassed about in that lower right-hand drawer. He had copied some of the pages from the diary and read them to Mr. Clifford over the phone. Mr. Clifford had seemed very grateful.

"Clete," he had said, "you are one of the most loyal people I have ever met. Some day you might have a much more important job at Cliffhaven. In the meantime, watch out for George these next few days just in case he suspects. He's an awfully vengeful man."

There comes a time, thought Henry, trudging up the road

with Margaret ahead of the six trusties, *when one must take a chance with life*. He remembered that January, years ago, when the boy had fallen through the ice at Echo Lake. Four men had seen the accident. Two had hung back for fear of falling through themselves. Henry and the other, much younger man had run out over the ice, slipping, stumbling. The boy's head was still above water, and he remembered thinking *Risk a life to save a life* just as the other man yelled, "You stay here!" and plunged into the icy water and, swimming, pushed the boy toward Henry till he could grab the trembling arms and pull the boy onto the ice. The other man lifted himself out on his strong arms and said to him, who had done nothing, "Thanks, mister. Sorry I yelled. I thought you were going to dive in, too, and there'da been nobody to haul the kid in." The man, he learned later from the newspaper report, was a volunteer fireman, used to reacting fast in emergencies. Why hadn't he told the other man to stay put and dived in for the boy? Was it cowardice? What of the two men who had remained on the shore? Would they have watched the boy drown from a distance, afraid for their own safety? Or had they merely hesitated on seeing two others rush to the boy's aid? There were those who would never risk their lives, a decision carried through life like armorplate against the possible touch of love. And at the other extreme all those volunteer firemen all over America, welcoming the danger of being at risk for strangers on a moment's notice, like boys, thinking themselves immune from death, playing at war. And in between? Everyone else, calculating the odds, as he was doing now, thinking of the six trusties behind him, each armed with a club. Yes, he would fight any one of them bare-handed, try to twist the club out of his hands. He would have beaten the man with his own club, anything to be free of this place. But six of them were not odds, they were certain defeat. Was there not a value in resisting anyway, showing these cretins who worked for the enemy that a Jew can fight back? Or was it authority and government ordering him to obey, the face of the state trooper calling him kike, that had sapped from him the necessary iota of insane will needed to lunge into battle against a half dozen adversaries in the hope of somehow getting away?

Henry, he chastised himself, you think too much and do too little.

He looked at Margaret, just ahead of him to the right, her hips moving in the upward climb. She reminded him, strangely, of seeing a locomotive moving slowly out of a station, its wheels and levers moving its weight mechanically. She must be terribly tired, as he was, from the long scramble through the brush. Neither of them was used to this kind of physical test. From time to rare time he had thought of Margaret as a physical being. Beneath her skin, the sensitive and lovely envelope, were strong muscles on a skeleton, an alimentary tract puckered at each end, functional, similar to other bodies, except in this case belonging to the totality called Margaret and imbued with the mind and character and charm that individuated her and brought to her physical being his love for all of her. She had borne not only Stanley and Ruth but him in the comfort of her arms during a quarter of a century of nights, this other person who was half of whatever they constituted together. He had never stopped loving her.

Right now that thought was subverting his attention. He needed to concentrate on breaking away. If escape was possible, was it possible for them both, or did it mean that he might stand a better chance if he escaped alone? He would, of course, come back with help to release her and the others, but would these Cliffhaven people in the meantime revenge themselves against her? Or would they refrain because as a Gentile she was not the object of their special venom? Or would they attack her with zeal because she was a defector married to a Jew?

You see, Henry thought, I am thinking Jewish thoughts—on the one hand, on the other hand—when I should be acting, as a Gentile would, as a *sabra* would.

He heard the motor scooter before he saw its single light come around the bend, recognized Clete, who slowed down, extended his legs from the sides to balance himself as the scooter stopped. What a fool to expect a smile of friendly recognition from Clete, who merely nodded at him and at Margaret as if their capture was foredoomed. Clete exchanged a word with one of the trusties, then twisting the accelerator on the handlebar, went sailing behind his headlight down the road they had just exhausted themselves climbing.

Frank Fowler's assembled family had overheard his phone call to Clete. As he passed through the dining room, he saw them look up from their meal with what he took to be interest. *None of them had the guts to do what he did.*

"Don't get yourself in trouble, Frank," his mother said.

Frank stopped. "With who?"

"You hush your smartass mouth," his father said. "Our family's been here near on fifty years. Whatever those new resort people do is none of our business."

"Bullshit," Frank said.

"Who are you saying bullshit to?" his father said, standing.

"Not to no one, just to what was said about our business. Ain't our sales way up since Cliffhaven started? I gotta go."

"Finish your dinner," his mother said, motioning her husband to sit back down.

Frank went outside. *What a bunch of liars his family was. Long before Cliffhaven was up there they'd talked about the L.A. Jews, and the Frisco Jews, and the New York Jews. They knew. They just had no guts to do anything about anything.*

"Here's your card, mister," he said to Fetterman. "I called Cliffhaven for you, and they said they could put you up."

"You mean the place just here?" Fetterman asked, glancing at the Cliffhaven sign past the gas station.

"Yeah, it's real neat."

"Expensive?" asked Fetterman.

What's a rich Yid worried about that for? "I guess they'll take your credit card," Frank said.

"But is it expensive?" Fetterman asked. He saw Frank glance at his Mercedes. "I know what you're thinking," said Fetterman with a smile. "It's my old man's."

Sure. How many's he got?

"My old man's in the hospital," Fetterman went on, trying to be friendly. "Cancer. He lets me use the car."

Frank was relieved to hear the motor scooter and a moment later see its headlight turn off the Cliffhaven road. "Hi Clete," he yelled eagerly.

Clete nodded to Frank. Coldly, Frank thought. But Clete gushed at Fetterman.

"Welcome to Cliffhaven, Mr. Fetterman," he said, extending his hand. "The sign says reservations only, but we have a spare room this evening, and Mr. Fowler here thought you'd welcome a stopping place for the night since you've come all the way from L.A."

Frank liked the "Mr. Fowler." He forced himself to listen carefully to Clete's pitch. Maybe he'd get a chance to do that someday.

"Yes, indeed. My name's Steve Clete and I'm your guide. I'll just hook up my scooter to your car with this gizmo and we'll be on the way."

"Just a moment," Fetterman said. "How much is it a night?"

I hope he's not going to make a break for it, thought Frank, after all the trouble I've taken.

"Just sixty for a single," Clete said, "and that includes breakfast. It's a three-star restaurant, you know. You have a credit card?"

Fetterman nodded.

"No problem. Want me to drive your car up? The road's kind of tricky at night."

"All right," Fetterman said, getting in on the passenger side. "Key's in the ignition."

"Hey, Frank," Clete said, holding the driver's door open. "Can you get the chain?"

Frank nodded, ran ahead as Clete started the car up. When they got to the gate, Frank had already lowered the chain, and when they passed over it, Frank put it back up. Clete waved to Frank. That boy was okay.

As they started up the winding road, Clete thought it was lucky the trusties and the Browns had gotten a good head start. It'd be a mess to explain if they were all still down here. *Brown is a real fuck trying to escape.*

"Mr. Fetterman," Clete said, "you a businessman, in L.A. I mean?"

"Student," Fetterman said.

"What college you go to?"

"UCLA."

He sure wasn't very communicative. Awful lot of Jews go to that UCLA.

"Some people try to make it all the way from L.A. to San Francisco in one ride, but it's harder'n hell on this road."

"My girl's up at Palo Alto."

"Terrific," Clete said. "My girl works right here at Cliffhaven, which is convenient. Not too convenient for you, Palo Alto."

"I guess I could have made it on U.S. 101, but I get sleepy on freeways if I keep going all day. I thought this road might keep me awake."

"Well," Clete said, "it's a mighty pretty road."

Fetterman said nothing. He seemed preoccupied. Clete thought he'd better keep the conversation going because they were going to pass the others on the road soon.

"Your girl expecting you tonight?"

"She's not expecting me."

"That's good. Will you want to phone her anyway?"

Fetterman seemed a bit embarrassed. "We had a kind of argument on the phone. That's why I'm driving up. I thought I'd surprise her tomorrow."

The headlights of the Mercedes caught the backs of several of the trusties trudging up the road. The sticks they were carrying were clearly visible. When they heard the car, they moved to the side of the road, revealing the Browns. Clete honked so Brown would move to the side of the road.

"Kitchen help," Clete said. "Night shift coming to work."

"We could give some of them a lift," Fetterman said, motioning to the rear seat.

"Against the rules," Clete said, wishing Brown would get his ass out of the way. He was glad he'd thought to keep the car's air conditioning on and the windows up.

He saw Henry Brown suddenly turn toward the passenger side of the car. He was yelling something.

Brown was shouting now, the stupid bastard. One of the trusties was on him. Clete accelerated up the road, hoping the gizmo would hold. If he lost the scooter, he'd keep going anyway, not take any chances.

"Some of those night workers are real weirdos," Clete said

to Fetterman, who had turned to look out the rear window. "We keep them away from the guest areas, naturally."

Henry Brown realized two things at once. His warning had been useless, and the angry trusty, who had waited till the car was around the bend, was now coming at him with a raised club.

"Watch out!" Margaret yelled.

Henry raised his left arm to ward off the blow. "There's no reason for that," he shouted, as the club came down on his forearm, sending a shock of pain to his shoulder. He went for the man's throat, which may have been a mistake he realized too late as the man swung his club sideways, hitting him squarely in the side of the head. The flash of pain seemed luminous as he fell.

Margaret knelt at his side as the other trusties formed a half circle, keeping their distance. She put her hand, then her ear, to his chest. There was a small amount of blood oozing from the side of his scalp.

Margaret looked up at the trusty who had hit him. Her glare was ice. "I'm a doctor," she said as if to explain what she was doing.

It didn't matter. The trusties closed their semicircle, and two of them picked her up by her armpits and dragged her, resisting, up the road, leaving the trusty who had clubbed Henry to watch his prostrate form. "We'll send a car down," one of them said before disappearing from sight.

Henry could feel the throbbing in his head, the ache in his left arm, knew that his feigning unconsciousness had fooled the trusties but not Margaret. She would be worried enough. It amazed him in the midst of his pain how an idea had careered through his mind. He wondered about that trusty. A Jew who had quickly taken a club to another Jew on behalf of these crazies. What kind of man was he? Where was he from? What in his past had made it possible for him to turn into a *Kapo* capable of violence? He needed a moment or two more. His breathing was still hard. If only the man would come closer.

As if in answer, the trusty came over and then, setting his

153

club down, knelt by Henry's side. In one continuous motion Henry turned toward the squatting trusty and brought his good right arm around with whatever force he had in his body behind it, smashing the man in the face, knocking him easily off balance, and in a second, Henry, like the animal he felt himself to be, dug his right thumb into the man's left eye socket hard. The trusty's scream of pain seemed loud enough to be heard in heaven. Henry put his hands around the man's throat. His left hand throbbed with pain from the pressure, but he kept both hands locked until he knew the man was unconscious. Alive but unconscious.

He picked up the trusty's club before fleeing downhill into the woods.

Jacob Fetterman proved to be an unusually observant young man. When Clete showed him the room, he was genuinely impressed with its modern splendor. He had never stayed in a place this fancy. His parents were camping enthusiasts who at every vacation opportunity, even long weekends, took their children and themselves into a reachable wilderness. Once, when Jacob was eleven or twelve, they were caught in a terrible downpour within sight of a motel, but Jacob's father insisted that they erect their tents and spend the night as they had originally planned, out-of-doors.

"It's very luxurious," he said to Clete.

"I'm glad you like it, Mr. Fetterman. Will you be dining with us this evening?"

"It's kind of late."

"The kitchen is still open. It's a three-star restaurant, you know."

"I'm pretty pooped after all that driving," Jacob said. "And I had a snack on the road. I think I'll just turn in. What's that?"

His eye had caught the small camera at the juncture of the wall and the ceiling. It was the first time in Clete's experience that someone had seen it right off the bat.

"Oh that," Clete said. "You won't be needing that."

"What is it?" Fetterman insisted.

"We try to have all the newest things, you know, like the Jacuzzi near the swimming pool. Well, some folks like to tape themselves, lovemaking, that kind of stuff. They have a good time here and sort of like to watch reruns back home."

"That's a hard place to reach up there."

"It's the right angle. We use a small ladder. Anyway, if you're not going into dinner, I'll say good-night unless you have any other questions."

"Well," Fetterman said. "You know those creepy-looking people we saw on the road, some of them were carrying what looked like clubs. I mean, is it safe here?"

Clete laughed. "Of course, it's safe. Those weren't clubs, they were walking sticks. Most people who walk up that road use walking sticks. It really helps. Now I'll just park the Mercedes in the lot and leave your key at the front desk."

"Oh thank you very much," Fetterman said, taking two singles out of his wallet. "I appreciate your help. I'll probably get a real early start tomorrow. I'd like to get to Palo Alto as early as possible."

"Of course. If you need anything, just call the desk and ask for Clete."

"Thanks."

When Clete left, Fetterman looked up at the camera again. He'd heard about motels that showed X-rated movies, but this was a new twist. Incredible what people do.

He was putting his pajamas on when a thought occurred to him. *Clete hadn't left the room key.*

Clete dangled the room key in front of Paula at the reception desk. "New one for you, honey. Jacob Fetterman, room 34. Smart young fellow. Spotted the camera."

As Paula took the key, the door was swung open by one of the staff members in the blue-and-orange Cliffhaven uniform. Out of breath, he yelled, "Your guy Henry Brown's on the loose again. Just found one of the trusties unconscious on the road."

"Shit," Clete said. "He can't get far. Where's his wife?"

"Locked in her room."

"Good. Let's round up a couple of the guys." He held his hand out palm up to Paula.

She reached into the desk and pulled out a standard California Highway Patrol .38. Clete put the pistol in his belt and held his hand out again. Paula put the clip of bullets in his hand. "Remember Mr. Clifford's warning."

"Don't worry," Clete said. "I know the rules."

12

It was the shortest help-wanted ad Daniel Pitz had ever seen:

RESORT MANAGER, BOX 1665

At first he thought it was a dumb ad. With that little said, a hundred guys could answer. But somebody who didn't really need a job wouldn't answer something like that. That eliminated the merely curious. You couldn't phone and find out more. You had to write. To a box number at the *L.A. Times.* You couldn't guess what kind of place it was or who you were writing to. It was all up to you. Your letter had to do it all. Nobody would get in touch with you unless your letter made you sound like the right type for them, whoever them was.

Dan Pitz decided that somebody smart had placed that ad. He liked smart people. Whenever he thought of himself, it was not as good-looking, which he was, or physically strong, which he also was, but as real smart. When he had got caught pulling the fire alarm in grade school, his homeroom teacher had said to him, "You think you're smart?" When he answered, "Yes ma'am," she had slapped his face. Well, he'd gotten even on her, hadn't he? Four flat tires on her car.

Dan spent all of Sunday afternoon and part of the evening composing his letter carefully.

"Dear Sir or Madam," it began, "I am intrigued by your laconic advertisement."

He chose the word "laconic" carefully. It proclaimed that the applicant was a man of good vocabulary who assumed the recipient would be also:

> I have managed resorts successfully both in California and in the East.
>
> My father died when I was eight years old. My mother and an older sister raised me. I have a B.A. from UCLA, with a major in Drama and a minor in Psychology.
>
> While in college I had several bit parts in motion pictures, but after graduation found the entertainment industry uncongenial. I got a lucrative position as salesman in a well-known clothing emporium, but found the owners uncongenial. My break came when I was selling real estate on commission. Some people I dealt with were impressed by my abilities and offered me an opportunity to be deputy manager of a motel. At the time the manager died in an accident, the motel was in the red. Within three months of my appointment as manager, the motel was making money. The owners asked me to take over a much larger motel and restaurant they had in central California, and I was able to turn that around also. After a successful eight-year career with the same ownership at various locations, I was lured East to manage a very large and long-established resort in the Catskills. I found the environment uncongenial and have since returned to California to pursue my career here.
>
> I am single, have no dependents, and am free to relocate provided the responsibility and remuneration are appropriate to my experience. References in California are available on request.

In the living room of their mansion, Merlin Clifford showed the pile of replies to Abigail, who used a pair of gold-framed eyeglasses that hung from her neck by a black satin cord to glance through them. Clifford watched his wife's expressions. She wasn't liking what she saw either. When she looked up, he handed her Daniel Pitz's letter.

"This man's a pompous ass," he said. "But interesting."

Abigail Clifford read Pitz's letter several times. "You'd better find out more about what he means by uncongenial," she said.

"I can guess. I have several other matters to explore with this young man."

"How do you know he's young?" she asked.

"He hasn't mentioned anything that would clue me to his age. If he thought he might be too old for the job, he would have mentioned his high energy. The writer of this letter takes high energy for granted. Unless he's left out a lot of employment deliberately, he's young and worried about it. Also, Abigail, there comes a time in life when even a pompous man says money instead of remuneration."

Abigail had to laugh.

"Mr. Daniel Pitz?" the man's voice asked.

"Speaking." The caller, Dan thought, had a very authoritative voice.

"I'm calling in response to your letter applying for the position of resort manager."

"Yes, sir."

"How old are you?"

There was a moment's silence.

"Please don't lie," the voice said. "It's something that is objectively ascertainable."

"I'm thirty-six."

"Good," the voice said, to Dan's relief. "You said your father died when you were eight. What was the cause of his death?"

"A trauma."

God, thought Clifford, he really is pompous.

"What kind of trauma?"

Again a moment's hesitation.

"Please, Mr. Pitz. I'm a busy man."

"I'm sorry. I still have difficulty with it. He died of a gunshot wound."

"From the police?"

"No, no. A holdup."

"Where?"

"In . . . his store."

159

"Your father was a shopkeeper?"

"A liquor store."

"I see. Is your mother alive?"

"No. Excuse me, but is all this relevant to the position?"

"Extremely. Did your mother die of natural causes?"

"An auto accident."

"I see. Your sister is alive?"

"She died in the same auto accident."

"How long ago was that?"

"Let's see. May third, eleven years ago."

"Do you recall the date on which you became manager of that first motel?"

Pitz gave the date to the caller.

"I will phone you again in two days' time unless my inquiries produce negatives, Mr. Pitz."

"Do you want my references?"

"No."

"May I ask your name, sir?"

There was a click on the line.

Daniel Pitz thought a lot about that phone call during the next twenty-four hours. The man must have been impressed by his résumé to call, but the questions didn't make sense. That man didn't know any more about Dan's ability to run a resort after the call than before.

Dan decided he'd better keep looking. He was writing a reply to an ad for an assistant manager when the phone rang.

"We spoke two days ago, Mr. Pitz. I've had some inquiries made. You are now the leading candidate for the position. My name is Clifford. I will expect you for an interview at my home tomorrow at the cocktail hour, say five. Is that convenient?"

Dan Pitz's throat felt dry. "Yes, of course," he managed. Clifford gave him the address. "Bring with you a list of the books you've read in the last five years. Please don't come early," he added, "and if you're more than ten minutes late, don't bother." He hung up.

Punctuality was only one of Merlin Clifford's tests. When he hired somebody, it was damn well going to be permanent.

* * *

When he was in real estate, Dan Pitz had handled the houses of some well-to-do people, but never anything like the Clifford mansion. There was an impressive stone-and-ironwork gate with a gatehouse. The guard was not some elderly man dozing on the job, but a fellow who looked like he could strangle a dog. He was expecting a man named Daniel Pitz, but insisted on two pieces of identification. The guard then telephoned the main house to say that the guest had arrived at the gatehouse at five o'clock and was on his way up.

The lawn and shrubbery seemed the kind it would take a small army of gardeners to keep up, but not a soul was in sight. The house itself, set back about seventy-five yards from the road, was in the Spanish style that suited southern California. In fact, it looked like a mission more than a home, with tile roofs at various angles, parapets, openings in the stonework that looked as if they were meant for riflemen or archers. Dan always worried about a prospective employer's financial stability. He didn't want to get caught in someone else's bankruptcy, but these folks looked like they were here to stay.

He heard the dog growl, then saw it, a German Shepherd between himself and the entrance doors. The German Shepherd his father had kept in the liquor store hadn't done any good. The intruder had shot them both.

"Here, boy!" A Japanese man had appeared at the door, and the dog immediately went running to him and disappeared inside the house.

"Mr. Clifford is expecting you," the Japanese man said. "This way, please."

Dan was ushered through the entrance hallway—the floor was marble in a checkerboard pattern—to a huge living room with peaked windows two stories high. He couldn't believe the size of the intricately woven carpet. At its other end a man of sixty or so put his pipe down in an ashtray and stood up, then advanced across the carpet, his hand out. The woman he had been talking to stayed put, watching him.

"I'm Merlin Clifford," the man said.

"Daniel Pitz, sir."

"Welcome. Please come sit down. My wife wants to meet you as well. Abigail, this is Mr. Pitz."

Mrs. Clifford raised her head for a better look. Handsome young man. Though she now drew her lovers from a different stratum of society, in the old days she had permitted some of her husband's employees to service her from time to time, and she still found herself inspecting each newcomer to see if he would do.

"What will you drink?" Mr. Clifford asked the moment Dan was seated on the edge of his chair.

He liked beer, but that wasn't for now.

"I prefer whisky," he said.

"Ice and soda?"

"Yes, please."

The Japanese man had reappeared.

"Scotch and soda for Mr. Pitz, and the usual for Mrs. Clifford and myself." Mr. Clifford turned to face Dan Pitz. "Do sit back, you'll be more comfortable."

Dan did as he was instructed.

"Now then," Mr. Clifford said. "Did you bring your reading list?"

Dan handed it over. It was short and included the names of novels that Dan remembered wanting to read. Most of them he hadn't gotten around to. To his surprise, Mr. Clifford just put the list in his inside breast pocket without examining it.

"We will get on much better," Mr. Clifford said, "if you assume I already know the answers to any questions I ask. Understood?"

Dan nodded. For a moment, glancing around at the vast space in the room, he felt small.

"I am a student of language," Mr. Clifford said. "One unusual word showed up in your short letter three times."

"Oh?"

"Do you remember which word?"

"No, sir."

"Uncongenial."

Dan blushed.

"What do you mean by uncongenial?"

"Oh," Dan said, "the same as everyone else does. Not right. Different. Bad different."

"Do you remember the connections in which you used the word?"

"I think I said I found some of my employment uncongenial?"

"I think you found some people uncongenial. In the motion picture industry. The owners of the clothing store. The people at the resort in the East."

"That's right," Dan said.

"Were they all Jews?"

Dan took his handkerchief out of his pocket and rubbed his wet palms. Then he realized what he was doing and, embarrassed, shoved the handkerchief back where it belonged. *Clifford couldn't be Jewish, could he?*

"What do you mean?" Dan asked.

"You know very well what I mean. Was the common denominator of the people you found uncongenial the fact of their Jewishness? Are you circumcised, Mr. Pitz?"

Dan looked over at Mrs. Clifford. Her gaze did not relent. "Yes. Most men my age—I'm not Jewish, if that's what you're getting at."

"I established that before inviting you here. I just want to clarify what you meant by uncongenial. Is there something about Jews you don't like?"

Dan felt he had to take a chance.

"Pretty much everything," he said, smiling in Mrs. Clifford's direction and noticing that she now smiled, too. Mrs. Clifford was thinking that while she didn't want the bother of becoming regularly active with employees again, she might enjoy this young man just once or twice.

"Explain that," Mr. Clifford said. "If you will. What don't you like about them?"

"Well," Dan said, spreading his fingers as if he were about to play the piano. "They're very aggressive. I mean in school they were the pushy ones, trying for the straight A's, scholarships, things like that. They were always running for student government. Both kids who ran our Drama Society were Jews, and I felt it wasn't fair that Christian kids did all the acting and the Jews ran the place."

He hoped that would satisfy Mr. Clifford. You could get yourself in a lot of trouble saying things like he just did. You had a feeling the Anti-Defamation-whatever-the-hell-its-name-was recorded everything you thought as well as said about the Hebes.

"Go on," Mr. Clifford said. "I'm interested in your views."

"About Jews?"

"I believe that's what we're talking about."

Dan looked over at Mrs. Clifford. She was smiling in that special way again. She wasn't a bad-looking woman, attractive, in fact, if a little bit older than he would have preferred. Still, older women could be great in the sack, all that experience and nothing to lose. Dan felt encouraged.

"Well, everyone knows the people on top in the film business are Jews. The ones—"

"That's not quite true," Mr. Clifford interrupted. "The Chairman of Fox is not a Jew, nor is the head of production. Zanuck is not a Jew."

"But they predominate," Dan said hastily.

"Go on."

Dan wondered whether he was on the right track. "Well, the ones I got to work with, lower down the ladder, they were flashy types, just like I later found in the clothing business, which is why I liked real estate better."

"Aren't there plenty of them in real estate?" Mrs. Clifford asked.

Dan turned to her. He knew when a woman was interested. "Oh certainly, but you can avoid them if you want to."

"Are you uncomfortable with Jews?" Mr. Clifford asked.

"Well, yes."

"But you wouldn't want to do them any harm, would you?"

Mr. Clifford noticed the momentary twist in Dan's lip, not quite a twitch.

"You don't have to answer that," Mr. Clifford said, already having had his answer. "Do you think you would have difficulty working with them?"

"Jews?" Dan asked.

"Ah," Mr. Clifford said, "there are the drinks." He waited

till the Japanese had served Mrs. Clifford and Pitz, then took his own drink. Dan watched the Japanese leave the room.

"Don't worry about his overhearing anything, Mr. Pitz," Mr. Clifford said. "He's been with me for years. He's like a son."

Dan saw the look Mrs. Clifford shot at him at the mention of a son. That might be worth exploring privately with her. His view was that you always needed something on the other guy, and women were a good way to get what you needed. He smiled at Mrs. Clifford to let her know he knew of her interest.

"I was asking," Mr. Clifford said, "whether you would have difficulty working with Jews."

"Is this a Jewish resort the ad was for?"

"I wouldn't call it that," Mr. Clifford said. "There are Jews there."

"What about the owners?"

"The owners are Mrs. Clifford and myself."

"It isn't one of those, er, restricted places then?"

Mr. and Mrs. Clifford looked at each other.

"Mr. Pitz," Mr. Clifford continued, "I want an absolutely honest answer to the next question."

"Certainly."

"Are you capable of murder?"

Dan Pitz sat frozen.

"Please remember my earlier warning," Mr. Clifford said. "Are you capable of murder?"

This wasn't a courtroom. He could say anything.

"Isn't everyone?" he asked, his palms sweating again.

"I'm not asking about everyone, I'm asking about you." Mr. Clifford seemed annoyed. "Can you kill if necessary?"

"I think so," Dan said.

"Good," Mr. Clifford said. "I'm glad you chose not to obfuscate. Just for Mrs. Clifford's elucidation, I should tell her that your mother and sister died in an automobile accident under circumstances remarkably similar to the ones obtaining when the manager of your first motel died, am I right? Please don't be alarmed, Mr. Pitz, I'm not about to inform the police.

From the dates you supplied on the phone, I was merely able to have the newspaper accounts of the time researched. I would guess that you used rubber cement, is that correct?"

How the hell could he know?

"What kind of fuse did you use, Mr. Pitz?"

"An ordinary display fireworks fuse."

"How much rubber cement did you use?"

"Just half a gallon."

"Why was no container found?"

"Oh," Dan Pitz said, "I transferred it to an empty half-gallon milk carton."

"Very, very clever, Mr. Pitz. According to the news account, your mother and sister were in the front seat and you were in the back seat when you noticed something was wrong with the car. You had them pull over, you got out to see what was wrong, and suddenly the interior of the car was a mass of flame from an explosion, and there was nothing you could do but watch your mother and sister being incinerated."

Dan coughed into his hand. "Well, actually, not having done this before, I lit the fuse, got out, and ran like hell. I ran back only after the explosion. There were one or two cars coming down the road, and I thought I'd better be close to it."

"The newspaper had you trying to pull them out of the fire."

"Not really," Dan said. "It was one big ball of fire right away even before the tank went."

"Where was the container?"

"I had it in a paper bag in back. I just put it right behind the front seats."

"When the car stopped, you lit the fuse, and got out?"

"That's it."

"Were you pleased with the results?"

"What do you mean?"

"I mean, how much did you inherit as a result of the untimely death of your mother and sister?"

"Well . . ."

"Well is not an amount."

"About twenty-seven thousand dollars and some furniture."

"Thank you," Mr. Clifford said. "And having used that technique successfully, you tried it again for job advancement purposes, is that right? According to that clipping, you weren't anywhere near the car."

This Mr. Clifford was worrying Dan.

"Do go on," Mr. Clifford said.

"No, I didn't want to be connected with it. I picked a fairly isolated road. I said I needed to get something out of the paper bag I'd put in back. The manager stopped the car. I opened the back door, lit the fuse, and ran like hell. Never looked back. A mile or two away on another road, I hitched a ride on the back of an open truck. The driver never got a good look at me. I was back in the motel when I got word of the accident."

"Very clever, Mr. Pitz. Actually, what I'm most interested in was how, once the manager was out of the way, you got that seedy motel into the black so quickly. Can you elucidate?"

Maybe this fellow Clifford is taping this conversation.

"I want to assure you, Mr. Pitz, that I am not making a record of this conversation, but if you'd like to satisfy yourself, please do look around."

This guy reads minds. "No, no," Dan said.

"You trust me then?" Mr. Clifford asked.

Dan thought for a moment. "I can't afford to trust anybody."

"Suppose I were to go to the authorities? There's no statute of limitations on murder."

"It'd be your word against my word," Dan said.

"My word and Mrs. Clifford's word."

Dan smiled. "Guess I'd have to kill you, too," he said.

Mrs. Clifford guffawed.

"Very, very good, Mr. Pitz. Well, then, continue about the motel."

"The manager was a very fusty guy, old-fashioned, wouldn't rent to a couple without suitcases. He had some kind of excuse, but it was really on moral grounds."

"Oh?"

"I suggested to him that we could take in a lot more if we rented by the hour, your only real cost was the sheets and it would always be just one of the beds, but he wouldn't do it."

"I see."

"You know bed vibrators were very common even then, but

he wouldn't go for them. And he would never have agreed to show the kind of movies on closed circuit that a lot of adults like to see when they check in at a motel."

"And you were anxious to get all these innovations going?"

"Yes."

"And under your direction the motel thrived?"

"Yes."

"Pity you had to kill the manager to prove yourself, but then if you hadn't, this interview would not be taking place. I suppose I should explain why your ability to deal forthrightly with obstacles and your finding Jewish people uncongenial helps qualify you for a position as manager of our resort. Mr. Pitz, let me tell you about Cliffhaven."

Ten minutes later Dan Pitz felt he had passed a point of no return. He had learned enough about the Cliffords to have a real hold on them. They didn't seem concerned. Did they have a hold on him?

Dan had learned that Cliffhaven was only six months old, but that the assembling of the real estate and the building had started a year and a half before that when Mr. Clifford had officially retired from the business he had built—something to do with oil-drilling equipment that had been extremely profitable and had made him rich. Mr. Clifford had principles. He was interested in social experiments.

"Can I order you a refill?" Mr. Clifford asked.

"I'd better not."

"Good," Mr. Clifford said. He didn't want a boozer managing Cliffhaven.

"It isn't as if I've invented anything new," Mr. Clifford said. "The Hebrews were unpopular in various societies long before the birth of Christ and for two millennia afterward. They are a real challenge, however, to those of us who would prefer that they keep their own company somewhere else, because they have a way of surviving, you must admit . . ." he moved his chair a mite closer to Dan's, "that is uncanny."

"It is," Dan said. Clifford seemed very rational, very sane.

"Did you realize, Mr. Pitz, that we have eight times as many of those people here in these United States than Hitler had to contend with in all of Germany?"

Dan nodded.

"And they have a great deal more direct and indirect influence on the government. That's why I see my social experiment as a challenge. The fact that Cliffhaven has been successful for half a year is, historically, a fantastic achievement, don't you agree?"

"I'm not too sure what actually goes on there," Dan said.

"Oh you'll have plenty of opportunity for that," Mr. Clifford said. "Just think. We have sequestered, serially, some several hundreds of them and there's been not one leak, not one newspaper story, no hint of what we're doing. Yet people know. Locals. Some of the state police. Others. You see, Mr. Pitz, there are a lot of people who tacitly approve of our experiment. That's the clue to our success. People don't interfere. Now then, Mr. Pitz, I hope you'll stay for dinner."

The Japanese man served with the expertise of a butler. Dan wondered if he was the cook, too. Surely, for a place as large as this, they must have other servants. But where were they? Were they kept from seeing visitors?

Just as dessert was being passed, Dan heard the very distant ring of a telephone. His instinct was to rise to answer it. Mr. and Mrs. Clifford did not move.

They seemed as if they were expecting him to say something.

"Isn't there a chance that whatever is going on at your place will be discovered?" Dan asked.

"That question must be very important to you," Mr. Clifford said. "You've been silent for nearly twenty minutes. Who do you think might discover Cliffhaven?"

"Anyone."

"The guests never leave."

"The staff? Don't they leave the premises? Vacations and so on?"

"Of course. You'll find them very loyal. I think I can demonstrate that to you."

The Japanese was standing there. Dan hadn't seen him come in.

"Telephone, Mr. Clifford," he announced softly.

"I said no phone calls."

"Important, sir."

Mr. Clifford seemed a bit put out as he rose to take an extension phone behind the screen in the corner. Dan could not make out any of the words. He wanted to take the opportunity to say a few words to Mrs. Clifford, but not in front of the Japanese, who just stood there as if he were invisible.

Dan noticed the flush in Mr. Clifford's face as he rejoined them. "Sen," he said to the Japanese, "we must be in Cliffhaven tomorrow, hopefully well before noon. If we left at three A.M., would that be sufficient time?"

"Yes, sir."

"Well then, Mr. Pitz, you're in for some unexpected excitement. I trust you'll stay a short night with us and join me for the trip? You'll have a chance to see Cliffhaven firsthand."

Dan hesitated. "I insist," Mr. Clifford said. "You can take advantage of one of our guest rooms here. Sen, Mr. Pitz will be staying over. Be sure to wake him at half past two. Will a half hour be sufficient for you to get ready, Mr. Pitz? So that we'll waste no time, Sen will have a breakfast box and a thermos of coffee for us in the car. I trust four or five hours of sleep will do you, Mr. Pitz, you're a young man. Well, Abigail," he said, turning to his wife, "we have a little problem at Cliffhaven, and I'm so anxious to see how Mr. Pitz might solve it. Mr. Pitz, of course I don't expect you to spend your time for nothing. Your salary in the East was thirty thousand dollars."

How the hell did he know that?

"I will pay you for tomorrow at that rate, pro rata, but double to make up for the travel time involved. One of our new guests, a Mr. Henry Brown, has managed to break loose for the second time. My people are sure he hasn't escaped from the premises, that he's on the grounds somewhere. Not to worry. We have his wife. She will be interrogated tomorrow. It should be interesting for you to observe."

He is doing this to observe me, Dan thought.

"By the way, Mr. Pitz, at Cliffhaven you will be meeting the present manager, George Whittaker, and I trust you will be discreet. You see, Mr. Whittaker believes I am looking for a number two for him, not a replacement."

"Of course," Dan said. *Why is Whittaker losing his job? Maybe I won't want it after I see the place.*

"Mrs. Clifford will show you to a guest room upstairs. You'll find clean pajamas, if you use them, in the drawer of the bureau, as well as underclothes in all the usual sizes for tomorrow. We're quite prepared for guests here as well as in Cliffhaven."

13

In the darkness Henry came upon a patch of leaves no bigger than a coffin where he could lie down. He fell to his knees, then slowly let the rest of his aching body down, turning sideways. He put his hands under his cheek as he used to when he was a child.

He must rest, he told himself. Even for a few minutes.

When he and Margaret planned to see a movie on a weekday evening after work, he always took ten or fifteen minutes for a siesta before dinner, trying to drain his mind of thought. He must do that now.

Think of nothing.

This bed of leaves is quite comfortable. It would be easy to fall asleep.

Must not fall asleep.

Rest. Make the mind a blank, but do not fall asleep.

He opened his eyes. You can't fall asleep with your eyes

open. Above him the bracken-like jumble of growth seemed protective. The tops of the redwoods were splayed against the night sky.

Make the mind a blank.

Count the stars.

Were those sounds from the road he was hearing?

He sat up. It was no good lying here. It was too good lying here.

Slowly, he got to his feet. He couldn't be far from the road.

Should he flag a police car on the road? *Not around here.*

There was a gas station just near the entrance. Might someone there help? They would look at him, dirty face, dirty hands, torn clothes. They'd think he was crazy.

Would any motorist in his right mind give him a lift?

Henry could hear the activity down on the road, scooters, a car, another car. They are assembling a posse.

Must not get caught. *They still had Margaret.*

He lay down again on the leaves, thought of Margaret lying beside him. Listen, he told himself, this is like lying down in a snowdrift. It was a way to wait for death.

Got to get moving.

He remembered the time of infinite energy, in his teens and twenties, when he could do anything for however long. Once, when he was twenty-two, he'd caught a flu with fever that lasted for a week. When it was over, he sat up in bed, then swung his legs over the side. When he rose his legs were suddenly unresponsive to his will, and he fell back onto the bed and stayed there for hours, thinking the former infallibility of his body had gone, until reason returned and he tried slowly to get out of bed, stood up slowly, then sat back down, and gradually brought himself back to normal strength over a period of more than a week.

It was like that now. He was demanding more of his body than it could give. He had fallen back onto his bed. He had to get up. Slowly.

On his feet he did not feel woozy. All he had needed was the short respite. He could go on. It would be easier to descend the rest of the way through the dense brush by using the same kind of rhythm monkeys use to swing from branch to branch, letting momentum do much of the work, grabbing a branch with his right hand, letting his body swing forward and down to grab something with his left hand before letting go with the right. It was all right. He was making it. It couldn't be much farther now.

It was then that he heard from below the yapping of the dogs.

He was eight years old, walking with Bobby down near Van Cortlandt Park near the golf course, when the dog, a collarless mongrel, had come snapping at them.

"Don't run," he had yelled to Bobby, but Bobby had run like hell. The perverse dog, instead of following the running boy, stayed to guard Henry, snapping from a distance of four or five feet.

He decided to walk around it as if he weren't nervous. Just when he thought he was safe, the crazy dog suddenly lunged at him, biting, tearing at his pants cuffs. He remembered the pain shooting up his leg, the sudden blood. He kicked off the biting dog, ran the way Bobby had run.

At home his horrified mother washed his wound down with water, then took him to the doctor, who insisted on the tetanus shot. The doctor said that if they found the dog, they could avoid the rabies series. The policeman came. He rode with his mother in back of the police car to where it had happened. They looked everywhere. No dog. Finally, he was made to take the dreaded series of rabies shots. He remembered weeks of discomfort in school and having to hobble. From that time on he carried the fear of dogs in him.

When he was older, Henry understood his self-deception. Being bitten and getting the shots was bad, but his fear came from something else: Animals were irrational. You can't argue with them. You could convince people, talk them out of a vicious intent.

Thinking of that now, Henry was embarrassed by his naïveté. Could he talk the people who ran Cliffhaven out of their vicious intent? Were human beings less vicious to each other than animals were? To believe that was to believe in the sin that led to all others. Human nature, the subject of so many heated discussions at his house, was the ultimate trap of the idealist. Man could be a pig. Or a vulture. Under duress, a hyena.

Henry listened carefully, for he suddenly thought he heard the sounds of more than two dogs. The old fear was with him, unshakeable.

From the sounds, they were working their way up from the road with the dogs, planning to cut him off. But could they if he went the other way, toward Cliffhaven? Was that crazy? They would be looking for him down by the highway. Or on the way down, but not the way up. Did the dogs have his scent from some piece of clothing he had left behind?

He remembered the story of the prisoner at Sing Sing in the sixties who had escaped from his cell, and the search parties had combed all the adjacent towns uselessly because, as it turned out, so many frantic hours later, the man was still behind the walls, hiding in an outbuilding. Did he remember that now as a God-given clue to what he should do—get out of the woods where the dogs would eventually find him and get to where they wouldn't look, the place he had escaped from? Or was he losing his mind, becoming his own captor?

The yapping sounded closer. He had no choice. Back up to Cliffhaven was where he had to go.

The branch-holding routine he had worked out for going down was much harder going up. The only hopeful sign was that the yelping faded. He was alone and moving faster in a direction they hadn't expected him to go. Maybe the handlers thought the dogs were following the wrong scent, and were trying to reorient the dogs.

It seemed an eternity before he reached the perimeter of Cliffhaven, circled around in the end of the woods away from the resort buildings, until he came to the long, flat-roofed building set far apart from the others and so different in style. It was built of cinder blocks, not wood, and looked like some oversized utility building. It might have been a small factory except for the absence of windows anywhere.

He'd have to cross about seventy-five yards of open space to get to it. Would he be seen? It was dark, but he'd be silhouetted against the woods.

He couldn't take a chance, and so, exhausted as he was, he

crawled the entire distance, moving his arms like a duck as he had been taught in the army, dragging his body, keeping close to the ground. The knuckles of his right hand were bleeding from the small stones. It seemed not to matter. His body moved like an automaton.

Once against the building, he stood. It was good to stand. He edged around the building to the other side. Should he chance the one door? What if there were someone inside? Would there be any way to get inside a building without windows? There was no sign that the building was air-conditioned.

He tried the door. It was locked.

Henry listened for sounds within the building. Machinery? Nothing. He listened for the dogs and could not hear them.

He had not seen the fourth side of the building. Carefully he made his way around. Luck. A metal ladder going to the roof. Could anyone see him? He'd have to chance it.

He clambered up the ladder. The rungs were very narrow and hurt his feet. He mustn't fall. From the distance, he had not realized the building was nearly two stories high.

Swinging himself over onto the roof, he was glad to see there was a two-foot parapet all the way around. They could come up after him the same way. He tried to pull the metal ladder up. It was very heavy, and he couldn't get any leverage, yet he managed to lift it off the ground, then hand over hand to pull it up a few inches at a time. It was too heavy. He had raised it perhaps a foot or two off the ground. He couldn't hold it anymore.

It fell to the ground unevenly, tilted, and toppled over. He had lost his means of getting off the roof. Nothing seemed to matter anymore except the possibility of sleep.

He huddled against the parapet, holding his knees. His body hurt so.

What the hell. He didn't have to fight sleep anymore. Stretching his hands under his cheek, he was almost instantly lost to the world.

14

The night was coming to an end when Margaret stretched her arms out for Henry.

He wasn't there.

She woke abruptly, remembered she was alone behind a locked door.

If they found Henry, would they bring him here? *They might not even tell you if he were alive or dead.*

If he had escaped onto the road, would he be able to find willing help? Could the wound in his head be worse than she thought it was? Had they flung his body into the woods?

When Margaret was thirteen she had imagined herself to be vulnerable to every ailment of mankind. But by the time she was fifteen, she believed that all of the serious ailments— including death, which she thought of as the ultimate ailment— were things *other people got*. By the time she had finished a year of medical school, she had a sensible view of her vulnerability; she could catch or get or be visited with any or many of life's physical and mental catastrophes, but care, antisepsis, attention to diet, keeping one's distance from friends with active colds could all contribute to health.

In contrast to Margaret's rationality, the young men of her acquaintance thought of themselves as special vessels of the Almighty, impervious to harm, whether driving a car or off to war. They were fools. Two of them died in car crashes. Most of the others went off to the army, jocks in brain and body, unmindful of how vulnerable their fine physiques were to Asiatic fungus, malaria, disabling dysentery, concussion, and shrapnel, their heads reverberating with the song of youth, *It can't happen to me.*

Henry was not like them. He was not a jock, nor was he a whiner. He had been an optimist in all things except one.

They were in a rowboat in Central Park on a sunny Saturday in June when he announced to her, "I want to tell you something about my being Jewish."

It all seemed so irrelevant to her. He didn't indulge in any religious practices. He didn't act different. He certainly didn't look Jewish.

"Before we get involved any further," he said, shipping the oars as if to avoid even the distraction of rowing because of the importance of the point, "you should know that to Jews anything can happen. Anything bad."

She had tried to laugh it off, the idea of a perpetual sword of Damocles, but he was insistent. "Margaret, I love you."

Of course she loved him, too. What was he getting at?

"Your involvement with me could lead you into the circle of danger."

"Cheer up," Margaret had said. "Hitler's dead."

"He was just a stage," Henry said.

"It's a lousy century," Margaret said.

"The Middle Ages were pretty bad. For Jews, I mean, as well as others. Luther traded on it. Then the Russian pogroms. The Polish pogroms. You can find the emotions anywhere."

"Here?" she had said.

"Anywhere."

Had either of them, after that day on the lake, ever given it a second thought? She hadn't.

There was no point in trying to get to sleep again. It was morning. Yet the temptation was to lie there because getting up meant knowing what you would do. She wanted to think.

Were some of Henry's notions Jewish notions? When she was about to drive the car, he'd remind her, not always but on occasion, to turn off the ignition while she was getting gas. When Stanley was first sent away to summer camp, Henry prepared for him a written list of warnings:

1. *Don't go swimming without another boy swimming close to where you are.*
2. *Don't go in the water unless a lifeguard is present.*
3. *Roughhouse with pillows okay, but no sticks, rocks, or anything else that can really hurt people.*
4. *In public toilets put paper on the seat before you sit down.*
5. *Cut meat into small pieces. People have choked to death on food.*
6. *Be polite to strangers, but never get into a stranger's car under any circumstances.*
7. *Don't wander off. Always let your counselor know where you are.*

Anybody could pass those warnings on to a child, but actually drawing up a written list—was that Jewish? Had he ever warned Stanley out of her earshot about the hazards of being Jewish as he had her?

Stanley. They said they would phone him from Santa Barbara. Would he be alarmed if they didn't call? Would Ruth be worried? She'd have no reason to. Not yet.

What of all of the people who've been here for months? Didn't anyone come looking for them? If they hadn't announced their intentions to go to Cliffhaven, where would one look? There are bureaus of missing persons everywhere, aren't there? Now that's something Stanley would do, he'd pursue the matter. We were supposed to meet in L.A. Henry was to call him. Oh my God, she thought, if he comes looking for us and gets here, they'll simply have one more prisoner. Is that what happens? Those who track their kin to Cliffhaven are also among the guests?

The distinct sound of a key in the lock startled her. Quickly, Margaret got out of bed and slipped into her robe just as the door swung open. It was that very tall young woman, dressed in the same uniform as Clete, who had been taken away by the two men in the dining room, Clete had gone after them. And that was when they seized the opportunity to escape. What did Clete say her name was, Charlotte?

She was carrying a tray. "Good morning," she said as if nothing had happened.

"Is your name Charlotte?"

She nodded.

"You're Clete's friend."

Charlotte set the breakfast tray down. "Sometimes," she said.

"You took his car to San Diego."

"I didn't get very far."

"They came after you, like they came after us."

"You better eat this stuff before it gets cold, Dr. Brown."

"You're a prisoner just like we are."

"That's not true." Charlotte was trying to control her anger. "It's just that they have rules. They're letting me make up for being AWOL."

"How?"

"I don't have to answer you."

"How?"

"By being in charge of you, dear," Charlotte said. "Now eat."

Margaret looked at the tray. On it was a very large glass of orange juice, a small beaker of coffee, toast, marmalade, a glass of milk, and a covered dish in the center. A feast before dying? Charlotte lifted the cover to reveal scrambled eggs and bacon.

Margaret had not thought of food; now, reacting like Pavlov's dog, she was suddenly, instantly hungry.

Why was she not eating in the dining room?

Out loud she said, "Why am I not eating in the dining room?"

"You won't be doing that until your husband is found," Charlotte said.

Thank heaven. They're still looking for him. Maybe Henry got away!

"You better eat before this stuff gets cold," Charlotte said.

"I'd like to wash up first." Margaret wanted to change. She didn't like eating in her nightgown.

"You'll wash later," Charlotte said. "I brought the food hot. You eat it hot."

Eating with Charlotte looking on made her feel more like a prisoner than anything else that had happened so far. After a few mouthfuls she no longer felt hunger. Her body was warning her; if she ate more she'd get sick.

"You'd better finish," Charlotte said. "We don't know when you'll eat next."

There must be stuff in the food to tranquilize me, Margaret thought.

"I'll throw up if I eat more," Margaret said. "I really can't. I need some air. Can you take me outside? Can we take a walk?"

"You're not walking away again. The only thing I'm allowed to do is leave you in the rec room. Locked."

"What's in the rec room?"

"Basketball. Volleyball."

"Who do I play with?" Margaret asked. The idea of socializing with Charlotte was repugnant to her.

"You play with yourself," Charlotte said, laughing. "I mean by yourself. I got work to do. I'm taking you to the rec room. Get dressed."

Anything but this room, Margaret thought. "All right," she said, "I'll go to the rec room."

"Say please."

Margaret looked at the tall young woman. *Think of it as a game*, she told herself.

"Please," Margaret said.

"Okay."

On the short walk to the rec room, Charlotte and Margaret encountered Carol.

"That the escapee's wife?" Carol asked.

Charlotte nodded.

"I'm taking her to the rec room."

"I just put my infraction in there."

"Terrific," Charlotte said. "They can play with each other."

Girls' jokes, thought Margaret, *are like boys' jokes.* She wondered who the other resident was.

The rec room, it turned out, was much too small to be a real gymnasium. It had a polished wooden floor and only one basketball hoop. The volleyball net was wrapped around its standards in the corner. The rest of the room was bare, except for the other resident, who stopped bouncing the basketball when they opened the one door.

"This is Dr. Brown," Charlotte said.

"Phyllis Minter," the other woman said, nodding only at Margaret.

"Don't try anything funny," Charlotte said. "There's only the one door."

"I can see that," Margaret said.

"It's bolted from the outside."

"What do I do in case of fire?" Margaret said. *What's the point of baiting her?*

"Don't play with matches," Charlotte said. "I'm to be back for you as soon as Mr. Clifford arrives."

"Is it supposed to be a privilege to meet the sickie who invented this place?"

"You're looking for real trouble," Charlotte said.

"I already have that," Margaret said. "Shouldn't I be looking for something else?"

"Mr. Clifford will deal with you."

"I have nothing to say to him or to any of you."

"Dr. Brown, Mr. Clifford is bringing a new interrogator with him, and there'll be several of the men from here."

"I won't talk to any of them."

"My instructions are that when I get you over there, you're to wear handcuffs behind your back and nothing else."

"What do you mean nothing else?"

"The person being interrogated is always in the nude," Charlotte said, backing out, then shutting the rec-room door. Phyllis Minter and Margaret heard the promised bolt slide home.

"What are they doing that to you for?" Phyllis asked.

"My husband's escaped."

"I heard about that. Listen, can they hear what we're saying? Is the place bugged?"

Margaret surveyed the periphery of the ceiling where it met each wall. No camera. "I don't know," she said.

"I don't care if those bastards hear me. I want to do what your husband did, get the hell out of here." She looked at Margaret, who she guessed to be perhaps ten years older. "Are they going to rape you?"

"They wouldn't dare."

"Oh they'd dare."

"Charlotte said they were going to question me."

"Don't be naïve, Doctor. You are a medical doctor?"

Margaret nodded.

"Want to play? Basketball, I mean."

"I haven't played in what, twenty-six years."

"Let's just throw it around."

Phyllis dribbled the ball toward the other end of the room, then lightly threw it up. It circled the hoop and dropped through the net.

"Here, you try," she said, throwing the ball to Margaret.

Margaret caught the ball clumsily. "I don't know if I can." She bounced the ball once, twice, then stopped.

"What are they giving you special attention for?" Margaret asked.

"I talked to a truck driver from the outside," Phyllis said. "I thought he might give me a lift down. He was scared shitless."

How naïve, Margaret thought, *trying to hitch a ride out of a place like this.*

Phyllis thought Margaret was reacting to her choice of words. "Sorry," she said. "I use words like that all the time. I'm not a doctor. I'm a nothing."

The young woman's toughness denied her self-deprecation, Margaret thought. She reminded her of Bacall in those early Bogart films.

"I didn't know nothings can afford to come to a place like Cliffhaven," Margaret said.

"I have money," Phyllis said. "Pass the ball."

Margaret threw the ball to Phyllis, who caught it as if she were used to catching it.

"Are you married?" Margaret asked.

Phyllis laughed. "On and off." She dribbled the basketball in place, stopped. "Look, I want to get the hell out of this cockamamie place. How did your husband escape?"

"We both got down to the highway by going through the woods."

"What happened?"

"There were half a dozen trusties waiting for us."

"So what, they're mostly fogies."

"They all had clubs," Margaret said. "And there was a state trooper."

"Didn't you tell him they were keeping you prisoner up here?" Phyllis said, her voice rising.

"He called us kikes," Margaret said.

"I'd cut the balls off a guy like that," Phyllis said and threw the ball at the basket in anger. It hit the backboard, rolled around the basket, missed. The ball bounced, then less and less. Phyllis made no attempt to retrieve it.

"On the way back up," Margaret said, "there was a fight. While the others brought me back up here, he must have overcome the trusty who was left to guard him."

"Terrific," Phyllis said, her eyes showing her excitement.

"They say he's still on the grounds somewhere."

"I'm sure he'll get away," Phyllis said. "He'll blow the whistle on the place, right?"

Margaret did not want to quash the hope in the younger woman's eyes.

"All we got to do," Phyllis said, "is keep whole in the meantime, right? Listen, can I trust you?"

"Yes," Margaret said.

"I have a knife. You take it. If they try anything in that interrogation, you can use it."

"I couldn't. Besides, if I were undressed, where would I hide it?"

"Use it on them when they try to undress you."

"No, no," Margaret said, "put it back in your boot. What good would it do against half a dozen men?"

"If they go after you, just jam it into their you-know-whats. You'll see what good it'll do."

"I don't think I could," Margaret said.

"I could," Phyllis said.

"Then you keep it."

"If your husband finds you, take me with you. Please? I'm in room 27. Please."

"I'll remember," Margaret said.

"Terrific," Phyllis said. "Where you from?"

"Just north of New York."

"Gee," Phyllis said. "I'm from here, California I mean, but I was born in Brooklyn. Why don't we throw the basketball around, it'll take our mind off things."

Dan Pitz found the ride up Highway 1 exhilarating. As a youngster he had hated the people he saw inside chauffeured limousines. Now he was riding in one himself, a prospective future manager for Mr. Clifford, a resourceful, accomplished, rich man.

When they were about halfway, Mr. Clifford said, "We are paying double pro rata for the day, but if you and I agree that you will work for me, I will pay you precisely the annual salary you received at your last position."

"Plus an expense account?" Dan asked.

"You won't need an expense account at Cliffhaven. Everything is provided." He looked over at Pitz. "The reason I pay the same is to make sure that it is not just the money that attracts you to our work."

"I understand."

"You have one serious liability," Mr. Clifford said.

He's tracked down some of the people I've had affairs with.

"You are not," Mr. Clifford continued, "what I would call a natural reader. You may have read a lot in school, that is immaterial. You do not now have the habit of ingesting information from books. Your reading list was full of trivia. Pity."

"I've been busy," Dan said.

"Have you been too busy to fornicate?"

What was he getting at?

"People have time for what they want to do," Mr. Clifford

said. "I suppose you haven't read Kosinski, Bellow, Kazin, Trunk."

"I can't say that I have."

"It is very important in our work to understand how Jews think. Today's Jews. I don't want robots working at Cliffhaven. You must understand your work in its social and historical context. I will give you a list with a time schedule for each book. I will ask you two or three questions about each as you finish."

Dan, who had hated school, thought *maybe this job isn't for me.*

"Perhaps this position is not for you," Mr. Clifford said.

He reads minds. He knows too much about me for me not to take the job. If he offers it.

"Well, my boy," Mr. Clifford said, patting Pitz once on the forearm, "nothing to worry about. Just some catch-up work to do. You'll be surprised how easy it is, once you get used to it."

They arrived at the entrance to Cliffhaven just after eleven o'clock. There were two uniformed staff members at the gate, and as soon as they saw the limousine in the distance, one of them lowered the chain. The other was Clete, who signaled to the driver.

Mr. Clifford pushed the tab that lowered the electric window.

"Hop in, Clete," he instructed.

"Yes, sir."

Mr. Clifford nodded to the Japanese driver and they started up the road to Cliffhaven.

"This is Daniel Pitz, Clete. He may be joining us in a senior position."

Dan shook Clete's hand.

"What's the story?" Mr. Clifford asked.

"Well, sir," Clete said, "no real change from last night. They both got out of a rest-room window in the dining room. They made it down to the highway, but George had six trusties down there."

"Yes, yes, I know," Mr. Clifford said impatiently. He turned to Pitz. "George is George Whittaker, manager of the resort."

"On the way back up," Clete said, "Henry Brown—that's the escapee's name—tried to shout a warning to a new customer I was driving up. He got clubbed by one of the trusties—I didn't see that—and the others took his wife—she's a doctor—back up. Apparently Brown wasn't as badly hurt as we thought, and he somehow managed to overcome the trusty guarding him and took off. George decided we'd better use dogs, but we couldn't track him."

Mr. Clifford seemed pensive for a moment. "Perhaps he's still on the property somewhere."

"You think so, sir?" Clete asked.

Dan Pitz took a chance and volunteered. "If he got away, you'd have heard one way or another by now," he said.

"Very good," Mr. Clifford said. "I was thinking the same thing. Especially if he encountered an obstacle at the road the first time—"

"We took the dogs down to the road," Clete said, "and worked our way up."

"If he heard the dogs," Mr. Clifford said, "he'd have back-tracked. Maybe he's hiding under your bunk, Clete. It was your fault they escaped, wasn't it?"

Clete nodded.

"This is the first time you've disappointed me. You've spoiled a promising record. You'll have to make up for it."

"We'll find him," Clete said.

"Oh yes," Mr. Clifford said. "Assuredly."

Dan expected Cliffhaven to be like one of the resorts he had worked at previously. He was overwhelmed by the magnificently designed buildings, a row of triangles against the mountains and the sky.

"It's certainly beautiful," he said.

The last of the buildings looked the same as the others from the outside, but inside it had been designed as a private residence. The living room had a two-story-high, vaulted ceiling, with the highest wall giving the appearance of being wholly of glass. Dan noted another wall that had filled bookshelves ten feet high. He hoped he wasn't going to be made to read all that.

"Whom will you want for the meeting with Dr. Brown?" Clete asked. "Besides George."

"You can stay, Clete. Tell George to bring Robinson and Trask. Who's taking care of the woman?"

"Charlotte," Clete said. "She's the best woman we've got."

"Good. Let's get started."

Margaret and Phyllis Minter had worked up a sweat playing basketball. The physical activity made Margaret feel better.

The Minter woman interested her because there was no one like that in her circle of friends or acquaintances. Had she and Henry grown too narrow without realizing it?

When Charlotte came to take her back to her room, she and Phyllis parted as if they were old friends.

"Break it up," Charlotte said and led Margaret away.

Back in Margaret's room, Charlotte ordered her to take a shower.

"Are you going to watch?"

"Why would anyone watch an old bag like you?" Charlotte said. "I'll be back in ten minutes. You hurry."

Good, Margaret thought, as Charlotte slammed the door and locked it. *She's angry. Angry people are less in control. Maybe I can make Clifford angry.*

In the shower, she could not shake her thoughts about Henry. *Please, God, let him not come to harm.* For the last quarter of a century, she had been there to advise. They collaborated on the solution to problems. When Ruth, at one, seemed to be developing knock-knees, it was Henry who insisted that she ignore the advice of three orthopedic specialists to put Ruth's legs in metal braces linked to each other so that the child could not move at night. "I'm not interested in warping her mind with fear for the sake of her winning a beauty contest," Henry had said. And, eventually, they found an orthopedist who prescribed shoes for the toddler that did the trick without harm. And when Henry procrastinated about the mailboy who was stealing paychecks and managing to get some of them cashed, she was the one who said demoralizing everyone else by inaction was a greater sin than picking up the phone and letting the police deal with the young man. In the end their decisions were right because they served as devil's advocates for each other. She needed him now.

She hated the idea of being unprepared for any sort of questioning. She could refuse to answer. Once, standing at the curb, she had seen an elderly woman get off a bus, right leg first, and step into a three-inch hole in the pavement, snapping her brittle limb just above the ankle. A citizen can choose to be a good Samaritan, but a doctor has no choice. Margaret saw what the injury was almost immediately, kept people from moving the woman before the ambulance attendant could apply splints. What she hadn't expected was that her name would be taken and that the old lady would sue the city of White Plains, and that she would be called as a witness. A lawyer friend of Henry's named Harold Arnold had cautioned her. She was a witness not only to the diagnosis but, more importantly, to the accident. She had seen the elderly woman actually step down into the hole. Was she exercising sufficient caution, looking where she was going? Was the bus driver at fault, stopping so near a deep hole, or could he not see it? Or care? The plaintiff's lawyer would try to twist Margaret's testimony one way, the attorney for the city of White Plains another. The best thing for a witness to do under almost all circumstances, Harold Arnold maintained, was to say the least. "I don't know." "Yes." "No." "I don't remember." These Cliffhaven people who would be questioning her, thought Margaret, would get nothing out of her. She would stonewall them.

Charlotte had said she would be interrogated in the nude. That would make her more vulnerable only if she was unprepared. What if they beat her? What if they tried to molest her? These people would dare anything.

Margaret thought *I should not have showered. Why should I look clean for them? I am showering for myself. The main point is to get through this somehow and come out alive at the other end.*

Toweling herself dry, she examined herself in the full-length mirror. There were the slight stretch marks that had never gone away. The veins on the underside of her left knee that she thought about whenever she donned a bathing suit. She would never subject herself to an operation purely for cosmetic reasons. Her hips were good. The skin of her thighs was unblemished. Her breasts were okay. *What did it matter? Why think about things like this? Stay alive.*

She wondered if Henry thought of her body differently than she did. *Where was he at this very moment?* She was not used to not knowing where he was.

She would make it as difficult for them as she could. Margaret put on panty hose, and then slacks over them, a brassiere, and then a shirt that buttoned all the way and tight cuffs that buttoned at the wrist. Every inch of clothing would be fought for.

Margaret sat in the armchair looking at the door. She heard it unlock. Charlotte's expression was a mask of ice, frozen to protect herself.

"Let's go," Charlotte said.

"Go where?"

"To Mr. Clifford's residence."

"I'm not going anywhere," Margaret said, still sitting.

Charlotte went immediately to the phone. "This is Charlotte in room 20. Would you send up two of the fellows from security and help me get a resident to Mr. Clifford's quarters. I've got cuffs."

When she hung up, Margaret was standing. *She had to resist with her mind, not her body. She needed to conserve energy.* "I'll go," she said.

Charlotte picked up the phone, a slight smile on her face. "Cancel that request. The resident has agreed to go peacefully."

In the living room of Mr. Clifford's house, Margaret's eyes went immediately to the faces of the four men she had not seen before. Clete's face she would remember. She had to be sure she remembered the others well enough to identify them later.

"My name is Clifford, Dr. Brown. This is George Whittaker, manager of Cliffhaven, Daniel Pitz, Oliver Robinson, Allen Trask. Clete you know."

Nobody moved to shake hands. Had she expected them to?

"Charlotte," Mr. Clifford continued, "would you please get Dr. Brown ready?"

"Ready for what?" Margaret said, flinging the words.

"Charlotte," Mr. Clifford said, "hasn't Dr. Brown been briefed about the purpose of our visit?"

"Yes, sir."

"We have some questions to ask you, Dr. Brown. You'd better have some illuminating answers for us."

"I don't wish to speak to you, any of you," Margaret said.

"Your wishes are not relevant," Mr. Clifford replied. "Charlotte, get her ready."

Margaret let Charlotte show her the way down the hall because she wanted to get out of that room. She wanted to find a door to run through, a window to break and climb out of.

She had climbed out of one window in Cliffhaven already, and through the woods, to no avail. She must not let defeat settle on her. Henry had escaped. She could too.

Mr. Clifford's Japanese manservant passed Charlotte and Margaret in the hallway as if they did not exist. He handed the elegant attaché case he was carrying to Mr. Clifford.

"Oh thank you, Sen," Mr. Clifford said. "You were able to find what I asked you to?"

"Yes, sir," the Japanese said.

"You may go," Mr. Clifford said. "I expect to stay here until the escapee is found. I'll let you know when we'll be driving back."

"Very good, sir," the Japanese said. "I'll check in with the reception desk from time to time as usual."

Charlotte led Margaret up three stairs and into the most elaborate bathroom she had ever seen. The room was huge, with two rectangular excavations, one a square Jacuzzi, one a rectangular bath that could easily hold four or five. Along one wall was an enormous blue-tiled shower. The vanity wall was completely mirrored. From the high ceiling dangled something Margaret had never seen in a bathroom before, not even in the great hotels of Europe: a crystal chandelier.

"Undress," Charlotte said.

Margaret turned to face the girl and walked to within three feet of her. "I will not," she said, locking onto Charlotte's eyes.

"Dr. Brown," Charlotte said, "you're not the first woman to be interrogated here. They always undress, sooner or later. Later means after we've had to try one of the things we've been taught."

"Do you realize you're committing a crime?"

"That's outside. What I do here is follow the rules of Cliffhaven. Now undress."

"I will not."

Charlotte opened the door of the bathroom and called out, "Clete."

In an instant, Clete was there.

Charlotte said, "Your Dr. Brown isn't being cooperative."

"Oh I do wish you'd cooperate," Clete said, as Charlotte got a pair of handcuffs out of her jeans and handed them to Clete.

Margaret saw how the game went. Clete stood behind her. If she turned to face Clete, Charlotte was behind her. The thing to avoid now is the handcuffs, therefore face Clete. When she turned, Clete threw the handcuffs to Charlotte. Margaret spun around. Clete immediately grabbed both of her arms and with the forearms of a gymnast yanked Margaret's hands together behind her back. Charlotte came around to snap the cuffs on.

"Now all that dancing around wasn't worth it, was it?" Charlotte asked. "Thanks, Clete."

Clete left the room.

"Now," Charlotte said, "with those handcuffs on, I'll have to undress you."

"Don't you dare!"

"Okay," Charlotte said, "have it your way." She lit a cigarette, dragged hard on it to get the end lit well. Then, holding the cigarette pointing forward in her left hand, she approached Margaret.

Margaret backed away.

"Careful, dear," Charlotte said, "you'll fall into the Jacuzzi."

Margaret turned to look behind her and immediately Charlotte was upon her, her right hand grabbing Margaret's shirt above the first button and with one tremendous rip tearing it straight down the front.

"You're an animal!" Margaret said.

"You're the one who married a Jew. Who's the animal?" Charlotte said.

There was a knock on the door.

"We're wasting time in there," Mr. Clifford said. "Need the boys to help you?"

"Are you going to let me take the rest of it off," Charlotte asked, "or are you going to fight?"

Fighting is pointless. If she can't remove my clothes, they will. The point is to resist their questions. Let them see me naked. What do I care? Or is this how they whittle your resistance down?

"Well?" Mr. Clifford's voice said.

"I think she'll cooperate," Charlotte said.

"Hurry up then," Mr. Clifford said, and his footsteps retreated.

"Can I put the cigarette out?" Charlotte asked.

Margaret nodded.

Charlotte went over to the toilet, lifted the lid, and dropped the cigarette in. It sizzled once. Charlotte flushed the toilet.

"Need to use this, dear?" Charlotte asked.

"Don't call me dear."

"Do you or don't you?"

"I don't."

Charlotte, behind Margaret, unbuttoned the right cuff of Margaret's shirt, pulled it gently through the handcuffs. She repeated it with the left cuff, then removed the rest of the shirt. Still behind Margaret, she undid the clasp of the brassiere. It fell from her breasts but was trapped by her handcuffed arms.

Charlotte came around to Margaret's front.

She's looking at my breasts.

"I wish you hadn't worn trousers," Charlotte said.

"I'll take them off and my brassiere, too, if you'll let me out of these handcuffs."

Charlotte considered. She'd need Clete to put the cuffs back on. They certainly weren't going to question her without them.

"I think I'd prefer to do it," Charlotte said.

Charlotte wormed the brassiere through the cuffs, then undid the button of Margaret's pants and unzipped the front. Margaret felt strange. She'd never been undressed by a woman before.

"Damn," Charlotte said when she discovered the pantyhose underneath. With a yank at each hip, she pulled them down sharply, tearing them.

Margaret was afraid of falling over the bundle around her feet. With difficulty she kicked her shoes off and stepped out of the debris.

"Thank you," Charlotte said, opening the bathroom door and pointing. "You lead the way."

Margaret caught a flash at her nakedness in the mirror. *Think of them as naked, too.*

"Come on," Charlotte said, pushing at her back.

Margaret was careful going down the three steps. She held herself erect, pulled her stomach in as she entered the living room. Mr. Clifford beckoned her to a straight-backed chair around which the men sat in a semicircle of armchairs.

"Thank you, Charlotte," Mr. Clifford said. "I'll phone when I need you."

Margaret wished Charlotte wouldn't go. The animals were staring at her.

Margaret sat down. When she crossed her legs, Mr. Clifford smiled, as if her modesty were a weakness to be tolerated.

"Well then," he said, "Dr. Brown, you must be aware that your husband very foolishly has tried to escape from our control."

Margaret said nothing.

"You needn't say anything," Mr. Clifford said, "unless specifically asked. Undoubtedly you and your husband, after your first abortive walk down the road, must have planned what you would do next. How did he plan to get out of Cliffhaven? You may answer now."

Margaret remained silent.

"I am, of course, expecting you to cooperate. You see, Dr.

Brown, you really don't belong in Cliffhaven except for the unfortunate fact that you, perhaps as a young and unwise woman, married a Jew."

"Mr. Clifford," Margaret said, noting how they all immediately perked up when she spoke. "Why do Jews preoccupy you so? They have never preoccupied me."

The man named George Whittaker said, "Dr. Brown, your function here is to answer questions, not ask them."

"Oh that's all right, George," Mr. Clifford said. "This is going to be a basically friendly discussion among Gentiles, isn't it, Dr. Brown? Well then. You cannot have passed through forty odd years of life in this country without having observed the degree of Jewish influence on the press. If they don't own all the newspapers, they certainly own and control the most important ones, not to speak of the other media, CBS, NBC, Hollywood. Our cultural exposure, popular and esoteric, is constantly being irradiated by Jewish thought. While there has never been an actual Jewish president, Dr. Brown, I am certain you have observed that there has always been a Jew or two at every President's ear, calling the shots. Roosevelt had one, Truman had one, Eisenhower, Kennedy, Nixon—all of them. We've kept pretty close track of them despite all the name-and nose-changing that's gone on. Now, you may say, what's wrong with all that influence?"

Was he waiting for her to reply?

"Jews are migrants, Dr. Brown," he continued. "They do not belong here or any other place anywhere except perhaps that trivial bit of land in the Middle East, yet these transients corrupt our society. They are a secularizing force. They believe in nothing except their techniques of haggling, advising, huckstering, profiteering as nonproductive middlemen. They are exploiters and userers, these alien foreigners who have nothing to do with our America!"

She could see what a spellbinder he might be with these young California nitwits.

"Would your husband have been as successful in business as he's been if he weren't Jewish? You see, there is only one answer. Further migration. The Jews, when pressed, have usually resorted to bargaining, at which they are very good.

But eventually, the Jewish response to pressure of the kind we are arranging here—once it is known—is to get out, to emigrate, to take their secular deviltry somewhere else. And as a Gentile, if you had not made that one mistake, you would have to agree with everything I have said because it is clear, logical, and supported by history."

He stood up and walked over to Margaret. She was a bright woman. He would have liked to try his genetic theory out on her. She'd understand the implications of what van den Haag found. But not in front of the men.

"Where did your husband plan to hide?"

"I don't know."

"Don't lie to me!" Clifford slapped her face hard. "He must have told you."

Through her anger, she saw Clifford's red-veined face. That slap cost him more than me. They're all looking at him. All that pompous speechifying and then he slaps me.

"George, take over!" Mr. Clifford said.

George Whittaker was a very tall man who liked to take advantage of his height by standing whenever possible. He stood to say, "Dr. Brown, you are an intelligent woman. You may not agree with everything we say at this moment, but surely you must know that there are hundreds of influential people in American politics who can't wait for a movement such as ours to succeed. This country has been troubled enough by their having to kowtow to the Jewish vote. Ask any congressman if he isn't sick to death at times of the Jew lobbies?"

"I don't know what you're talking about," Margaret said.

"Ask the Arabs!" Whittaker raised his voice. "They can't get a word in edgewise in this country!"

Dan Pitz thought it was time for him to make his move if he was going to impress Mr. Clifford. "Excuse me," he said. "Could I pursue a somewhat different line of thought?"

"Of course," Mr. Clifford said. *God, that Whittaker was short-tempered for a man who's supposed to be an executive.*

"Dr. Brown," Dan Pitz said, "why did you marry your husband?"

It will be easier for me if I speak, Margaret thought.

"Because I loved him."

"That's a very conventional answer, Dr. Brown. A cliché. Weren't you at all troubled by the fact that he was Jewish?"

"He was troubled. I wasn't."

"He was?"

"He didn't want to see me involved in any danger."

Dan looked over at Mr. Clifford, who seemed intensely interested. Good.

"Do you find that people who expect trouble generally deserve trouble?"

"No. There are a lot of innocent victims in the world."

"Do you think that your husband's employees think of him as an innocent victim?"

"My husband's employees are very loyal to him."

"Of course. That's how they keep their jobs!" He wasn't getting anywhere. He had to go for broke. "Dr. Brown, I'm glad you're a doctor because you'll be able to decide the following matter with a lot more knowledge than a layman would have. If a woman . . . Are you paying attention, Dr. Brown?"

"Yes, I am."

"If a woman had a gasoline-drenched tampon placed in her vagina and the tampon was ignited, do you think she could love her husband or anyone else ever again? Is that what you want?"

Dan caught the startled reaction of the others—Robinson, Trask, and Clete. His soft approach had caused them, too, to be taken by surprise.

"You are all sadists!" Margaret was screaming.

Whittaker was watching Mr. Clifford to see his reaction. This new man Pitz could be a threat.

"You are all monsters!" Margaret yelled, knowing that she had lost control of the situation, the one thing she didn't want to have happened.

Clifford's decision was made. Pitz knew how to deal with these people.

Clifford stood up. Amazing what the right technique could do. "Call us what you like, Dr. Brown," he said. "Scream if it pleases you. Do you think it will bring help?" He went over to the huge window and pulled the drape. Outside, a few

197

people had stopped to listen. When they saw him, they continued on their way. Spineless vermin.

Turning to Margaret, he said, "We once had Jew-loving Roosevelt in the White House. Did he come to the aid of the European Jews? Not on your life. *In extremis*, Dr. Brown, the Jews are alone, you hear me, alone. We are going to win, and the only choice you have is to separate yourself from the interests of your husband or share his fate. Which will it be?"

With her hands cuffed behind her back, Margaret could not dry her eyes.

"Last chance," Clifford said. "Will you tell us what his plans were?"

"The truth is," she said, "I don't know. But if I knew, Mr. Clifford, I wouldn't tell you."

"Well, well, Dr. Brown, what a brave thing to say. The fact is that you have insufficient experience with human nature. Under duress, everybody talks. The only open item in any individual case is how much duress and for how long. You make the choice. You suffer the consequences."

Margaret looked at each of them in turn. And as her gaze met each of theirs, they turned away, just for a second but long enough for Margaret to feel a touch of victory. And so she said quietly, "God help you all. None of you are Christians."

Clifford would have killed her on the spot, choked her with his bare hands, but with his senior staff watching, he had to set an example. He didn't want them to react violently to insolence. There were methods, procedures for dealing with this. He said, "God help your husband when we find him, Dr. Brown, as we most assuredly will. And in the meantime, you'll need some help yourself." He turned. "Oliver and Allen, see that this woman puts some clothes over her ugly body and take her to the lockers."

"Yes, sir," Oliver said. "How many hours, sir?"

"Since the lady wants to be a Christian martyr to Jewish scum, I'd just leave her there."

Clifford watched the two men take Margaret away, then turned to Dan. "Mr. Pitz," he said, "could you really do that tampon thing?"

Dan didn't hesitate. "Of course, sir."

"Very good. Clete, I've got a plan for finding your vagabond. First, I'd like you to take Mr. Pitz on a tour around Cliffhaven, introduce him to all the niceties of our three-star ghetto. I want him to like this place."

"Yes, sir," Clete said.

"Be back here in twenty minutes. In the meantime, George and I are going to have ourselves a little talk."

When they were alone, Mr. Clifford sat on the couch quite close to Mr. Whittaker, knowing that proximity always unnerved him.

"What did you think of our newcomer, George?"

"I'm sure Pitz will be very helpful to me."

"He's got one interesting qualification you didn't have when you arrived here, George."

"What is that, sir?"

"He's killed three people and gotten away with it. Of course, you've disposed of many more than that number since coming here, but it took you a little getting used to. George, I'm concerned about the laxness in security under your administration. Was Clete responsible for Brown's escape?"

Whittaker thought *he likes that son of a bitch.* "No, sir," he said. "Clete is top rate."

"I agree. Therefore, you accept the responsibility."

"It won't happen again."

"Not if you can help it?"

"Right, sir."

"George, I have some evidence that you have several times in this past year had sexual relations with Mrs. Clifford right on these premises, is that not true?"

Clifford watched George hesitate.

"Would you like to see the film?"

"It was on her initiative, sir."

"Does that excuse it?"

"No, sir. What else could I do?"

"You could have refused her. It won't happen again?"

"No, sir."

"George, I have a much more serious matter to discuss with you. Why do you keep that diary?"

199

Whittaker blanched. "What diary, sir?"

"Oh, do you keep more than one?"

"No, sir."

"Just that one?"

Whittaker had always despised people who resorted to the Fifth Amendment on the witness stand. Right now he wished he could do so.

Mr. Clifford turned to his attaché case, snapped the two locks open, click and click, and removed the diary. He held it in front of Whittaker's face. "Why?" he asked.

Whittaker hung his head, trying desperately to think.

"I'll tell you why, George. You wanted a record showing that everything you did as manager of Cliffhaven was following an instruction of mine, so that if Cliffhaven is ever exposed, you could plead that you were only following orders, is that not true?"

Whittaker was relieved that there was a knock at the door.

"Come in," Mr. Clifford called.

Clete and Dan Pitz came in.

"Ah," Mr. Clifford said. "How do you like the place?"

"It's terrific," Dan said.

"I'm glad you like it," Mr. Clifford said. "Clete, I want a meeting of the entire staff as soon as possible. I want to instruct them in my plan for recapturing Brown. I also want to announce that George has resigned as manager and that Dan Pitz is taking over effective immediately. Clete, perhaps you could accompany George to pick up his things in his room and then give him a ride off the premises."

George reached to pick up the diary.

"I think that'll stay with me," Mr. Clifford said.

The moment George Whittaker and Clete were out of the building, Whittaker turned on him.

"You son of a bitch! You told him about that diary!"

"What diary?"

"Don't pretend with me."

"Well, you listen to me for a change," Clete said. "You drummed loyalty, loyalty, loyalty into my head, didn't you? It wasn't loyalty to you you were talking about, right, loyalty to Cliffhaven, right?"

"I'll get you, Clete."

Clete took the .38 out of his windbreaker pocket. "My instructions are to see you off the premises. If you resist, I use this and cart your body away, that clear? Now, let's get your gear packed."

George Whittaker decided that his life was more important than revenge. Besides, revenge could come later. Would he dare blow the whistle on the whole place? And incriminate himself? That bastard Clifford really had things figured out, didn't he?

As they reached Whittaker's quarters, he said to Clete, "I've got a lot of stuff."

"That's okay," Clete said. "The last van that came in with guests will hold your stuff."

Whittaker took his time packing because he wanted to think. Clete volunteered to help him. Clete wouldn't be helping him if he didn't want to get him off the premises as fast as possible. He began to think of what job he might want to try next. He couldn't use Cliffhaven as a reference, could he? Mr. Clifford was smart. He'd give him a terrific reference.

When they got the gear loaded into the van, Clete took the wheel, George beside him. He could see how nervous George was. He didn't like dealing with nervous ones.

"Hey," Clete said, "since you've got all this stuff, I thought I'd let you have this van till you get to wherever you're going. When you settle in, give me a ring and I'll arrange to have it picked up."

Whittaker was suspicious, but said, "That's nice of you, Clete. You're just driving me as far as the highway?"

Clete didn't answer.

"Clete," George said, "don't you want to hook a scooter to the van for the ride back up?"

Suddenly Clete picked up speed, heading around the back of the dining hall, and George said, "Hey!" but Clete kept his eyes riveted to the road heading for the gully. George frantically tried the handle on the passenger door, but Clete had followed regulations, fixing it so that it could not be opened. *Time to go,* Clete thought, pumped the brake hard once, twice, it was still going twenty, what the hell, he opened the door on the driver's side and with one movement leaped out, as he had many times before, rolling as he had learned to do, hearing George scream the way some of the Jews did as the van went straight off the edge of the precipice, thinking Pitz was tougher than George, and they'd have a real good time when they found Brown.

15

Henry woke with the thought *there are Gentiles out there who would be horrified if they knew what was going on in this place.*

Above him it was bright daylight, blue sky with only a few scattered clouds drifting in from the Pacific. He had slept as if drugged.

Henry stretched, feeling the ache in his back. This place is Clifford's invention. His followers obey him. How many followers would Clifford find outside?

Weren't all of the staff members outside when he found them?

Henry touched the side of his head. It still hurt.

You are a nice Jew. Not like the others.

What was your father's name before it was Brown? Braunstein?

If you Jews are always in trouble, there must be something about you that causes trouble, don't you think?

I think one must not get paranoid. I must give my will strength. Remember, there are Gentiles out there who try to compensate for history, who like Jews too much. They have a taste for worriers? Are they attracted to the Jewish intellectuals, sprinkled everywhere, who think by talking, who are forever on the trail of solutions for the insoluble? Bullshit. They are attracted to Jews out of guilt!

Henry, you're going too far. It isn't always this way. *From time to time every Jew looks over his shoulder and finds that there's no one following him.*

Henry laughed. He felt his body coming to life. He stretched again.

Time to act. Carefully, Henry raised himself so that he might see over the low parapet. At a great distance some of the guests were meandering slowly down to the dining hall for breakfast. He wondered if any of them had kept kosher at home. What did they do here?

They ate what they were given.

At home, if you were hungry you went to the refrigerator. If you were not at home, you stopped in a restaurant, or picked up something at a takeout place. He smiled at the thought of the credit cards in his pocket. Margaret called them his plastic security blankets. Not they, not all the money in the world would get him food without his surrendering. Would a hundred dollars get him a toothbrush, toothpaste, and a cup of water? What was that 1930s book by Michael Gold, *Jews Without Money*? This place was filled with them.

Looking carefully over the parapet again, Henry saw stragglers heading for the dining hall. If Margaret was among them, he could not see her. If she were here, she would say *be logical. Homo sapiens, use your brain.*

He remembered when she had said those exact words. Two years after he had started his business, the fulfillment center was a round-the-clock worry. Some days the incoming customer complaints were more numerous than the orders. There were cash-flow problems, and the personnel turnover created the endless process of training many new people who would soon leave. It was like trying to fill a leaky pail with a teacup, and so he brought his worries to Margaret's dissecting table.

Homo sapiens, she said, *use your brain.* "What do people want from your so-called fulfillment center?"

"They want what they ordered, not something else."

"And?"

"They want it quickly, but what can I do? The least able, lowest-paid clerks are the pickers. They are dull. They don't even respond to incentives."

"Yes, they do," Margaret said. "Negative incentives. They don't get into trouble if there's a policeman watching."

That got them started. It was an exciting evening, starting from scratch as if the business did not yet exist. Knowing what you know now, how would you set it up? they asked themselves.

To avoid wrong shipments your order pickers had to fill hundreds of orders a day, each one perfectly. Yet it was one of the lowest-paid jobs in the plant. They were the unskilled—no previous experience, the ads said. You couldn't have highly skilled people as pickers, the cost per order would be prohibitive. Moreover, it's the kind of job that would drive most people bananas. People who could pick four hundred orders a day of miscellaneous items without getting some of them screwed up didn't want to do that kind of work. So you had to surround those who did with a system that would police them.

Negative incentives, she had said.

He could hire two inspectors to sit at the end of the collection points where the baskets were brought, and have them double-check the orders. If they caught only five or six mistakes in a day, was it worth their salaries? The point was, the order pickers would be more careful, knowing that their baskets would be checked. It was like the presence of a policeman, worth his salary as a preventer of crimes that wouldn't happen.

His highest-paid clerks were in the customer correspondence section. Their work would be cut enormously if the orders were picked right in the first place and shipped out promptly. Promptly. He'd set up a system where every day the people who opened the incoming orders would be the first on the job, then the order processors, then the pickers, then the packers. The order openers, first to arrive, would be first to leave, but only when every order in the day's mail had been okayed and passed on to the order processors. When the pickers had received the last incoming order, the order processors would leave. The pickers would leave when the last basket successfully passed the check-out point. The packers, last to arrive, were the last to leave. On Monday everybody would work long hours to take care of three days' worth of mail. On Friday everybody could get away by noon or one o'clock to take an extra half-day holiday each weekend.

It took six weeks for Henry to put the new plan into effect. The workers loved it, especially the new hours. The good people stayed. The task of teaching newcomers almost disappeared. The fulfillment center could guarantee same-day shipment. The customers got their orders filled promptly and correctly. The customer service department with the highest-paid help got cut down to one person, who sometimes had idle time. And all of it shaped the business into the success it became out of an evening's thought.

On hands and knees Henry crawled around the perimeter of the roof, checking the activity in each direction. *Use your brain.* What interested him suddenly was the view in the direction from which he had come: the nearest wooded area.

To escape from jail is one thing. To escape from a jail that has no right to exist is another. The solution is not escape but the destruction of the jail. Peering over the parapet at the woods, Henry, as if stimulated by Margaret's absent collaboration, had an epiphany, an illumination of how one person, if lucky, could liberate all the inmates of Cliffhaven and expose the place to the glare of the outside world.

He felt the high excitement of possibility. Could he recruit anyone else to help? Who? What if they proved to be unreliable? The beauty of the plan was that he could pull it off, if necessary, all by himself!

Henry heard the unmistakable sound of footsteps on gravel. Quickly, he crabbed himself over to the other side of the roof and peered carefully over the parapet.

He couldn't see anyone.

Taking a chance, he raised himself enough to look over the parapet and down. Almost immediately below him, two stories down, was a resident wearing the trusty armband. The man had set down a bucket and mop, and was opening the door with a key. Suddenly, the man looked up and Henry jerked his head back just in time.

He hoped it had been just in time.

The trusty was an older man, past sixty, frail-looking. There was no way Henry could get off the roof safely. If he jumped, he chanced breaking a leg or worse from that height. If he got hurt now, his plan was doomed.

He was about to look down again and attract the man's attention when he heard the door slam. The man was inside.

Henry surveyed the roof, squinting his eyes against the reflection of the now-bright sun. He could see a slightly raised rectangle in the center. He crawled closer to it, realized it was a kind of flat skylight that had been painted over. He could try to break it with his fist, but he might cut himself. The noise might attract somebody outside the building. He could stomp it with his foot. No need to, it had a catch, caked over with paint, and some roofing material with aluminum in it. Lucky; the beginning of luck. He scraped the catch with a fingernail. No good. He scraped it with one of his keys. That did it. He got the catch free enough to lift it, and then with all of his strength yanked at the skylight, lifting it away from the roof. As soon as it was open, he was on his knees peering down.

The trusty holding the mop was looking up, petrified. Henry held a finger to his lips.

The man was saying something in a voice too thin to hear.

"I can't hear you," Henry said, raising his whisper to an audible level.

"You're the man they're looking for," the trusty said.

Henry saw the old man put the mop down and glance toward the door.

"What is your name?" Henry asked.

The trusty hesitated. Henry had to keep the old man from betraying him.

"My name is Henry Brown. My wife is a prisoner here, too."

"You're not supposed to use words like prisoner," said the trusty.

"What is your name?"

The old man put his fingers to his lips, then spoke. "Morton Blaustein. My wife is here." He jerked his thumb at the wall.

"I don't understand. Mr. Blaustein, listen, I want to come down and talk to you. There's a metal ladder outside along the wall that could reach up here."

"They'll kill me."

"Nobody will know."

"They always find out everything."

"Not anymore. I want to tell you my plan. Please, Mr. Blaustein."

The old man shook his head.

"You have to do it," Henry shouted. "Our lives depend on it!"

"I don't want any trouble, mister."

If life is trouble to this man, is freedom too much trouble? Had he resigned himself to mopping floors forever?

"Listen, I can give you more trouble than they can, Blaustein."

The old man looked up at him. Was that a look of fear?

"Get the ladder!" Henry ordered, his voice demanding obedience.

The old man headed toward the door. Would he run for it? And squeal?

"Blaustein!" Henry shouted, his fist a gesture at the man.

Blaustein glanced up for just a second. Was that a derisive look? Or frightened?

The old man went out the door. Henry listened for his footsteps in the gravel. He was heading around the building, not away from it.

It seemed to take an eternity, then the old man came back in the door, empty-handed.

"It's too heavy," he said. "I can't lift it."

Henry wanted to throttle him, for being a coward, for not being strong enough. They both heard footsteps from outside at the same moment.

God, thought Henry, there isn't time to close the skylight gently. If he closed it quickly, the clatter would attract attention. *Don't do it.*

Henry lay down as quietly as he could so he could look

past the edge of the skylight. He saw the orange-and-blue uniformed Cliffhaven man shove a younger man, no more than twenty, through the door. "I've got a new helper for you, Mr. Blaustein. Teach him to be polite."

"Fuck you," the young man said.

The Cliffhaven person laughed and shut the door behind him. Henry listened to him walk away. When he looked down into the building again, Blaustein was pointing up at the skylight. Henry recognized the young man.

"Hey!" Henry said. "You're the fellow in the Mercedes they got last night."

"That's right," the young fellow said.

"I'm the guy on the road who tried to warn you."

"No shit?"

"How come they've got you on clean-up duty the first day?"

"That guy Clete said I was a wiseass. What are you doing up there?"

"I can't get down. It's too far to jump. Listen, I've got a plan for getting out of here. I'll take you with me if you'll get the ladder that's outside and get me down."

"Sure thing."

"I'm not supposed to let you out of the building," Mr. Blaustein said.

The young man laughed. "Try and stop me."

He went out the door, glanced around to be sure he wasn't observed, then went around the building, found the ladder, got a grip on its middle, lifted it off the ground, and carried it into the building.

"Shut the door," he told the trusty.

"You're going to get us killed."

"Just shut up and do as I said," the young man said.

Henry liked that. He's fresh from the outside, not like some of the others around here. He hasn't been worked over yet.

The young man put the ladder on the floor, and moved it so that one end was just under the skylight. Then he went to the other end, put one foot on the bottom rung.

"Okay," he said to Blaustein, "lift the other end."

"I can't," Blaustein said.

"Then come here and do what I'm doing."

Blaustein obeyed. The young man went to the other end, lifted up a bit, then higher, then over his head, and started walking the ladder into a vertical position. Henry could see it wasn't easy. He was able to reach down and grab the end. It barely touched the rim of the skylight.

"A bit higher," he said.

The young man nodded. He motioned the old man away, got hold of the fourth rung from the bottom, jerk-pulled it toward him, moving its position the requisite few inches.

"Okay," Henry said. "I think it's safe." He started down, with the young man holding onto the ladder, steadying it.

When he got to the bottom, relieved, he stuck his hand out. "Thanks. My name's Henry Brown."

"Jacob Fetterman," the young man said. "Jake is okay."

"The trusty's name is Blaustein," Henry said.

Jake nodded in Blaustein's direction, then said, "What the hell is this room?"

Henry noticed that two walls were covered with long rows of Stars of David. Next to each star was a nameplate.

"What is this place, Blaustein?" Henry asked.

Blaustein looked at each of them in turn. "This is where they keep score," he said.

For a second they were all silent.

"You mean these plaques were all people here in the last six months?" Henry asked.

Blaustein nodded.

"Your wife?"

Blaustein shuffled over to the wall and, stooping, pointed a sad finger at a plaque near the floor. "She lasted three weeks," Blaustein said. "She was always a fanatic about the Sabbath. We were given a chance to work on the farm. She refused to work on Saturday because it was the Sabbath. She said she'd work on Sunday. They wouldn't allow it."

"Didn't anyone ever come looking for you?" Henry asked.

"Of course. My son came. Within a week he found us. They took him also. That's what killed my wife. She yelled at Mr. Whittaker they could do anything they wanted to her, but to let the boy go. He laughed at her. He called her a Jewish mother. 'I'm proud to be a Jewish mother,' she yelled at him and spit in his face. Finished."

"Jesus," Jake said. "What happened to your son?"

"He works with me on the farm. Including Saturdays. Twice a week I clean this place, and he cleans the lockers."

"Lockers?" Jake asked.

"Just hope you never find out," Henry said.

"You were already in the lockers?" Blaustein asked. "What did you do? I thought you just came here."

"What kind of farm is it?" Henry asked.

"Very profitable."

"Tell me."

"You'll see soon enough," Blaustein said.

"Blaustein, how long have you been here?" Henry asked.

"Six months. From the beginning. I was here the first week."

"What will happen to you?"

"Nothing," Blaustein said. "I'm a trusty."

"Is your son a trusty?"

"Not yet. I'm hoping."

"Why would you want your son to be a trusty?" Henry asked.

"It's the only way to escape being taken for a ride like my wife," Blaustein said.

It's frightening to see a pale face blanch, Henry thought. "What's the matter, Blaustein?"

"I said too much. Only trusties are supposed to know."

"What does going for a ride mean?" Henry asked.

"I'm not saying anything."

"Yes, you are," Henry said. He moved very close to Blaustein.

"What are you going to do to him?" Jake asked.

"Keep out of it!" Henry said, his eyes inches from Blaustein's eyes. *Bluffing is the heart of business. God, help me bluff,* Henry thought.

In a whisper Blaustein said, "It's a very American expression, taking somebody for a ride."

Henry stepped back. "A car ride?"

Blaustein nodded.

"Where?"

Blaustein shook his head. "Must he hear, too?" Blaustein pointed at Jake.

"Yes."

"It doesn't have to be your car," Blaustein said. "Just some car that brought guests here. They tie your hands. There can be one, two, three guests in the car, all hands tied. One of the Cliffhaven people drives. Up that way." His pointing was meaningless.

"What way?" Henry asked.

"Where the cliff is. There's a road. It starts just behind the dining room. It ends at the cliff. The gully is eight hundred feet down. The driver leaves the car in gear and just gets out. The car goes over the edge with the guests, all the way down. Sometimes we hear the sound. To those of us who know what it is, the crash of a car in the bottom of the gully is like the sound of a firing squad. They told me my wife had a heart attack in the lockers. Maybe she was still alive. They didn't take her to the hospital. They took her for a ride. All the names here are of people in the bottom of the gully. Sometimes . . ." Blaustein looked at Henry and then at Jake. "Sometimes, if you go real close, you can hear screaming from the gully long afterwards."

"The ones who don't die on impact?"

Blaustein nodded. "Maybe you two can become trusties. You won't have to go for a ride."

Henry looked at Blaustein's face. He wasn't as old as he had at first thought, just so defeated-looking.

"Were you always a coward?" Henry asked. "Or did they make you one?"

Blaustein let a fragment of a smile flicker onto his face. "Mr. Brown, listen. Before Cliffhaven, I was an accountant. I add up the past. I don't have a handle on the future."

"Well," Henry said, "you've got a handle on yourself, which is better than most people have. We're not going to stick around, Blaustein. And I can't afford to have you squeal on us. Will you come along with us peacefully?"

"Do I have a choice?"

"You do not have a choice," Henry said.

"Then," Blaustein said, "you are the same as Cliffhaven."

"You'll come with us?"

"What about my son?" Blaustein said.

"There's no way we can get him now," Henry said. "But if my plan works, we'll be able to set everyone free. We've got to get into the nearby woods. Will you come?"

"They'll kill me or you'll kill me, what's the difference?" Jake said, "When will that creep come back for me?"

"Not for two, three hours," Blaustein said.

"Good," Henry said. "Let's go. The spot we want to head for is the wooded area about seventy or eighty yards from the back of the building. Let's lower the ladder. We don't want them on the roof looking for us."

Jake and Henry carefully took the ladder down and laid it on the floor.

"Now," Henry said, "I'll go first. Stick close to the building, there's less chance of being noticed. Blaustein, you go second. Jake, you follow, make sure Blaustein keeps up. When you get to the back, crawl to the woods."

"Crawl?" Blaustein asked.

Henry got down on the floor and demonstrated.

From the floor Henry said, "You ever in the army, Blaustein?"

"No."

"Jake?"

"No, but I've seen movies on TV."

"Watch me. Think you can do it?"

"Sure," Jake said. "Mr. Blaustein, I'll be right behind you."

"Okay," Henry said, getting up. "Let's go. Jake, shut the door behind you. Quietly."

"Will do."

Henry went out the door and around the building, his eyes taking in all directions. Nobody. Where were they searching for him? Down below? Had they given up? Did they think he had escaped to the road?

At the back of the building, he lowered himself to the ground and started off.

Left elbow, pull forward.

Right elbow, pull forward.

Left elbow, right elbow, like an automaton. Keep your mind

on the movements you make, not on your destination.

Left elbow, pull, right elbow, pull.

It seemed a much longer distance than it had when he crawled to the building. He could feel the heat of the sun on his back. His knuckles were beginning to bleed again. Had Blaustein started out? He didn't hear anything.

Almost there. Keep going.

At the edge of the woods Henry stood up, moved rapidly into concealment, turned to watch. Blaustein was no more than a quarter of the way, Jake just behind him. Why was he crawling so slowly? Then he saw Jake moving around Blaustein, passing him, and crawling like a large lizard toward the woods, leaving Blaustein behind.

Could anyone see them? Were they safe from view?

Jake reached the woods. Henry grabbed his shirt. "Why the hell did you do that? I said to stay behind him."

"He was going too slow."

"That was an order. If this thing is to work, you've got to obey orders."

"Okay, okay."

They both saw Blaustein stand up in the middle of the clearing, look around uncertainly.

"He's going to run away," Jake said. "I'll get him."

"No, you don't," Henry said.

Blaustein was running toward them. Breathless, he arrived in the woods. "I couldn't crawl any more," he said, "I'm sorry."

"I just hope you weren't spotted," Henry said.

He peered out, watched, listened. Nothing. Thank heaven, nothing.

He turned to the two of them. "Now both of you listen carefully. There are small patches of clearing scattered through these woods. What I want us to do is to move as much brush as possible, and any dead wood that we can carry, anything, into the clearings that are close to the perimeter. We'll stack the brush close to the woods, not in the center. Pile it up for a bonfire. I want at least one big stack close to the woods in every clearing."

"What are you going to do?" Blaustein said.

"We're going to set fire to those stacks as near simultaneously as the three of us can manage. These woods go clear around Cliffhaven, except for the road, which will act as a firebreak unless the fire jumps across."

"Hot damn," Jake said. "This stuff is dry as hell."

"That's right. With these woods on fire, there'll have to be a massive fire-fighting effort. They'll have to bring in the pros."

"Won't the buildings catch?" Blaustein asked.

"I hope not. There's enough space between the woods and the buildings."

"Burning debris could get airborne and land on a building," Jake said.

"I hope not," Henry said. "There are a lot of people in Cliffhaven. Including my wife."

"What happens to us when the woods start burning?" Blaustein asked.

"We'll have nowhere to go except into the compound," Henry said.

"They'll catch us," Blaustein said, envisioning a scene of terror. "They'll kill us for it! This isn't a plan, it's suicide!"

PART 3

16

Stanley's friend Kathy lived off campus in Santa Cruz, in an apartment shared by four girls. They each had a bedroom with a doorknob that locked and a common living room and kitchen. The rules were you could feed yourself and one fellow in the kitchen and a fellow could visit you in your room, but if he stayed the night he had to vamoose before breakfast because the girls just didn't want to go through the hassle of being seen in disrepair by someone else's boy friend early in the morning.

"Can I speak to Kathy, please?"

Stanley heard the girl's voice yell, "Kathy Brown, telephone!"

When Kathy got on, Stanley said, "Can I come over now?"

"I've got my period."

"Jeez, Kathy, that wasn't on my mind."

"It wasn't on mine either, you boob. I'm just telling you because you were worried, worrier."

He had forgotten.

He felt the ping in his conscience. It was just two weeks ago when Kathy had said she wasn't wearing her saucer, as she called it, and he'd said he'd be careful but wasn't. Kathy'd cried, saying it was a perfect time for conception. He worried. And then forgot.

"I'm sorry," Stanley said. "I mean, I'm glad."

She had a nice laugh, Kathy did.

"So I can come over?" he asked.

"Sure. The living room's a mess from last night's party. Everybody's been in class all day. Never mind, we can talk in my room."

Kathy answered the doorbell. The living room served not only as headquarters for the four girls, but also as a drop-in place for at least two dozen friends. It still had last night's paper plates with scraps of pizza ends, beer bottles, and crumpled napkins all around. There was a couch, but the real furniture of the room was three huge boldly colored cushions on the floor. On the walls were relics of an earlier period, posters of Hendrix and The Who, and, thumbtacked to the wall by the previous occupants of the apartment, a pair of bikini panties around which legends continued to grow.

As Kathy led him through the debris, he noticed the nothing dress she was wearing, a gauzy one-piece sack, colored like madras except you could see through it, vaguely, like the outline of her pants.

"You bought another one of those," Stanley said.

"I've had this," Kathy said. "Just haven't worn it lately. When I do, people look at my boobs, not my face."

"Nice face."

"Thanks, I'm waiting."

"For what?"

"For you to say nice boobs. What's the matter?"

"What do you mean what's the matter?"

"You're still worried."

"Yeah," Stanley said.

"You look worried. You're worried half the time." She closed the bedroom door, got up on the bed, crossed her legs.

"Sit," she said, pointing to a spot on the bed. "Tell me."

He still wasn't used to sitting cross-legged the way she did. It amused her to see him struggling with what came so easily to her.

"Okay," he said. "You know the plan for the weekend. We fly down Friday morning and you're supposed to show them around. Only we don't know where to meet them. He was waiting to have a standby room confirmed or get a different hotel. He said he'd call from Santa Barbara. He never called."

"Well," Kathy said, "the day isn't over."

"He wouldn't wait till the last minute."

"Maybe you weren't in when he called," Kathy said.

"Sure I was in. Or my roommate was in. He always calls when he says he's going to call."

"Jesus, you're a worrier," Kathy said. "Suppose they just found someplace they liked and stayed a couple of days, something like that."

"Then he would have called so I didn't worry. If he says he's going to be in touch, he's in touch. I called the Beachcomber in Santa Barbara, they never checked in. They had a guaranteed reservation, which means they get charged for the room even if they don't show. That's not like him."

"Oh Stanley, one night's hotel bill is not going to break your old man. I hope you're not going to be like that."

"Like what?"

"I like to coast when I travel. Want a beer?"

"Not now. Look, I have this instinct, see, it's like I can tell something's wrong."

"That's bullshit. You don't *know* anything. You just guess on the gloomy side. Are all Jews like that?"

"Like what?"

"Gloomy."

"Listen, most of the comedians are Jewish."

"Yeah, and are they gloomy."

"You're a big help. I think I'm going home to make some phone calls."

"You just came."

"I don't want to run up your phone bill."

"You can always pay me back for toll calls when the bill comes."

"I guess I could."

"Why don't you try that place in Big Sur? What's its name?"

"Something like Cliffhaven."

"Call. Get it over with."

While the information operator was getting him the number, Stanley thought *What they'll tell me is they left. And if they didn't arrive in Santa Barbara, they cracked up the Ford somewhere in between. Kathy says I worry. I got reasons to worry.*

He wrote the number down and then dialed.

"Do you have a Mr. and Mrs. Henry Brown registered there?"

The girl at the other end was consulting somebody, but she had her hand over the mouthpiece and he couldn't hear more than mumbling. When she got back on, she said, "Nobody here by that name. Sorry."

"Well, were they registered? Yeah, this week."

Again, mumbling.

"I'm sorry, sir," she said, "there's been nobody here by that name."

"You sure?"

Stanley turned to Kathy. "She hung up."

"Well, if she's handling a switchboard, she doesn't have time to dawdle, I suppose. What are you doing now?"

"One more call?"

"It's all right."

He dialed a number. "Ruth? It's me, Stanley."

To Kathy he said, "It's my sister, don't get jealous."

Then into the phone, "Yeah, I met them in San Francisco like a good boy, and they were down here at college for a couple of hours. Have they called you? Dad was supposed to call me. What's that? No, I'm not worried, I was just checking. Okay, okay, if he calls or Mom calls, just tell them to keep trying me. You're going out where tonight? Well, don't forget your diaphragm, Ruthie. Bob Zuckerman? That's an idea. Yeah, I've got his number. Thanks. Good-bye."

To Kathy he said, "For a sister, she's all right. Nobody called. She said to try Bob Zuckerman."

"Who's that?"

"Oh a guy. I guess he's Dad's best friend." Stanley fished the three-by-five card with all of his phone numbers out of his wallet. He dialed Bob Zuckerman's office.

"He's in a meeting," his secretary said. "Can you call back?"

"I'm in California, in a friend's apartment."

"Leave me that number. I'll have Mr. Zuckerman call you."

"I won't be at this number."

"Wait a minute. Looks like it's breaking up."

Bob Zuckerman's voice was too high for a man. And he sounded like he was tired even when he wasn't.

"Stanley? What's up?"

"Has my father been in touch with you?"

"No, why would he be?"

"He's in California this week."

"I know. Didn't he see you?"

"Sure. He was supposed to be in the Big Sur area Wednesday, Santa Barbara on Thursday, and fly home Saturday from L.A. I was supposed to fly down tomorrow to meet them there."

"Well?"

"He was supposed to call me from Santa Barbara. He never checked in at the Beachcomber."

"Maybe he checked in at some other hotel. Or stayed longer in Big Sur. What's to worry?"

"They say he never checked in at the place in Big Sur. He always calls when he says he's going to call."

"Stanley, your father can take care of himself, he's a big boy. Even if he gets sick, he's got a doctor at his elbow. What are you worrying about, kid? Listen, if he calls me when he gets back, I'll tell him to give you a ring, okay? Got to rush now. Take care of yourself, Stanley, and stop worrying."

Stanley jammed the phone down onto the receiver.

"He's a shit."

"What's wrong now?"

"No help." Stanley imitated Bob Zuckerman saying *Take care of yourself, Stanley.* "Asshole."

"You're working yourself up for nothing."

"I'm getting another number. What do you call it, Missing Persons Bureau?"

223

"You're crazy."

"Okay, I'm crazy." He got up and left without saying good-
bye.

The phone rang in Stanley's room. He pounced at it.

"It's me," Kathy said. "I tried getting through for two hours.
I haven't been able to work on my term paper or anything.
I'm sorry I got you angry."

"Me, too. I mean I'm sorry I blew up. This is not a joke.
The missing persons thing doesn't know anything. I remembered the names of the places they said they might stay at in
Carmel, and I found the place they were in one night. I phoned
the Beachcomber again and they still haven't showed. I tell
you there's something really wrong and it's wrong somewhere
between Carmel and Santa Barbara. Maybe they had an accident. Maybe it was so bad they're both, you know, can't talk,
tell anyone to get in touch, something like that?"

"Now you got me worried. What are you going to do?"

"I was thinking I would drive down Highway 1 just like
they did and see what I can find out."

"That's crazy. You'll miss classes."

"I can't pay attention to that. I have to go."

"I wish I had someone worried about me sometime like that."

"You do. Want to come with me? You'd just miss one class
Friday. You don't have anything important Fridays. You said
so yourself."

"What about wheels?"

"Jerry? If I paid him something?"

"He might."

"I'll call Jerry."

"Call me back, crazy."

"Jerry said okay. First, he said ten dollars a day and I pay
for gas, et cetera, but when I told him why I needed wheels,
he said to forget the ten dollars. What about you, you coming?"

"Please wait till tomorrow morning. I can finish my paper
and have Betty turn it in for me, okay? Besides, maybe your
father'll call by then and you won't have to go."

"I'll be at your place at seven."

"How about eight?"

"I wanted to get an early start if we're waiting till tomorrow."

"Eight is early."

"Seven-thirty?"

"Haggle, haggle. Okay. Listen, if you hear from him, call me right away."

Stanley put the phone back in the cradle, then lifted it again almost immediately. He didn't want to make a fool of himself, but his mother had always said *Trust your instinct.* When he dialed the Cliffhaven number again, the same woman's voice answered.

"Listen," Stanley said quickly, "don't hang up on me. My name is Stanley Brown. I'm trying to locate my parents. Are you sure they aren't there?"

Damn, if the woman didn't hang up on him again.

At the reception desk the young woman looked up at Clete. "If he wasn't suspicious before, he'll be suspicious now," she said smiling.

"Good girl," Clete said. "I'm looking forward to this one."

17

Margaret, this fire is for you, Henry thought, as he and Jake, arms and legs working like mechanical cranes, threw twigs and brush together in bonfire heaps the size of a man. *At Masada they died fighting.* That's a lie. They killed themselves. They did their enemies' work for them. *Not me.*

Henry glanced at the younger man. Jake's body, drenched in sweat, seemed to work so much faster than Henry's. The refrain went: Jake was younger, Jake was stronger. Jake's head, Henry would bet, wasn't a crowd of conflicting thoughts.

"You worried about being an arsonist, Jake?"

All Jake did was laugh. He was the age one sent to war. Cliffhaven was the enemy. Burn it down.

To get to New York City from the suburbs, Henry couldn't avoid the tip of the South Bronx, its skeletal brick shells a monument to building-by-building arson, a city within a city incinerated.

"That's high enough, Jake," Henry shouted, and Jake moved on to start another pile.

Those Spanish people are crazy, Henry thought, while driving through on the Deegan, it's their own homes they are using as tinder toys. They are not civilized, meaning *we don't do this kind of thing*.

Break the branch, pile it up. Take the brush, pile it on. When this one's lit, thought Henry, these young redwoods circling it will catch like orange crates.

Breaking branches hurt the hands. No time for pain. Gloves would have helped. We're doing it with our bare hands, getting a redwood forest ready to blaze. Bad means to good ends. Codes meant to be broken in self-defense. This wouldn't be necessary, would it, if someone, anyone, had paid real attention to those boy-scout-looking storm troopers in St. Louis and New York, those crazies marching in Chicago? Outside, you ignore them. Inside, it's too late.

"Next one!" he yelled to Jake, and they moved on.

The mob drops bodies along roadways in Queens, streets in Brooklyn, highways in New Jersey, do even the police care? *As long as they don't bother us.*

"Hurry up, Blaustein, Jake is way ahead of you!"

Man in Texas kills twenty-seven people of a certain category only. *As long as he doesn't bother us.* Remember the kid in the city—thirteen years old—has murdered twenty-two people by the time he is caught. Asked is he sorry now, no, he yells, he's mad about being arrested. *We are untouched.*

"You're doing great, Jake!" Encouragement, like to the men at the plant, feeds the adrenalin.

And these religious communities, closed off till someone raises an alarm about a missing daughter. The daughter, a pleasant-looking young woman, slightly plump, completely rational in manner, says to the television cameras, I have found happiness with these people. *Case closed.* Is Cliffhaven different in kind or only degree? Was there any way that Margaret and I, in the car on the highway below Cliffhaven, could know that up that road was a closed society waiting to envelop us because we, I, fell into a category Cliffhaven had selected as its victims?

Paranoids of the world, don't go near resorts, is no answer. Now we know. Now we do something. Henry, he told himself, finishing another brushpile, this is no time for thought. An alarm has to be set off that will be heard by the rest of the world.

"How many brushpiles have we got now?" Henry asked Jake and Blaustein. "Sixteen?"

"Seventeen," Jake said.

"Not enough. We've got to ring the periphery."

Blaustein said, "You could make a hundred and then get caught."

"Should we ignite what we've got?" Jake asked.

"One plane could water-bomb the area we've covered," Henry said. "We must have a fire that can't be put out right away. What I want from both of you is to build as many more as you can in the next two hours."

Jake, a boy suddenly seeing himself leaderless, cried out, "Where are you going?"

And how could Henry answer that so that it made sense? Could he tell him a thought, more like a cry than a thought, had entered his mind as if it came from Margaret?

"Do Jake and I work together or separately?" Blaustein asked, nervously.

If he asked the question, Henry thought, *Jake had better keep an eye on him.*

"Together will be faster," Henry said.

Jake, piling up brush, had stopped in mid-motion. "Where are you going?"

"Don't stop," Henry said. "I'm going to release the people in the lockers so they don't get incinerated. Jake, look at your watch. If I'm not back in two hours, light the brushpiles as fast as you can."

"With what?"

"Take a branch about this long," Henry extended his arms. "Here, I'll show you." He picked up a dry branch. It was too long. He put one end on the ground, stomped hard on it about a foot from the end, breaking it. "There," he said. "That's about the right length." He tied his handkerchief around the end. "Use your T-shirt. Tear it up. Make two torches. This way we'll have three of them so we can run in opposite directions, lighting them. You take a third of the area, Jake, and I'll take the rest, skipping every other pile. Blaustein can follow right behind me, lighting the alternate piles. That'll be quickest. Got it?"

Jake held his fingers against his mouth to command Henry's silence.

He turned to look. They all saw the two Cliffhaven-uniformed men walking just beyond and to the right of the building where the score was kept. The men were looking over in their direction.

"They can't see us," Jake whispered.

"They always capture everybody," Blaustein said.

"Shut up," Jake said. Then to Henry, "You'd better not risk going out there."

"They're leaving," Henry said. He picked up the stick he had used to demonstrate how to make a torch. "I'll take this with me, just in case."

"Don't be foolish," Jake said. "You'll be caught."

"If I don't return, just do as I said."

Henry waved at them with his free hand. Only Jake returned the wave. He wondered what Blaustein was thinking.

Henry wove his way through the woods for several hundred yards in the direction of the building that housed the lockers. There would be a long way to crawl to get there unnoticed. Crawling was much more exhausting than running. Besides, how could he crawl carrying this big stick? He could throw the stick away. Suppose he needed it. He could run to the building. That would attract attention. At the edge of the woods, he looked for activity between himself and the building. None. He would chance walking, calmly, as if he belonged there. If someone spotted him, he'd simply run back to the woods, and they'd light the brush fires immediately. If only they'd had a chance to rehearse this!

If the building housing the lockers had its front door locked, how would he get it open? Were there windows? He couldn't remember.

His heart skipped when he saw the open door. First, a feeling of elation, followed by alarm. If the door was open, one of the Cliffhaven people must be in there. He could hear the sounds he had heard during his four-hour ordeal.

This is not a sensible thing to do, he thought, as he walked in the door. The Cliffhaven man—he looked like Clete from the back—was fussing with someone at the other end of the room. The man turned around. It wasn't Clete, someone a bit older, with a moustache.

"What are you doing here?" the moustache said.

It was the young man against Henry's stick.

"Hey, you must be Brown," the man said.

The moustache doesn't seem frightened. *He doesn't know I'm going to try to kill him,* Henry thought.

"Give me that stick," the moustache said.

He's used to people obeying.

The moustache was walking straight toward him. The woman he'd been shoving around was crouched against the far wall, staring at Henry.

He is assuming that I am passive like the others, Henry thought. He's a fool.

When they were five feet apart, the man stopped. "Give me that stick."

"Sure," Henry said and, in the same moment, stepped forward with his left foot and, holding the stick as if it were a baseball bat of his youth, swung it with all the strength he could muster against the man's head. The man's left arm came up to ward off the blow, and Henry's stick glanced off the man's forearm, hitting his cheekbone with a sickening crack.

"You son of a bitch," the man said, tottering a step or two backward, spitting blood. The club, now in the position of readiness for a tennis backhand, came back around with a force Henry didn't know he had. It hit the man in the right jaw, and with an inarticulate cry he collapsed at Henry's feet.

Henry watched the blood ooze from the man's mouth, reddening the ends of his moustache. The blood dribbled onto the concrete floor, assuming the shape of a large red amoeba, searching. *I hope he doesn't die.*

Except for the woman hunched against the far wall crying,

the place was suddenly silent. What had the people inside the lockers made of the commotion?

"Listen to me," Henry shouted. "You are being freed. I am going to open the lockers. Margaret! Are you here, Margaret?"

The babble of voices from inside the lockers made it impossible to distinguish any one voice.

"Please," Henry shouted against the din. "Go to the center of the resort, near the dining hall. You'll be safe from the fire there. Don't go near the woods or you'll burn to death! Margaret?"

He couldn't hear for the noise. Suddenly, he caught the body at his feet stirring. Blood was now bubbling out of the nose as well as the mouth and ears. Henry could not bring himself to club the man again. He started opening the lockers one after the other as quickly as possible, glancing at the prostrate form in the middle of the room. That man needed a hospital.

Out of the lockers started to emerge pathetic creatures, men and women without wills, some in great pain from the cramped confinement.

Henry opened the lockers one after another, his arms working in rhythm. The occupants tumbled or slid or fell to the ground in front of him.

Where was that freckle-faced man who'd been put in for eight hours? The eight hours were long up, he'd be somewhere else. God, how long have some of these people been in here, days?

"Don't be crazy," Henry shouted. "You're free. Get going. Move out the door. Head for the dining hall."

It was then he heard her voice and his name, just a few lockers away. With a twinge of guilt he skipped the next three or four lockers and opened the one he thought the sound came from. The man inside was dead.

Quickly, Henry opened the next locker and it was Margaret. He had never seen her bereft of life and strength. She came forward into his arms, and he eased her onto the floor. Her lips were dry, her legs stiff and aching from the cramped quarters.

Henry looked up to see one man trying to crawl back into his locker.

Henry grabbed him by his shoulder. "No, no," the man wailed. He was out of his mind.

"Let's go!" Henry shouted, waving them toward the door. Then he knelt beside Margaret.

"Can you walk?"

She nodded. "Sure. Just give me a minute."

"We have to get out of here."

Henry shouted at the others. "You've got to get out of here. Move!" The idiots wouldn't leave.

A tall, sinewy man of about thirty came up to Henry and said, "I opened the rest of the lockers, but they seem afraid to leave the building. Some are too sick."

"When did you get put in?" Henry asked.

"Just a couple of hours ago. I'm okay."

He didn't look like the others. He might be strong enough.

"Can you help me with this woman?" Henry asked.

"Sure thing."

Together they helped Margaret to her feet. She rubbed her thighs. "I'll be okay," she said.

"We'll have to make time getting to the woods," Henry said to the sinewy man.

Outside they moved as rapidly as they could. Suddenly, a thought hit Henry as if it were a hammer blow. He hadn't thought of the people in the locked rooms. If the fire reached the buildings, they'd be burned alive. *You couldn't help everyone.* Perhaps help from outside would come before the building caught.

Safely in the woods, they stopped to catch their breath just as Henry spotted Jake, waving. He ran over to him.

Jake had just finished securing Blaustein to a sapling with his own belt.

"He tried to get away," Jake said. "You can't trust him. Is that your wife?"

Henry nodded.

"Who's the other one?"

"I don't know."

Margaret and the younger man had now come over.

"Margaret," Henry said. "This is Jake. He's been helping me."

Jake nodded.

The other man stretched his hand out to Henry. "My name's Shamir," he said.

"Henry Brown. My wife, Margaret. This is . . ."

Jake held his hand out. "Jake Fetterman."

Henry said, "How long have you been in Cliffhaven, Shamir?"

"Since last week. I'm doing fine. I've been in the lockers twice already."

"What did you do?" Henry asked.

"The staff member who took me to my room the first night said something about me not looking Jewish, so I said he didn't look too Jewish either, something like that, and before I knew it we were arguing, and I told him to just do his job and shut up. So what he did was get permission to put me into the lockers for four hours before I had unpacked my bag."

"Terrific. Who steered you to this place?" Henry asked.

"Well, I'm a photographer. I was hitchhiking from San Francisco to San Diego. I've done it lots of times, not to save money particularly, to meet people. Somebody in Frisco suggested Cliffhaven, great views for a photographer."

"Did they get whoever was driving you?"

"No, no," Shamir said. "When I saw the Cliffhaven sign, I asked to be let out. I walked up here carrying my small bag, and boom, I'm a prisoner. They took my cameras, two good ones. This one they didn't see."

Shamir took a tiny Minolta out of his change pocket.

"I have some terrific pictures, if I can get out of here, I thought, so I waited till dark, then walked down the road same as I came."

"Trusties brought you back?"

"You, too?" Shamir asked.

Henry nodded.

"What's your plan?"

"We're going to set fire to these woods. How many brush-piles, Jake?"

"I did six or seven more, good ones, before I saw that bastard Blaustein trying to sneak away."

"One moment," Shamir said to Henry. "Can you point to

where your furthest brushpile is in that direction?"

"I think about there," Henry said, pointing.

"And in the other direction?" Shamir asked.

Henry nodded to Fetterman. Jake pointed to where he had erected the last brushpile.

"Excuse me," Shamir said, "but if you're aiming at a conflagration, you may not have extended the line of brushpiles far enough around the circle. A bomber dropping ammonium nitrate—if one got here soon enough—could extinguish the blaze in two or three passes."

"How do you know this?" Henry asked.

"Just what I read. Never been involved in fire fighting, but I put in two years with the Air Force."

"Whatever fire-fighting equipment Cliffhaven has," Henry said, "I'm sure they don't have airplanes."

"Listen, if this forest goes up, the fire fighters'll have to call in all the help they can get, including the military. These woods are bone-dry. Tens of thousands of acres went up a year ago."

"Cliffhaven won't call in outside help."

"Then we have to," Shamir said.

"All the phones go through the switchboard." Henry looked over at Blaustein, tied to the tree. "Isn't that so?"

Blaustein coughed, said nothing.

Henry walked over to within two feet of the tied man.

"What's the matter, you sick?"

Blaustein shook his head.

"Then talk. Is there a phone that doesn't go through the switchboard?"

Blaustein coughed again.

Henry raised his hand, then slapped Blaustein's face hard.

"You didn't have to do that," whimpered Blaustein.

"Answer me."

"There's a direct telephone in Mr. Clifford's house, the last building over."

"I hope the lines don't burn before we can get to it," Shamir said. "Well, then, shall we do another group of brushpiles along that way?"

"No," Henry said. "We'll go with what we have. If they come looking for us in these woods, we might find ourselves caught before we light a single one. That's a chance we can't take." He glanced over toward Margaret. "Can you help?"

"Sure," Margaret said.

"Okay," Henry said. "Let's start at the two extremes and work our way toward here. Shamir, Jake, we'll each light a fourth, then meet back here. Let me have a match, Jake."

"I don't smoke," Jake said. "Don't you?"

Henry looked at Shamir, who shrugged his shoulders. "You mean," Henry said, "after all this, we have nothing to light the torches with?"

18

Mr. Clifford usually arranged for his meetings with the staff in a corner of the dining hall so that he could stand on the raised corner level and see the faces of everyone he was talking to. Today he felt the same exhilaration he had felt when he had heard that the Japanese had bombed Pearl Harbor. Nothing stimulated him like the prospect of battle. His face had better color than usual. Even Abigail would have thought him commanding as he waited for silence in response to his raised hands.

"Ladies and gentlemen," he began, "this is not, as you know, a regularly scheduled meeting, but as a matter of some urgency I have two announcements to make."

They were all there, the familiar faces, except for the half dozen on duty in the compound. Allen Trask would do a good job of briefing them later.

"You all know that one of our guests, a man by the name of

Henry Brown, escaped our custody after beating one of the trusties unconscious. He will of course be rather severely punished for that infraction."

The staff members laughed. They knew what he meant.

"First we have to catch him."

Again laughter.

"We always do."

Clifford loved the way his audience responded, this time with applause. He remembered their first escapee, a very tall man with bushy hair, who had broken his leg stumbling through the underbrush heading downhill toward the road. Eventually he had had to call for help. The dogs found him. The fellows hadn't even bothered to return him to his room. They were under instructions. Do the same thing as you would with a horse that had a broken leg.

"In the present instance, we believe the man still to be on the premises. His wife, who accompanied him to Cliffhaven, is being kept secure for him—"

He nodded in response to the laughter.

"—in the lockers. There's a staff member in the locker building, just in case. In the meantime, as you will learn in a moment, I have a plan to regain control of this individual that will involve all of you. And that will, as usual, succeed."

He held his hands up to acknowledge their approbation, and then moved them in such a way as to bring a silence that was absolute to the large room.

"You all know that keeping a diary or daily record of any kind in Cliffhaven is forbidden."

There were nods here and there. Clifford took the time to look at each part of the audience.

"Several months ago," he continued, "I asked at a meeting of the entire staff whether anyone was keeping a diary. Everyone answered in the negative. One person in this room was lying."

He noticed eyes darting glances.

"Though I am not present here a good deal of the time, I know sooner or later everything that goes on in my absence. Does anyone doubt that?"

Clifford, who was well read in history as well as genetics,

knew that the respect and admiration of his staff was not enough. He wanted what Napoleon had with his troops. Adulation.

"I had proof presented to me that George Whittaker, who I had entrusted to manage Cliffhaven, had covertly committed treason against that trust by keeping a self-serving diary to whitewash himself should Cliffhaven ever be defeated by its enemies."

Staff members looked around to see where George Whittaker was sitting.

"You won't find George in this room," Clifford said quietly. Perhaps Whittaker had been popular with some of the people. He had to be certain his decision was accepted by all.

"Cliffhaven," he said, "is the beginning of a national movement. I am sure you are all proud that Cliffhaven is the single most successful experiment of its kind in the history of the United States."

He allowed them to applaud. Were some not doing so? As he glanced around the room, he saw the last ones join in, till everyone was clapping. Then he continued, "With the discovery of Mr. Whittaker's treachery, I had no alternative but to accept his immediate . . . resignation."

They were waiting for the rest, he could see that.

"Our collective security—I am speaking of everyone in this room, in this enterprise—is dependent on complete trust. The question then was: Could I trust George Whittaker as an ex-employee on the outside? Something I know—and which you may have guessed—is that our enemies on the outside would gladly pay great sums of money to get someone like George Whittaker working for them, even testifying falsely against our cause. That thought may or may not have crossed George Whittaker's mind. Indeed, it may have crossed the minds of one or another of you. If that is the case, you must know my response. I have a huge investment in Cliffhaven, monetary as well as ideological. I will not see it jeopardized by anyone . . ." Clifford looked around the room to emphasize the point. "For any reason."

They needed the lesson.

"As a consequence of an action he initiated—keeping that self-serving diary—George Whittaker stepped across the line.

Therefore, he is no longer with us, not in Cliffhaven, not anywhere."

They understood.

"His treason has been punished. I hope it is the last case of that kind I will ever see here."

He studied their faces. The meeting, he judged, had been valuable.

"Now," Mr. Clifford said, "for some good news. It is my pleasure to introduce you to the new manager of Cliffhaven, Mr. Daniel Pitz."

The applause was sporadic. Mr. Clifford let a slight frown cloud his visage. The applause increased, and increased again until it became unanimous and loud. Dan, getting up on the platform next to Mr. Clifford, drew the conclusion that some of the staff had liked Whittaker. Or maybe they were just scared, working in a place that seemed not to tolerate ex-employees. Whittaker was a fool for having kept a diary where it could be found.

Dan waved a hand at the group, taking in their faces, wondering if some of them might be sexually useful to him in time.

"Mr. Pitz," Mr. Clifford said, "has managed several resorts previously and has had a highly successful career. Beyond that . . ." Dan noticed Clifford was beaming at him now. He hoped the old man wasn't going to say too much.

"Beyond that, Mr. Pitz has certain unique qualifications for his work at Cliffhaven."

That's all, please, Dan thought.

"I'll say no more," Mr. Clifford said. "You'll all have a chance to meet with him as the days progress. Now, I want to say that just before this meeting I had a talk with Clete, who was superintending the Browns at Cliffhaven. I have come to the conclusion that he was not at fault in Brown's escape. However, I have told Clete, as I am now telling all of you, when you have your first talks with a new resident it is important to ascertain who might or might not be a troublemaker. Most of our residents give us little or no trouble, as you know. If you think we have picked up a potential troublemaker, let Dan know right away."

Mr. Clifford saw Oliver Robinson, who had been left in

charge of the compound during the meeting, coming in the back of the dining hall. Robinson ran to the rostrum, whispered in Mr. Clifford's ear. A buzz went through the audience.

"Well, then," Mr. Clifford said, straightening up, his face showing a tinge of color it had not had before. "It seems that I was correct about Brown not having escaped the area. The guests undergoing punishment in the lockers have been released. Fortunately, only two of them have chosen to go with Mr. Brown to commit whatever further mischief he is up to. But another newcomer, Jacob Fetterman, a young man, seems to be unaccounted for, and a trusty by the name of Blaustein, a previously reliable man, seems to be missing from his clean-up station. I therefore want to put my plan into effect immediately. All together you—under the direction of Messrs. Pitz, Trask, and Robinson—are to form a ring around the outer perimeter of Cliffhaven. You are to be close enough to the next person right and left to be seen by each other. Then on signal, everyone, at a walking pace, is to move forward to the center of the compound. Search every building in your path. If you come upon locked rooms, open them and verify that the occupants are there. Check the roofs. When you are certain that you have examined every hiding place, move on. We will scour the entire grounds, and within an hour Brown, Fetterman, and the two new escapees will be back in our control. I trust no harm has come to that older man, Blaustein, who has been with us for half a year and has performed valuable service."

Clifford was pleased with himself for having avoided mentioning that one of the new escapees was Brown's wife. He hated her as if she was a Jew. When they were caught, she would suffer Brown's fate.

"Well then," Mr. Clifford said, "let us go and solve our little problem."

With Margaret present Henry felt a renewed determination. His adrenalin was running. He couldn't believe that he would be thwarted now just because neither Jake nor Shamir had matches. He'd have to go back into the compound to get matches from someone. He glanced at Margaret. Leaving her here meant being separated again.

The sound that intruded on Henry's thoughts was a racking cough. It was Blaustein tied to the tree.

"You sick, Blaustein?" he asked.

It was Margaret who interjected sharply, "He's not sick. That's a smoker's cough."

"Jake," Henry commanded, "look in Blaustein's pockets." Jake did and found the matches.

"Thank God," Henry said, taking them.

The matchbook cover was damp from Blaustein's sweat. He struck one match. It flickered for a moment, then went out. The others watched as he felt the matches to see if any were a bit drier, pulled one out, and with his thumb on the match head, struck it. "Pray," he said.

The match stayed lit. Quickly he lit one torch with it, then with the flaming torch lit the other three torches as he gave them final instructions. Then he said, "Let's do this as fast as possible."

"I'll burn to death," Blaustein said, strapped to the tree.

"If we untie him," Jake said, "he'll run."

"I won't, I won't," Blaustein pleaded.

"You can't trust him," Jake said. "We're wasting time."

Henry went up to the old man. "Blaustein, if this were medieval times, I'd cut your tongue out and let you go. You better keep up with me so I can keep an eye on you. You try anything and I'll kill you, understand?"

Blaustein nodded.

Henry unstrapped the belt from around the tree. Blaustein rubbed his wrists.

Jake was already off with his torch for the far end. Now Shamir ran in the same direction to start at the halfway mark, as the plan called for. In minutes the first mounds of brush would be ignited.

"I'll go to the end," Henry said to Margaret. "You start at the halfway mark and work your way back here. Will you be all right?"

"I think I'm going to enjoy being an arsonist. You watch out for him."

"Come on, Blaustein," Henry said. "You run ahead. That way."

And they were off to light the pyres.

241

19

As the Cliffhaven staff spread out in a fan around the perimeter of the resort, each careful to keep the person on his right and left in view, they looked toward Dan Pitz, standing in the center where most of the group could see him, his arm raised for the start signal. Some of them wondered how he got the job, how Clifford found him. They didn't envy Dan, those that thought about it, having an escapee on his hands the first day.

Some of the staff members had been at Cliffhaven long enough to remember the man named Matusky, one of the first guests, a broad-shouldered fellow in his forties who had had the gall to wear a skullcap in the dining room; who had defied orders to remove it indoors; and who, finally, when taunted about his special shawl and head-bobbing prayers, had gone berserk, punching out with fists like pig iron at the staff member who had goaded him. It took two or three men to wrestle him to the ground. It was George Whittaker who had stomped his heel into Matusky's mouth. Just once, but several of the man's front teeth had come loose and his mouth had filled with blood. Somehow he had struggled to his feet and then spit a mouthful of blood straight at Whittaker's face, yelling *"Petlyura!"* before he was wrestled to the ground again and rendered unconscious with repeated kicks to the head.

Matusky was the first to get more than twenty-four hours in the lockers. When he was let out, four or five staff members had gathered round the locker, expecting to see Matusky crumpled like a sack of potatoes, his trousers drenched in his urine, begging for mercy. Instead, when the locker opened, Matusky stepped out like an enraged bear, opened his fly, took out his thing, and sprayed a stream of piss at the staff members. Each, in turn, backed away from this madman who had let his bladder fill to bursting in order to hose them down, screaming epithets at them in Yiddish, or Hebrew, or Polish, or Russian, or some unknown combination of curses charged with guttural sounds.

And so Matusky, finally chained but not silenced, was the first taken for a ride to the gully. In the building where Mr. Clifford decided to keep score, Matusky's name was on the first plaque in the left-hand row. It was in that building that Mr. Clifford assembled the guests—there were only twenty or thirty at that time—and showed them the blank plaques waiting for their names if they followed the path of Matusky to defiance and death. Mr. Clifford admonished them to behave and live. But knowing that Jews could not be trusted to keep their word, and that as a people they had a history of useless resistance that stretched from Masada to Warsaw, he decided that discipline had to be reinforced with some chemical help. He arranged for their food to be laced with a small part of the harvest from the marijuana farm.

As the young men and women of the staff spread out around the perimeter, Clifford thought that perhaps he should pursue the idea of a sperm bank from the best of these young men, to hasten the process, double the genetic thrust. Suddenly he was impatient with his plan to round up Hebrews. The process was too slow and needed doing on a much larger scale. Craving allies, he thought himself a fool to have counted on a man like Jordan to share his vision or his leadership. All of the great movements were inspired and led by a single person who commanded the compliance of others. His obligation was not to expect others to start compounds modeled on Cliffhaven but to do so himself! The thrill of the idea excited him as he thought of a place he had visited not far from Houston that was as suitable as the Big Sur area. If he were to do it himself— and he would, of that he was now certain—he would simply call it Cliffhaven Two. And now that it had a name, it took on a reality in his mind that caused his heart to beat faster. As soon as this nuisance was over—perhaps tomorrow—he would begin to work on Cliffhaven Two. He must tell Abigail. He wondered if she would like the challenge of actually running such a place, taking her position in history as a woman as he had as a man.

"Let's do this fast," he said to Dan.

Dan surveyed the staff members around the perimteter, all in place, then moved his arm down smartly. "Let's go!" he yelled, "Go, go, go!"—knowing that few would actually hear him. He watched them trotting, picking up their pace, running toward the center of the compound where the buildings were.

Clete, near the middle of the inward-moving ring, had his eye on Mr. Clifford. At first it seemed the old man was talking to himself. Then it seemed as if Mr. Clifford was seeing something beyond the ring of staff members running toward the center. Now Mr. Clifford was pointing, but Pitz wasn't noticing.

Clete broke from the circle and ran full-speed to Mr. Clifford.

"Hey!" Pitz yelled. "Where the hell are you going? You're breaking the ring!"

"What is it, Mr. Clifford?" Clete said, pulling up puffing. Then he followed Mr. Clifford's gaze.

"I saw someone running in the woods right there," Mr. Clifford said, pointing. "I can still see him. There!"

Clete could see the figure also. Just that moment a brush fire flared where the figure had been.

"Jesus!" Clete said.

"Get him!" Mr. Clifford said, and in an instant, Clete was

running toward the ring of staff members, through it, and past it to the woods. His peripheral vision caught brush fires starting in other locations. What the hell was going on? Clete kept his attention on the running figure darting through the trees, tracking him the way a machine gunner would track a moving target.

Jake realized he had been spotted. If only he'd stayed deeper in the woods. He stopped in front of his proudest brushpile, perfect for a bonfire, and ignited it. It flared like sudden daylight, and by it he could suddenly see Clete and Clete could see him.

"You son of a bitch!" Clete yelled.

Jake held the torch in front of him as if to fend off a wild dog.

Clete picked a broken limb off the ground. He'd get this fucking Hebe.

It's stupid to stand and fight, thought Jake. My job is to get the brushpiles lit. And so he turned his back on Clete and took off, carrying his torch toward the next pile, moving as fast as he possibly could, hoping the torch wouldn't go out.

They were both fast, but when Jake stopped to ignite the next brushpile, Clete caught up and with the wood in his hand struck at Jake's legs at knee-level from behind. As Jake started to topple backward, Clete swung the limb against Jake's back with enough force to shatter a spine, and even as Jake cried out, dropping his torch, Clete shoved the boy straight into the bonfire he had just created.

Jake's single scream cut through the night like a scimitar. His hair and clothes afire, Jake struggled to regain his balance; *something was dreadfully wrong with his back,* he thought, his body wouldn't cooperate anymore with the will of his mind. Mustering his remaining life's energy and calling for the help of God, Jake tried to thrust himself out of the blaze. At that moment, Clete, with the tree limb in his right hand, smashed the burning boy across the face. Jake, his vision red with blood, his face a whirling pool of pain, fell backward into the heart of the bonfire.

Clete couldn't take his eyes off the still-living body wholly aflame, blackening, crisping. This is what we ought to do with all of them, he thought, instead of fucking around with them the way Mr. Clifford was with his crazy genetic whatever-it-was. Clete had a vision of an army of trucks picking up Jews everywhere and bringing them here so he could smash them and burn them the way he had Jake, getting it over with all at once. Maybe he and not Mr. Clifford or that new guy should be running this show!

Clete trotted back to where he had left Mr. Clifford. Sure his face was scratched from the brush and there was a snag in his jeans, but he felt fine, terrific, his adrenalin running through his veins like speed.

When he reached Mr. Clifford, he said, "I got him, sir."

"The others, the others," Clifford said, pointing to the bonfires burning far to the left, and then to another group of them, still farther. The sound of the individual fires were now becoming one indistinguishable roar as the wind whipped the flames through the over-dry forest. Hundreds of yards of woodland circling Cliffhaven were bursting into flame.

We need to put the fire out, thought Clete, then kill the fucking Jews the way he'd done that what's-his-name. All it took was leadership.

Clete yelled at several of the staff members who had stopped their forward movement. He motioned at some of them to join him. Two did. He'd remember who the others were. He'd get them afterward. He took the two who obeyed with him at a fast trot toward the utility building in which the fire equipment was stored, leaving Mr. Clifford standing stock-still.

Dan ran over to where Mr. Clifford was standing, a frightened man.

"Those Jews did this," Mr. Clifford said. "The ones that escaped."

"What kind of fire-fighting equipment do you have here?" Dan asked.

"Those Jews did this," Mr. Clifford said.

"Mr. Clifford," Dan said, taking a chance, grabbing the man by both shoulders. "Fire-fighting equipment."

"That's where Clete went." He pointed.

The staff members, no longer in the closing circle, were breaking ranks, mesmerized by the fire.

Dan raced after Clete.

Inside the utility building Dan was astonished at how little there was, a small pumper, two ordinary 32-foot ladders, a lot of hose coiled up in the back of the pickup truck.

"Jesus," Dan said. "How are you going to put that out with this?"

Clete was starting up the pumper. "The old man put his emphasis on prevention. If we had a fire in a room, even the dining room or kitchen, we could handle it. But the woods!"

The two staff members who had followed Clete were starting the pickup truck.

"This is crazy," Dan said. "You've got to call in the Forest Service."

"That's exactly what Clifford didn't want," Clete yelled, putting the pumper into gear. "We have to be self-sufficient. Let's go!"

Dan climbed in alongside him and they were off.

"Where's your water supply?" Dan asked.

As they bumped over the ground, Clete pointed at the water tower.

"That dinky thing? How much does it hold?"

"Not enough."

"Don't you tie in to community water anywhere?"

"No, just our wells. Mr. Clifford didn't want to give outsiders that power."

"What power?"

"To cut off our water supply."

"Jesus!" Dan said. He grabbed Clete's arm.

"Don't do that while I'm driving," Clete said.

"Let me off near where Clifford is," Dan yelled over the roar of the engine.

"I'm heading for the water tower," Clete said, pointing straight ahead.

"Then let me off here," Dan yelled. *I'll deal with this son of a bitch later.*

Clete slowed just enough for Dan to hop off, then roared away in the direction of the tower, where staff members were already gathering.

Dan watched the pumper, thinking at least they have fire

drills in this place. He trotted over to where Mr. Clifford was.

"We mustn't let any of the residents escape," Mr. Clifford said.

"Mr. Clifford," Dan said, hoping to penetrate the fog the old man seemed to be in, "I was a volunteer fireman. With those woods ablaze, you've got to call in help."

"This is your chance to demonstrate your resourcefulness, young man," Mr. Clifford said. "I hope I didn't make a mistake in hiring you."

"I think the buildings are safe, sir."

"That's right. There's at least seventy-five yards from the woods to the nearest buildings. It was planned that way. That open space will act as a firebreak."

"Sir," Dan said, "if there's enough heat generated in the woods around us, this middle area's going to pull in smoke from whatever direction the wind is blowing. See over there." From the north a dense gray cloud was drifting languidly toward the buildings.

"I'm going to my quarters," Mr. Clifford said. "I want to telephone my wife."

Dan walked along with him.

"Why are you accompanying me?"

"Because of them," Dan said, pointing to the residents who were congregating in clusters at a distance. Most of them were staring at the fire. Some were looking straight at Mr. Clifford.

"They wouldn't dare," Mr. Clifford said, thinking *they're afraid of the fire.*

Dan Pitz did not give a damn about the old man. He wanted that telephone. "I'll come with you, anyway," he said, "just to be sure."

When they reached Clifford's house, Mr. Clifford turned to Dan Pitz. "You'd better get back and direct the fire fighting."

It was worth risking. "Shouldn't we phone for outside help?" Dan asked.

"Never," Mr. Clifford said, again wondering if he had made the wrong choice. It was too late, Whittaker was dead.

"You'll have to put it out yourself," he said to Dan.

20

Stanley saw the chain across the entrance to Cliffhaven and braked the car to a stop just before it.

"I'm sure this is the place," he said.

"I hope you're right," Kathy said.

Out of the sentry box came a fellow dressed in an orange-and-blue outfit who looked to Stanley like one of those roller-skate waiters at a drive-up fast-food place.

"Hi," Stanley said, rolling his window all the way down.

"We're full up," the fellow said.

Stanley said, "We're not checking in. I'm just seeing if my parents are registered."

The fellow's expression shifted. "What's your name?" he asked.

"Stanley Brown. This here's Kathy."

Kathy nodded.

The fellow at the gate thought a moment. Wasn't Brown

the name of the man they were looking for topside? If this kid is his son, Mr. Clifford will be real glad to get him.

"Hold it just a second," he said, "while I check up top."

He went into the sentry booth and tried the phone. Stanley was getting impatient.

Then the fellow came out and said, "I can't get through. Whoever's at the switchboard isn't picking up."

"Try again," Stanley said. "This is important."

"Sure," he said.

The moment he was back inside the sentry box, Stanley held a finger to his lips to keep Kathy from saying anything, opened the car door quietly, left it open, unhooked the chain across the Cliffhaven entrance, then hopped into the car, slammed the door, and was off. In the rearview mirror he caught the fellow waving at him and yelling something. *Fuck him,* Stanley thought.

He had to slow down when the road narrowed. He didn't want to run off the winding road and break an axle on Jerry's car.

"Wonder what they do when a car is going up at the same time one is coming down?" Kathy said.

"One of them lifts up in the air so the other can pass," Stanley said. "There must be some bypasses on this road."

"You'd think—"

"What?"

"The kind of place your parents would stop at—I mean they wouldn't stay at an ordinary motel, would they?—would have a better road than this."

"Maybe they figure people won't run off without paying their bills. Too easy to catch on a road like this."

"What's the matter?" Kathy asked.

"Take a deep breath."

She did. "Woodsmoke?"

Stanley nodded, moved forward slowly, went around another S-curve, stuck his head out of the side window, and looked up. That was definitely smoke drifting across the horizon.

Stanley drove a bit faster, as fast as he dared, then suddenly saw the man running down the road toward them.

"Look at that guy," Stanley said.

The man was waving his arms across one another as if to warn Stanley to stop.

He did and got out of the car. "What's up?" he shouted.

The man was terribly out of breath. "The woods are on fire. The whole place is going to burn down. Please turn around, get to a phone, call for help, firemen, police, everybody."

"My mother and father might be up there," Stanley said.

The man's expression collapsed. "You're Jewish?" he asked, then glanced over his shoulder.

"What's that got to do with anything?"

"Get out of here fast. Sound the alarm."

"But my parents—"

"Son, the best thing you can do for your parents if they're up there is to get help quickly. Here he comes."

"Who?"

They heard the clatter of feet running.

"Turn your car around. Quick!" the man yelled.

Stanley looked at the width of the road. This guy was a nut.

"I'll go up and turn around at the top," Stanley said.

"They'll never let you. Please do as I say."

They could hear the footsteps louder now.

"Let me come with you," the man said, just as an orange-and-blue uniformed staff member came into view.

"Mr. Meyer," the staff member yelled. "Where are you off to?"

"I've always obeyed," Meyer said. "I don't want to burn to death."

"We're going to have that fire under control," the staff member said, puffing. "You come back with me."

What kind of place is this? Stanley thought.

"Let's get out of here," Kathy said.

"Yeah."

He got in, turned left as far as he could, then turned the wheel all the way round, then backed up, turned the wheel, repeated the process till the car was facing partly downhill.

"Get in," he said to the man.

"He won't let me," the man said.

This is crazy, Stanley thought.

The staff member gestured to the man to come along. The man looked with longing at Stanley's car. The staff member now stood right in front of him. The staff member shook his head. *No.* The man shook his head. *No.*

Stanley looked up at the sky, visible above the dense woods. He could see sparks as well as smoke.

He took off down the road, faster than he'd come up, tires squealing on the turns.

"Jesus," Kathy said.

"That a comment on my driving?" Stanley said.

"No," she said. Then repeated, "Jesus."

As he neared the chain barrier, Stanley thought, what would he do about the creep in the sentry box who had tried to stop him? In the movies, he supposed, you'd just crash the car into the chain, hoping it would uproot one of the two-by-fours holding the chain. He couldn't do that to Jerry's car.

"Kathy," he said, "I'm going to stop just this side of the chain, then I'll get out and run to that gas station just down the road. You come there, too. Fast as you can, okay?"

She nodded.

"I can't hear you," he said, concentrating on the last part of the winding road.

"Yes," she said.

Stanley ran right by Frank Fowler, who was pumping gas for a van, and into the house. Matilda Fowler put her newspaper down.

"Yes?"

"Where's your phone?"

"What?"

"Please let me use your phone. There's a big fire up there." Frank was standing in the doorway. "Up where?" he said.

"Up at the resort. Cliffhaven, whatever they call it."

"They take care of their own problems," Frank said.

"Not this. The woods are going up all around them."

"Hey!" shouted the van driver. "Where's my change?"

As Frank went to make change, his mother pointed to the phone. "Just tell the operator."

Kathy came in.

"Yes, young lady?" Matilda asked.

"I'm with him," she said, just as Stanley heard the operator answer.

"I want to report a fire in Cliffhaven. Big Sur." He gave her the number he was calling from. In a moment he was talking to someone else. "Yeah, Big Sur, place called Cliffhaven. I didn't get up to the buildings, just on the road. The woods are on fire. Yeah, all around. Please hurry."

Stanley hung up. Kathy looked worried sick. He put his arm around her.

It was Kathy who saw, over his shoulder, Frank Fowler standing in the doorway with a shotgun.

"What did you do that for?" Frank said.

The oldest surviving resident of Cliffhaven, Moshe Perlman, was a man of sixty-eight who, perhaps because of his full white beard, looked as if he were eighty. The sight of the conflagration had paralyzed him at first because he was certain it was an act of God. It was necessary to be grateful. He put on his skullcap, which he had not worn since his second day in Cliffhaven, and started rocking. *Sh'ma yisroel adonoi elochenu adonoi echod* . . .

Two residents, seeing the old man, went over to him and each took him gently under an arm.

"Come," one said. "It is getting very hot here."

Moshe Perlman, who had wanted to leave the second he was up in Cliffhaven because the place seemed too posh for a man with his plain tastes, was persuaded by his wife to live a little and to stay. She was twenty years younger than he, and he often acceded to her wishes. When she didn't show up in the room the second day, his first thought was that she had taken up with a younger man. But he had seen her nowhere about that day or the following, and, frantic with worry, he had asked the *goyim* who kept him prisoner to tell him where his wife was, but all they did was laugh and say what did an old man need a wife for?

"Come," the first resident said to Moshe Perlman. "It will be safer in the swimming pool."

"I don't swim," Moshe Perlman said.

"We are just going to stand in the shallow end and stay wet," the other man said. "See, others are already there."

Perlman let them steer him to the pool. Perhaps God would let him drown. It didn't matter anymore.

Blaustein, the accountant, was not used to physical exertion. Henry had to keep urging him ahead. He had set his share of brushpiles on fire, and they were now skirting wide around the ones set by Margaret to avoid the heat as they hurried to their point of origin.

Just then he saw Margaret up ahead. "Hey," he shouted.

She spotted them, Blaustein stumbling along behind Henry now.

"The heat," puffed Blaustein. "It's unbearable."

"Good work," Henry said to Margaret.

"What took you so long?"

Henry jabbed a thumb in Blaustein's direction. "I should have left him tied to the tree." He pointed across the open space to the flat-topped structure on whose roof he had taken refuge. "It's the closest," he said, as Margaret, as if on cue, lit the last brushpile and threw her torch into the pyre.

"All set?" Henry asked.

She nodded. "What about the others?"

"They'll see us if we stay on this side of the building. All right, let's go, all together."

They ran to the building, Margaret hoping against hope they would not be seen by anyone from Cliffhaven. After this inferno, she was certain that if Henry were caught again, they wouldn't bother playing cat-and-mouse with him. Their rage would mean his instant death.

Shamir, who had just touched off his last brushpile, could see the three figures moving unrhythmically across the open ground like a troika of uncoordinated dancers. Time to join them, he thought, and he started running back near the edge of the woods, warding off sizzling sparks as if they were bullets. It was too hot. He left the concealment of the woods and headed for his comrades at an angle across the open ground, hoping he wouldn't be spotted.

A minute later he collapsed on the ground beside them, panting.

"Got all mine," he said. "Yours?"

Henry nodded.

"Where's Jake?"

They all looked far off to the right. Most of Jake's brushpiles must have been ignited because that part of the woods was roaring away, but at the farthest end, nothing.

"He didn't finish," Henry said.

"I wish he'd get here," Margaret said, and in that moment realized that if Jake had not made it to all of his brushpiles, something might be very wrong.

"Could he have fallen, broken a leg, be unable to move?" she said.

Across the part of the semicircle entrusted to Jake, the nearest areas were completely ablaze. The dry brush had flared like kindling, the smaller branches had smoldered and caught, and now the trees themselves were burning.

"He probably took off," Blaustein mumbled.

"Just a kid," Henry said, standing. "Stanley's age. I'm going to find him."

"In that blaze?" Shamir said.

Margaret felt the crow of panic fluttering its wings in her chest.

Henry was off, running toward the part of the woods where Jake must have lit his last bonfire.

"Come back," Shamir yelled. "Don't be crazy!"

He's not crazy, Margaret thought. It's his nature.

Margaret, Shamir, and Blaustein watched Henry, the tiny form of a running man, disappear just at the edge of the blaze.

Margaret thought *I am praying to both our Gods, Henry. I can't trust the one who's been looking after Jews.*

"Come out," Shamir said, as if to himself.

Time froze. Then, suddenly, they saw the tiny figure burst out of the woods, running toward them. Margaret stood. When

Henry was halfway to them, they saw the streaks of charcoal on his face.

Shamir got up. As Henry approached them, Shamir yelled, "Are you all right?"

Henry waved his hand as if to say *never mind me.*

He was drawing in deep breaths like a long-distance runner. Margaret put her arms around him. "Are you hurt?" she asked.

"I'm okay," Henry puffed. "Winded. Couldn't find Jake. I hope he's not in there."

Blaustein ventured, "Like I said, he probably took off."

He probably didn't, Henry thought. He slid down against the wall of the building, then rested his arms and head on his knees.

When Henry's wind returned, he looked up to see what the others were watching. What they were witnessing was the phenomenon of spontaneous combustion, the forest on an uphill grade, the heat rising in billows, brush higher up smoldering and flaring even before the fire reached it. Margaret could understand the fascination that pyromaniacs had for the grandeur of flames shooting upward as from a mammoth oven, turning dry solid wood into crackling limbs that in moments broke, falling into the inferno.

It was then that Henry kissed her, unmindful of their companions, of their breaths, of where they were. A kiss of life.

When their faces parted, Margaret saw Blaustein staring at the ground between his knees, a man embarrassed by the emotions of other people. Shamir was pointing.

Henry rolled over and, shielding his eyes, looked in the direction of Shamir's finger. At a great distance he could see a group of Cliffhaven staff members linking up sections of hose, ants trying the impossible. There was no way mere water from a hose could smother the roaring forest now. He looked at his companions with an expression of wry triumph. They had succeeded in ringing at least three-quarters of Cliffhaven.

He let his head rest against the softness of her breast, as he used to do under the trees in Central Park when they were courting. Had all those years passed? Ruth, Stanley, a lifetime spent like a brass shell. After this they would savor the minutes.

It would have been easy to let himself slip into sleep, but he felt Margaret's body tense. He opened his eyes to see, as she had, three trusties come around the corner of the building. They came within ten feet of where the four of them were sheltering.

They recognized Henry as he recognized them. They were among the ones who had stood in front of the chain, blocking the way to Highway 1.

21

Dan Pitz, wishing he had never answered the advertisement, viewed the fire not with the fanaticism of a convert but like an outsider appraising the chances objectively. The roadway down might act as a firebreak, but a conflagration of that magnitude could easily send a flaming piece of debris across the road and they would all be trapped, not only the residents, who were now milling about near or in the swimming pool, trying to keep as much distance between themselves and the heat as possible, but the staff also. This fire could incinerate them all. Mr. Clifford might prefer wiping out all traces of the project, but he'd be damned if, after burning three people to get where he did in life, he was going to end up a roasted chestnut.

Dan was glad to see Oliver Robinson and Allen Trask running to join him. They didn't need to exchange many words. "It won't work," Robinson said, pointing at Clete and the others in their pathetic attempt to fight the fire.

Dan Pitz said, "We could get the staff down the road and leave two or three guys rear-guarding it with guns to keep the residents from following."

Robinson had wanted George Whittaker's job. Now he was glad he didn't get it.

"You think Mr. Clifford will give me a reference for one day's work?" Dan asked.

Robinson laughed. Trask said, "I suppose we better get the old man out of here."

Just then they all heard the helicopter and turned their faces skyward.

Buzz Ballard, piloting the Bell Ranger and in charge of its Helitac crew, was forty-six. His strongest memory of childhood was the whah-whah-whah sound of the siren that would get his father, a volunteer fire fighter, into his clothes in the middle of the night, giving his mother a peck on the cheek just in case, and then the sound of the car starting up, and young Buzz was always at the window of his room, watching the blue light on his father's car rotating like a disappearing beacon in the night.

Once, over Thanksgiving dinner—turkey, cranberry sauce, mashed potatoes, gravy, and pumpkin pie—Mr. Ballard was asked by Mrs. Ballard why he did it, meaning all those volunteer hours, and his father had answered not so much to her but to Buzz by saying, "Doctors cure most of their patients, but not all of them. Lawyers get some of their clients off, but some go to jail. We never lose to a fire. We get it sooner or later."

Buzz, at eighteen, had been trained as a Marine pilot just in time to catch the tail end of the Korean War. And when he was given his certificate of honorable service and went into the reserves, the idea of fighting fires by hanging on to a truck and then holding a hose seemed slow for the speed he was accustomed to, letting the nose of his jet down just a bit to bring its airspeed to five hundred and sometimes five fifty.

And so Buzz found his place in the air arm of the U.S. Forest Service, where the slowness of a bomber was made up for by the excitement of unleashing a massive torrent of chemical from the air. Later, as Buzz worked his way into choppers, he found renewed excitement in being, as was often the case, the first man to survey a virgin fire of great dimensions. He liked the chill of recognizing its extent and seriousness, and being the first voice to report back in, the go signal for what he saw as a war against flames that if unchecked could consume part of the world.

Taking the Bell Ranger down to three hundred feet, he got Ed Ballantine back on the radio.

"Here are the coordinates, Ed."

Then Buzz said, "Fire is in an incomplete ring around nine or ten large buildings in a compound, all part of some resort. My estimate's one fifty to one-seven-five people visible outside rooms and buildings. Don't see anyone heading down the road by foot or car. What's that?"

Buzz listened for a moment, then switched back so he could talk. "No buildings burning yet. Pattern of the blaze indicates origin in multiple locations. Wouldn't rule out arson."

Ed, who fought fires from a desk, was cynical. "The insurance companies sure make it easy for motel owners who can't cut the mustard."

"Ed, this is no motel. It's a big place. I'd hate to see more of Ventana go up so soon after that last one. Recommend putting bombers with ammonium nitrate on standby. This'll take one thousand men for starters. You'll need dozers airlifted. If we can keep the road clear, ground tankers could get up. If the fire jumps the road, we'll never get the tankers through. You'll have to use air tankers period. Ed, I think you'd better get the Indians in off the reservations the way this is going. There could be poison oak down there burning. The area north of the buildings looks very rough for pack mules. Hey, wait a minute."

Buzz brought the helicopter down lower and made a pass over Cliffhaven. Almost everyone was now staring up at the solitary Bell Ranger.

Buzz pulled upward and away to where he could get a better view of what had caught his eye.

"Hey, Ed, that fire could jump the road about two hundred

yards downhill. It narrows between big rocks. Very thick brush on both sides. Better get the Coast Guard rescue choppers at Monterey plus Fort Ord's Hercules if you want to get these people out in time. Ed, you better drop some organized heads into the compound real quick from the look of things. I'll stick long as I can, over."

A few minutes later he got back on.

"Lot of people crowding the low end of the swimming pool now. It must be hot as hell down there. Isn't room in the pool for everybody. Also we're getting uphill combustion, I'd say upwards of twenty acres flaming or gone. This is a fast one."

Ballard checked his fuel gauge, then made a sweep of the periphery.

"Hey, Ed," he called. "Choppers on the way? Good thing. Listen, something crazy. The parking lot here's got just a few cars and a pickup truck. Doesn't make sense with all those people. But just east of this place there's a gorge I just buzzed. It's filled with auto junk, most of it complete cars. Think there's some kind of racket going on here? What? No, more'n a hundred. If they've got gas in the tanks . . . You'd better get a command post set up fast. And, Buddy, better get here soon, my fuel gauge's telling me to head home. Over."

Henry looked up at the trusties and decided he'd better stand. Shamir had thought of the same thing at the same time. Pity Jake wasn't here, that would make three against three.

Blaustein, still slumped against the wall, spoke to the trusties first. "I didn't do anything," he said.

The leader of the three looked at Blaustein with contempt. Then he spoke, his hand encompassing the blaze. "You started all this."

It wasn't a question. Henry acknowledged the deed with silence.

The leader of the trusties seemed nervous about what he wanted to say.

Finally, it came out. "We three think you did right. We were wrong to play ball with Clifford."

"And now you're afraid of being punished."

261

The man nodded. This is as it always is, Henry thought, the sides change, the worm turns.

"What should we do?" the man asked.

"Fools," Henry said. "For a start, take your armbands off."

All their heads turned at once. Blaustein, who'd sidled along the wall, now suddenly stood and ran as fast as he could.

"What's the matter, Clete?"

Dan Pitz's voice had come up right behind him. Clete signaled for the hose he was holding to be turned off. When the water pressure eased, he put the hose on the ground but kept his foot on it to keep it from rolling about, spewing the remains of the water.

"It's like trying to piss at a bonfire," Clete said. "We're making no headway at all."

"It's too bad Mr. Clifford won't let us call in the pros."

"And let them see what we've got here?" Clete wondered about this new guy's guts.

Certain now that no one was within hearing distance, Dan said, "I'm sure that chopper called in the feds."

"Then we've got to do something about all those people in the swimming pool." Clete was looking in that direction.

"Jesus, some of them are heading toward the road."

"I have an idea," Dan Pitz said, "if you'll listen."

"I'll listen okay."

"I'll make a deal with you," the new manager said. "When this is over . . ."

"Yeah."

"I won't identify you, if you won't identify me."

Clete looked Dan in the eye. So this was the tough guy picked by Clifford.

Dan put his hand out to clinch the agreement.

Clete extended his right hand to shake Dan's, and also his left to grab Dan's underarm just above the elbow, and with that perfect grip, threw Dan Pitz to the ground on his back. He could see the surprise in Pitz's face and took advantage of it to put his knee in Pitz's chest as he pinned his arms.

"You stupid son of a bitch, you're worried about *me* identifying you, you chicken-livered idiot? What about all those Jews? Maybe they won't remember the face of the new guy, I don't even know if they've seen you, but they'll sure as hell remember me. Now listen!" Clete let Pitz's left arm go and put his right fist in Pitz's face. "I'm going to get the weapons from the closet behind the reception desk. We'll distribute them to the staff members we can find real quick and set up a barricade at the road. Any Jews try to get down it, we shoot. Understand?"

Dan nodded. He would have nodded whatever this nut said, as long as he could get away. In a second Clete was gone, running toward the reception building.

Luckily, he knew where Ann kept the key. He opened the second drawer on the right and lifted the tray from the cash box. It wasn't there! He rummaged through the various keys quickly—ah, there it was! He opened the cupboard. There were twelve guns of various makes, mostly .38s. He scooped up several boxes of ammunition from the bottom of the cabinet, stashed them and all the guns but one in the canvas log carrier by the fireplace. It wasn't a good way to carry anything, but he didn't see any better way. He was off, shoving his own weapon behind the belt of his jeans.

He couldn't see Dan Pitz anywhere. He looked anxiously around for Robinson or Trask. Not to be seen. What he did see were about eight or ten of the Jews within a hundred yards of the road. They were dripping from the pool, most of them. And glancing around, as if expecting to be caught if their plans were known. Where the hell was Charlotte? He could sure use her.

Quickly, Clete found five staff members, then saw four more and called them over, handed out the weapons, explained what the Jews were doing, and what his plans were. He jammed the extra gun into his waistband, handed out the ammunition, and had everybody load up, while he did the same. He threw the log carrier to the side and then, on the run, the others following him, went to head off the residents at the top of the road. He remembered the sawhorses and the two-by-six painted with "No Exit" behind the sentry house—he could use them, but they wouldn't really hold a crowd back. He'd make a barrier of bodies, that would keep them away!

In no time Clete had the armed staff members lined up in front of the barrier, several of them frightened by the changed circumstances.

"Don't you worry none," Clete said. "When I'm through, there won't be any witnesses."

"What are you going to do?" asked the staff member next to him.

"Everybody!" Clete yelled, feeling a rush of excitement as the idea in his head bloomed. He had the feeling he was a natural leader, long repressed, now out from under jerks like Dan Pitz and raring to go. "Count your rounds," he shouted.

The residents approaching the barrier stopped their forward movement.

"Okay," Clete said, so the staff members could hear him. "Let's make every shot count. We'll put the bodies in the dump truck, and the ones we don't shoot, we'll put them in the big van and run it and the truck into the gully. Remember, no witnesses!"

There were more than a dozen residents now not more than ten yards away. Way behind them, after the stragglers, a whole mob from the pool was headed toward the barrier. Let them come, thought Clete. It's easier if they head for us than if we have to chase after them.

"Remember," Clete said, raising his pistol to eye level, "don't waste shots. Aim for the one directly in front of you. Everybody ready?"

The others took aim, some of them unsteadily.

"Fire," Clete said. His shot hit the man he was aiming at in the center of his chest. He could see the reaction on the man's face, a great gasp as he fell backward. Clete got a lot of satisfaction from being that close, but something bothered him. The volley he had heard didn't sound like a dozen shots. He glanced right. Obviously some of the guys had not fired. Slim, the tall guy from Pasadena, had lowered his pistol to his side.

Clete went up to him. "What's the matter, Slim, chicken?"

Slim didn't say anything.

Clete was a lot shorter than Slim and felt that way as he

stood close. Slim didn't see Clete raising the pistol to his
midriff, he just felt the sudden blow into his belly as the shot
resounded. He fell, writhing, and Clete stepped on his right
wrist and got the gun away from him, then left him lying there,
screaming.

"Anybody else chicken?" Clete asked, shouting so he could
be heard against the roar of the fire.

Nobody said anything.

He then ordered them to take aim. The residents, meanwhile, were backing off, and Clete ordered the line of staff
members forward. He wanted his targets within easy range.

It was at that moment that he saw the figure running toward
the periphery of the compound perhaps a hundred and fifty
yards away, but he recognized her. That Minter woman, the
one he hated most, was trying to make her escape through the
brush that was not yet burning. She was a fool. That area would
be ablaze in minutes.

"Hold everything," he yelled, signaling the others to lower
their weapons, and took off after her. He'd make an example
of that cunt. He'd execute her in a really fine way in front of
everybody.

She saw him coming and knew who he was. She also saw the
upraised pistol in his hand. Phyllis Minter could have made
the woods, but she deliberately stopped, turned, and waited
for him.

"Well, if it isn't little prickle with a big gun," she said.
"Looks like your fun park is burning down."

"Just the woods, jewbaby. We're keeping the rest intact
for all your relatives. Now march!" Clete waved the pistol in
the direction he wanted her to go.

Phyllis had no intention of obeying orders from this weasel.
She held her middle finger up.

Clete hated obstruction from anybody, but especially from
women and Jews. He slammed at Phyllis's upraised finger with
the butt of his gun.

"You missed," she said, pulling her hand smartly away.
Then, with her knees bent, she reached into her boot for the
knife she had secreted there.

Clete had his plan in mind. He'd make her undress in front of everybody right by the barrier, and then he'd shoot her point blank into the furry triangle, tearing her cunt to pieces. He'd just have to get her knife away first.

"Come on, jewbaby," he said, "let's have the knife." He held out his left hand for it, keeping the muzzle of the gun pointed in her direction. Were the others watching from a distance?

"Sure," Phyllis said. "If you promise not to shoot."

"Why would I shoot you, baby? You know what I want to do to you. How can I do that if you're dead?"

Phyllis made as if to lay the knife down in Clete's out-stretched palm, moving two steps closer to do so. She'd noticed that Clete didn't have as much know-how in handling a gun as some of the men she'd known; he was pointing it at the sky, not at her. With a determination born of her lifetime of griev-ances, she suddenly thrust the knife at Clete's chest.

Clete's instinct was to block her arm the way he'd been taught, but the upraised palm of his left hand put him in the wrong position, and as he brought his gun arm slamming around it was too late, he felt the puncture in his chest, my God, she had the strength of a man as she shoved the blade all the way in. He looked down and saw the handle protruding grotesquely and felt himself falling forward as she stepped back to be out of his way. It was important, he thought, not to fall face down on the handle, and, as if everything were working in slow motion, he found the strength to turn as he fell, falling on his side, then rolling onto his back, looking for Phyllis Minter through the haze of his eyes. The bitch he had wanted to get more than any other was standing not four feet away. In the distance people were running away from the barrier at the road, scattering everywhere, and what was that up in the air, helicopters? It was all the fault of the Hebewoman, dis-tracting him, tempting him to murder as she had tempted him to sex. He raised the gun, holding it in both hands so his aim wouldn't shake, though he knew he was shaking, and though Phyllis Minter stepped back and instinctively ducked her head, that wasn't where Clete was aiming when the gun roared.

* * *

Henry, Margaret, and Shamir had come from around the corner of the buildings in time to see, at a distance, the barrier at the road, with several bodies lying on the ground nearby like a scene from a war newsreel. They saw the row of armed staff members, all looking in the direction where Clete was fighting with a woman Margaret immediately recognized as the one she'd played basketball with.

Henry saw clearly, in a way he would never forget, the woman push the knife into Clete's chest as if all the strength in the world were suddenly hers. He was halfway there, sprinting, by the time Clete, on his back on the ground, raised the pistol at the woman.

"Clete!" Henry shouted with all his might, hoping to distract him, but Clete, on the ground, heard nothing but the inside of his own head saying, "Fire."

The bullet shattered Phyllis's pelvis, plunging into her intestines. She thought of her father, as she fell, who had not been shot in the war and had then received his fatal bullet in a Manhattan taxicab. Her vision was blurred, strangely, as were her thoughts. She had no heir to mourn her, she thought. Perhaps she would not die. Oh God, she didn't want to die.

Henry kicked the gun out of Clete's hand, but it hadn't been necessary. He was unconscious. When Margaret caught up, she knelt by Clete's side for a moment and saw what had to be done. Mustering strength, she pulled up as much of Clete's T-shirt as she could get in her hand and pressed the wad of cloth against the hole in his chest. It was probably no use unless he could be gotten to a hospital right away.

"Please, Margaret," Henry was saying, "the woman."

Of course, the woman. She should have tended to her first. "Hold this," she instructed Shamir, showing him how to press down on the wad of cloth to stem the blood flow.

"If we put a tourniquet around his neck, the blood would stop," Shamir said, but his remark went unheard.

Shamir held the blood-soaked cloth tight against Clete's chest with his left hand and with his right fished into Clete's pockets. He found what he was looking for in the first one, a yellow-

and-blue plastic Cliffhaven tag with Clete's passkey. Now they could open the rooms that still had residents behind locked doors.

Kneeling next to the Minter woman, Margaret noticed two things. How beautiful her face was, despite the pain, and how desperate her condition seemed. There was obviously a great deal of internal bleeding. She guessed, and she was given to correct guesses in matters of this sort, that the bullet had shattered bone, and the bone fragments had in turn become multiple bullets, tearing her lower abdomen as if she'd been hit with a bursting shell. What good was it to be a doctor now, without morphine, without surgical equipment, or blood to replace the blood that was staining the ground?

Margaret did what she could for Phyllis Minter. The rest needed to be done in an operating room by a surgeon very soon. In dreams you ran away from terror but your legs wouldn't move fast enough, and you wondered could you get away in time. In life the future was more precise. Within ten or fifteen minutes this woman would die, she was already on her way to death, and nothing available could stop it.

A familiar sense of despair crowded Margaret's mind as she stood up slowly. She looked at Phyllis Minter's face. At least, she wasn't conscious. *Good-bye* Margaret said in her mind.

Then, remembering the rest of the world, she looked about. A staff member she recognized as Charlotte was bending over Clete.

"Is he dead?" Charlotte asked Shamir.

"No," Shamir said, "but he will be. Here, you hold his T-shirt against the wound. I've got something to attend to."

When Shamir raised the red-soaked cloth slightly, the wound spurted. Charlotte straightened up. She hated the sight of blood, but even worse was the shattering effect of seeing the man she'd spent more time with than any other man in her life lying there, his eyes glazed with a prescience of death. He would never fuck her again, her or anybody.

"Come on," Shamir shouted at her. "He's one of yours."

Charlotte took several steps backward, then turned and started to walk toward her quarters, which Clete would never visit again, wondering how quickly she could pack. She had to get out of this place before the Jews turned on her.

Shamir saw Charlotte break into a trot. "Hell," he thought. "Henry! Come here, hold this. I've got some doors to open."

22

Blaustein was glad to have gotten away from the *meshugganer* and his Gentile wife. That man puffed himself up with hope like a balloon. Who did he think he was, Moses?

Keeping in touch with reality had kept him alive for six months in this place, Blaustein thought. Henry Brown was a man to keep away from. He was going to get himself killed, by one of Clifford's people, by the police, by someone.

From a distance Blaustein saw that, despite the heat, which was getting worse by the minute, people were swarming out of the swimming pool. Some of them were heading for the road. The fools would be stopped. Then he saw the small group gather around someone he recognized. Dr. Goodson was not one of Blaustein's favorite people. He thought Goodson's so-called experiments nonsense. You didn't need to be deprived of essentials to know that they were essential.

Squinting, Blaustein could see that they were beating the shit out of Dr. Goodson. You see, he thought, the Jews are

270

going to end up killing each other. Some of those who had grudges against him were in that group. He'd better get to Mr. Clifford fast.

The curtain across the big glass window was drawn; he couldn't see whether Mr. Clifford had anyone with him.

Blaustein didn't go to the front door. He was no fool. He went around to the back door that led into the kitchen. It wasn't locked. If he were Mr. Clifford, he would lock all the doors!

In the kitchen his eye caught first the long row of copper pans, gleaming as if they were decorations instead of utensils. What waste! thought Blaustein the accountant, who had kept his wife sensibly to two pots, one big and one small.

He heard the footsteps. A voice snapped, "What are you doing here?"

"Oh, Mr. Clifford," Blaustein said, his body scrunched into obeisance.

"What do you want?" Clifford said.

"I had nothing to do with it."

"Do with what?"

"The fire," Blaustein said. "Henry Brown started it. I tried to warn the staff but he tied me up."

It always put the other person at a disadvantage when Mr. Clifford employed his technique of coming very close to the person he was speaking to.

"You helped him set those fires, Blaustein," Mr. Clifford said.

Blaustein stepped back.

"He made me do it."

"You're a jellyfish, Blaustein. Get out of here."

"I was one of your first trusties, Mr. Clifford, don't you remember?"

"You'd have been dead long ago if I hadn't picked you."

"Yes, I worked for you hard."

"You owe your life to me," Mr. Clifford said. "And then you go help that son of a bitch burn the place down. Is that gratitude?"

"They forced me to do it," Blaustein whimpered. "I was only following orders."

Mr. Clifford laughed.

Blaustein said, "I came to tell you who did it as soon as I could."

Mr. Clifford opened the kitchen door. "Get out of here before I kill you, Blaustein. Go down to the pool, maybe the others will kill you."

When Blaustein scampered off, Mr. Clifford closed and locked the door, then, hearing what he thought to be the distinct sound of helicopters, went to the phone to try Abigail again.

Replacing the Bell Ranger piloted by Buzz Ballard, Buddy Arnold's Helitac chopper, hanging high above Cliffhaven, reported developments to his headquarters in Monterey.

Buddy watched the first three Coast Guard rescue choppers, much smaller than his, come in high and then let themselves down carefully past the great circle of flame and smoke into the center of the compound. He could see the last people skittering out of the swimming pool, running toward the choppers. People were heading toward them from every which way. Buddy hoped they'd keep their distance. Rotor accidents can be nasty.

An ensign from the first chopper had his hands up, stopping people from getting closer. He appeared to be asking questions, gesturing at the buildings. Someone pointed to the locker-room building. Buddy could see the ensign run in the direction of a far building, followed by two of the people he'd been talking to. The ensign was in the building four or five minutes before he came running back to his chopper. Buddy picked him up on the radio instantly.

"This is Charley two-five-oh on the ground."

"Receiving," Buddy said. The ensign's voice sounded husky, choked up.

"This is no resort," the ensign said. "This is something else. Put medical on alert. I reckon thirty or more bad cases requiring attention."

"Cases of what?" Buddy asked.

"Look, I don't know. That building, inside's the worst I ever saw in my life. A whole bunch of empty lockers, and a roomful of filthy sick people most of whom are afraid to leave the building because they think they'll be killed. You better get some federal law-enforcement people down here, too. We'll need all the help we can get. Meantime, I'll try to get priorities organized for lifting people out four or five at a time. We'll need stretchers for some. We've only got eleven men down here."

Buddy thought he heard the ensign trying not to cry. Must be one of those newly commissioned kids who's never seen combat.

"I'll relay all," Buddy said.

"Thanks."

MONTEREY, California (AP): Another forest fire was reported today in the Ventana Wilderness, where thousands of acres of redwood forest burned in 1977. Early reports indicate the fire started in the periphery of an isolated resort halfway up the coastal mountains in the Big Sur area of central California. The U.S. Forest Service says it is preparing to bomb the fire with ammonium nitrate, a substance that has proved effective in the past, according to a spokesman. Trained fire fighters from other states have been summoned. Meanwhile, Coast Guard rescue helicopters from Monterey and helicopters at the Fort Ord military base have been summoned to help the Helitac crews evacuate the people trapped in the mountainside resort. The first rescue teams are already on the ground. No word has been received yet on casualties, or the number of people at the resort at the time the fire broke out. The resort, named Cliffhaven, is only six months old.
TO ALL EDITORS . . . URGENT . . . UPDATE VENTANA WILDERNESS FIRE STORY . . . FIRST RESCUERS REPORT NATURE OF CLIFFHAVEN RESORT UNUSUAL . . . MAYBE MUCH MORE CONSEQUENCE THAN FIRE . . . FIRE MAY HAVE BEEN ARSON SET BY RESORT RESIDENTS . . . REPORTER FLYING IN WITH HELITAC CREW . . . MORE

The ensign and three corpsmen separated the people in the lockers into four categories. Two of the women were found unconscious, their breathing shallow. They would be evacuated first. About ten others, mostly men, were in bad shape, some with high fevers, some still retching, all filthy from their own body wastes. The place stank to high heaven. The people the ensign assigned to the third group were clearly in pain from being in cramped quarters for a long time. Some of them could barely shuffle. Eight or nine others must have been placed in the lockers recently. They were ambulatory in minutes. It was to this group that the ensign addressed his question.

"What's this place all about?"

A moment ago they were all thanking him as if he was their savior. Now they were silent.

"This is a vacation resort, right?" he asked.

Someone nodded.

"What happened?"

They looked at each other.

The ensign tried once more. "Why did they do this to you?"

It was a gray-haired woman, old enough to be the ensign's mother, who finally answered.

"We are Jews," she said.

The stretchers had been lashed securely to the runners of the helicopter. On them were the two unconscious women. Five of the others from the locker building were crowded into the cabin, one of them wailing. They were ready to go and the ensign was motioning people back, but the woman at the rear of the mob kept shouting something at him. Finally, Margaret was able, with Henry's help, to push her way through.

"I'm a doctor," she said. "That woman"—she pointed to the one lashed to the near runner of the helicopter—"I think she's not just comatose."

The pilot, anxious to take off and make room for the other chopper hovering nearby, was yelling something that sounded like "Let's go!" But the ensign could not stop Margaret, who brushed past his outstretched arm and then squatted beside the woman's stretcher. She put her head to the woman's chest, then yelled to the ensign, "Tell him to turn the engine off, I can't hear!"

The woman was not breathing. Margaret put her finger deep into the woman's throat. There was no debris, and so Margaret, bending forward, put her mouth to the woman's mouth and began exhaling rhythmically, while Henry, who had now joined her, alternately pressed and released the woman's chest with both hands, as she had taught him. It was no use. Margaret got up and with a sad hand, waved the chopper away.

As the triple blade swirled the dust and dirt, Margaret, keeping her head low, retreated with Henry to the circle of people waiting their turn.

On impulse, Henry put his arms around her. She turned to him, and they were both suddenly hugging each other with a ferocity of found life.

Frank Fowler kept the shotgun aimed at Stanley. He didn't care about the girl. There'd be no Cliffhaven when all those fire people were through with it. This guy had ruined his chances for a job up there.

Frank's mother said, "How long you going to keep them standing that way? Cop come he's going to take that thing away from you and maybe lock you up, Frank."

What did she know? Cliffhaven didn't mean anything special to her.

"What'd you have to telephone for?" Frank said, his voice shrill.

"I told you. The place was on fire. They probably phoned in from up there before I did."

"No," Frank said. "I know them up there."

"Come on, put that gun away," Stanley said nicely. *This guy's a nut.*

"You said your mother and father were up there, didn't you?" Frank said.

"That's right."

"You Jewish?" Frank asked.

Stanley thought about that once in a while. Which half was Jewish was his joke to himself. Every other cell, was his answer.

"Not as Jewish as Jesus," Stanley said. "Point that shotgun somewhere else, will you?"

"You're taking the name of our Lord in vain," Frank said, his face reddening.

"I'm not taking anything in vain," Stanley said wearily.

Then, to the lady he said, "Make him put that away before someone gets hurt."

Frank's mother said, "Do as he says, Frank."

"I'm not taking any orders from any fucking Christkiller!"

Kathy was nearest the door, so Stanley said to her, "Go get a cop."

"No, you don't!" Frank yelled, swinging the shotgun in Kathy's direction, at which Stanley took three quick steps forward and grabbed the barrel, trying to wrench it away.

"Stop it!" screamed Frank's mother at both of them, as Frank stepped back and yanked hard, and Stanley lost his balance, though not his grip, and tried to keep the barrel deflected downward even as Frank pulled the triggers and the barrels roared, the shot at point-blank range tearing into Stanley's legs and feet and the floor. As he crumpled downward, seeing the blood and wondering why he felt no pain, he could hear Kathy scream and scream and scream.

23

To Henry the sight of the helicopters bringing in fire fighters and equipment produced both a sense of achievement and a question. He had struck a match and now an army was assembling. But would these same strong, well-trained men have come with the same sense of mission to save Jews as they had to put out a fire?

Shamir had returned from his door-opening mission. Now he was busily click-recording everything with his small camera. Henry envied him. After all his activity, Henry's present role as a spectator bothered him. And so Henry went up to the gruff-voiced fellow in a navy wool cap who seemed to be in charge of the incoming men, and said, "Excuse me, can I help?"

The fellow turned and said, "Fuck off, mister. Leave this to the professionals. Stay over there." And the man pointed to where the remaining guests of Cliffhaven, some sitting, some lying down in place, waited their turn to be evacuated.

Henry saw that Shamir, who had overheard this exchange, was about to erupt in anger and quieted him with a hand.

"There's something I'd like to do," he said. "Are you finished taking pictures?"

"For the moment."

"Do you know where Clifford is?" Henry asked.

"I know where his place is," Margaret said. "I don't know if he's there."

Henry looked at her. How did she know something he didn't?

"I was there," she said, as if in answer. "I'll explain later."

And so Margaret led Henry and Shamir through the noise and bits of charred debris carried by the wind to the last of the buildings. A black limousine with a driver at the wheel was parked at the rear of the building. Perhaps they had come just in time.

"Let's go by way of the front," Henry said. Then to Shamir, "Let's understand each other. We turn him over to the authorities, that's all."

"My preference would be to throttle him," Shamir said.

"It is possible," Margaret said, "that I have greater cause than either of you to hate the man personally, but Henry is right. We are not policemen."

She is wrong, thought Henry. It turns out, if we would survive, that we are all policemen.

Inside, Mr. Clifford was just finishing his advice to Abigail. "My dear," he said into the phone, "with all the outsiders swarming around, there's no chance. Sen is parked outside ready to go, but don't wait for us. I suggest Argentina. If first class is booked up, take a coach seat, I'll make it up to you. I should be there within a day or two. I love you too, dear," he said.

As he hung up, he heard the crash of something against the two-story-high window. He was glad he'd had the sense to pull the drapes.

Outside, it was Shamir who had flung, like a shot-putter, the melon-sized whitewashed rock. Henry saw the jagged hole radiate breaks like lightning forks. The upper part of the window, as if in slow motion, started to settle, then suddenly came down, the rest of the huge window breaking in a storm of noise.

Shamir beamed at Henry with the expression of a boy who has worked great mischief successfully. He stepped through the debris and over the bottom, motioning Henry and Margaret to follow him inside.

With one fierce pull, Shamir tore down one side of the drapes.

Mr. Clifford watched the three of them come into his living room. He recognized Margaret immediately, of course. The older man must be her husband, the escapee who had caused all the trouble. He was ready for them, the .38 in his hand.

"You are trespassing in my home," Mr. Clifford said calmly. "What do you want?"

"I'd like your insane head mounted above the mantelpiece in my home," Shamir said.

"It is perfectly legal to kill trespassers who threaten violence," Mr. Clifford said, his gun hand trembling perceptibly.

"We're turning you over to the authorities," Henry said.

Mr. Clifford laughed. "I would have no compunctions about shooting all three of you Jews."

Margaret thought *he counts me as a Jew.*

There was the distinct sound of footsteps from the kitchen at the rear of the house.

"Who's there?" Mr. Clifford yelled.

"Sen, sir," answered the voice of the Japanese. "Bag in car. Need help, sir?"

He is going to shoot us, Margaret thought.

"I know what you're thinking. You are wrong. I have never personally taken a human life."

At which Shamir took a step toward him.

Immediately, Mr. Clifford swung the pistol toward Shamir's face. "Though Sen has had experience and would be happy to accommodate me."

Then, without a further word, the three of them watched Clifford back up, then quickly vanish into the kitchen. They heard the rear door slam, the engine start, and they followed in time to see the limousine roar off.

Henry and Shamir ran hopelessly after the car, yelling "Stop it! Stop it! Clifford's in that car!" but none of the fire fighters within view took more than a second's notice of the limo as it avoided their equipment, then picked up speed. Henry, puffing, stopped because he could run no farther. At a distance he could see the black car heading for the road down, around which were clustered perhaps a dozen or so guests. Did any of them realize who was in the car? Henry could hear the driver honking. Some but not all of the people there moved quickly to the side of the road as the car drove through, hitting at least three or four of them. One, a woman, went sliding along the hood of the car, and seemed to smash into the windshield. Henry turned to see if Margaret were following, and she was now, at a walking pace, and he was glad because she would be needed.

Henry, out of breath again, found the woman who had slid into the windshield about a hundred and fifty yards down the road. She was not someone he recognized. Whoever she was, she was beyond help. Henry walked slowly back up the road, wondering when the nightmare would end.

Matilda Fowler took the shotgun from her son's hands, then looked down at the girl, whose clothes were now bespattered with the blood of the boy she was kneeling next to.

"You better go," she said to Frank. "Fast."

Frank, who had never been farther than Monterey in the north and Santa Barbara in the south, said, "Where?"

"Oklahoma. I'll give you the name and address of some kin. Take all your money and a change of clothes. Now git."

The only actual violence Kathy had ever seen in her young life was when a neighborhood dog had been run over on the street where she lived. She'd been six then, and when the policeman had come and seen how badly injured the dog was, her mother had tried to pull her back into the house, knowing what was coming. But Kathy had resisted long enough to see the policeman draw his service revolver, point it between the dog's questioning eyes, and pull the trigger. The sound had not been as loud as little Kathy had expected it to be from the noise of gunfire she'd heard on television. The dog's head had merely flicked back, and then the dog was lying down as if asleep.

Kathy was totally unprepared for what the shotgun had done to Stanley's legs. There seemed to be dozens of black blood-holes from his knees to his ankles. What could you do about so many wounds, especially with Stanley screaming and crying? She knew that a tourniquet must be applied to stop the bleeding. She could do that with Stanley's belt, if she could get it off him, but he'd just bleed to death from the other leg's wounds. She could feel herself on the verge of panic and ran outside. Frank Fowler was getting into an old car. He might shoot her, too. Then she saw the convoy of three yellow buses coming north on Highway 1 fast, and got into the middle of the road to flag them down. The driver of the first bus wasn't about to stop for anyone and planned to pass her by swerving into the oncoming lane, when he saw that the girl was spattered with blood, and he hit his brakes, let go, then hit his brakes again, hoping the bus behind him wouldn't plow right up his ass.

Several of the fire fighters in the first bus quickly debarked. The man in charge went over to Kathy, who, breathless and crying, told them her boy friend had been shot.

The man in charge followed her into the building, took one look at Stanley, who was now unconscious, and then ran back out to the buses.

"Please," Kathy screamed after him. "Don't leave him."

The man in charge had no intention of doing so. In quick time he cleared all but two of the men out of the first bus, and divided them into the two remaining buses and had them take off. They were on the way to the nearest helipad, with only three minutes lost. With the two remaining men, he got Stanley, somehow, into the first bus. On the way to the hospital, he fixed tourniquets around both of Stanley's thighs.

Kathy, holding on to a seat back as the bus careered on the curves, said to the man in charge, "His mother's a doctor." And as soon as the words were out she realized how irrelevant they were.

Just to make talk, the man said, "Where you kids from?"

She told him from the college at Santa Cruz. And then, as if an excuse for their presence in Big Sur were needed, she added, "He thinks his parents were up in that place where the fire is."

* * *

In the emergency room, Kathy, who had had so few choices to make in life so far, was asked if she wanted to wait. They were administering blood and saline solution, then taking X rays preparatory to surgery.

She asked a nurse, "Can I stay with him?"

The nurse shook her head. "After he's out of the recovery room. That'll be hours."

"I have to tell his parents," Kathy said.

The three men from the bus offered to drop her off somewhere on their way to the helipad.

"I've got nowhere to go," she said. "Can I go with you? His parents are up there and they don't know."

The man in charge said, "That blaze is no place for someone who doesn't have to be there."

"But I have to be there or they won't know," Kathy insisted.

The man, who had teenage children of his own, looked at the two other men, then said to her, "Okay."

It was only when they were airborne that she said to the nice man, "You know, I don't know what his parents look like."

When Kathy stepped out of the helicopter, the man in charge said, "Stay away from the fire zone, kid, and good luck!" He and the other two ran off at a trot. The helicopter pilot was waving to her to get out of the way, he needed to be off again. Ducking as the blades whirled faster over her head, Kathy ran, crouching, toward where people seemed to be gathered.

"Does anyone know Mr. and Mrs. Brown?" she asked one group after another. These people seemed strange, as if they'd been beaten by life. Maybe it was the terrific heat, she thought.

"Does anyone know anyone named Brown?" she asked.

Then a woman was coming over, Kathy could *see* the resemblance to Stanley and she said, "Are you Dr. Brown?" And Margaret, seeing only the blood on Kathy's clothes, felt suddenly as if a cleaver had cut her in two from sternum to pelvis.

"Where is Stanley?" she said, knowing the answer had to be very bad.

* * *

Margaret had once had a recurrent fantasy that the main reason she had become a doctor was to develop the skills that would save the life of a child of hers because she was there and knew what to do. Instead, now, as she and Henry and Kathy were sitting in the helicopter, holding hands, Henry to whom she had never felt closer, and the girl, who was a stranger and her living contact to her son, Margaret thought how far she was from Stanley now when he needed her.

Of course, journeys like that seem to take forever. First the helicopter, then the seemingly endless drive to the hospital. They had escaped from Cliffhaven into a nightmare that seemed worse because there was nothing you could do about it until you got there, and even then you might be reduced to a spectator.

Margaret explained to the doctor in the emergency room who she was. The fact that she was the boy's mother drew a practiced reflex of sympathy. Her announcement that she was a doctor, however, elicited a touch of real warmth. He said the operation was still in progress. The X rays had shown multiple fractures of both legs. They wouldn't know the amount of tissue and nerve damage till later. Did she want a cup of coffee?

No, she told the doctor, she wanted to go into the operating room. She didn't tell him her experience had taught her not to trust other doctors.

"If you'll follow me," the doctor said, "I'll show you where to scrub up, Dr. Brown."

"Give me one minute," Margaret said. She found Henry sitting on a bench in the waiting room.

"Where's Kathy?" she asked.

Henry wanted to scream at her *forget Kathy, how is my son?*

He swallowed because his vocal chords seemed stuck together. "Kathy went to the ladies' room." Finally, he couldn't control himself and said, "Tell me."

What could she tell him, that Stanley was badly hurt? He knew that. That he was in surgery? He knew that.

"Will he be able to play tennis?"

"I don't know," she said, thinking she was justified in this one lie. She rushed off to follow the doctor.

Forty minutes later there was still no sign. Henry thought of ways he could die if an exchange could be worked out for Stanley's life. At this moment he detested the rational part of his mind that told him such exchanges were not possible.

In the operating room Margaret watched the intricate procedure. It seemed to take forever. Stanley's unconscious face was whiter than she'd ever seen it. He looked dead, perhaps because of the rubber mouthpiece between his lips, keeping the air canal open. The movement of his chest was very slight. Fluids were dripping into his arms.

Finally, the surgeon turned to her. "I think we recovered all of the shot," he said. "In one respect we're very lucky. I've seen shotgun wounds that made restoration impossible."

The huskiness in Margaret's voice betrayed her. "You weren't contemplating amputation?"

"I was sure we'd have to when I went in. He will need further surgery. In a few weeks time, he might be well enough to be flown back East provided he can travel horizontally. It may mean buying a row of seats. And someone will have to accompany him."

She hadn't heard a word the surgeon said except by implication, that Stanley would live. Her heart was pounding.

She had to hurry down to tell Henry. *Stanley is alive.*

Margaret saw Kathy and Henry standing next to a California state trooper, holding a pair of handcuffs in his left hand.

"What's going on?" Margaret said.

"How is he?" Henry asked.

"It's almost over. He'll be all right. What's going on here?"

"You his wife?" the trooper asked.

Margaret nodded.

"He's under arrest," the trooper said. "One of the evacuees named Blaustein's given an affidavit that your husband set the fire up there. Said he saw him do it." To Henry he said, "You have a right to remain silent. Anything you say may be held against you."

"But . . ." Henry said. Then to Margaret, "Can I see him in the recovery room?"

"You're not going anywhere except with me, mister," the trooper said, snapping the cuffs on Henry's wrists.

"Now just a minute!" Margaret said, enraged.

"Better save it for the judge in town," the trooper said. "I'm just doing my job."

24

Henry was arraigned before Judge Sylvester Bonington, a disappointed man who had once dreamed of sitting on the Supreme Court. Now sixty-four, he no longer looked at prospective cases as vehicles to call his work to the attention of politicians and the public. Set on retirement, in his last year on the bench he was determined to be judicious.

When Henry Brown was brought before him, charged with deliberately setting fire to a federal forest preserve, Judge Bonington had already heard the early news about Cliffhaven and knew that if Henry Brown were to go to trial, that event, in case he should preside, would make Bonington a household word. The temptation percolated only for a few moments in Judge Bonington's brain before good sense took command.

Since Mr. Brown was from out-of-state and wanted to contact his lawyer back home for his recommendation of California counsel, Judge Bonington appointed a local lawyer named

Hilkey to advise the accused until his own counsel was arranged. Arson was a serious crime, and the judge wanted Hilkey to address himself to the issue of bail. The accused had no roots in the California community, yet he seemed to be a respectable businessman with no previous convictions.

Hilkey, a decent man, was horrified to hear what Henry and Margaret told him during the hour and a half they were together. He shared their grief, for he had lost a son some years earlier and knew the particular pain of unfairness the Browns must be feeling. He decided to ask the judge for a meeting in chambers with someone from the district attorney's office present. When they were all assembled around the conference table in what Judge Bonington referred to as his office, the judge asked Hilkey if he was ready to address the issue of bail.

"Your Honor," Hilkey said, "since the arraignment is incomplete, I should like to ask for your indulgence while I address myself to the circumstances surrounding the underlying charge."

The assistant district attorney thought it unwise to object. And so Hilkey filled the judge in on what had happened since the Browns had arrived in Cliffhaven. He did not omit Henry's four-hour experience in the lockers, nor Margaret's interrogation or the method the newly appointed manager of Cliffhaven had proposed to extract information from her about the whereabouts of her husband, nor her incarceration in the lockers. Hilkey concluded with the shotgunning of the Browns' only son, who had come searching for his parents and who had alerted the authorities to the fire. While his information on this matter was hearsay at the moment since he had not personally interviewed the young lady who had witnessed the shooting or the mother of the alleged assailant, he thought it necessary to mention the matter to the court.

"Your Honor," he said in conclusion, "what we have here is a vast array of crimes, including kidnapping, assault, murder, and mass murder, all allegedly occurring in one place in the state of California, and with few of the perpetrators in custody. It seems that all of the agencies of law enforcement, state and federal, have a monumental task before them that should not include the prosecution of the one man who used the only means at his command to expose Cliffhaven and cause the release of the more than one hundred persons still alive on the premises. Your Honor, I do not see how, under the circumstances, a grand jury would indict, nor do I see, in fact"—and here Hilkey looked at the young district attorney—"how the prosecution would want to ask for a true bill. I move that the charges against the accused be dismissed. Mr. Brown has undertaken to make himself available for depositions and affidavits as required in other cases, and has agreed to return to California for such purposes should his presence be required."

The judge consulted with the assistant district attorney, who then asked to make a telephone call to his office. On his return all he said was, "Okay, we'll drop the charges."

Hilkey thanked the district attorney and the judge, and told Henry Brown he was free to go on the stipulated conditions. Mr. Hilkey, who had studiously learned to control the appearance of emotion, was upset to see his temporary client, a grown man, sob. What he couldn't be aware of was that Henry Brown's grief was not only over his inability to help his son. His heart was thudding with despair, feeling himself for the first time in his life a refugee in the country of his birth.

25

Three months later in their home in Westchester, north of New York, Henry and Margaret Brown awaited a visit, arranged on short notice by Webster Lynn, then the number two man in the Justice Department and widely believed to be the likely next attorney general of the United States.

It was raining hard as Lynn stepped from the taxi that had taken him from the Eastern Airlines shuttle at LaGuardia. He opened his umbrella and walked unhurriedly up the seven broad flagstone steps leading to the Browns' front door. The second occupant of the taxi had not been expected.

Once inside, Lynn introduced the second man as Francis X. Stanton. Mr. Stanton had water on his hat and was anxious that none of it held by the brim drip onto the parquet flooring of the Browns' hallway. Margaret took Stanton's hat gingerly to the kitchen as Henry hung his and Mr. Lynn's coats. She brought back a paper towel, which Lynn used to dry his briefcase. Stanton, much taller than Lynn, bent over in a slight bow as he performed the obligatory ritual of opening his wallet and showing his FBI card.

"You're much better looking than your picture," Margaret said. "Are you here to protect Mr. Lynn?"

Lynn, anxious to keep everyone in good humor for a few minutes longer, apologized for Stanton's presence. "I really didn't realize he was joining me," Lynn said, "until this morning."

Stanton, Margaret observed, seemed embarrassed, perhaps by Lynn's lie. A kindness was in order. "Mr. Stanton," she said, "your people were very quick to pick up Mr. Clifford at the airport before he could get away."

Margaret thought Stanton actually showed a slight blush. "It was simple enough to check that his wife had fled to Argentina. We had nearly forty agents at the airport before each of the next several flights to Buenos Aires. His disguise was amateurish. The man who supplied him with the false passport reported in to us immediately, as he always does. It was relatively easy."

Lynn interjected, "It would have been boggled if it'd been left to the California authorities."

It was Henry who said, "Perhaps Clifford should have hidden out somewhere in California. Will his wife be extradited?"

"To tell you the truth," Lynn said, "no. Accessory charges would seem most tenuous to Argentina. And to a prosecutor, I might add."

Margaret offered them both coffee. She wondered what kind of woman Clifford was married to.

As Lynn and Stanton settled down in front of the welcome fire, Lynn, clearly in charge, decided to pass a few more civil moments with the Browns before getting down to what was troubling the administration.

"How is your son?" he asked.

"His spirits are up since he's returned home," Henry said. "I'll defer to my wife for a medical opinion."

Lynn had been led to expect that Henry might not be entirely friendly and was glad to turn his attention to Dr. Brown.

Margaret said, "Stanley's scheduled to go into New York

Hospital in less than a week for a second operation on his left leg. Everything has to be done in stages. It'll be another year before we'll know if he'll be able to cope without a wheelchair."

"I certainly hope so," Lynn said. "I trust you've both gotten over your own bad experience."

By bad experience Lynn was not referring to Cliffhaven but to a letter addressed to Margaret that began, *My dear Dr. Brown, lest you derive some satisfaction from the detention of Merlin Clifford, please be advised that those of us who believe in his cause will use all of our many and varied resources to protect his civil rights and to secure his earliest possible release. Moreover, a sister resort to Cliffhaven, already in operation at another location, has taken in several members of the Cliffhaven staff who escaped the dragnet ...*

When Margaret had gotten to the last paragraph of the letter, she was instantly on the phone to the local police. *While we are all very busy right now, Dr. Brown, rest assured that as soon as convenient we shall dispatch two loyal marksmen to eradicate your family for its role ...*

The policeman who came dismissed it as a crackpot letter. As a precaution, however, he suggested that the Browns contact the postal authorities, who had an investigative division. Henry, who considered the postal service the chief enemy of his order-fulfillment business, elected to turn the matter over to the FBI, which, because the letter threatened bodily harm, accepted jurisdiction.

The FBI, which had missed Cliffhaven, could not afford to ignore the letter, but it didn't have much to go on. In Washington the lab managed to raise some latent fingerprints, which were quickly identified as those of Margaret and of the local policeman. The unsigned letter was typed on a rather common electric typewriter and mailed from a shopping mall in Ohio that was frequented by tens of thousands of persons each week. There were no misspellings. Bureau offices in Cleveland, Columbus, and Cincinnati were asked to check all resorts in isolated areas that could accommodate one hundred or more persons. Nothing was found. The special agent in charge of the case thought the letter was probably mailed to Ohio from another state for remailing. "The man who wrote that letter," he said, "is not a dummy."

"It is very important," Lynn continued, "that you both testify at the California trial. As you know, the prosecution is in the very capable hands of the U.S. Attorney for the Southern District of California."

"Would you like a drink?" Margaret asked.

"No, this coffee's fine, thank you," Lynn said, hurrying to his point. "My office is involved solely to convey the President's view that this case is of grave national concern."

"I will tell you," Margaret said, "why I have decided not to be involved any further."

"I hope you still have an open mind on that subject," Lynn inserted quickly.

"There have been four phone calls since that letter," Margaret said.

Stanton leaned forward. "I heard you thought they were all from the same person."

"It sounded like the same person to me."

"I meant the same person who wrote the letter," Stanton said.

"He used one of the same expressions."

"What was that?"

"He said loyal marksmen."

Stanton said, "I understand our local people have put a recording device on your phone. I'm sure they've told you that all you have to do, Dr. Brown, is lay the phone down quietly. He'll go on talking, but you don't have to listen as long as we're recording it."

"Mr. Stanton," Margaret said, "if your wife were on the receiving end of phone calls like that . . . you have a wife, I presume?"

Stanton nodded.

"She'd be upset by phone calls like that."

"Damn right," Stanton said.

"But you see," Margaret said, "I've been a physician for

twenty years. I've become inured to crackpots. It's an occupational hazard of anyone who's involved with the public on an intimate basis. I am not shockable, not by words. But I am concerned about threats of physical harm. I've met those people face to face. So has my husband. So has my son. More importantly, right now my obligation is not only to my patients but to my most important patient, Stanley. I'm not going to leave him either here or in a hospital and traipse off to California. If you want further affidavits, fine, but I'm not going anywhere till Stanley's well."

Mr. Lynn looked as if he'd been waiting for this moment. "Doctor Brown," he said, "one of the reasons I am here today is I have authority to offer you and your husband accommodation in the Witness Protection Program after you testify. Your son could go with you."

It was Henry who stood up. "Are you crazy?"

In the weeks after Cliffhaven, when he seemed to be on the precipice of a nervous breakdown, Henry'd raised his voice a good deal. Margaret had given him a tranquilizer to take three times a day, but he'd given them up almost immediately because they made him feel sleepy.

"Change our identities?" Henry said a bit shrilly. "Move somewhere else?"

Margaret, distressed by Henry's momentary loss of control, intervened.

"Surely," she said, "even if we were willing, a physician with an active practice could not—"

"Doctor Brown," Lynn said, "I assure you we've thought of the expense as well as the complexity in your case. Your husband has a thriving business. You have a practice and hospital connections. Nevertheless, we'd be willing . . ."

"Never!" Henry said.

"Of course not," Margaret added, gently taking Henry by his arm and urging him to sit.

"Well," Lynn said, addressing himself squarely to Margaret since she seemed in control of herself (*she isn't Jewish* is what he thought), "I'm certain one of your hesitations is that the tampon incident would come up. I don't see any reason why

293

you should volunteer that story. I certainly would arrange for the U.S. Attorney not to examine you on that point unless the defense brought it up."

"Why in heaven's name would the defense bring it up?" Margaret asked.

It was Stanton's role to be the nice guy in the sister act. He leaned forward and said, "Doctor Brown, I think it is only fair for you to know that an agreement has been reached with Daniel Pitz's attorney. Since he was only employed at Cliffhaven for less than one day and during that time hadn't harmed anybody, the government has agreed to exchange his testimony for a . . ."

Henry, standing again, his eyes blazing, said, "I know it! Say it!"

It was Lynn who said it. "For a suspended sentence. His testimony will be invaluable."

"Then you can't have mine," Margaret said, motioning to Henry to please sit down.

"I'm afraid we will," Lynn said. "You see, under the law we have to advise the defense of the witnesses we will call. The moment Clifford's lawyer sees Dan Pitz's name on that list, he'll question Clifford privately about Pitz and learn that the tampon idea was Pitz's. It is inevitable that the defense will bring it up to try to impeach Pitz as a witness, whether or not you are present. However, having you as a witness will enable us to make it clear that Clifford and the others were present, that Clifford was in charge of the interrogation, and that Pitz was merely trying to show off to Clifford by coming up with something shocking. Now, Dr. Brown, before your husband gets upset again, let me say that the affidavit you gave in California about your experiences at Cliffhaven is a cornerstone of our case. Since this is a criminal prosecution in federal court, the government, I'm afraid, can compel your attendance at the trial to testify, and that if you refuse, you can be fined and imprisoned, and the trial adjourned until you agree to testify. You are welcome to check this with your personal attorney, of course."

"I can't believe that," Margaret said.

"Nevertheless," Lynn said, "it is the law."

"I can say 'I don't remember' over and over again. That won't help you, will it?"

Lynn coughed ever so slightly. "It is a felony to lie on the stand, Dr. Brown. Moreover, and please do check this with your lawyer, the response 'I don't remember' can be prosecuted as a false declaration under Title 18 of the U.S. Code, 1623."

"I thought this was a free country," Margaret said.

"It is," Stanton intervened. "And we'll surely try to get the man who wrote that threatening letter to you."

"You want to bet?" interjected Henry.

Stanton smiled. "The Bureau doesn't bet."

"As for Stanley," Lynn said, "if you're concerned about his welfare, I'm sure Mr. Stanton can arrange for the Bureau's local office to have someone with him at all times, here or in the hospital, while you are in California."

"He needs medical attention," Margaret said, "not a policeman."

"I'm certain you can arrange for another physician whom you trust to be on call," Lynn said. "We can probably even arrange for you to be compensated for the additional expense. We can promise you that you won't be gone more than three days, including travel time. You do realize that you must go."

It is normal for governments to be brutal, Margaret thought.

"I'm glad we have that resolved," Lynn said. "And now," he turned to Henry, "I'd like to raise the other subject. I understand from one of my colleagues that you've consented to give an extended interview on your experiences at Cliffhaven to *U.S. News and World Report*."

Henry wasn't surprised that they had found out.

"I've discussed that matter with the U.S. Attorney for the Southern District of California, and we agree that an extensive interview by you given before the trial would greatly impair the government's case."

"How?" Henry asked. "I'll tell nothing but the truth, exactly what happened, step by step."

"Don't you see," Lynn said, "that by doing so you will provide the defense with opportunities for a fishing expedition? The whole truth can give the defense all kinds of handles for impeaching your testimony. When you freed the people in the lockers, you gravely injured one of the staff members. You beat him brutally with a club, though he in no way injured you. Don't you see how that might look if the defense attorney brought it out? You set fire to a protected wilderness area, causing millions of dollars worth of damage. Why are we not prosecuting you?"

"You didn't make a deal with me," Henry said.

"Of course not, but it can be made to look as if we did. We much prefer that your testimony be carefully organized and gone over when you return to California, and that you discipline yourself to speak to the agreed matters under questioning by the prosecutor and in cross-examination by the defense."

Stanton said, "It's for your own good, Mr. Brown. We want to put these people, Clifford and the others, in jail where they belong. We're on your side."

For a moment Henry seemed detached, as if he were remembering something. When he spoke, Margaret noticed with relief, his voice had its normal pitch.

"I had the impression from *The Los Angeles Times*," Henry said, "which I had sent to me for several weeks after we returned, that some considerable part of the California citizenry was more concerned about the number of perpetrators still at large, presumably in California, than about what happened at Cliffhaven."

Lynn coughed. "It is perfectly natural for people to be concerned about their safety. I think there's enough evidence that at least some of the people who worked at Cliffhaven were criminal types—"

"By criminal types," Henry interrupted, "you mean types who would commit crimes other than crimes against Jews?"

Lynn had tried to get a fix on Henry Brown before leaving Washington. He had not expected that much belligerence.

"*The Los Angeles Times*," Henry continued, "is looking to the police power of the state to clean up the residue of the Cliffhaven mess—I think they used those exact words in an editorial. Maybe that's good. Maybe that's better than *The New York Times*, which addressed the conscience of humanity three times on the subject of Cliffhaven."

"Surely," Lynn said, "the conscience of humanity is out-raged by what happened."

"I agree," Stanton nodded.

"In my judgment," Henry said, "there is no historical evidence that the conscience of humanity exists at all. I mention these two important newspapers merely to describe two attitudes toward the events at Cliffhaven that *leave me cold*."

For a moment Margaret thought Henry's voice was slipping again, but she was wrong.

Henry said, "That's why I've chosen to give my testimony my way. Tape-recorded and complete. On the record for people to read no matter what happens at the trial. Moreover, Mr. Lynn, I don't intend to drop the matter after the trial. I've never had a penchant for public speaking. I have one now. I will speak to Jewish groups, Church groups, mixed groups, student groups, anyone who will listen. I will engage a public-relations firm that knows how to do these things and tell about Cliffhaven on radio and TV—"

"Mr. Brown!" Lynn was standing. "I hate to disabuse you, but in another three months your story will be very old news. No one will listen. The trial is the place for you to make your record."

"I am not naïve, Mr. Lynn. I know what happens at trials. I saw Clifford's limousine deliberately career straight through those people, but in court all that might prove is that his driver may be guilty of vehicular manslaughter. Clifford could deny having anything to do with it!"

"I want to assure you," Lynn said, "that I personally intend to see to it that not one clause of the grand jury indictment against Clifford is thrown out. I have the full backing of the administration for my position on this case."

"Oh I'm sure," Henry said, "that the President is once again anxious about the Jewish vote. I'll tell you something, Mr. Lynn. Neither you nor the President are going to be members of that jury. Those jurors don't have to give a damn about the Jewish vote. I've seen several persuasive stories to the effect that Clifford is probably going to get a very light sentence because of the difficulty of proving many of the items in the indictment beyond a reasonable doubt. Mr. Lynn, I have no reasonable doubt. I was in the lockers. I saw the plaques that kept score. I know why there were no children visible anywhere. But the assembling of proof! I don't want my legacy to be a trial that whitewashes what happened there!"

Lynn, seeing that his tack was not working, thought to try another, especially since—he darted a glance at his watch—the cab would be arriving momentarily to take them back to the airport.

"Mr. Brown," he said, "why not ask *U.S. News* to simply hold off their interview till after the trial? That's reasonable, isn't it?"

Henry laughed. "Because they're in the news business, not in the post-mortem-of-a-trial business. I already broached the subject and that was their answer. Before, or not at all."

"Well," Lynn said, standing, "you certainly defeat the popular mythology that Jews have no guts. I'm sure Mr. Stanton agrees with me. My concern is not to wreck the trial by undue disclosures in the press. I could of course have the U.S. Attorney for the Southern District ask the judge to slap a gag order on you and *U.S. News*. You'd be in contempt if you proceeded with the interview prior to the trial."

"I am in contempt," Henry said.

Margaret observed a slight smile on his lips, perhaps too slight for the others, who knew him less well, to notice.

"If I were you," Lynn said, "I shouldn't want the court to come to that conclusion. I trust you'll discuss this among yourselves and phone me tomorrow."

When the cab honked to announce its presence, Henry and Margaret saw Lynn and Stanton to the door.

"Please don't get wet on our account," Lynn said, as they went down the stone steps and entered the waiting taxi. Through the window he raised a hand, waving it just a mite. *To show we are all friends,* Henry thought.

As the door closed on their departing visitors, Henry asked Margaret, "Do you see what I'm doing as crazy?"

"No," she said. "As aftercare."

Margaret led the way to their chairs in front of the fireplace.

Henry stared at the flames. A fire used to make him feel comfortable.

Margaret, worried about his recent silences, said, "Has it any use?"

"What?" Henry asked.

"What you're planning to do."

Henry seemed lost in thought, alone somewhere. Finally, Margaret interrupted him. "Human nature," she said, "will never change." She sighed. "All we do in intensive care is police the body better."

They heard the cowbell they had put at Stanley's bedside. He needed something.

Margaret was immediately on her feet. "I'll go."

"I'll go, too," Henry said.

Margaret was about to say that Stanley probably only needed something he couldn't reach, but it was just as well that they both went.

All Stanley needed was to have his water pitcher refilled. The medication he took was dehydrating.

They sat on either side of the bed, silent until Henry said, "I'm glad, in a way, they're forcing you to testify."

Her eyes queried his meaning.

"Oh," Henry said, "Cliffhaven was a Gentile invention. I think it's time the innocent among the Gentiles confront the consequences of such inventions. We Jews after all are only the victims."

Stanley, lying between them, said, "We half-and-halves get caught in the middle."

"Yes," Margaret said, patting her son's hand.

On their way back down the stairs, Henry stopped at the landing. He watched Margaret go down the rest of the flight.

At the bottom she stopped, then said, "You never answered me. Will you do the interview and all those other things?"

Henry's every instinct was to say *of course*, but there was a vast difference now. Speaking out could dominate his life. He had never volunteered for committees, never been the chairman of anything. He was a private person on the verge of becoming a public person, a condition from which it was impossible to retreat. If they knew your face, even if they couldn't place it, they would pump your hand. You were theirs.

The fear he remembered came in dreams. He would be standing on a rostrum somewhere, hundreds of faces looking up at him, waiting for him to speak, but his vocal cords would not respond. It was a childish fear. Awake, he was the executor of his own will.

Margaret, looking up at him on the landing, must have known how important the moment was. He would not be coming down the stairs like a naïve Moses carrying tablets nobody would pay much attention to. He had been born into the Devil's best century. America was not immune. He was not immune. Men who had come out of the trees did to each other what no apes did. He couldn't change their natures, but he must tell what he knew, for hope was the only medicine that would not become obsolete in time.

As he came down the rest of the stairs to Margaret, she said, "You will." It wasn't a question.

"Of course," he said at last.